POWER & WAY

PAUL LOCANDER

CHRISTMAS LAKE PRESS

Published by Christmas Lake Press 2025
www.christmaslakecreative.com
Copyright © 2025 by Paul Locander
ISBN 978-1-960865-36-6

This book is a work of fiction. Any resemblance of characters to real people, living or dead, is purely coincidental.

POWER & WAY

*For Amy, Geoff, Judith, my family . . .
and my father.*

Prologue

My father was born Francis Raymond Campbell on a cold West Virginia day in 1930. He claimed to have grown up on the rugged shores of the Bluestone River, where he often fished for bass, filling his bucket with shining trophies—smallmouth, largemouth, white, spotted—and allegedly the rare golden, a mutated king of the murky deep. Why his mother named him Francis no one will ever know; however, I'm sure he changed it to "Frank" thirty seconds after the first bully's fist connected with his head. Perpetually skinny and often cruelly teased, he responded to these taunts by throwing himself face-first into the grass, eyes squeezed shut in shame, breathing dirt as the sun scorched his back, waiting for the footsteps of his enemies to recede. The tactic took his tormentors by surprise, and when it was finally quiet, he would stand back up, brush himself off, and continue on his way. He also liked to repeatedly share this tidbit of non-sensical trivia with me: that he was conceived upon the top of a 1929 icebox. Like most of his stories, it was unsupported by fact and had a twist of romantic martyrdom to it. This, of course, annoyed me no end, which was probably the point.

A self-taught man, my father considered himself to be highly intelligent. He was well read, loved classical music, and possessed surprising artistic talent when confronted with a blank canvas or a blob of clay. He was also blissfully unaware of his blind spots. He carried a long list of frustrating half-truths, odd idioms, and the lingering effects of a youth raised entirely by women. His mother, Emma, frail and ancient in my memories, was a wisp of a woman—a mere leaf in the wind of matrimony. She had married at least four times (that I knew of) and gifted Frank with a conga line of uninterested father figures, none of whom he mentioned more than once. Emma was inseparable from her dear sister, my great-aunt Hattie, whom Dad always spoke highly of. He offered no detail about her other than her possessing a remarkable chin and a pronounced nose that arrived well before any of her other body parts entered a room. The one and only Aunt Hattie story he shared with me was her recollection of my great-grandmother, Kitty Belle Braun, who had bounced off to South America to become Argentina's first woman gunslinger and was never heard from again. Even if, like all my father's tall tales, this one was an exaggeration, I chose to hold on to it as an actual truth, entertained by the old sepia-toned newsreel playing out in my head: "Long gone—Kitty Belle Braun."

As for my Campbell grandfather, he disappeared well before my father reached kindergarten, something a lot of men did back in the 1930s when work was scarce and heading for the hills was a strategy practiced in great abundance. In the decades that followed, Arthur Campbell managed to track down the only son he had left behind, calling him out of the blue on a singular Sunday evening just before dinner. Dad said he simply hung up on him. He then told me his father hanged himself from a dead tree in the backyard of an abandoned Los Angeles home immediately afterward.

Dad never spoke of him again.

By the time World War II came about, my father had bailed out of the senior stages of his eighth-grade education and beelined to the local recruitment office, only to be booted back out the door for being too young to fight—let alone write his name with any semblance of legibility (he was more skilled in drawing than penmanship). Even when Dad lied about his age to the Navy, the Marines, the Army, and probably the Salvation Army, they all must have taken one look at the scrawny kid from the Greenbrier Valley and catapulted him out onto the street with a gruff, "Come back when you've grown some hair on your chest, kid!"

So—and again with no verifiable proof whatsoever—Dad boasted of a life as a mercenary. He claimed to have furiously fought the Japanese in Burma, only to step on a land mine and receive the gift of a concave chest, which ultimately sent him back home a war hero to whom no one paid any attention. He told me that story once, and after I shot him a look that screamed "bullshit," he allowed it to fade into fatherly legend. And though his possessing a concave chest was true, the reality was that my father the "war hero" was a 4-F the moment he was born.

With his "mercenary career" now behind him, Dad went to work as a brakeman for Atlantic Eastern, a small regional railroad that laced together the towns and coal mines of West Virginia with five locomotives and a rail yard of rotting wooden coal cars. Although he was born a West Virginian and could swing the accent to a non-sensical level, he chose to maintain a Midwestern drawl in case he ever needed to abandon his home state.

And that's when he met Mom.

Born Fay Anne Guinness in July of 1937, Mom was a brunette beauty who loved floppy hats, Lucky Strikes, and convertibles. She also had horrid taste in men. I mean, she married Dad.

My father boasted more than once that he had stolen my mother from a grotesque soul by the name of Hollis Peete, a miserable man who was hatched upon this Earth with a mean streak as wide as the Ohio River. Hollis had also managed to find enough knuckleheads to elect him sheriff in what felt like perpetuity.

Mom and Dad were married on a New Year's Eve, and I promptly popped out seven months later, so I can only assume it was a shotgun wedding. By then, Dad was already well-versed in his work routine: getting up at 4:00 in the morning, in the locomotive cab by 5:00, out by 3:00 in the afternoon, in the M&M Bar at 3:05, and shit-faced drunk twenty-five minutes later. He'd be kicked out at 2:30 the next morning just to stagger home and do it all over again in a couple of hours. Dad worked hard, drank hard, and fathered his essentially fatherless son even harder.

To be fair, Dad had no idea what to do with a son. God knows he didn't have the patience, let alone a competent role model to work from. If I had been born a Dorothy or a Mary, it likely wouldn't have been a problem. I would have had dresses and ponytails and a doting father. Instead, I was born Kevin Michael Campbell, and it was all downhill from there.

Dad was usually absent, while Mom seemed continually overwhelmed with the effort of raising a son while living the life of a boozer's widow. She was relatively forgotten about by her parents, who preferred to revel in the accomplishments of her younger brother. They made no measurable fuss when she stayed out late, dated sketchy young men, or eloped with Dad. For as lovely and loving as Mom was, she was also a mess. My father was often hard on her, maybe even cruel for all I knew. She wasn't easy on him, either. Mom spent many nights alone in our sparsely furnished, dinky home filled with shelves of trashy novellas, Tom Jones spinning on the turntable, Dad's semi-talented paintings crafted by a shaky hand, and his plentiful collection of handsomely named bottles like Johnnie Walker and Jack Daniel's. And with turning random stints as a candy striper at the hospital, she also discovered her affinity for easy-to-pocket mind-bending medications.

Mom would often get a head start on Dad with the drinking, especially whenever she spent a long afternoon with Nutty Maude McMillan in her weird Victorian at the top of Branch Hill Lane. It was a spooky place that reminded me of the foreboding house in *Psycho*. And when she did get a jump on him, the fighting would rage well into the evening, usually within two minutes of Dad walking through the front door, already hammered himself. And I would watch and listen from the so-called safety of my half-open bedroom door, fiddling nervously with a toy train in my robe pocket, while a familiar knot grew and grew in my stomach.

Mom died not much later.

It was a warm August night when Mom woke me up. I was eight when she led me to our four-door sedan in my blue pajamas. With a noxious mix of vodka and ill-gotten barbiturates, Mom slipped off to sleep and wrapped our car around an enormous oak on Sumter Road. My mother never saw sunlight again. With a broken leg, I was pulled from the back seat by the kindness of Sherman Gale, an angelic soul in a white 1960 Volkswagen Beetle, who then fell to his knees as my mother was incinerated in the fire that started moments later.

My mother was gone. And it was entirely on me that it happened at all.

Afterward, I was mostly left to my own devices. I was painfully shy, skinny, occasionally picked on, and hung out with only a few whom I would consider friends. The middle school years were not much better. My father spent more time staring into his beer glass than watching me do homework. I ventured into my teenage years with a love of fast cars, a chronic shortage of girlfriends—save one who managed to fall and stay in love with me—and a subconscious following in my father's well-worn footsteps.

Once out of high school and after a failed attempt at anything resembling a college education, I found my way to the Union Pacific Railroad and into the cab of road locomotives. I wound up becoming the local union president, mostly because no one else wanted to do it. Thus, I drudged a bit further in my career than my father ever did in his. Not that it impressed him, or impressed him enough to say anything about it.

So as much as my father had no idea what to do with me, I had absolutely no idea what to do with him. Frank Campbell was someone I could never read, much less please. He was impossible to talk to, and after Mom passed, he raised an impenetrable wall that wouldn't even come down for the sound of his only son's voice. We were out of sync and lived at different frequencies, separated by a cavernous, undefined disconnect. After a while, I stopped trying to relate to him, staying in his life only out of obligation and a faint hope for some acceptance and approval.

Trust me, I'm no prince of perfection either, so it wasn't entirely on my father. Or at least I think it wasn't. Or maybe it was. Looking back on this so many years later, the memories have begun to fade as the presence of today shoulders out all the yesterdays. The guilt I've carried so long from that gut-wrenching August night and the scream of my mother is something I have tried so hard to bury. Even now, I couldn't say it would be any different if my father were still alive. Our disconnected lives continue to live on in the lengthening shadows he continues to cast.

You see, I've lived in a self-imposed prison with my father as the warden. He was always there watching my every move, judging my every step. And no matter how hard I've fought it or tried to deny it, I am my father's son.

1

Frank Campbell snapped awake and clutched the steering wheel of his twenty-year-old Ford F-150 when a short freight train noisily plodded by behind him. The squeal of steel upon steel and the hollow slamming of empty rail cars jarred him back to consciousness with an involuntary kick of adrenaline. He had nodded off in the old train yard, just enough to close out the world and drift into complete nothingness—his preferred state of mind. Almost nothing turned off the noise in his life. His daily existence was a cacophony of random thoughts driven by memories that mercilessly invaded moments of his life at any given hour.

At sixty-five, Frank considered himself downright ancient, especially anytime he looked in the mirror. Something he tried to keep to a minimum simply because he loathed the face looking back at him. In all, the years had not been kind to him. And for the cruelty of God, it showed. Starting the day by drinking brandies at 4:00 in the morning likely didn't help, which is what the battery of idiot quacks told him whenever they marveled at the block of concrete his liver was becoming. Frank detested them. They were committed to keeping him alive far longer than he cared for. Thus, he gave them a deaf ear anytime they dispensed medicinal wisdom upon him.

By the time the freight train had rattled away, Frank's adrenaline rush had subsided enough to ease the pounding in his head, but it returned viciously when a face suddenly appeared in the windshield.

"Wake up!" the face barked, nearly launching Frank's spine through the roof of the truck.

"Jesus fuckin' Christ!" Frank yelled as Tom Ryder receded from the windshield with a shit-eating grin. "You scared the livin' shit out of me!"

Tom smiled before moving toward a brooding, decaying, crusted black 1954-vintage General Motors GP-9 diesel locomotive that idled on a siding nearby. To the untrained eye, it was nothing but a brick of rusted iron with wheels.

Tom was a few years older than Frank but didn't look it. A towering man, he stood an easy six feet, four inches in work boots that helped keep his thinly framed body upright. Even with a full head of wavy gray hair, Tom had done a better job of holding on to his youth, something Frank dismissively attributed to genetics.

Frank slid out of the pickup with a wince, hauling his daily backpack of tools and lunch behind him. It weighed all of twenty pounds, but today it felt like fifty. He slammed the door shut and hobbled alongside Tom toward the decrepit locomotive, affectionately dubbed "The Brick."

Tom watched Frank move as if one leg were two inches shorter than the other. Today, Frank was far more gimpy than usual. "Hip crankier this mornin'?" Tom asked.

"Meh, it woke up pissed off," Frank grumbled. His pace slowed as he strategically metered the pain. Frank was barely six feet on a good day, and his additional thirty pounds of questionable eating and drinking pulled on his now sagging spine, which shaved a couple of inches off his once youthful height. Like Tom, he, too, had managed to keep most of his hair, with Frank having the advantage of being naturally free of invading grays. Frank would eagerly trade all that in for a working hip but wasn't about to let the cluster of certified clowns at the Medical Center open him up.

Without a word, Tom pulled the backpack from Frank's shoulder and threw it over his own. Frank was quietly grateful for the immediately lightened load.

Tom was one of his few remaining pillars of stability, a constant from a time fading faster than he could grasp. For thirty straight years they had worked together, and even though tomorrow would be his last day, tonight Tom was retiring with a blowout party that Frank dreaded. It was closing another chapter Frank wasn't ready to complete, making him feel all the more hollow. If asked what Tom meant to him, Frank would be hard pressed to explain the bond, let alone willing or able to articulate the details.

"You know," Tom said, looking on at The Brick as it collected a new coating of damp fall leaves that would only add more rust to her frame, "I think I'm actually gonna miss this piece of shit."

"Want me to wrap it up as a retirement present?" Frank snarked. "Park it in your driveway?"

Tom grinned as he climbed the crew ladder. "You've always known the way to my heart." He pulled open the heavy cab door and stepped inside.

Frank moved on, passing along the locomotive's fifty-six-foot length for the walkaround, noting the deeply faded stenciling on its side—"Power & Way"—an artifact from the engine's short time in the sun. A remnant from when it was used to build the electrification of what is known today as the Northeast Corridor. Now it was a hand-me-down to the two-bit company Frank and Tom had spent the last three decades working for.

The Brick was a 260,000 pound, fifteen-foot-tall slab of iron and steel. With horrid visibility, the GP-9 locomotive was powered by a mid-century diesel-electric motor that painfully doled out 1,700 horsepower to the rails. A thing of beauty it was not.

With the walkaround wrapped up, Frank climbed the crew ladder and closed the cab door behind him, immersing himself in the pungent cocktail of oil, lubricant, and diesel fumes. He planted himself on the cracked cushion of the worn fireman's seat and watched Tom release the brakes. As The Brick hissed and spat, Tom eased the throttle forward a click. With a shudder, she rolled on the steel rails.

Tom popped his head out of the window, checking the track ahead and behind, something he'd done thousands of times before. But under Frank's watchful eye, this would be the last time. It was a moment that wasn't lost on Frank, who watched the silhouette of his friend in the cab window, backlit by the glare of morning light. It was an oddly ghost-like image that spawned a frightening hollow feeling in his chest.

"Stop looking at me like that," Tom said. "I'm retiring tomorrow, not dying."

Frank felt differently. The hollow feeling continued to grow, taking up permanent residence alongside all his other long-held sorrows and misgivings. He narrowed his eyes and looked out at the long line of tracks ahead disappearing into the morning fog.

2

Kevin stared through his truck windshield at the M&M Bar with the same enthusiasm he shared for a root canal. Through the brightly lit windows at the end of the parking lot, he spotted his father at Tom's side, charming a gaggle of partygoers with his alcohol-fueled wit. The vision alone amped up his annoyance to the point of throwing the Silverado into reverse—he wanted to spray gravel across the county as he frantically drove home. Or across the state. Or deep into Canada.

"Engine off." Trisha's voice instantly obliterated his fantasy.

Kevin turned the key, and the truck settled into an uneasy silence. "Remind me why we're doing this again?"

Trisha threw an eye roll as she turned to dig their fidgety and squirming three-year-old son, Michael, from his car seat in the back of the crew cab. He was on the wrong side of a sugar high, instigated by his discovery of a poorly hidden box of Twinkies. "Shiloh, give me a hand?" Trisha asked while Michael's back arched.

With the help of his seventeen-year-old sister, Michael was now free to climb over the seat and into his mother's arms. "We're here because we love Tom, and all of this is for him," Trisha continued, "so let's keep it civil, yeah?"

"Yeah, Dad," Michael piped up. "Keep it Sybil."

Kevin didn't answer. He sagged out of the truck, knowing full well his wife was right; this was about Tom and not something to be overblown into an emotional loggerhead with his father.

Once the truck's doors were closed, Shiloh pushed her father ahead as if he had a stuck parking brake. Not exactly a mature attitude for a man in his mid-forties, Kevin would readily admit. However, the estrangement from his father wasn't all that mature either.

With domestic hostilities imminent, Trisha Marie Pettit Campbell was a perfect grounding rod for Kevin. She knew her husband's foibles, weaknesses, and strengths, along with his irrational, non-sensical addiction to quixotically seek his father's approval. He was maddeningly loyal, even though Frank didn't deserve it. Intellectually, Trisha understood, but never emotionally. Frank was a pill to his son. Distant, aloof, and forever disappointed and dismissive of the man she'd loved since she arrived from Nashville, Ohio—a little town with two Amish buggies and a cemetery loaded with graves from the Grand Army of the Republic.

After nearly twenty years of marriage, Trisha knew the signs of a storm brewing better than anyone. Kevin was already on edge and his father was likely hammered. They were late, due to procrastination on Kevin's part. So, as setups go for probable familial combat, this was ideal.

The M&M was a noisy, rustic bar nestled off the beaten path just outside of Granite Point, West Virginia, setting it apart from the more typical dive bars in town. It was the go-to gig for all the after-work train crews since the first rails were laid through the valley. The building was old, with a stylish rusting green dumpster in the back. The parking lot was a combination of cracked concrete, old gravel, and petrified rail ties used as parking curbs.

On the inside, the M&M was adorned with an array of Pittsburgh sports paraphernalia, co-owned by Mitch and his father, Miles, who was rarely seen. This was perfectly fine with Mitch, as his father was a Philly fan; hence, there was always a disagreement about the establishment's preferred décor.

Kevin and his family were showered with hellos and hugs the moment they were through the door. Even amongst all the smiles, Kevin's only thought was to slip out the back and disappear for the next three hours, which would get him to, say, the far side of Ohio. Once in eyesight, Kevin and Trisha waved to Tom.

"Oh Christ, run for it, everyone," Tom bellowed as he rumbled in to bestow a spine-snapping hug on Kevin. "The union's here!" Kevin hugged as much as he could in return. Once he caught his breath, he shot a glance at his father, who was stewing off to the side.

"Nice of you to show up," Frank said to his son in a caustic tone that sent Kevin away to find people happier to see him.

The clock slowly ticked away in agonizing fashion for Kevin, who managed to find a safe spot in the corner of the bar at a table far from the hazards of his father. His seat was tucked away from the noise of small talk and jokes he had no hope of hearing the punchlines to. However, it was still close enough for him to take in the cast of characters that populated the many corners of his little hometown.

Cutting off his view, Tom pulled up a chair and sat across from him.

"You know," Tom said, sliding a fresh beer in Kevin's direction, "your dad isn't going to be that far behind me. Pretty soon we'll both be fishing in the Blue River."

"Well, with the pension you've got coming, you can probably fish anywhere you want," Kevin said.

Tom scoffed. "That's about the only thing I've got coming." He downed his beer and stared into its clear bottom. "That and the two dollars a month from Social Security. It's like being an inch from welfare and dumpster diving for dinner."

"There's always a trailer park in Mexico," Kevin offered.

"Fuck that," Tom coughed, recoiling from the thought. "I'd rather starve to death here."

Kevin looked on at Tom, who appeared suddenly wistful.

"Besides, who the hell do I know down there?" Tom added. "All the faces I know are here. I mean, look at all of them. Everyone here is like family."

Tom then eyed an elderly couple making an early departure. "Like the Gales. Fifty-six years together. Gotta respect that. My one and only marriage didn't last fifty-six days."

Kevin smiled slightly and watched as the door swung shut behind the ancient Gales. Through the rain-speckled window he could see them hunched over, Sherman Gale struggling to open an umbrella and hold it over his wife as they shuffled through the parking lot. Kevin knew little of the Gales beyond Sherman falling to his knees after pulling him from the car that one ghastly night. Kevin owed his life to this quiet man, a veteran who helped bomb the Third Reich into the fate it deserved, and since came home with a glassy look that telegraphed a horror Kevin could not imagine.

Walking in past the Gales were the Amboys.

"Or these two," Tom continued, nodding his head toward the door. The Amboys were the crazy granola couple who lived up in the old McMillan Victorian at the top of Branch Hill and declared upon their tie-dyed souls they were being haunted by none other than Nutty Maude McMillan herself. Maude would have tea with them on rainy afternoons and ramble on about her afterlife affair with Elvis.

Tom chortled at the sight of them and returned their enthusiastic wave. The Amboys were eccentric in their off-beat clothes and eco-friendly Birkenstocks.

"They made millions selling their business, and where do they land? Here," Tom added.

"Cheaper than a lot of other places," Kevin remarked.

Robert and Sheila Amboy were empty nesters who had fallen for the decaying, out-of-place mansion with its expansive views of the valley. Everyone steered clear of the McMillan home with its fenced yard and decorative "No Trespassing" signs—except for dumb kids who would go on ghost hunts in the middle of the night. It was the perfect haunted house with its sprawling floorplan, incredible lead-glass curved windows, and ornate exterior décor.

The house scared the shit out of Kevin. He never set foot in it after his mother was gone. It was a place of confusing memories and aching haunts, although he would've loved to have had tea with crazy old Maude at least once.

"Do you know who's going to be paired up with Dad now that you're about to become history?" Kevin asked.

Tom turned back around and thumbed behind him. "Your daughter's boyfriend."

What levity Kevin was enjoying immediately dissipated. He looked beyond Tom to Kyle Samuel, who stood at the bar amongst a cluster of coworkers, stealing looks at Shiloh, who had immediately beelined to the safety of her friends the moment they walked through the door.

"Relax, he's a good kid," Tom said, eyeing his glass for the blessing of one more drop.

Kevin knew that, but it didn't change the fact that Kyle, at the age of twenty-one, was too old for his daughter of seventeen.

Kyle had been a high school senior when they met in Shiloh's freshman year. Sparkling gray eyes accented by a neatly trimmed beard made him look like a prince—if Appalachia had princes. The moment Kevin saw Kyle, he knew his daughter was in big trouble. It was one of the rare occasions when a high school senior fell for a freshman, and a freshman was bestowed the dubious honor of going to the Senior Prom, much to the objections of parents on both sides and the envy of Shiloh's friends.

To Kyle's credit, he didn't try a thing on prom night nor was he expecting anything to happen. He received a notable amount of grief from his carnally starved friends and was nearly thrown off an overpass when he told them all he did was hold her hand and steal a kiss. Kyle also made sure he had Shiloh home fifteen minutes before Kevin's threat of statutory rape deadline expired. And he was completely content with that. Kyle knew Shiloh would be worth the wait, and, over the next three years, he watched her grow into a woman.

"Hey, look on the bright side," Tom chuckled. "Paired up with Frank, that kid's life will be a living hell. He'll want to retire at twenty-two."

Kevin took a little solace in that. Not much, but some.

Tom nudged Kevin and pointed toward the opposite end of the barroom. "By the way, you're about to lose your wife, Kev."

Kevin turned and found Tom pointing a bony finger toward "Bolt" Murphy, whose real name was Sebastian Clarence McCoy, a moniker he detested about as much as Francis Campbell hated his.

"Shit," Kevin hissed, to Tom's amusement.

Tom spoke into Kevin's ear before standing. "That's one of the reasons I stayed unmarried." And with a firm pat on Kevin's shoulder, Tom made his way back to Frank and a refill of his drink.

Kevin looked on at Bolt, who hovered around Trisha like a summer gnat. Bolt fancied himself a cowboy and hoped the name would get him riding gigs and Hollywood stunt roles, and draw in long-legged rodeo queens—like Trisha Campbell. He'd spent a good part of the evening following her around, percolating Kevin's patience.

Many knew Bolt's story. He had driven his hand-me-down Dodge pickup to Texas the day after he graduated high school. Within a week of driving across the state line, he signed up for an open bull riding competition at a county rodeo, accompanied by a newly minted bar-hopping girlfriend he'd found in a honky-tonk outside of Fort Worth. He lasted 1.45 seconds on the bovine and not even one with her. A vicious bull stomping left him with a fractured skull, no girlfriend, minor brain damage, and a broken back. He returned to West Virginia with medical bills, empty pockets, and a new name that possessed no value.

After a few years he had scratched out an existence roping together Granite Point's "Western Days Invitational," which drew crowds from four counties and thousands of dollars for the Chamber of Commerce, who used the money to hang Christmas decorations on lamp posts up and down Main Street come the holiday season.

Now in his mid-forties, Bolt was lean, muscular, and spoke with a voice that possessed some silk.

And Trisha made his soul ache.

Trisha was very conscious of this and maneuvered herself to a group of a few core friends, allowing her to shed Bolt onto other hapless prey. Once free, she stole a quick look toward her husband to ensure he was safe from his father and that the young homewreckers of Granite Point continued to steer clear of him. Even with his fatherly hang-ups, Kevin was still attractive enough to catch wandering eyes. Yet he barely seemed to notice. Trisha's own eyes never tired of taking in his tall frame that filled out the worn leather jacket she'd gifted him for Christmas years ago. He sported a hardened look with vulnerable eyes set under dark hair that refused to gray or thin. She knew she'd gotten lucky with him.

Trisha's life in Granite Point was short of idyllic. Being a latecomer to Granite Point High School and the bottom-dwelling Fighting Owls football team, Trisha found friends hard to come by, save for a few cheerleaders bent on recruiting her to their squad of back-biting conceitedness. Her sister, Michelle, had better luck fitting in; however, many girls at Granite Point High steered clear of Trisha the teenage barrel racing princess from Ohio.

Then she met Kevin Campbell.

Kevin was just like any other boy she would catch gawking at her. They all harbored full-time crushes, but what made Kevin stand out was his bravery to do more than just stare. He actually had the courage to say hi. This thin, unassuming tall kid with a defiant flop of hair would smile at her, hold the door open for her whenever she was behind him in class, and wave to her from across the cafeteria. So, when he asked her to the junior prom in a full sweat and with a waver in his voice, Trisha said yes without even thinking about it. Kevin was the only soul in West Virginia who made her feel at home.

Kevin filled the role of the dutiful boyfriend brilliantly. He attended every one of her barrel racing events, no matter how dusty it made his deep blue Dodge Charger or how much pungent crap stuck to the bottom of his shoes. And though she knew he always felt out of place amongst the horses and riders, he happily drove her and her trophies home, scraping his soles carefully afterward.

After graduation, Trisha's parents were ready to move once again, eager to explore Florida's big three H's: heat, humidity, and hurricanes. And while her sister opted to head back to Ohio for medical school and her meathead wide-receiver boyfriend, Trisha elected to stay in Granite Point with the high school sweetheart who saved her teenage years. She had also grown accustomed to the reality that Granite Point, West Virginia was now home.

"Kyle is staring at you," commented Caitlin, who looked beyond Shiloh's shoulder to the prince who was too pretty to ignore.

"Yeah, I know," Shiloh replied without turning around. She could feel Kyle's eyes cooking the back of her skull.

"You should go talk to him," Caitlin added, urging Shiloh to create new fodder for the town's gossip mill, "or are you afraid your dad will murder him in front of everyone?"

Shiloh glared at her with annoyance. Though Caitlin had been Shiloh's friend since childhood, lately they hadn't been as close, and this was a good example of why.

"Why do you stir up shit when you don't need to?" asked Ashley, who was both kind and loyal to Shiloh, which needled Caitlin to no end.

"I'm just sayin'," Caitlin claimed. Along with her competitive shallowness with Ashley, she held an additional, unspoken contempt for Shiloh because she possessed a catch like Kyle, while the best Caitlin could do was attract flies that only wanted to get her into a room at the Easy Stay Motel for an hour.

Shiloh wisely remained mum, possessing no interest in starting a pointless spat.

"You know," Caitlin prodded, "if you ignore him long enough, he's gonna look someplace else."

"Like where?" Ashley sniffed. "At you?"

"Well, if Shiloh doesn't want him . . ."

Shiloh simply shook her head. She knew Kyle had zero interest in Caitlin; he found her as intelligent as a five-watt light bulb.

Of her friends, Shiloh was the one who had spent the last four years growing up on her own. Once Trisha dropped the pregnancy bomb on her, Shiloh found herself on an accelerated path to adulthood with a growing collection of secrets she wouldn't share with anyone. They stretched from the benign, like when she had spent a year going to school sans underwear, to the more exploratory with an equally adventurous and curious Ashley. It only took one sleepover for both to decide that being a lesbian wasn't the way either one wanted to flow, especially once Shiloh offered up her virginity to the twenty-one-year-old Kyle Samuel shortly after the start of her senior year. She found him far more appealing, hence the biggest secret of them all.

Shiloh loved Kyle. She found him funny, kind, handsome, and the best her little hometown could offer. And that was just it. Her whole world was framed by a ridge of mountains to the north; rail lines that sliced right through from east to west; and a steel truss bridge that crossed the river to the south. Except for visiting her aunt in Ohio, nothing else in the world existed beyond TV, movies, and magazines with pictures of Italy, Africa, and the Alps.

Shiloh caught Kyle's eye and waved slightly to him before anyone could see. She then looked over to Beau Harper, who sat at a lonely table where everyone ignored him.

Beau was a good-looking kid, Shiloh's age, tall, brown-eyed, and autistic. And there he sat, content with a pair of headphones on, watching the miniature screen of a camcorder displaying endless footage of passing trains he'd recorded over the years—that was until Shiloh parked herself across the table from him and pulled one headphone off an ear.

"H-hey, Shiloh," Beau scratched out, sadly cursed with a stutter and a heartbreaking crush on the pretty girl now sitting across from him.

Shiloh leaned over the table and peered at the screen of the camcorder, then settled back into her seat and stared at him. "Third power equals twenty-seven?" she asked.

Beau didn't answer. He just stuck his nose back into the screen.

"I'm not tutoring you for my health, you know," Shiloh said, pulling the camcorder down. "Third power equals twenty-seven?"

"X equals three," Beau answered immediately without having to really think about it.

Shiloh cocked her head at him. "Yeah, you need a math tutor," she said sarcastically, knowing a sandbagger when she saw one. "You're so full of shit."

Beau gave her a slight smirk, slipped his headphones back on, then watched Shiloh head back to her friends out of the corner of his eye, a slight ache in his heart. Beau's mind was a noisy place, clogged with repetitive visions of trains and anything that spun in circles or on an axis. He was incredibly bright, with a large heart for animals and gifted with a fly-paper memory for numbers but little ability to remember conversations or facts of things that held no interest to him, which made communication a challenge. Only a rare few could see through it, and Shiloh was one of them.

Watching the exchange from afar was Kevin, nursing the new beer Tom had given him. Even without knowing her conversation with the Harper kid—who was considered more than a bit odd by everyone in town—he admired his daughter's big heart.

"You know," said the husky voice of Dana Harper, "your daughter is really the only one who talks to him."

Kevin turned to find Dana taking a seat at the table with him, carrying her beer and a folded piece of paper. So much for the corner table being a haven of quiet.

Dana was Kevin's age, and much like his father, was significantly hardened and worn down by life. The two had gone to school together and even dated once. But life and genetics were kinder to Kevin.

"Well, except that he's always too close to the tracks when he's filming," Kevin answered, "Beau's a good kid."

"So's your daughter," Dana added as she handed the paper to Kevin, who opened it and scanned through her union dues renewal form.

"Yeah, well, she gets that from her mother," Kevin replied, deflecting anything angelic over to the true source of everything good he considered in the realm of humanity.

"I think you had a hand in there somewhere. But here you are, hiding in the corner like Beau."

"That's because we both know it's the safest place to be."

"Until you're backed into one," Dana countered. "Beau doesn't know safe from a hole in the ground. Lately he's been slipping out in the middle of the night on his bike after I've gone to bed."

Kevin paused, trying to imagine an autistic teenager pedaling his ten-speed around in the middle of the night. He then signed Dana's renewal form. "Slipping out to do what?" he asked.

"What he always does."

Kevin handed her the form back and then watched as Michael climbed up next to Beau to watch his camcorder screen with him, the late hours starting to catch up with his son, who was now up way past his bedtime. "Videoing trains in the middle of the night is an awesome way to get yourself killed. Maybe have his father talk to him?"

"Well, if you can find his father and pull him off of his latest teenage girlfriend for two minutes, let me know," she answered. "Until then, it's just me trying to be in two places at the same time."

Kevin could only nod. He had no magic answers for that problem. Dana's ex-husband was a town nightmare who drove a rotting '74 Mustang II with an even more rotted muffler and a well out-of-date mullet under an odorous and threadbare ball cap that needed to be burned.

"Have Jimmy sign the bottom," Kevin said, nodding to the paper Dana was folding back up. "Then give it to Sarah and they'll fix your paycheck."

"I don't give it to Phil?" asked Dana. Phil, who worked in payroll, could be an easy doppelganger for her ex.

"Give it to Sarah. Phil can't even operate a light switch, let alone a four-function calculator."

Amused, Dana stuffed the paper into the back pocket of her jeans, a pair that was at least two sizes too small. Kevin was always great at bringing anything bright out of her, and she couldn't help but feel he was the one who got away. When Trisha had showed up with those long legs, that impossibly slender waist, a wide, toothy smile framed by to-die-for dimples, and sandy blonde hair criminally perfected by her cowgirl hat, Dana was doomed. Trisha possessed intelligent dark eyes that sucked Kevin in like a pair of black holes. And being five feet and too many inches too short, Dana was divinely sentenced to a gymnast's build that made her look like a bruiser version of Mary Lou Retton. Trisha had her outgunned in every department. To make things worse, Trisha was nice, which made her impossible to hate. So instead, after high school Dana did the only thing she could: fall for Randy "the Mullet" Schwartz, and that was that.

Dana turned, spotting Shiloh settling in at a table, where Frank and Tom immediately began dispensing Blackjack wisdom upon her. "At least your dad's teaching your daughter crucial life skills," Dana commented.

Kevin followed her gaze and sighed with enough volume to be heard two tables over.

"Take your victories where you can find them," Dana added. "It's better than teaching her how to do shots."

Kevin had to concede that. There were times he enjoyed watching Frank interact with Shiloh; he displayed obvious affection and patience for his granddaughter. Even blitzed, it was visible. It was one of his father's rare virtues that Kevin admired but further drove home the reality that he should've been born with a name like Molly.

"Amazing that after all these years, the two of you still can't find a way to get along," Dana followed up.

"We found something better," Kevin answered. "Peace in a détente of mutual disappointment."

"That makes no sense. Maybe you two should lower your standards," Dana said as she left the table and walked toward her son.

Kevin couldn't imagine their standards getting any lower, but Dana had a point.

It wasn't much later when the party began to thin. Even as Kevin managed to hide out for much of the evening, many still found him to chew his ear on subjects from big block Fords to union advice on retirement accounts. Beyond Trisha, Kevin was still a bit of a loner. He'd had difficulty making friends in his later years and failed in many ways to keep even a few. Those he grew up with in school either faded into other friendships, married, or moved away. Inside, Kevin felt that Trisha was all he needed, and, in the years that passed in their marriage, Trisha had failed to prove Kevin's mindset wrong.

With merciful timing, Kevin's eyes fell upon his wife as she pointed to Michael, who had become an exhausted bag of bricks in her arms, his head lolling to the side. With a final downing of his now rather nauseatingly warm beer, he waved to Shiloh that it was time to go.

Shiloh deflated a bit. Her grandfather had moved her on to Texas Hold 'Em after she'd clobbered him and Tom by winning seven straight hands of Blackjack, so she wasn't quite ready to leave. She quickly folded with her four queens, slid her collection of potato chip winnings to Tom, and pushed back from the table far before Frank was ready to see her go.

"That's it?" Frank complained. "You're leaving?"

Shiloh kissed both old farts goodbye and headed toward Kevin, who was now at the coat rack.

Frank's annoyance was palpable. Before Tom could get a hand on him, Frank swayed from the table toward his son, who was failing to make a quick getaway to avoid what was now inevitable.

"Where the hell you goin'?" Frank slurred, stumbling after his granddaughter.

"School night," Kevin replied, grateful for having a legitimate reason to make a hasty exit.

"Yeah, well, that wouldn't have been a problem if you got here when you were supposed to. Where were you?"

"Out boning the Ladies Auxiliary," Kevin quickly fired back with a conditioned response after years of the same old shit. "Where do you think I was?"

"Kevin . . ." Trisha discreetly tugged on her husband, urging him to stop before he even got started. Kevin looked at her briefly before moving off with the coats from the rack.

"Hey!" Frank barked at his son. "We're not finished here."

Kevin stopped as the remaining crowd in the bar went dead silent, and Tom wiped a hand across his face.

"Trust me, you're finished," Kevin said while Trisha's face tightened and Michael, now fully awake, watched from her arms.

"Apologize," Frank ordered, pointing at his friend.

"For what?" Kevin shot back. He was already well entrenched to repel his father's effective effort to make him feel like a five-year-old. Before he could open his mouth for the next salvo, Shiloh crossed between them.

"Grandpa," Shiloh said, slipping on her coat. "You're being an asshole." She then took her little brother into her arms and headed for the door.

Trisha smiled slightly as Frank stewed on being called out by his granddaughter, even though he had to admit Shiloh always called it the way she saw it.

"Your daughter," Frank said, pointing toward Shiloh outside.

"Your blood," Kevin threw back. He then exited with his wife.

Frank just stared at the door his son disappeared through.

"Come on, Frank." Tom appeared beside him before Frank could storm after Kevin. "Let's go get some air."

"Air?"

"Yeah, you know. Breathe?" Tom responded and maneuvered Frank out the door into the cooling night.

The moment they were outside, they watched Kevin's crew cab hit the pavement and roar off into the dark. Tom leaned against Frank's pickup, his breath swirling around him. "You keep doin' this to him," he said, "it's gonna bite you in the ass."

"Aw, I was raised the same way and I turned out alright," Frank dismissed him.

Tom scoffed. "You were raised entirely by women, Frank. I wouldn't say you were raised the same way."

Frank ignored that and swayed into the middle of the parking lot.

"He's a good kid, Frank," Tom kept at it.

Frank looked back at him, surprisingly able to stay upright and mostly coherent.

"Last time I checked he's the only one you got," Tom offered. "Might come in handy someday."

It took a few moments for Frank to concede that, but he'd rather eat rotted squid than admit it. Frank then looked around, imagining a long-departed kingdom. "Remember when we owned all of this? This was our town."

Tom looked around with him, only seeing a parking lot of rusted pickups, mud puddles, and an overflowing dumpster. "All we owned was the market for hangovers. We worked, drank, rinsed, and repeated."

"It's just another word for dying," Frank said with a hint of defeat.

"What is?"

"Retirement."

"You truly are a ray of sunshine, Frank, you know that?" Tom stated as he herded Frank back inside.

And it was then that Tom noticed the sheriff's cruiser skulking at the far end of the parking lot, its lights off, illuminated only by the dim orange glow of a rusted lamp post. He could just make out the dark silhouette of a large man visible in the driver's seat, watching, waiting. Tom immediately soured at the sight. He scratched the side of his face with his middle finger, then disappeared back inside the bar.

3

It was well after 10:00 PM when Kevin slipped out of the house and walked toward the detached two-car garage, which was affixed to a modest-sized barn decomposing faster than he could keep up with. The Campbells owned one of the larger four-bedroom, two-bath, two-story clapboard homes just outside of town that was free of the stereotypical lawn and porch appliances found further down the highway. The house was in better shape than most, freshly painted in white with a green roof, set on enough acres for an occasional horse to run and trample freely in the mud.

Pushing the garage door in, Kevin flipped on the light switch that brightly illuminated a screaming yellow 1940 Ford Business Coupe Street Rod. The Dodge Charger was long gone, liquidated to purchase the rock still attached to Trisha's finger. So, for now the street rod was his pride and joy, an auto cinema-worthy of George Lucas's *American Graffiti*. Tinkering with it was one of the few distractions—the other being a long hot shower spent staring at his feet—that gave Kevin any sense of solace.

Standing at the front bumper, he stared at the mirrored-finish chrome of the hand-built engine, trying to get the energy up to at least turn a bolt. The only energy he found was to shiver in the autumn evening chill. He glanced at the large heater still sitting in the dusty box it came in three years ago and again chastised himself for not putting it in over the summer when it was warmer and daylight was far more plentiful.

With the physical reality of holding a frigid wrench, the thought of cranking on a frozen bolt with exposed knuckles was less than appealing. Instead, his mind was adrift, much like a sailboat sitting directionless in the water on a windless day.

The echoes of the party and the well-predicted run-in with his father sat like lead in his psyche. He looked about the cluttered garage that was his domain, a domain slowly invaded by the realities of family life. Aside from the large workbench that had become more of a storage shelf, the garage held an inventory of parts for the Ford he had collected over the years, pushed aside by the necessity of a tractor mower, endless bins of Christmas decorations, camping gear, bikes, and an ATV that made trucking around their ten acres far easier than pushing a wheelbarrow.

The cold and the hour sapped any incentive in Kevin to do much with the car short of closing its hood and calling it a night. And if it wasn't for the thump he heard from the barn, he would've done just that. Kevin leaned to the side, peering toward the doorway of the barn and into the eyes of a large palomino American quarter-horse with a dainty braided mane that stood with a snort in the middle of it.

Really, Trish? Kevin thought. He closed the hood and walked toward the mare, who met him halfway once he was inside the barn. With a nudge of her head, the horse mushed Kevin back a step and then nestled into his chest. He'd had his fill of horses from Trisha's bygone racing days, but horses loved him anyway.

"You like her?" asked Trisha, who had walked in behind Kevin as quietly as a cat stalking its supper. She was bundled up in fuzzy boots and layers of anything that would keep her warm, topped off by one of Kevin's work coats and one of his cleaner Union Pacific baseball caps. "Her name is Freedom."

"No," Kevin answered without turning toward his wife, "her name is Bankruptcy, and there's nothing *free* about her."

"Oh, come on," Trisha tossed back, "she's beautiful."

Kevin threw a glance at the cruel God above who had bestowed this unwanted blessing upon him. He knew firsthand that one horse alone was more expensive than a midlife crisis comprised of two boats and a blonde, an analogy Trisha would immediately roll her eyes at. He had gone down the road of one-time horse ownership with Trisha before, not long after they were married. That particular nightmare, as he liked to call it, nearly pushed them over the cliff and into the Valley of Fiscal Destitution.

"Please tell me we didn't buy a horse," Kevin asked with a pleading tone.

"No," Trisha answered as she took Freedom by the bit and led her into an open stable. "She came from Bolt Murphy."

Horseshit, Kevin thought. "Bolt Murphy couldn't afford a horseshoe, let alone an entire horse."

"No, but the Amboys can," Trisha countered, easily remembering once upon a time when she hadn't had the luxury of a horse of her own. She closed the stable gate and gave the mare a scratch behind the ears. "She sorta belongs to Sheila."

Kevin stared with a slight sneer, his thoughts loud enough to be picked up on by every phony tarot card reader this side of the Continental Divide. *More horseshit—Sheila Amboy is sixty-five with bursitis and a hip made from parts on sale at Joe Bob's Mountain Hardware Store. There's something else going on here.*

"And stop staring at me like that," Trisha said without looking at him. "Sheila's granddaughter wants to learn how to barrel race."

"So, they got her a horse?" Kevin challenged, although he knew very well that every barrel racing student in the county came with either their own horse or a loaned one from somewhere or someone. Even when Trisha was riding in high school, it was on a horse from an older rider who loved Trisha's ability to make it a winner.

"Well, not quite," Trisha admitted. "Bolt told Sheila I'd be willing to try Freedom out before she went ahead and bought her."

"Of course he did," Kevin snarked. "You haven't been on a barrel horse in, what, ten years?"

"Are you saying I can't do it?" Trisha snapped, daring him to continue that train of thought.

"Not if I want to see tomorrow," Kevin retreated. "But you do realize what he's doing, right?"

Trisha stared at him. *Please.*

"Seriously," Kevin pressed. "The guy is methodically trying to worm his way into your life so he can work his way into your pants."

"You have a lot of issues, you know that?" Trisha retorted before walking back toward the garage. "Sheila's paying me to take the horse out. The money doesn't hurt, and it lets Bolt add barrel racing to the event."

"One, his name is Sebastian Clarence," Kevin pointed out as he followed the swaying of Trisha's hips still visible under the long sweater and heavy coats. "And two, he's only doing this to add *you* to the event so he can mutilate your married name over the loudspeaker."

Trisha stopped at the coupe to hand Kevin the tools he had left on the fender. She was very much a neat freak, and the garage drove her insane.

"I doubt he'll use it," Trisha answered just to needle his jealousy a bit.

"Very funny. But seriously. You haven't raced in years."

"I can handle a horse around the barrels far better than you can handle your father, and you've been doing that for much longer."

Ouch, Kevin thought and cocked his head at her. "That hurt."

"Trust me," Trisha added, knowing she'd stung her husband a bit more than he deserved, "tonight was embarrassing for everyone."

"And yet, somehow, that isn't making me feel any better," Kevin answered, collecting his tools from her hands to toss loudly into the toolbox with deafening clangs of metal against metal.

"Hey, look at it this way," Trisha said, leaning into him with affection. "At least you won't be waking up with *his* hangover. Can you imagine how he's going to feel in the morning?"

Kevin could. And even that little bit of solace etched a grin across his face.

4

The following morning, Frank was blessed with a hangover powerful enough to kill a large, fully antlered moose. And if that wasn't enough, he had to use most of his dulled brain power to quell the nausea that swilled in every corner of his digestive system. He attempted breakfast, which consisted of a squished packet of instant oatmeal and a slice of dry toast, only to jettison it all into the garbage after one bite. His stomach wasn't having any of this, and neither was his brain, which remained in the "off" position. Even the thought of coffee made him want to retch.

Frank also had to endure Kevin's unbelievable superpower of finding every damn pothole, crack, dip, and broken stretch of pavement as he drove him to work. With every bang and shudder of the truck, Frank grimaced with skull-splitting pain. His son was doing this on purpose. *He had to be.*

"Go back," Frank said, pointing behind them. "You missed hitting a telephone pole back there."

Kevin glanced at him with no sympathy whatsoever.

"There is no God," Frank muttered.

"Maybe try a ginger ale next time," Kevin suggested. "Might work better than sticking your head in a blender."

Frank glared at him and then closed his eyes, warding off the pain that daylight delivered like a hypodermic needle to his optic nerves.

Kevin sped on, tempted by a poorly nestled manhole cover that might just drive Frank's head into the roof, but he steered around it at the last minute. Then AC/DC's "Thunderstruck" came on the stereo, set to WSPR, also known as "97.3, The Hound," broadcasting from the top of Granite Signal Hill, whose DJs somehow knew their morning listeners needed to be audibly slapped awake. He cranked up Angus Young's guitar riff just in time to nearly end his father's existence right then and there, and if Frank had had any steam left, it would have come out of his ears. He sagged lower in his seat, eyes clenched shut in pain.

But wait, there, on the side of the road was something far better to torture his father with. Coming into glorious view as they crested the last hill into town was a heavenly offering of karmic splendor—a sight that wrenched a slight shit-eating grin on his face. It was then that Kevin realized his ability to avenge his father's cruelty might have no limits.

"Uh-oh," Kevin said.

"Uh-oh, what?" Frank asked as he looked ahead. It took him only a moment to take in the horror before him. "Oh, HELL no . . ." Frank barked in a near panic.

Closing in was the wiry figure of the widow Mrs. Olivia Edith Hobbs, a wicked octogenarian standing with her arms crossed next to a beaten-up 1975 Chevy Impala. To Frank, Olivia Hobbs was the epitome of evil, a nasty nightmare from his childhood who he always said should have stood trial at Nuremberg with all the other fascists.

And, of course, Kevin knew all of this and began pulling over anyway.

"WHAT are you doing?" Frank panicked.

"Saving an old lady."

"Sav—" Frank snapped. "Are you out of your fucking mind!?"

"Oh, come on. She's harmless."

"She's Josef Stalin in support hose!" Frank barked, wondering if he could grab the wheel to send the old bat sailing over the hood. "Keep driving!"

Frank felt like a trapped cat in the truck's cab as Kevin pulled to a stop next to Olivia Hobbs and rolled down Frank's window.

Frank stared straight ahead. He couldn't bear to look at the Wicked Witch of Granite Point and Everything East of the Mississippi.

"Looks like you've broken down again there, Mrs. Hobbs," Kevin said.

"Damn thing's a piece of shit," she snarled in a venomous huff.

"Need a lift?" Kevin asked while Frank grimaced.

"Oh, that would be lovely," she answered with deceptive old lady charm and a pleasant smile at Kevin, only to narrow her eyes at Frank, who reluctantly slid over as she climbed in and reached for the door handle.

"Don't slam the—" Frank said a half-second too late.

With nefarious splendor, the old woman slammed the door with authority, nearly killing Frank on the spot. Even Kevin winced.

"You know, I could look at your car for you," Kevin offered. "It's probably something simple."

"Oh, no. I wouldn't want to be a bother."

"Too late," Frank muttered in a weak attempt not to be heard, causing her to glare at him.

"I see you've been drinking again, Francis," Olivia Hobbs said with a dramatic sniff. "I can tell."

Frank sniffed back at her. "And I see you've been using Raid again. Still can't find the right pest-control deodorant?"

Her eyes darkened. "My Bobby used to say, once a drunk, always a drunk."

"He would've known." Frank smirked.

Frank remembered Bobby Hobbs clearly. He was a portly man with a pinched face that reminded Frank of a real-life iteration of Elmer Fudd. But whereas Olivia Hobbs, with her chicken legs, heavy heels, and muted wardrobe from the long-dispatched Sears outlet on 4th, was just downright nasty most of the time, Bobby Hobbs was actually a pleasant guy to be around—even though his wife drove him to the bottle almost daily. With Frank's father lost to the winds of the Depression, Bobby Hobbs provided a few tidbits of normalcy by sharing some of the simple things in life a father might teach a son, like how to use a screwdriver, work a handsaw without slicing one's fingers open, and change a tire without getting killed by a bumper jack. Frank even worked at the Hobbs Gas Station for a summer—until that fateful day when the Gales took out the ethyl pump with their '47 Buick and erased it from existence in a fire that took two days to put out. Upon the ashes of the Hobbs Gas Station, Karen's Coffee Shop was built, and Kevin swore the coffee had a faint taste of motor oil. Bobby Hobbs was one of just a few men in town who showed Frank snippets of a boy's life that his mother never could, and when he passed away a few years later, Frank truly missed him.

But Olivia Hobbs remained as ill-tempered and inhospitable as an agitated hornet. She played favorites in the classes she taught—classes students survived more than they endured—and Frank Campbell, or Francis as she insisted on calling him, was her least favorite of the many troublemakers who darkened her fifth-grade classroom doorstep. She only tolerated the kid because her husband took a liking to him.

Olivia Hobbs turned and squinted at Frank. "You wanna know how you can spot a drunk?" she asked rhetorically. "By the eyes. You can always tell a drunk by the eyes."

"Well, that makes sense since he probably spent a lotta time looking at *you*," Frank tossed back.

"You're a rotten man, Francis Campbell," she fired in return. "You were rotten when you were a kid, and you're just as rotten now."

"Well, maybe it had something to do with my teachers."

"Ha! I was a great teacher, and you needed discipline."

"No. You're an escaped Nazi and you should be in a straitjacket," Frank retaliated, raising his gnarled hands for Kevin to see. "See these knuckles? You think they're swollen from my cracking them? Uh-uh. Ask Babe Ruth with a yardstick here."

Kevin drove on, simultaneously satisfied and rather repulsed by the image of Frank's young hands being split open by three feet of wood wielded by the old woman. He envisioned his father stoically absorbing the corporal punishment that had led Mrs. Hobbs into a forced retirement.

Soon enough they passed under the welcome sign for Granite Point, a blue-collar railroad town on the edge of extinction.

"Criminal," Olivia Hobbs quipped darkly.

"Mule," Frank countered with disdain.

Kevin had barely pulled up to a corner in the town's center when Mrs. Hobbs flung open the door and landed on the sidewalk with her sensible shoes. With surprising agility she marched off, white hair standing up like a rooster's comb in the wind, utterly flustered. The world was an intolerable place for Olivia Edith Hobbs. It had the audacity to surround her with all its obnoxiously pretty fall colors, pleasant morning temperatures, and the impending holiday season that made her miss her Bobby even more. Even though he had spent many evenings hugging inexpensive bottles of scotch as his wife raged around the house, Bobby loved her regardless. He'd somehow managed to live with an affable smile in the midst of her Category 5 storms. She certainly had her moments, and he found them worth going through hell for due to one single trait he was convinced she possessed: Olivia Hobbs cared for everyone, even the students she professed to despise, like Frank Campbell—a kid who continued living, seemingly, for the sole purpose of agitating the hell out of his wife. Bobby Hobbs had grown up without a father himself, understood Frank, and vowed, when the opportunity arose, to put him on a better path. And for that one summer, when Frank was wiping windshields and pumping gas, it seemed that Bobby's plan was working—until everything went up in flames.

Frank watched as Olivia Hobbs rumbled away, taking a leg swing at a large orange tabby that dared to cross her path. "Indisputable proof God doesn't exist," he hissed, then made his own way out through the same door.

"You don't want me to drop you off at the yard?" Kevin asked.

"NO!" Frank barked, his hidden West Virginian accent making a surprise cameo appearance. "Christ knows who else you'd pick up!" He then fumed off down the street with an angry limp, turned to cross it, then jumped back as Beau nearly ran him over with his bike. "Goddammit! Is there anyone in this fuckin' town that isn't tryin' to kill me?"

Kevin grinned, his day pretty much made. He watched Beau pedal on, video camera and tripod slung over his shoulder, then parked his truck in front of Karen's Coffee Shop at the corner of 3rd and Center. Once inside, he found Puck watching Stanley Kamp hanging a trendy, mostly unpronounceable coffee menu over the counter. Stanley was an energetic fifty-five-year-old, aching to stretch beyond the confines of his little diner, while Puck was in his late twenties, a man who never launched into life beyond the junkyard he inherited from an uncle who drank himself to death.

"Hey, Puck," Kevin nodded before looking at Stanley. "Stanley, what are you doin'?"

"Showing this podunk town the future," Stanley replied, lowering himself down the ladder. "What do you think?"

"It's great," Kevin answered. "What is it?"

"What do you mean, 'what is it?' It's gourmet coffees. A grand, international collection to suit any taste, even if they're from around here." Stanley leaned toward Kevin confidentially. "Karen's given me two months to make this work. Then it's—" He imitated a throat slash, referring to his tolerant and practical wife, who was more than happy to let her husband run the diner in her name. "So, what are you guys gonna try?"

Puck leaned toward the sign. "What's an 'Ethiopian breakfast blend'?" he asked, squinting at the type above him. "I thought they were all starvin' over there."

Stanley rolled his eyes as Kevin cracked an amused grin. "Kevin, save me here," Stanley pleaded. "You're educated. Try somethin'."

Educated? What the hell has Stanley been smoking? I couldn't survive one semester in community college, Kevin thought while he scanned the sign and sneered just enough for Stanley to catch it.

"Dammit, Kev!" Stanley whacked Kevin on the shoulder in exasperation. "Expand your horizons. Look beyond your shoelaces for once. How about the Orange Colombian? It's supposed to have zing."

Kevin continued to stare at the sign with a twist of the nose.

"The Arabian Sidamo?" Stanley continued, growing more annoyed. "The Komodo Dragon? The double-espresso full-caf Sumatra?"

Nothing. Kevin was silent as Puck looked out the windows at a wood-paneled station wagon wobbling by.

In defiant defeat, Stanley stiffly poured a plain cup with his eyes never leaving Kevin, who held up a dollar bill. Stanley snatched it in disgust. "Peasant," he said.

Kevin grinned while the first of the new small cell phones in his pocket began to ring. Stepping away from Puck while Stanley watched, he answered the call from Dana Harper.

Stanley looked on as Kevin's smile faded and his demeanor shifted. Something was wrong. Very wrong. In an instant, Kevin was outside and heading for his truck. He spotted Beau setting up his camcorder less than a foot from the nearby trackbed and adjoining railroad crossing. He seriously didn't have time for this. "Beau!" he called out. "BEAU!"

Beau tried to ignore Kevin at first. He knew very well what Kevin was going to tell him to do. But eventually he looked over anyway.

"Too close!" Kevin barked at him. "Back up!"

Beau stared at him. He was stalling, having no interest or desire to move the tripod. He was happy where it was.

"I'm serious, Beau! Move back!"

Beau reluctantly did, moving back just enough to let Kevin climb into his truck and speed off. Once Kevin was out of sight, he moved the tripod right back where he'd had it.

Granite Point had been built around the rail lines that stitched through its hilly countryside. Back then, the Atlantic Yard Office was ideally located—a few blocks from the town's center. The building was old and nondescript: a faded beige paint job, faded logo, faded flat black paint on the bars over the windows and doors. The yard was small, with no more than six rail sidings and a pair of tracks to house the long-haul road prime movers or the decrepit old switchers from the Eisenhower era. And on a distant track sat The Brick, idling under a cloudless blue sky.

Frank stepped through the office door into chaos. He found coworkers snapping at each other while others suffered inwardly with a blank stare. Some gazed listlessly down at their boots, or at the envelope they held in their hands. An envelope that held the blueprint for many lives that were now ruined.

And it was then Frank's stomach fell a painful mile.

He had heard the company was running into money troubles, something management would neither confirm nor deny. It had seemed to be nothing more than a rumor born from the overactive imaginations of those who had already downed three beers at the M&M with nothing else to talk about.

Frank glanced toward the glass-walled main office just as Kevin stepped inside. He could see Dana giving him a dramatic rendering of whatever the hell was going on. Sitting there with her was Shiloh's wannabe boyfriend, Kyle Samuel. Why he was in there, Frank was unable to fathom, but Kevin's presence offered Frank a thread of solace.

With a dry swallow, Frank limped over to his locker, not even close to being ready to see what fate awaited him. He passed more envelopes haphazardly taped to locker doors for those who had not arrived yet or already knew their fate and had chosen to avoid coming in altogether.

With dread, Frank finally reached his locker.

No envelope.

He exhaled as part of him shook slightly in nervous relief.

"I guess old gimps come cheap, don't they?" said a voice nearby in a deep accent from the Hatfield-McCoy region of the state.

Frank turned to find Sal Pitt sitting behind him on the bench. Sal was a man sunk in his forties, already well-worn by only a decade on the rails and bitter from always being a dollar and a foot short in life. He crinkled up his pink slip and tossed it aside.

"Aw, leave him alone," said another voice nearby in Frank's defense. "He didn't do anythin'." This was Chad Colt, a kid just short of twenty-five. He was one of the rare ones who took a liking to Frank and was someone Frank didn't mind tolerating. He was a good kid, happy to help Frank any time he needed it.

"Why don't you go fuck yourself, ass-wipe," Sal snapped, his drawl snarling in anger.

Chad lunged at him and the two quickly enveloped themselves in a tangle that sent Frank backward against his locker. Others instantly pried them apart, with Kevin rushing in and pulling Chad away with a single arm.

"Alright!" Kevin yelled. "Everyone knock it off!"

Kevin's arrival and his union presence did little to tame the mounting hysteria. In an instant, questions and pleas were gunned at him, forcing him to whistle loudly.

"Whoa, whoa, whoa!" he bellowed in a voice that overpowered them, establishing his control over the room. "Everybody, calm down! The last thing we need around here is full-blown panic!"

"Man," Sal responded, "I got two mortgages, three kids, and a wife who wants a divorce. All I wanna do is panic!"

And that immediately drove the noise level back up again, almost to the point where Kevin could barely think.

"Hey, shut the fuck up, all of you!" shouted a voice from the back of the locker row. This was Will Hamer, a tank of a man Frank had known for years but someone he rarely spoke to. "What I wanna know is what about the goddamn pensions? I've heard that we've all been fucked!"

The room fell dead silent as Will drew a bead on Kevin and tried to burn the question out of him. Kevin hung on the answer. Then, after a couple of agonizing moments, he revealed what he knew. "Yeah," he said as emotionlessly as he could. "It's gone. All of it. And those of you who didn't get pinked today will be gone in a couple of months."

The silence in the room turned into an absolute pall. Stomachs fell into hopeless depths of despair, and all the men could do was disperse as a defeated mass of disposed labor.

Frank stared ahead in shock and then looked at his locker and then, absent-mindedly, turned to an adjacent locker to talk to Tom.

But he wasn't there.

Frank recoiled at the sight of the envelope still taped to it. He quickly looked around, searching for his friend, who had now lost everything. He was soon up on his feet, scanning everywhere for Tom before bolting toward the door to the yard as Kevin looked on.

"Dad?" Kevin called out as Frank disappeared outside.

Even with his limp, Frank could move quickly. As close as he could get to a run, he beelined directly to The Brick that idled alone on a track siding at the far end of the yard. He could just see Tom in the cab as he hobbled quickly to the crew ladder and raced to the cab door. But the deafening BANG inside the cab stopped him cold in his tracks, the door glass blooming blood red. Frank stared at the door handle for a heartbeat before yanking it open and rushing inside.

He was greeted with a level of carnage generally reserved for a war zone.

Tom had placed his service issue .45 automatic against the roof of his mouth and pulled the trigger, opening the top of his skull against the roof of the cab and spraying blood on everything within the blast radius.

Frank stood frozen as Kevin arrived a moment later. He instantly stepped back from the sight, then pushed Frank aside in a hopeless effort to save Tom.

Shattered, Frank slid along the cab wall in retreat. Reaching the cab door, he turned to leave this moment of horror, only to go face to face with a blood spatter on the door glass. He sagged to the cab floor as Kevin watched him, sure he saw a tear emerge from his father's eye.

5

A cold autumn rain had moved in as daylight faded over the town on its first day of the apocalypse. With a hint of Armageddon, downtown was remarkably clear of any sort of traffic, and the hills that hemmed in Granite Point were obscured by a scattering of low clouds that hid most of the peak fall colors—not that anyone today would be in a frame of mind to enjoy them.

At the M&M, it wasn't much different. The parking lot was devoid of all but a couple of pickups, including Frank's, which Kevin spotted and pulled up next to when he drove in. With a grab of his ball cap, Kevin was out of the truck and darting for the door under sharp pellets of rain.

Inside, he found it just as vacant, apart from Mitch at the bar, who was now recleaning his tenth shot glass, and Frank, who was sitting alone at a table. Kevin took the seat across from Frank, noticing his blank stare, a collection of empty glasses, and a mostly uneaten burger in front of him.

"You wan' it?" Frank asked, glazed eyes slightly brightening, his accent rolling in with ease due to the endless run of CC Manhattans that pickled his liver.

Kevin shook his head slightly. "Let's go home, Dad."

"That's the last place I wanna go."

"Yeah, but hanging around here isn't going to do you any good."

"Why not? I've got everythin' I need right here. A roof over my head, a john down the hall, and a TV in the corner. What else do I need?"

Kevin looked at his father for a long moment, knowing this wouldn't end well. But still, he had to try. "There's openings down at CSX. I can check and—"

"Who's gonna hire an old gimp with a limp, huh?" Frank interrupted with annoyance.

"You've got experience."

"What I got is this incredible desire to be left the fuck alone," Frank shot back, glaring at his son. "Which is gettin' more incredible by the minute."

"Dad, look . . . about Tom. I'm sorry . . . I don't even know—"

"You don't know shit, Kevin. You never did and you never will. You're not remotely qualified to say anything."

Stung, Kevin stewed in silence as his patience quickly ebbed. He knew that Tom's suicide made little sense to anyone, particularly his father. To everyone who knew him, Tom was hardly the type. The opposite of Frank—often a cantankerous thundercloud—Tom was an orb of approachable light. And while no one had expected this, Tom's sudden end knocked Frank completely sideways with gut-wrenching grief.

But the years with his father had eroded any reservoir of tolerance Kevin could have tapped, and he quickly found himself of the opinion that the old man could rot in this bar for as long as he liked. With any luck, he'd drop dead right there, right now.

"You can go fuck yourself, Dad," Kevin said, leaning in, his words exploding in Frank's face. He stood from the table, violently jarring it in the process. "You know, dipshit, you're not the only one who loved Tom. And you wanna know the difference between an asshole and an asshole who drinks? Nothin'. They're both full of shit."

Frank closed his eyes and sagged from the exchange as Kevin brushed past him, nearly knocking him off his chair. Part of Frank wanted to call his son back to the table, but the word "disingenuous" paralyzed him into silence, and the alcohol-soaked part of him, as always, won out. He would never be able to articulate what drove the undeserving emotional dismissal of his son. Nevertheless, there it was.

Kevin planted a twenty-dollar bill on the bar in front of Mitch. "Call the shithead a cab when you're ready to throw him out," he said before striding out the door.

Mitch watched Kevin through the window and smirked when, on the third try, he finally wrenched the mirror off Frank's truck and chucked it clear across the parking lot. Mitch then looked up at the clock. With an inebriated Frank as the only customer, he concluded it would be a dead night and completely pointless to wait for it to improve. "Come on, Frank," Mitch said, "whatta you say we call it a night, huh?"

"How 'bout you pour me another?" Frank tapped the table. "Let's go."

Mitch considered that for a few seconds, then pulled out a new glass, shot water into it, and delivered it to Frank.

Frank looked at it with a slight sneer. "What the hell's this?"

"Water. Rumor's it's good for you."

Frank considered the glass before he poured it out onto the floor. He then pulled out his wallet and dumped what little cash he had onto the table. "There. Money. Lots of it. Now start pourin'."

Mitch stared at the puddle on his already water-stained wood floor. He clenched his jaw and fumed.

Frank tapped the table again.

"I don't want your money, Frank," said Mitch, forgoing the fundamental lesson: never argue with a dumbass drunkard. "What I want is for you to get the fuck out."

What followed was a brief stare-down punctuated by Frank firing the glass past Mitch's head. It crashed into a framed Steelers football jersey, scattering shards of glass in all directions.

Mitch eyed the water-splattered jersey. With his patience now exhausted, he pulled a Louisville Slugger out from behind the bar, ready to whack Frank's head deep into the cheap seats.

Frank immediately retreated and fumbled out of his chair.

Mitch steamed toward him and threw the table aside, winding up to club the old man into ground beef.

Frank scrambled out the door to the safety of the poorly lit parking lot. Outside, once he realized Mitch wasn't behind him, he skidded to a stop in the drenching rain. He now stood alone, lost in the suddenly cold air that pelted him with frigid drops, quickly turning to sleet. Frank's breath curled around him in a moment of complete emptiness. Tom was gone, taking not only a piece of Frank with him, but a time, a place, and all their shared memories. He closed his eyes and felt the earth sway beneath him.

He wanted his heart to stop, but it incessantly hammered on, which he considered to be utterly pointless. As his mind aimlessly wandered, he soon found himself back in the blood-soaked cab of The Brick, where Tom's thin frame lay slumped against the cab window telegraphing the only emotion Frank could now feel.

Envy.

Frank stepped forward into the unwelcome reality of the present. The world wavered, nearly folding him into the black puddle that now engulfed his boots. There was an irony to this, or at least a metaphor he felt. But he was too much of a self-proclaimed idiot and too drunk to define what it was.

It took the distant blast of a train horn to break the moment. Frank cocked his head, listening to the fading echo of the horn ricocheting across the hills. "I hear you, you piece of shit," he said quietly amidst the drone of sleet and rain.

With another blast of the horn, this time closer, a horrible clarity cut through the alcohol-fueled clutter that clouded his brain. He heard the rumble of a faraway freight train, a heavy consist of iron carrying a meager profit for a shitty little railroad that deserved none of it. A railroad that erased lives that depended on it and inevitably destroyed anything and everything in its path.

And now in a horrible epiphany that made sense only to him, he suddenly knew what to do, and there was no one else better to do it. He *had* to do it. For Fay. For Tom. And maybe even for his son. For what was right. Tonight, he would become a soldier of fate, delivering a level of justice his rising arc of courage would administer. He would be the hero, a man celebrated by all.

And why shouldn't he be?

6

It was coming up on midnight when Kevin quickly pulled into the Sebring Freight Yard, illuminated in brilliant white light likely visible from orbit. He was in a post-coital daze, following a rare moment when he and Trisha found five minutes of peace to tangle up and do more than just hold each other. She had easily read the turmoil inside of him the instant he stepped through the door, something that was common any time Kevin butted heads with his father. Trisha had changed that in less than a minute when she towed him upstairs and into their bed. At least they were able to finish before the phone intruded and drew him to the last place he wanted to be.

Now climbing out of the truck, Kevin bundled up in the freezing mist that enveloped the industrialized air of the freight yard: a sprawling complex of rail cars, railroad tracks, and locomotives spread out over a hundred acres of prime West Virginia real estate.

The yard was pierced down the middle by a main rail line that coupled the Appalachians to the Eastern Seaboard.

Kevin shuddered at the cold and pulled on a pair of well-worn work gloves. He was grateful that the drenching downpour subsided long enough for him to slog through the mud and steal a look at a passenger train that idled amidst all of it. Kevin immediately knew it was going to be a long, cold night, which made him miss his wife's long, warm legs even more.

With an exhale, he trudged his way through the loose gravel and spongy mud to a gaggle of Union Pacific yard workers clustered around the truck wheels of a flatcar.

"Alright," Kevin said as he arrived, "what's so fascinating that you all had to—"

The workers parted, revealing a derailed wheel and a trail of gouged wooden rail ties behind it.

"Aw, shit," Kevin sighed.

This isn't a problem, he thought to himself. It was a massive pain-in-the-ass that wasn't even in his scope of responsibility. He had a bad habit of answering the phone and solving problems others didn't want to deal with. This train wasn't just sitting stuck halfway in the yard with the derailed flat car fouling everything up, but the leading section of the train now clogged up one of the two main lines.

"Think we can use the jack from your truck, Kev?" asked a comedic voice from the growing bundle of guys around him.

Very funny. Kevin then looked over the thousands of tons of bright-yellow Caterpillar earth-moving iron sitting on the car that weighed about half of that. Next, he looked at his watch: 11:43.

"Where the hell is Forrest?" Kevin asked with consternation, searching through the faces behind him for the yard supervisor, who was as dependable as a three-cylinder minivan from Peru. "This is his knot to figure out."

The guys looked at each other for an answer, conjuring in Kevin's mind the image of a useless band of highway workers staring at a sinkhole, with traffic backing up for miles behind them.

"Why don't we try re-railin' it over there?" said another voice from the crowd, pointing to a rail switch in the distance.

"Really?" Kevin countered. "You'll rip up the ties and the switch. No. Best thing is to cut it out."

And that drove a collective groan from everyone.

"That's going to take most of the night," another voice complained from behind Kevin.

"Hey, this isn't even my problem, so if you guys have a better idea, I'm all ears," Kevin answered, waiting for someone—anyone—to speak up.

All he got was teeth-chattering in response.

Fine.

"Alright. So, we're cutting it out," Kevin added before motioning to the waiting passenger train. "Who's that?"

"Dunno," answered Forrest Brunner, the yard supervisor, who had now joined the crowd of onlookers. "The *Allegheny Limited*, I think."

Brunner was a large man, wearing an oversized coat that made him appear even larger, accentuated by a hard hat with a brim that sat low enough to meet his unibrow. He sported a peppered beard in bad need of a combing, which likely would free a minute population of small animals trapped inside it.

Kevin stared at him and then pointed to the derailed truck that sank another inch into the weakening rail tie that held it up. He also took a small step aside, upwind of the man.

"Yeah, I see it," Brunner admitted. "Tryin' to figure out how we're gonna move it 'cause this consist is due by mornin'."

"Yeah, well, that's not going to happen," said Kevin. "Put the *Limited* on track two so he can get out of here. Otherwise you'll be backed up into Buffalo."

Brunner nodded, pulled a walkie-talkie from his belt loop, and spoke into it while walking off.

With some level of questionable confidence, Kevin decided things were well enough in hand for him to make an escape. Fighting off a shiver and burrowing further into his coat, he trudged on to his truck, which took him close enough to the *Limited* to spot a ten-year-old boy in one of the passenger car windows, mesmerized by everything outside. With his mop of hair and big, dark eyes, the kid reminded him of what Michael could grow up to look like in a few short years. Which, of course, fired a pang of guilt through him, as it emphasized how little time he actually spent with his son. But that was a perpetual 'Campbell' conundrum for another day. Kevin continued to look on at the child, who was now waving to him. Kevin smiled slightly and waved in return. He opened the door to the truck and immediately spotted Beau Harper in the distance, speeding along on his bright red bike, then disappearing behind a set of boxcars.

"Goddammit . . ." Kevin growled, climbing into his truck. This was the last thing he needed. He fired the engine up and went after Beau in a spray of mud. Popping onto the road, he accelerated into the night and scanned the darkness, looking for a kid with absolutely no fear of much of anything, including getting run over by a train.

Soon enough, the road reached an end, butting up against a collection of weeds and a scrappy grove of trees and brush. Kevin stopped and climbed out. There were ten directions Beau could've disappeared into, each one giving the kid hypothermia if he were to stay out here too long.

"Beau, I know you can hear me," Kevin called out, honestly wondering if Beau was pedaling his way to the shortcut to Prowler Flat. "Go home!"

He heard nothing in return. Just the idling of his engine and the intensity of rain picking up around him. He took a quick look at his watch. It was now 11:52—way too late to be dealing with this level of bullshit. "I'm serious, Beau. Come out and I'll get you home."

Still nothing.

Already moving beyond frustration, Kevin considered calling in the cavalry to sift the kid out. But that would involve dealing with Hollis Peete, who possessed the empathy of a surly blowfish. Beau could easily wake up in a jail cell with Dana bailing him out with money she didn't have at 4:00 in the morning.

Fuck it. Kevin climbed back into his truck and drove off.

Beau poked his head up from behind the scrub and watched Kevin's taillights disappear down the road. Once out of sight, he climbed back onto his bike and pedaled toward Prowler Flat. He knew the footage he would get tonight would be totally worth it.

7

The blue and red lights of Deputy Preston Moulds' cruiser lit up the rain-soaked pavement of Route 341 like a roller-skating rink; the droplets of frozen rain on his car and Frank's pickup fractured the light into the darkness around them.

Preston Moulds was a Granite Point native. He'd graduated high school with Kevin, although neither was more than an acquaintance to the other beyond Preston having been a possible competitor for Trisha's affections. Preston had perfect posture, perfect teeth, a perfect six-foot-three height, and a perfect ROTC haircut that he looked perfectly perfect with. The girls of Granite Point High had swooned at the sight of him. At least they had in Kevin's mind. He knew Trisha had noticed Preston more than once in the hallways, but it'd never gone anywhere beyond that. Preston was even-keeled and had stayed that way when he'd entered law enforcement after four years in the Army. He was a stark contrast to his boss's erratic and snarly persona. Preston couldn't stand Hollis Peete, who himself found Preston annoyingly practical, patient, and a true poster boy of the sheriff's department—all traits Hollis detested with a passion. Preston was also good-looking with grounded empathy, which needled Hollis even more.

Preston looked ahead into the reflective glare of Frank's tailgate with resignation. Once again, he'd pulled Frank over; the fourth time this year and likely the end of Frank's driver's license. Hollis was going to relish screwing Frank on this one, and there was precious little Preston could do about it, especially when he had just stopped Frank for driving directly over the center line. At least he had his headlights on this time.

Preston grabbed his hat and gave a quick look at the time. It was 11:55.

Pushing against the cold damp air, Preston approached Frank's truck. He gave it a once around, immediately noticing a pinched, mud-crusted front bumper, mud-plastered fenders, and the missing driver's door mirror that Kevin had slung into the neighboring county. He then pointed his flashlight into the truck, finding a soaked Frank squinting from the blinding beam of unwanted illumination. Preston tapped on the window.

Inside the truck, the cab was sopping wet, with Frank a ridiculously drenched disaster. Dirt was haphazardly splattered on his clothes, and he was doing his best to hide his right hand.

Preston again tapped on the glass. "Roll down the window, Frank," he ordered.

Frank did, pulling in slightly from the rain and trying to focus past the brilliant shaft of light in his face. "Preston?" he asked.

"Yeah, Preston. What are you doing out here at this hour?"

Frank's brain went vacant. "Uh . . . goin' that way," he replied, pointing straight ahead.

"Yeah, I wouldn't count on it," Preston dismissed. He next noted the mess within the cab. "You been four-wheelin' with the windows down, Frank?" And then Preston noticed the blood on Frank's hand that was also smeared on the center console. "Jesus, Frank. Who have you been shaking hands with—Freddy Kruger?"

Frank again moved his hand out of sight.

"You're killin' me, Frank. Hollis has a noose with your name on it and now he's gonna hang you with it."

Frank stared blankly ahead.

"Come on, Frank. Let's go."

"Where?" Frank slurred slightly, oblivious to what Preston was about to do to him.

"To someplace warm and dry," Preston replied as he tried to open the locked driver's door. "Unlock the door, Frank."

"No," Frank mumbled, "I think I'd rather go home." He started the engine.

"Goddammit, Frank!" Preston barked as he tried to open the door again. "I'm serious! Unlock the fucking door!"

That wasn't going to happen. Frank spun his out-of-season snow tires and squirreled onto the road in a shower of more mud, spewing Preston with road debris and sending him scrambling for his patrol car. Inside, Preston stared at Frank's fleeing pickup in disbelief through his rain-splattered windshield. He didn't even have time to consider what any of this meant, but the vision of Hollis willfully violating Frank's civil rights by hanging him on the steps of City Hall was at the forefront of his mind. He mashed his foot to the floorboard while Dispatch frantically called for him.

Frank sped on, his eyes on the rearview mirror as Preston accelerated toward him. He briefly wished Preston would bump him just enough to send him sailing over the Route 18 overpass he was about to cross.

His mind was a muddled mess.

Just as everything had made sense a short while ago, it now made no sense whatsoever. But even through Frank's mental fog, he knew he was falling into a bottomless hole that would be impossible to escape from. He considered just pulling over again, but he knew what that would mean. And maybe he deserved it. Better yet, maybe Preston would just shoot him in the head and leave him for the wolves to clean up. But that kind of luck was meant for lottery winners rather than for dumpster feeders like himself.

And yet, he was still running. The broken divider line of the dark road ahead blurred and twisted as he gassed beyond 65 mph. The truck skidded and slid, hydroplaning on the soaked pavement while Frank's mind bounced from one thought to the next. *The old Woodward Tank Farm is right there on the left. All it would take is just a nudge of the wheel, a punch through the chain-link gate, and only a moment of blasting heat before it would all be over, done . . . but even doing that would be wrong. I'd leave a mess for someone else to clean up.*

Frank's foot fell off the pedal and the truck decelerated, quickly coasting below 50 as he surrendered to the reality that he couldn't even come up with a clean and efficient way to dispatch himself. He felt like a coward. He felt it in his bones. In his gut. And in the end Hollis would be proven right, and Frank could do nothing about it.

The truck slowed.

Frank looked for a wide enough space to pull back over in what was now complete darkness. It took a moment for his brain to focus enough to realize the blues and reds from Preston's light bar, which had flooded his cab just a few moments ago, were now gone. He looked into the mirror and saw Preston's cruiser speeding off—in the opposite direction and away into the distance, disappearing behind a bend in the road.

The truck slowed to the point where it drifted off the road and thumped to a stop against a rut in the asphalt. Frank's attention remained on his mirror. Preston was gone. The only thing that accompanied Frank now was silence.

And the faint wail of sirens.

A twinge of guilt swirled in Frank's stomach. He had an instinct to follow Preston and the sirens, but now he was tired. The pain in his hand grew, and he could only think of sleep.

8

Prowler Flat was a small, unincorporated flood-prone locale parked five miles down the main line from Atlantic's Granite Point yard. On this October night in 1999, the hamlet was home to fifteen full-time residents living below the poverty line, along with countless vermin, a few livestock hemmed in with decomposing split rail fences that leaned with the wind, six barn cats, and one stray mutt named Dammit who barked incessantly and chased chickens for breakfast, lunch, and dinner. Along the rail line, tracks stretched to the old Baltimore and Ohio main line that fed Pittsburgh, Buffalo, and plenty of points out west beyond Indiana. It was equipped with a new signal light, a bright silver transformer that fed it, and a fresh trackbed compliments of Hurricane Andrew relief funds.

And tonight, Prowler Flat was also home to the wreck of the *Allegheny Limited*.

It was at 11:58 when the first calls came into the county 911 switchboard with frantic reports that a plane had just crashed into the heart of a town, obliterating the Fish and Jane Bait Shop, erasing the old Union 76 gas station with the classic dinging pumps, and hollowing out the old Bank of No One Remembers. Except for old Bud Mahoney, who lived right up near the newly graveled trackbed, no one knew it was a train derailment from the apocalyptic racket it created—the wheel trucks from coach 78564, blowing through his back door and landing on his La-Z-Boy, were a dead giveaway.

When the first responders arrived, they found a scene of complete devastation. Gutted passenger cars lay strewn across the torn-up trackbed like a psychotic sewing job, their insides opened and spewed out into the chaotic darkness. The *Limited's* twin locomotives were buried deep in the mud and dumped on their sides, much akin to a child's abandoned train set.

Kevin was amongst the first to arrive. He had just gotten home when his phone rang incessantly, much to the disappointment of Trisha, who almost got her husband back into bed for more of what they had started. But once she heard what had happened, she pushed him out the door before he could put on his coat.

Up on a rail car, Kevin kicked in a window and dropped inside, followed by a rescue team from Morgantown that had been in the area for training. Landing amongst the moans and cries of the passengers, Kevin would later recall it was much like standing within a scene from *Saving Private Ryan*. The emergency lights that survived the derailment did little to illuminate the horror. Kevin waded through, leading the way as flashlights behind him pointed past those who were free of the wreckage and zeroed in on those who were not.

He pushed onward, climbing through the twisted piles of seats and sheer destruction until he came across a bloodied mother frantically clawing at a contortion of steel and aluminum. He quickly dove in, wrenching enough of the crumpled metal away to send the young woman shrieking.

Kevin froze at the sight of the child. It was the dark-eyed boy he had seen only a short time earlier, now severed in half above the navel.

All he could see was Michael.

"Holy Christ," said a voice behind him.

Kevin was stiffly pushed aside by paramedics, who also had to navigate the boy's hysterical mother. Kevin shook enough of the vision off and pulled the woman away, then held her back as she lunged at her child when the paramedics abandoned the boy in favor of a savable soul nearby.

She then turned and pressed her bloodied and sobbing face into Kevin's chest and sagged, pulling him down with her.

Kevin just looked at the shattered child and closed his eyes.

9

ndrea "Andy" Mayland zipped up her bulky, navy blue investigator jacket and nestled into it. The morning air was cold, with a freezing wind that blew in over the hilltops and rustled the red and yellow leaves of the nearby trees. With the deep blue sky above, it would've been a beautiful day if it weren't for the steel carnage before her.

In her mid-thirties, Andy possessed a warm attractiveness: dark eyes and unruly shoulder-length hair knotted up under a snug baseball cap. She stood a few inches short of six feet with a moderate build and mud caked onto the soles of her boots. She bent an ankle to assess how much she would need to scrape off to walk normally.

"Andy?" said a voice behind her. She turned to find Ryan Horn attempting to walk upright through the debris and puddles that swallowed his ankles. He was a young and skinny intern with a squeaky-clean look that would probably get him carded for the rest of his life. Andy also knew the boy held a quiet crush on her, so she did her best to keep him at arm's length.

"They find the recorder yet?" Andy asked as she noticed a couple of people who followed behind Ryan closely.

"Oh, uh, yeah, they're cutting it out now," Ryan replied, not expecting the question. He then motioned to Hollis, who had already walked past him. "Andy, this is—"

"Sheriff Hollis Peete," Hollis said, cutting the kid off. He shook her hand and took his hat off, revealing a clump of thinning hair that went in every direction except up. He continued to hold on to her hand as he struggled to remove his eyes from hers. He was mesmerized and enjoyed a moment imagining himself nuzzled into the base of her neck after a bottle of wine, summoning some long-lost charm, a soft whisper in her ear, maybe a line from Elizabeth Barrett Browning . . .

"My hand back, please?" Andy asked while her skin crawled and a chill ran down her spine.

"Oh," Hollis answered quickly. With his fantasy shattered, he immediately freed her hand. "Sorry."

"Hi," Dana said as she moved in for her own introduction. "Dana Harper. I'm the yard manager for Atlantic." Given the remarkable dark circles under her eyes, it wasn't hard for Andy to discern this woman was exhausted. Dana had arrived at the derailment shortly after Kevin and as of this morning she was barely surviving on three cokes, a dropped donut, and no coffee.

Andy shook her hand. "Yard manager?" she asked with an air of confusion.

"I was the only one available."

Atlantic sent a yard manager to this? Okay, Andy thought, *red flag number one.*

She dislodged her boots from the soggy soil and led the way into the chaos that lay ahead. She noted the throng of media in the distance, no doubt postulating on anything and everything while telling everyone very little. She also eyed the emergency crews continuing to mop up around them, ensuring no one was left behind in this apocalyptic mud pit.

And she had been through all of this before.

"So, you own the right-of-way?" Andy asked of Dana, who followed her close behind.

"Everything from 55 and 106," Dana answered, slipping and balancing on the gravel while doing everything she could to keep up with Andy's surprisingly long strides. How this woman could move with such grace over such horror was a mystery. She made it look too easy.

"Any roadbed problems here before?"

"Uh, a few years ago. When Hurricane Andrew took the subbed out."

"So, you guys have been monitoring the soil since then, right?"

"Uhhh . . ." Dana stalled. That wasn't a question she was expecting, so "unprepared" was the best she could muster. "That I don't know. But I can find out." She hesitated. "Uh, I know this is a little soon, but when can we start clearing the wreck?"

Andy gave her a glance. *Really?*

"People are going to ask," Dana fumbled sheepishly. The "people" asking was really no one except for Atlantic's idiot CEO, who couldn't be bothered to visit the site himself. Dana imagined him frantically barricading his house from the employees who wanted to string him up like Benito Mussolini, and she knew he would demand Dana ask what she knew to be a stupid and utterly tone-deaf question.

"Two, maybe three months."

Dana stopped cold. "Months?"

"That a problem?"

"Um . . ." Dana fell silent. How in the hell would she explain this one to the dumbass who would likely fire her on the spot for even mentioning the word "month"? Not that she would likely have a job in a month anyway.

Andy moved on. Her eyes passed over the expanse of ruin around her that also reeked of hydraulic fluid. She then saw a lone man sitting atop a rail car that lay crumpled on its side. He was essentially catatonic, just as a sole survivor who stormed a beachhead would be.

"Sheriff, who's that?" Andy asked.

Hollis looked up. "Oh, that's Kevin Campbell. He's the president of the local union," he answered with a hint of disinterest, "and a driver for Union Pacific."

"He looks a little shell-shocked."

Hollis looked again. "Yeah, I guess," he answered, and then retreated as she just stared at him. "Hey, I'm not a psychiatrist. I have enough headaches in my life."

Andy continued to stare, her dislike for him reaching a new level. "Thanks. I think I'm going to look around here for a while."

"Okay."

Andy walked on, immediately sensing Hollis was close behind her.

"So," Hollis asked, "have you found a place to stay yet?"

"I'm sorry?" she asked. *Please, God, make him go away.*

"I mean," Hollis continued, trying not to stumble over his own brain and libido, "I can locate a hotel for you, maybe show you some of the restaurants in the area. I know of some great places."

To his credit, Hollis was a surprising optimist.

Oh my God, Andy thought, cringing inside. *Is the guy really hitting on me? Now? Are you fucking serious?*

"You're not asking me out on a date, are you?"

Hollis slowed and paused. He found himself somewhere between embarrassment and humiliation, a sensation he wasn't well versed in. It was one of the few times he had wished life came with a rewind button.

"Um, no," Hollis stammered, frantically trying to backpedal.

"Because that's what it sounds like."

"Uh . . . just trying to be hospitable."

Bullshit, Andy thought. A date with this guy wouldn't be much different than going out with a manners-challenged gorilla.

"Oh, good," she said as she walked on. "I have enough headaches in my life, too."

And with that she left Hollis, who had now backed off and disappeared into the sea of responders that continued to comb the ruins.

Andy next stood at the edge of the crumpled coach car and looked up at Kevin. "Mr. Campbell?" she called up to him.

The sound of her voice was enough to break his trance. He looked downward from his perch, sizing up this stranger, with no desire to communicate with anyone.

"I'd like to talk to you for a moment," Andy continued. "Would you come down, please?"

Kevin remained silent and still.

"Please?"

With a shallow breath, Kevin finally moved. He slid off the car, landing on the scattered gravel of the torn trackbed.

"Thank you," Andy said. "My name is Andrea Mayland. I'm with the—"

And Kevin walked right past her, cutting her off mid-sentence and leaving her looking on.

Kevin drove straight home, his mind frozen in a long, surreal moment that felt like a lifetime. He was truly in shock, unable to fathom, comprehend, or process what he had just been through and seen with his own eyes.

When Kevin entered the kitchen, Trisha and Shiloh recoiled at the sight of him. He hadn't realized the sheer amount of blood that covered his clothes. He looked like he'd been in a war zone.

"Oh my God," Trisha gasped, "are you okay?"

Kevin didn't reply. Leaving a trail of red clay mud behind him, he disappeared down the hall and up the stairs just as quickly as he'd walked through the kitchen door. He just wanted to get to his son and was ready to push the already half-open door to Michael's room when Trisha pulled him back.

"Don't," she said in a protective whisper. "You'll traumatize him for life if he sees you like this."

Kevin stared at the door, knowing she was right, but it did nothing to quell the immediate need to lay eyes on his child.

"Come on," she said, guiding him down the hallway into their room and away from the bathroom at the end of the hall, where an unseen Michael looked on in dead silence.

10

The phone in Frank's bedroom rang incessantly. It was loud and intrusive, especially since it was right next to Frank's ear.

The shrill, electronic ringing was an audible cruelty best saved for torture chambers, but it was enough to elevate Frank from the alcohol-induced coma he was in. He reeled from the audacity of daylight that poured in through a crease in his forty-year-old window drapes. And as he went to sit up, he was rewarded with the savagery of a hangover gifted to him by Satan himself. His head felt like lead. His brain screamed. His skull wanted to split into four—no, make that eight pieces.

Frank fumbled for the cordless phone that continued to pierce his fading sanity. Once found, he quickly hung up on the asshole calling him before the answering machine in the kitchen could catch the call. Frank then tossed the phone aside and plodded his way to the bathroom. Nausea washed over him the moment his feet touched the cold floor. Once in the bathroom he lowered his head onto the rim of the sink, and with whatever energy he could muster Frank quelled what swilled in his gut.

He then looked in the mirror. *Good morning, Death Incarnate.*

Frank wobbled out of the bathroom and propped himself up against the door jamb, which was much better than landing on one's face, a direction that was exactly where he was headed.

The room spun around him, and the nausea swilled again. He took a couple of steps toward the bed and stopped instantly, finding the dirt and blood smears on the bed sheets.

What the . . . ?

Frank rolled his right hand and revealed a dirty and grisly gash in his open palm. And now that he saw it, it immediately stung like hell. He quickly went back to the sink and ran water over it. His face tightened at the searing pain.

What the fuck happened last night? Frank struggled inwardly through the fog that lingered behind the pain. *It was late. Kevin . . . Kevin was at the bar. He left pissed. Kinda don't blame him, really. But what else . . .*

The fog cleared and Frank found himself at Prowler Flat. He remembered standing on the tracks as rain poured down on him in quarter-sized droplets. A crowbar gashed his hand as it slipped from his grip . . .

What the fuck was I doing?

The phone rang again, nearly sending him into the attic with a heart attack followed by a stroke chaser. He stared at the cordless handset, terrified to touch it. And yet it continued to ring until the answering machine picked up the call. Frank couldn't quite hear the words, but he knew the sound of Dana's tired and overwhelmed voice. He grabbed the phone and clicked it on, then pressed it against his ear. The color in his face disappeared as he listened to Dana calling him to go to work . . . at Prowler Flat.

Frank's soul went cold. The phone fell from his hand and broke apart around his feet upon the hardwood floor.

Frank would never have been able to describe the disembodied sensation he felt the moment Dana blurted the word "derailment" over the phone. In reality, Dana's delivery was so breathlessly rushed and linguistically munged he could only make out maybe four words out of ten. It was true his hearing was beginning to go after spending decades in a ridiculously loud locomotive, but he wasn't hearing-aid-worthy deaf yet. But it didn't matter. Frank managed enough sentence math to piece together what she was frantically conveying. An instant later he wanted to desperately crawl out of his own skin.

From that moment forward nothing fit right. Not that much had before then. Beginning the dark morning when Fay's life ended, everything had changed. From the way the sun illuminated the world around him to the vicious cold that made his bones ache in the winter. And it changed even more when he saw Tom's opened skull and tall body sagged against the bloody glass of The Brick's cab windows. A change he wasn't even close to reconciling. But this . . . this was different. An air of inescapable culpability consumed him.

Frank trudged his way toward The Brick at Atlantic's Forty Yard, a collection of old tracks that sat below strings of rusted-out freight cars just outside of town. There waiting for him on the crew walk was Kyle Samuel, who, along with Frank and a few others, had managed to survive the layoff slaughter. He sized Frank up as he would a zombie.

"Dude, you look like shit," Kyle commented as Frank reached for the crew ladder with a painful grimace.

Frank paid him only a glance as he climbed the ladder, ready to retch on anything, everything, and anyone. Thankfully, the trip to the engineer's seat was mercifully short, and he settled in.

"Mile marker sixty-two," Kyle said, pointing ahead as he took the cab's other seat.

"Yeah, I know," Frank said in a soft voice that Kyle could hardly hear. "Prowler Flat."

"You heard, huh? Gonna be a shitshow," Kyle commented as he slid his window open. He then looked at Frank again. "You want me to take the throttle? You look like you've been worked over by a tractor mower."

Frank looked at him and placed a finger against his lips. *Shhhh.*

Kyle waited a few moments, until he couldn't help himself any longer. "How's Shiloh do—?"

"Still under eighteen," Frank quipped before Kyle could finish the question. Atlantic had snapped Kyle up a week after he exited high school, grabbed by a railroad hungry for young, cheap labor. And both Frank and Kevin were perfectly content with that, as it meant Shiloh would rarely see him, which also suited Trisha just fine. Shiloh's parents were not fans of their uncomfortably independent daughter dating someone who was already wading into the grinds of adulthood. But with her mother preoccupied with her obnoxiously cute little brother and her father hauling long freights to exotic locales like Kansas, Shiloh saw Kyle when she could. He'd even managed to extricate himself from work long enough to take her to her junior prom, so the young man was admirably committed to the young brown-haired girl who was morphing into womanhood.

The trip to Prowler Flat passed in thankful silence for Frank. Kyle would've usually chattered inanely until Frank's cranium melted, but he could tell Frank was barely holding on to life itself. So, any unnecessary blather would've resulted in Frank spontaneously combusting right there in the cab or tossing Kyle out through one of the locomotive's small windows.

Frank throttled the work train to a stop and stared at the overwhelming sight of metallic carnage. What passenger cars were not already horrifically sliced open were upended or accordioned together. As Frank absorbed the scale of what lay before him, the feeling of guilt grew stronger and was further exacerbated the moment he spotted Hollis loitering not far from a cluster of blue investigation jackets.

And somehow, by instinct, Hollis looked up from the mud and debris, directing his glare at Frank.

"See those blue jackets?" Kyle pointed out as he moved in next to Frank, looking through his window. "That's the NTSB. And the FBI's next. Wait and see."

Kyle grabbed his gear and jumped out the cab door while Frank stared out the window. The knot in his stomach tightened and he kept an eye on Hollis, almost waiting for his mortal enemy to point his fat finger at him.

But Hollis shifted his stare away from Frank and over to a muddy clutter of uprooted weeds, old rusted rail spikes, rocks, and twisted hunks of steel and aluminum around him. A distinct stench of mechanical fluids mixed in the morning air with the slightest hint of the nine who didn't survive the crash. It was a smell Hollis recognized from a war that was more than even he could stomach, which explained the odd familiarity he felt. For a brief moment, he could feel his old combat helmet lying loose upon his closely shaved head, his M-1 slung low in his arms, and the blasting, unforgiving Asian heat that drove sweat down his back while the head of the corporal in front of him exploded with the impact of a sniper's bullet, stinging Hollis' face with the contents of the man's skull.

And then with a blink, he was back in the middle of a grisly reality as the sheriff of a town that loathed him. Even for Hollis, what surrounded him was difficult to fathom. He moved on, skidding down what was left of the raised trackbed and landing on a bulge of soggy orange-red clay, his boots amongst fresh tread marks made from out-of-season snow tires. Hollis crouched for a closer look, his brain running down a memorized list of dipshits who never bothered to change their snow tires when spring arrived.

And there was one particular dipshit who immediately came to mind.

Hollis stood back up and returned his stare toward The Brick and its driver, who had since slid to the bottom of the cab, turning himself inside out.

Andy stared into the scars etched into the crumpled and puddled trackbed amongst the ruins around her. It was a jarring reminder of the strewn remains of a twelve-car passenger train that had lain scattered in a ravine in the middle of an Arizona desert just a few years earlier, only her second outing as a fledgling investigator. What followed immediately afterward turned her life inside out and upside down, and it'd been that way ever since. It was enough for that familiar ache to grow exponentially within her, causing her to wonder, *Was he here?*

The wreck of the *Allegheny Limited* would be her third investigation since Arizona but her first as the lead. Although many would consider it to be a promotion of sorts, it whipped up a small whirlwind of panic that clouded her confidence—her own version of imposter syndrome before it became a vogue term some decades later. Andy found it inevitable that it would only be a matter of time before someone figured out that she had no idea what she was doing, and that all she possessed was a convincing talent to fake it. Of course, no one ever thought that or said it to Andy, except for the demons in her mind, egged on by her lack of ability to chase one specific man down.

Was he here? the ache within Andy pressed again.

Regardless of Andy's self-doubt about her professional skill sets, she was, in fact, one of the strongest investigators in the country. Her talents became so coveted it created an ongoing push-pull bidding war that placed her in the middle of a bowl of alphabet soup—the NTSB, the CIA, the NSA, the LAPD, and ultimately the FBI, who wanted her the most. But Andy chose to stay where she was. At least for now. At least until she found *him*, and what he stole from her . . .

A cold gust of wind jogged her back to the present.

With a deep breath, she refocused. Her eyes drew in everything around her and her mind rewound all of it. She envisioned the trackbed, with its parallel rails hammered into the rail ties, stretching into the distance to the west and the graceful bends to the east. Next was the image of a train moving over those rails, then finding itself scattered and sliced open with its contents splayed akin to the splattered innards of a gutted fish.

Her eyes explored the rail ties beneath her, stretching for hundreds of feet before and behind her, pushed deep into the distorted gravel bed built with rocks nearly the size of one's fist, and the deep gouges carved into them by the flanges of the unforgiving steel wheels.

The *Allegheny Limited* had not jumped the rails. It was as if the rails disappeared beneath it.

Andy's brain recreated all of it within moments. With her intuition and the gifts only a divine entity could bestow upon her, she watched the two-engine set leave the rails, widened by a cause not yet known. With accelerating force, and the inertia driven by the sheer weight of the locomotives and the rail cars behind them, the *Allegheny Limited* would drive itself into the earth below, much like the *Sunset Limited* did in the Arizona desert in 1995.

Andy's internal ache churned, forcing her a step back while sending her focus into the ether. She wrenched her attention once again back to the present, purposely searching for something new to zero in on. Something she hadn't yet seen. Something she had so far missed.

Like the nearby track signal . . . and the something that protruded from its glass lens.

Andy's eyes narrowed. She actually did find something new, something that was indeed missed. She climbed the service ladder and spied a crowbar lodged into the housing.

"Shit," she muttered under her breath.

With that crowbar came a need for a whole new set of eyes. Federal eyes. And it was the first and the last thing she wanted.

A commotion erupted a good twenty yards away. Andy watched from the ladder as rescue crews raced past her toward a locomotive lying on its side. She quickly slid down the ladder and followed. What unfolded was chaos and a cacophony of voices as they dug frantically beneath the locomotive, throwing rocks and mud aside until a pair of legs appeared amidst the mangled wreckage.

Moments later, a young man was pulled from the entanglement, his body bloodied, battered, and broken in a way words could not capture.

Dana emerged from the circle of onlookers and screamed, quickly recognizing her son. "No, no, no, NO, NO!!!" She rushed forward and was instantly horse-collared by unseen hands.

Andy could only look on. She had lived this scene before, and she knew the anguish that was gutting Dana Harper. As Dana clawed and screamed to get to her son, Andy turned and walked away, reliving her own moments from a time long ago when she once had a family of her own.

11

Andy watched the blue and white government turboprop chirp onto the short, skinny runway of the county airport a few miles outside of town with dread. The plane braked heavily, stopping just short of the faded end of the asphalt strip where a stretch of chain-link fence served as the only barrier for a pumpkin patch. A whole new knot coiled in Andy's stomach as the twin-engine eight-seater taxied to the small airport shack where she stood waiting for it. She knew, instinctively, who was about to get out of that plane.

As the engines shut down, the turboprop's door opened and out stepped FBI Agent Robert Langsdon.

"Shit," Andy muttered under her breath while deflating at the sight of him as he slipped on his government issue Ray-Bans to deflect the West Virginia sun.

"Who the hell is that?" Ryan asked as he stood next to Andy. They watched Langsdon descend the plane's stubby ladder with a royal air; the only thing missing was a chorus of angels singing his praises as he strode from the plane.

Andy was immediately, and knowingly, queasy.

Langsdon was in his early fifties. He was seasoned, chiseled, sharp, and possessed an ego that would choke a goat. He led his compact entourage of FBI support personnel like a celebrity. As far as he was concerned, his shit didn't stink and no one pulled his pants up the way he did. He then stopped and towered over Andy with a wry smile.

"Seriously?" Andy asked, not buying any of the mystique, and then sized up the crew behind him. "That's it? Just you and Eddie Murphy's entourage?"

"Funny," Langsdon answered. "I heard you're going up in the world. Too bad you can't surround yourself with talent that's able to shave yet," he added, driving a glare at Ryan that stared the young man back a step. He then looked back at Andy. "So, what have you got to show me?"

Langsdon was up the signal's service ladder, looking over the crowbar while Andy, Hollis, and others watched below. With a gloved hand, he tugged it out of the housing and gave it another quick once over before handing it down to Andy. "You got me out here for a ten-dollar crowbar from Sears?"

"No," Andy answered with impatience. "Standard Operating Procedure did."

Langsdon looked at her and decided to let the familiar snippiness pass. He moved down the service ladder, pulled his gloves off, and tossed them absentmindedly to Hollis. "What else?"

Andy nodded toward the distance. "Train left the rails somewhere back there," she said, "and came to a stop just beyond that bend."

Langsdon's eyes followed the trackbed to where the wreckage had met its end. For all his issues with Andy, he also knew full well just how good she was at all this, and it would be pointless to debate any of it. "It's a little like Arizona, isn't it?"

Andy stared ahead for a moment. *It's a lot like Arizona.*

"So, tell me about the kid they pulled out," he asked while leading the way toward the mortally wounded locomotive that continued to lay stricken on its side.

"Still in surgery, the last I heard," Andy replied.

"Yeah, well, he'll be someone worth talking to when he's out," Langsdon said, stepping over the chunks of torn rail and debris in his path.

"If he wakes up," Andy added.

Langsdon gave her a quick look and continued toward the locomotive. "Hard to work on mysteries without any clues."

Andy knew the lyrics he'd recited instantly. It was one song of many that had often played in the background while she was entangled with a high school boyfriend in the back seat of his Vietnam-era Chevy Impala. "Really, that's all you have? A quote from a Bob Seger song?"

"Would you prefer 'Send in the Clowns'?" he answered without losing a beat. "It's obvious someone has a large burr up their ass if this was deliberate. Anybody got anything against anyone around here?"

"Yeah, open the phone book," Hollis chipped in from behind them.

Langsdon stopped to look back at him, oblivious to Hollis even being there. He then glanced at Andy and pointed a finger: *Who's that?*

"Sheriff Hollis Peete," Andy introduced them, "Agent Bob Langsdon, FBI."

"Robert," Langsdon corrected her, knowing full well she did that just to needle him. "And it's Special Agent."

Hollis approached Langsdon to shake his hand, which Langsdon did with reluctance. There was something about Hollis that rubbed him the wrong way, and he already knew, innately, that the existence of Hollis alone alienated just about everyone around him.

"So, what are you suggesting?" Langsdon continued. "We start with the As?"

"I'd start with the Cs," Hollis answered as he turned toward The Brick in the distance. "Starting with the name Frank Campbell."

Looking at Andy again, Langsdon asked, "Who the fuck is Frank Campbell?"

12

Autumn in West Virginia is something of unique beauty. Mornings are often laced with a low mist that weaves through the valleys and notches of granite or rests like a white blanket over the flatter countryside and the smattering of tiny hamlets. The sun illuminated the ambers and reds of the turning trees much like a Maxfield Parrish painting.

Many of the locals were accustomed to the bright palette of the season. For others, like Kevin, each autumn was adorned with the remnants of the Indian summer, making it his favorite time of year. With the horrors of the previous day, nature's cool morning glow was a welcome salve, even if it highlighted a railroad yard populated with bland industrial browns, grays, and soot. The only pop of color was the bright yellow idling Dash-9 locomotive Kevin sat in.

"Mr. Campbell?" a woman's voice called from below.

Kevin looked down from the cab window to find the same brunette NTSB agent who had tried to talk to him the day before. For the life of him, he couldn't remember her name. He also didn't recall her being so striking.

"We didn't get a chance to talk yesterday," she continued. "If you have a moment . . ."

Kevin considered her for a long beat. The last thing he wanted to do was rehash yesterday, but he also knew he would have to do this sooner or later. He nodded the woman in the NTSB windbreaker on up.

Andy made for the crew ladder, her long legs easily stretching the height of the first tall step. Arriving behind her was Bradley Gibson, Kevin's usual conductor for the last six years, about half his age with twice the lust. He looked Andy over, then smirked up toward Kevin, who thumbed him to get lost.

When Andy entered from the locomotive's nose door and climbed the short steps into the cab, it was obvious she was freezing. She was on the lean side, sporting only enough body fat to accentuate a sleek and flattering figure, but not nearly enough to keep her warm. She shivered in even the slightest of autumn breezes, and this cold morning was made worse by the thin jacket she was wearing.

"You want some coffee?" Kevin offered.

"Yes, please," Andy gratefully replied, riding out the chill that ran through her frame. "And it doesn't even have to be good."

"Yeah, well, I think you'll be surprised," Kevin answered as he grabbed his thermos and twisted off the top. "For diner shop coffee, it's alright. Hope you like it simply black."

"Simply black works for me," Andy answered as Kevin handed her a mostly clean Union Pacific mug. She gratefully wrapped her hands around the warming ceramic. "Thanks."

"You're with the FRA?" Kevin asked, referring to the Federal Railroad Association, which oversees anything and everything having to do with rails, derailments, and giving railroad companies indigestion.

Andy nodded as she parked herself on the conductor's seat. "On loan to the NTSB. I just have a few questions. It won't take long. Just some things that Sheriff Peete couldn't answer."

Kevin shook his head with a grin.

Andy easily picked up on it. "What?" she asked.

"There's a lot of questions that guy couldn't answer. Especially if it involves the truth, which, coming from him, has a probability of about zero. Much like someone else I know."

That was something Andy wasn't expecting, but she wasn't surprised either. She had only known Hollis Peete for less than a day, which was far more than enough. "Doesn't sound like you have a lot of confidence in your local law enforcement."

"Oh, I have a lot of confidence in our local law enforcement. Our sheriff is a different story."

"And that's because . . . ?"

Kevin stalled on the answer. He knew saying anything would lead down a conversational rabbit hole he wasn't ready for and didn't have the energy to go down, let alone climb back up out of. It was an episodic dose of a familial drama he'd rather keep to himself, and he had little interest in sharing it with someone he'd known for all of five minutes, no matter how pretty she was.

Andy waited for the answer regardless.

"Let's just say he nearly killed my father by pinning him into a boxcar once upon a time."

Andy visibly recoiled. "That's rather extreme."

"Yeah, the railroad thought so, too. He cried that it was an accident and the union bailed him out, but anyone with half a brain stem knew it wasn't. Anyway, that's why our trusted sheriff is right up there on my Christmas list of assholes."

"And your father is?"

"Frank Campbell."

A beat passed as Andy connected a dot. She recognized the name, as it had come with a hint of venom when it rolled out from Hollis' forked tongue. It was also a connection she kept to herself for now. But, still, you can't just throw something like that out there unless you tie it off. "Why would he do that?" she asked.

Once again Kevin stalled on an answer, which only made it worse. The conversation was already going in the wrong direction, and the only thing he was now interested in was keeping his mouth shut. His only hope was maneuvering this whole subject back into the closet where it belonged. "I'll just say it was over someone in particular and let's leave it at that."

"A woman?" Andy guessed.

Kevin stayed mum, not really needing to vocalize an answer to something so obvious.

Andy had already done the conversational arithmetic and knew instinctively that it was likely over Kevin's mother. But she also wasn't going to push this subject since it was more salacious than it was relevant. Granting Kevin's silent wish to talk about something else, she gracefully changed direction. "You want to tell me about the derailment at the Sterling yard?"

"It was a slipped truck," Kevin answered, taking a drink of his coffee from the thermos. "I wouldn't exactly call it a derailment."

"Not sure I would agree with that, but do you know who cleared the *Limited* through?"

"Yeah. Me."

"Why?"

"Because that slipped truck was going to take half the night to untangle. And we've got enough capacity problems with Atlantic as it is."

"So then, Mr. Campbell . . ."

"Kevin."

"Kevin," Andy answered with some welcome warmth. "When something like this happens, we look at everything, including—"

"Including figuring out if someone did this on purpose?"

Andy cocked her head slightly at him. He was well ahead of her, and it telegraphed that he had been through this before. "Something like that."

"Yeah, well, I'd be careful asking that kind of question around here," Kevin said in a tone that distinctly sounded like a cold, hard statement of fact. "You might find doors that won't open when you come knocking."

Andy wasn't sure if his words were a threat or just cautionary advice from a local. Either way, it was easy enough to push back on. "I wouldn't be the one doing the knocking. The FBI would."

Something immediately went hollow within Kevin.

"Thanks for the coffee," Andy said as she handed back the cup and pulled out her business card. "Just in case you hear anything. Mobile number is on the back."

"Thanks," Kevin said with some trepidation. He watched her exit the cab. She was beautiful and possessed an unexpected warmth that fogged his brain for the remainder of the day, especially as he caught himself trying to find legitimate reasons to call her.

13

The sky over Granite Point Cemetery was a deeply endless blue, the kind of blue typical of autumn and a welcome contrast to the milky skies of a humid summer. The weather for this day was more than perfect for Tom's service. It was a gathering of those who had known and loved him.

Frank, dressed in an old suit, was a stark figure amidst the throng. The faded fabric, somewhere between gray and black, was well worn, its style more suited to the days of the Ford White House. Not that he cared any. He rarely wore it, and it made him itch. He had little use for it outside of occasions like this one, and his distaste for such clothing was emphasized by the sloppy knot in his tie.

Across from him, Kevin and Trisha stood in attendance with the kids. Kevin kept his eyes on Frank, trying to fathom, measure, and assess the pain that roiled inside his father. Still, even at that moment on that day, Kevin struggled to read him.

Watching all of this from atop a nearby knoll was Hollis, who stood in his sheriff's uniform as the breeze tugged on his hat and rippled his oversized pants that flopped around his boot tops. He was not there as an ostracized attendee, but more of a wolf waiting patiently for the herd to disperse to reveal its most vulnerable and wounded prey, Frank Campbell.

Tom's suicide was of little importance to Hollis. His interactions with Tom were limited, mostly because Tom found Hollis to be utterly detestable. Their paths would only cross when they competed for the affections of desirable divorcees in their little town and neighboring hamlets, a competition Hollis was usually at the losing end of. It prompted a fair bit of jealousy from the perpetually single Hollis, who couldn't even make a date with a decaying tree stump and could only reconcile this by issuing Tom pointless parking and traffic tickets whenever he could. It was impossible for Hollis to compete with a lanky man who could charm a woman out of her heels. And even though they shared a history of being in the military, it was a brotherhood that never resonated between them. Nonetheless, Hollis looked on, his eyes zeroed in on Frank, who was mired in a private enclave of grief.

Frank was lost, and the concept of even considering the next day was incomprehensible. The only soul that disrupted this was Shiloh, who laced her fingers with his and anchored him amidst the drift he was in. She leaned against him slightly, giving him the support he wasn't even aware he needed. Still, it wasn't enough to halt the tear that ran down his cheek or keep his son from seeing it.

Kevin somehow knew the hollowness that chilled his father's soul. He could read it on his face, and he could see it in his eyes.

They stared into a void that was actively swallowing the man alive, and the sight created a pall within Kevin he had never felt before. It was a disturbing moment oddly accented by the sunlight that pushed through the thinning and brittle leaves of the trees above. It wasn't an aura, per se, nor was it a glow.

Kevin saw it as the first day that would mark the end of his father.

This would be the only way Kevin could describe it in the years that followed, and it frightened him. He had always imagined a time his father would be no more. Never did he once grasp the reality of it or attempt to pre-measure the depth of trying to reconcile it. Frank had been a darkening shadow upon his life for so long that he began to forget the wonder of what it would be like with him gone. He had subconsciously resigned himself to the reality of the present that existed for as long as he could remember. And now he saw a glimpse of tomorrow, when his father would cease to be, and he suddenly wasn't ready for it.

Kevin moved his eyes toward the lowering of Tom's casket into the horrible cavity of carved-out earth that awaited it. He found a grave to be a terrifying destination. The thought of being placed into a box—no matter how nice it may be—and then buried beneath a tonnage of dirt until Earth's inevitable demise made his mind scream in panic. A part of him wanted to dive onto the casket, throw it open, and haul his father's best friend clear of the suffocating darkness that loomed.

Tom's passing meant more to Kevin than he'd expected. It went deeper than the often-shallow empathy he held for his father; it erased one of the few remaining threads to his mother. With his maternal grandparents long gone, the only source of living history had lived within Frank, Hollis Peete, and Tom, who freely shared the stories that his father wouldn't, or couldn't, part with. Tom was more than happy to dispense questionable yarns and the misadventures of Frank, who never bothered to pass them along and preferred to spin out fibs and other invented bullshit instead. Kevin enjoyed the tales Tom would recite, including a drunken encounter his father had with a German U-boat on Chicago's Lakeshore Drive late one night in 1954, or how Frank was taken by a traveling salesman selling half-off cashmere sweaters, only to find the entire back half of the sweater missing when he got home. Tom showed Kevin a side of his father he never would've otherwise known.

But with Tom now gone, the only threads to Kevin's mother now lived with a man he could barely connect with, and a sheriff who stood upon the hill above—like a vulture.

The congregation slowly dispersed as the service came to an end. For Frank, it all dragged on like a prison sentence in hell, which was made worse by the military pomp Tom's first and only wife of less than two months, from some fifty-odd years ago, insisted upon. He had watched this woman receive the folded flag and play up the role of the tragic, money-grubbing war widow now eligible for his VA and Social Security benefits.

Frank observed this woman with disdain. She dabbed her crocodile tears with a wad of tissue and then felt Frank's eyes upon her. She was a tank of a woman with frigid eyes and pursed lips and a true love for no one except herself. And while she knew Frank could see straight through her, Tom's ex-wife was still empowered enough to give Frank her wrinkled and arthritic middle finger, which was capped by a nauseatingly bright red blunt fingernail. She then scurried off with a small gaggle of sour parasitic bipedal remoras, reminding Frank of why Tom only lasted two months with her.

Frank's day was destined to not improve. What lay next for him was having to spend the afternoon at his son's house with his snit of a wife and her brooding demeanor. Frank preferred to head to the M&M, drink Mitch out of business, and be spared the horrors of inane chitchat that even Kevin hated. And like an inmate plodding toward the gallows, he moved past his son and trudged toward his pickup.

Kevin watched Frank silently walk by him. Even with his father at another significant low point in his life, he still had no words for him. All Kevin could do was shepherd his family toward the sanctuary of their Chevy-made home chariot.

"My best friend was George Ray," said an ancient voice that turned Kevin around. Standing before him was none other than Sherman Gale.

"We didn't call him Georgie or anything like that," Sherman continued. "He hated that. George once punched this dumb kid from Idaho in the head 'cause he wouldn't stop saying it. He just downed his beer, dragged the kid outside, and dropped him like that. Ever since then it was 'Yes, sir' this and 'No, sir' that."

He smiled slightly at the memory.

Kevin looked quickly at Trisha, who stood by wide-eyed. Sherman had not said more than a handful of words to him since he pulled Kevin from the car and then helplessly watched Kevin's mother perish.

"George and I were at this pub one night," Sherman went on. "Explosions shook dust from the rafters. One after the other, getting closer and closer. We ran outside and saw this Luftwaffe sonofabitch taking off chimney tops with both engines on fire. He was unloading his bombs, you know, to get back up in the air. One of them dropped a block away. Blast blew me and George clear off our feet. I woke up the next morning in a hospital, but no one knew what happened to George. Couldn't find him ever. He was gone, just like he was never even there."

Kevin stood silently as Sherman looked off toward Frank with a sadness Kevin had never seen in anyone before. Even after all these years, Sherman Gale still pained for a friend gone for decades, and it was something Kevin found hard to understand, as close friends for him were hard to come by.

"Nowadays I don't even dream about him," Sherman added softly. He then looked back at Kevin. "How do you say goodbye to those you don't dream about?"

Kevin's brow knotted. The story unsettled him, and before he could muster anything that resembled a coherent response, Sherman had shuffled off toward his bride, who was as beautiful to him now as the day he married her.

The air around Hollis went deathly still as he continued to look on from the knoll. He next squinted upward, noting the autumn leaves resting motionless on their branches, and then felt a suffocating moment, much like fingers that invisibly wrapped around his throat.

The face of Tom Ryder appeared in the forefront of his mind.

Hollis was immediately incensed by the fleeting vision; the sensation infuriated him enough to start toward Frank, only to be held back when Langsdon's large hand clamped onto his shoulder with authority.

"There's a time and place for everything," Langsdon said, appearing behind him with a commanding whisper. "This isn't one of them."

Hollis sharply locked eyes with Langsdon. He wanted to slug the man simply out of frustration, but plowing a fist through the jaw of an FBI agent at a funeral was beyond even his personal level of decorum. Still, he couldn't hide the flash of regret across his face, and with a reluctant nod, he took a step back, surrendering his intention to torture Frank in a way he'd never imagined before.

14

The backyard of the Campbell home was generous in size, thanks to the large acreage that stretched to a thick tree line in the distance. It possessed a spectacular view of the nearby hills of pine and a palette explosion of elms and oaks. Beyond that was the ridge belonging to Signal Mountain that sprayed an even broader array of fall colors worthy of a watercolor painting. It was a view that Kevin loved, and a primary selling point to buy the overpriced home he would probably never be able to pay off.

Clogging this view was Frank, who sat in a lone lawn chair along a fence line with Freedom standing on the other side, comically straining her neck to give Frank an encouraging nudge of her nose. Frank was just outside of range and, instead, the horse snorted a thin layer of snot toward Frank's ear.

Frank was a picture of desolation with a half-empty beer can dangling loosely in one hand and a cigarette smoldering between his fingers in the other. His tie hung slack around his neck, and his suit jacket crumpled upward against the back of the chair. "When did you get this fucking mule?" Frank sneered as Freedom exhaled at him.

"It's a barrel racing horse and it's not ours," Kevin answered, noting that the mare must have found a way to unlatch the door to her stall with nothing but her incisors. *Great, the fucking horse is an escape artist.*

The smoke from the barbeque forced Kevin back a step as it fogged the backyard with a haze most typical of the worst polluted cities. Kevin's skills were many, but grilling wasn't one of them. With a wave of his arm, he attempted to dispatch the cancerogenic cloud of death around him and then turned his attention to his father. With an intuition buried deep inside him, Kevin knew something else brewed within the sulking man who continued to bob his head away from the horse that wanted to chew on him. Kevin knew it instinctively; he just couldn't put his finger on it. And the confusing prophecy of Sherman Gale, along with the vision of his father in the speckled sunlight, haunted him.

"Since when did he start smoking again?" Trisha asked quietly as she appeared beside her husband with a plate of raw patties, squinting from the acidic charcoal cloud that was only now abandoning the backyard.

"I don't think he ever quit," Kevin answered. He took the plate and began tossing the patties onto the grill, creating a new toxic cloud that was likely going to kill them all. "I think he decided to just stop hiding it."

Trisha returned to the patio table and sat across from Shiloh, who held Michael on her lap. With Tom's funeral service now behind them by only a couple of hours, the mood was a different kind of somber, mostly emanating from Frank, who rarely appeared at one of these family adventures in outdoor eating because he was such a pill to have around. And it always brought out the worst in Kevin. For Trisha, it was a frustrating obligation by her husband to keep including Frank whenever they had one. This is usually when she began fantasizing about living in California. Or Nevada. Or anywhere that was thousands of miles from her father-in-law.

And as much as Frank exuded an air of "leave me alone," which even the horse eventually picked up on, Michael completely missed it. At three, he only saw enough to know his grandfather was in a bad way, and that he smelled weirder than usual. With fearless empathy and the instability of toddlerhood, he wriggled off Shiloh's lap and headed to a small soccer ball on the grass.

Trisha and Kevin watched as Michael retrieved the ball and carried it to his grandfather's lap.

"So, what happened to your hand?" Kevin asked, nodding to Frank's bandaged right palm while watching Michael playfully lean against Frank's knee.

"Nothing," Frank answered. He brushed the ball away, not even remotely interested in playing fetch. This sent Michael smiling after the ball.

"Well, I'm going in and get something to drink," Trisha announced, rising from the table. "You want anything?" she asked Kevin, who shook his head.

"Do *you* want something?" she asked Frank, who just stared into the ether. Trisha looked at one, then the other, each lost in his own little world, and gave up. She tapped Shiloh to follow her inside.

By now, Michael had returned with the ball and placed it back onto Frank's lap with a smile.

Frank, again, swiped it off, this time with enough force to send it bouncing across the yard with notable velocity. "Not now," he growled slightly, trying to hold back from snapping at his grandson.

But for Michael it was now a game. With a belly giggle, he toddled after the ball and returned it like a puppy. He tossed it once again onto Frank's lap.

Frank snapped. From a dark place he didn't know existed, he erupted at the child with a resounding thunder that frightened even Kevin. "GODDAMMIT! I SAID NOT NOW, YOU LITTLE IDIOT! ARE YOU DEAF!?"

Michael recoiled and stumbled backward onto the grass.

Kevin stared at Frank, stunned by a monstrous outburst that even he had never seen before.

Michael's face crumpled, and he bolted toward the house just as Trisha emerged through the screen door. In an instant, she scooped up her sobbing son and glared death at Frank, who refused to meet her burning stare. He knew he had fucked up to an extent that exceeded what even he believed was unacceptable. Remorse was an emotion Frank rarely allowed himself to feel, let alone display. He'd undeservedly crushed his grandson, and it was a blow the child would not soon forget. Frank didn't want to hide under a rock; he wished to be pummeled to death by one.

"Get out," Trisha snarled.

Frank swallowed, sinking deeper in his seat and fiddling with his cigarette.

"Did you hear me? I said out."

Frank stared ahead. The afternoon was done and so was his welcome, which oddly suited him just fine at that moment. With misplaced defiance, he rose from the lawn chair, thumped his beer on the patio table, and was off, grazing past Kevin in the process.

Kevin watched his father exit through the gate toward his truck, leaving it open and allowing Freedom to race by at full gallop, with Shiloh after her in high-speed pursuit. He then turned toward Trisha while the patties burned on the grill. She scowled at him and went back into the house with her likely traumatized son.

It was after 10:00 PM when Shiloh parked herself at the top of the stairs to listen to what was happening downstairs. Mom and Dad were going at it. They rarely fought, but when they did it was loud and contentious and it always frightened the hell out of her. This bout was loud enough to haul her little brother from a dead sleep. He took up station next to his big sister, who pulled him onto her lap and held him tightly, her hand pressed lightly against his ear.

Downstairs in the modest kitchen that needed a refresh to expel the '70s decor, Trisha loaded the dishwasher as Kevin stewed at the table. She was pissed, and he knew it in high-definition stereo.

"… and I swear to God he's not going to treat Michael the way he's treated you," she continued in a rant Kevin began to tune out, which only made her amp her voice up in tamped fury. "Not in my lifetime."

Kevin pointed upstairs, urging her to tone it down.

Trisha just grabbed more dishes out of the sink, doing very little to keep the clanging to a minimum. She knew he was right, at least about the volume, but she wasn't inspired enough to manage the audio levels of her annoyance. It was one of Trisha's few failings: possessing a temper that could send animals of all sizes fleeing.

"Why are you doing this?" Kevin asked with unmistakable emotional exhaustion.

Trisha stopped and looked at him intently. "Really? Because I love you, you idiot, and I love our family. The last thing we need is for you to become more like your father."

"There's no point in talking to my dad when he's like that," Kevin answered, trying to keep his voice down at the same time. "You know that."

"Yeah, but it's okay for me to go head-to-head with him? For Christ's sake, Kevin, Michael's your son; you're supposed to defend him."

Kevin conceded that by picking at a wood rip on the table, which was enough to get her to stop the stacking in exasperation.

Trisha sighed loudly. She wasn't getting anywhere going after her husband this way, especially when he retreated into an emotional state so deep even she couldn't dig him out, let alone go to herself. Trisha loved Kevin fully, but his constant caving to his father was the one flaw she despised. For now, she had vented enough to at least turn the anger down a few notches.

"You know," she said as she sat across from him, "I've seen you take on the most militant of management and the most radical of union members. That's a strength even I don't have, but when it comes to your father, you're like a child afraid of his own shadow. But if you're not careful, babe, one day you'll look in the mirror and you're going to see him."

And with that, she left the table and the kitchen, calling it a night.

15

Frank's home was a 1200-square-foot A-frame with faded paint and a mixed era of furnishings. Long paid off, the house possessed memories that stretched from a marriage long ago to a little boy conceived on a queen-sized mattress (sure beats an icebox) in a modest master bedroom, a living room where he took his first steps, and a couch his mother always fell asleep upon. The walls were splattered with family pictures and artwork of his own creation, evidence of a man with better-than-average talent who had even created his own artistic logo of a railroad track within a circle. It was a dream that never found its way to the light.

But it was home. He'd lived in this little rancher for over forty years with a reality that he would likely die here—he was perfectly fine with that. As far as he was concerned, he didn't deserve anything better.

Frank twisted painfully in his lounge chair, his hip hurting more than usual. He crushed his eyelids together, trying to fight off the headache that was very effectively grinding his brain into mush. And the day alone was something he wanted to forget for the rest of whatever life he had left to suffer through.

After he was through fussing in his chair, his attention returned to the TV in front of him, where Andrea Mayland from the NTSB held court with the press. At the podium, she held an air of professionalism far exceeding her age. He expected he would meet this woman soon enough. At least she was easy on the eyes, which probably meant he was even more screwed.

". . . so, there'll be no comment on any of the particulars of this investigation until the FBI deems it appropriate," Andy said as she pointed to a reporter in the row in front of her.

"With the FBI getting involved," the reporter asked, "does this mean that the NTSB's job is finished?"

"I'm not sure how you came to that conclusion," Andy answered. "We're still very early into our investigation. The FBI's arrival at this point is standard procedure, and we'll work with them closely as well as with the local authorities."

Frank's stomach tightened. As well as his throat. He, again, tried to replay that night in his mind, but it remained blank. He knew he was there in some way. The ache in his hand made sure of that, along with the mud both in and on his truck in the driveway and the bumper that now pointed skyward.

He stared at Andy's name and then ran down the logistics of turning himself in. It would have to start with Hollis, who'd relish the spectacle of a public crucifixion and probably quietly arrange an early exit from prison in a body bag.

"What about Beau Harper?" the reporter asked, stuffing in another question. "Is he a suspect?"

"No one ever said that, either. He's just a person of interest."

Beau Harper, Frank thought to himself. *If the kid doesn't wake up, he could go down for it. Yeah, that could work. But what if he does wake up? I'm still fucked.*

"That's all, thank you," Andy said, closing off the press conference and leaving the podium.

Am I really that much of a coward? That's fucking low, even for you, shithead.

Frank's eyes drifted to his trembling hand, the ice cubes rattling against the glass. He tried to steady it, but he could only grab it with his other hand. He closed his eyes to settle himself. The moment he did that, he found himself between the rails at Prowler Flat, in the black of night and the pouring rain. It was bitter cold. And there in his hand was his crowbar, fresh from gouging out the hole in his palm.

His eyes snapped open, the pain in his hand throbbing.

"So, as you just heard, there's very little the NTSB is sharing right now," the reporter said into the camera on TV. "What I can tell you is there's a lot of interest in Beau Harper, who you may recall was found badly injured at the wreck site."

And they just had to plaster a picture of the kid on the screen, staring back at Frank. His guilt multiplied immediately.

"His condition is still unclear, but I can also tell you authorities are very interested in talking with this young man as soon as he—"

Frank fired his glass at the TV, shattering the screen and killing the box in a spray of electrical sparks. He had heard enough.

With no desire to linger at home and gaze at the field of shattered glass on the rug, Frank drove himself into town. He needed to escape from everything, including the smell of electrified dust that emanated from the remains of the TV already overdue to be thrown out anyway. But with the M&M off the destination list for now, Frank was down to only a few acceptable alternatives.

While the wipers dragged loudly across the windshield, mostly smearing rain droplets and dirt, Frank's drive toward Center Street carried that same persistent lump of lead in his stomach. Everything continued to be exponentially amiss. The thumping of his tires over one of the many track crossings that stitched through town brought a frightening vision of a town that could very well be ruins in a year.

He watched as a mix of vacant storefronts and little homes of people long gone rolled by. They harkened back to a time he only now realized he missed. There were parades long forgotten, buntings and flags on lamp posts for the Fourth of July, and the kids that hung out at the sundae shop next to the Western Auto store were all now faceless specters that echoed from summers long departed. Except for Kevin, whom he remembered seeing there late one night as Frank drove home from work. There was a pretty blonde girl who had her arms wrapped around him while they leaned against that tank of a car of his. Frank remembered how brightly blue it was, and how vibrantly it reflected the street and store lights. He also recalled how the sight made him yearn to be young again himself, when the feeling of the summer evening air would never pass.

He really did miss those days.

It wasn't long before Frank reached the center of town, where traffic continued to be a knotted mess with the impermanent challenge of news crews, their vans, and the herds of reporters that congested everything. It was a boon for the likes of Hollis, with his farcical parking tickets, and Stanley, serving food at a 24-hour clip. But it would be a boon doomed to fade by next week as the wreck of the *Allegheny Limited* became old news. And if Frank found himself to be alive by then, it would be a miracle.

After maneuvering around a news van from Pittsburgh, Frank pulled into the small parking lot for Harry's 5th Street Bar, a small hovel that was on that list of acceptable alternatives. The bar inhabited one of Granite Point's oldest buildings, a combination of brick and wood built in 1924 that boasted a severely faded ad painted on the second floor for a lady's hat shop gone since then.

On the inside, Harry's was dark and a bit too dreary even for Frank's usual liking. Tonight, there was a single soul at the polished bar, hunched over his drink and likely half-passed out. Wiping the bar down in front of him was Harry himself, a man nearing eighty with thin white hair and a stained apron that covered his protruding stomach.

Harry had stopped pouring money into what was once his jewel of a business years ago. Back then it was a watering hole favored by Atlantic's rail crews, done in by the likes of the much larger and brighter M&M. There was a useless pool table with a worn and ripped burgundy felt top, an old Seeburg jukebox that ate more coins than it played songs, a broken James Bond pinball machine in the corner, and paintings created by starving artists who also vanished with the breezes of yesterday. There were even a couple of small pieces Frank had painted near the table he landed at, which blended in with the rest of the forgotten oils on canvas with decades of nicotine that covered them like a yellow varnish.

Frank mindlessly swirled his mostly untouched drink, and then finally focused enough to down most of it with a foul grimace. Harry's taste in alcohol was highly questionable, and there were rumors most of his collection was spiked with homemade moonshine to help kick up his profit margins.

"Well fuck me a duck . . ." said a voice that pulled Frank's attention from the scratched-up tabletop. Peeling himself from the bar and slew-stepping his way toward Frank was Sal Pitt, the very man who declared Frank's gimpiness a fiscal benefit to the railroad that would eventually toss him out like everyone else. "One of the chosen few has decided to grace this shithole with his presence," Sal continued, his demeanor far more intoxicated than common sense would have it.

"Yeah, watch it, Sal," Harry snarled in a gravelly voice that still retained a little pride in his namesake.

"It's a shithole, Harry. Prove me wrong," Sal countered, his arms in the air. He then stood before Frank's table. "Hi, Frankie. You wanna buy me a drink with that paycheck of yours?"

Frank stiffened as Sal pulled out a chair and sat across from him, followed by Frank's mood quickly darkening when Sal grabbed Frank's glass and finished off his last drops.

"Another round on Frank, Harry!" Sal declared, waving the glass at him.

"I'm gonna be just as unemployed as you are, dumbass," Frank hissed at a man he detested almost, but not completely, as much as Hollis Peete.

"And yet you're still gettin' a paycheck while the rest of us go dumpster diving for dinner," Sal countered.

"How's that gonna be any different for ya?" Frank kicked back with no fear of poking an ill-tempered and rabid bear.

Sal stared at Frank and then barked out a fake laugh before he blasted Frank's chair away from the table with a leg. Frank fell and landed painfully on his back, the chair breaking underneath him and knocking the wind from his lungs.

Sal next threw the table aside and was about to pummel Frank's head into tenderized steak when he was suddenly yanked away by none other than Hollis Peete. Sal's vision spun as Hollis cranked Sal's arm behind his back and drove him toward the front door. Sal then felt Hollis' large boot delivering a kick to his buttocks that sent him through the door with almost comical velocity.

"Harry, you've got some trash out on the sidewalk," Hollis said as he straightened his uniform. "Suggest you have someone go pick it up."

By the time Frank regained his breathing, he felt Hollis grab him by the upper arm and swing him onto a chair at the next table with a wallop. The next thing Frank knew, he was looking at a tall, neatly dressed man sitting across from him. The kind of man who looked like he would belong to the Secret Service.

"Mr. Campbell, my name is Robert Langsdon," said the sharply dressed man with an alarmingly flawless posture. "I'm with the Federal Bureau of Investigation. It's nice to meet you."

Frank eyed the badge that hung from Langsdon's breast pocket and quickly forgot how to breathe.

"Say hello, Frank," Hollis said, bopping Frank on the shoulder.

Langsdon turned to Hollis with piercing annoyance. This wasn't how he wanted this initial conversation to go. "Sheriff," he asked, "would you be so kind as to help the poor individual you just threw out the door find his way home?"

Hollis looked at Langsdon sharply, taken aback by a leash that swiftly yanked on him to heel.

"Now, please," Langsdon added.

Hollis twisted his jaw in consternation at being humiliated in front of the man he hated the most. With a quick glance at Frank, he begrudgingly moved off, loudly shoving a stray chair out of his way.

Langsdon craned his head to watch Hollis mumble his way out the door and then turned his attention back to Frank. "I'm going to assume you two aren't exactly friends," he asked.

"Maybe," Frank answered just above a whisper, "once upon a time."

Langsdon studied Frank for a moment. He quickly did the math—not that there was much math to do. "Women can do that," he safely assumed.

Frank was too unnerved to answer or add anything to Langsdon's comment.

"You know, your name was the first the sheriff mentioned as someone of interest in that derailment mess out there," Langsdon calmly pressed, leaning back in the seat some. "In fact, it was the only name."

Frank's mind raced for a moment. "If Hollis Peete could pin the murder of Christ on me," Frank finally replied, "he would."

Frank was a bit brighter than Langsdon had expected. Not that it deterred him in any way. "Well then," Langsdon commented, "fortunately for you, bias is not grounds for prosecution."

Frank blinked as panic stirred within him. He desperately wondered what this man from the FBI was reading with his calm demeanor and pressing vocabulary.

The reality was, Langsdon was reading Frank like a dinner menu. He could see Frank's body language with his rigid frame and maybe a slight bead of sweat from the man's hairline. "Relax," Langsdon said with a friendly smile, "I'm just making conversation."

Bullshit, Frank thought. He obviously wasn't born yesterday and had enough years on this FBI guy to smell a lie with little effort.

"But I am curious to know why the sheriff, who obviously rules this fine little hamlet without question, would only mention your name and no one else's. I mean, aside from assassinating certain saviors."

Frank knew he was in a conversational minefield. One wrong move and it's life with no parole. He eyed the front door for a moment just as Hollis reappeared in it. The thought of bolting through it instantly dissipated.

"Or why you were stopped only a couple of miles from the derailment site," Langsdon pushed, "not more than a few minutes before it all happened."

Frank's brow knotted. He had no recent memory of being pulled over for anything. Not even for his broken license plate bulb that Hollis still hadn't managed to catch yet.

"What, you don't remember being pulled over?" Langsdon asked, pushing just a bit harder on Frank. "Suspicion of drunk driving?"

At this point, Frank wasn't sure if he could remember how to speak English. He had never blacked out before, and the reality that he might have done just that frightened him.

Langsdon easily saw this in Frank. It drew out a moment of doubt in the man's complicity in the derailment he'd been dragged out here to solve. But Langsdon could also read Frank well enough to know the man was living on a level of borrowed time. "You know, not everyone has a guardian angel that looks over them," Langsdon commented while he drew a hand across the table. "Even when they make, well, not the smartest decisions. Apparently, somebody was watching over you that night, seeing that you fared far better than nine other people did."

Frank clammed up as Langsdon stared him toward a shallow grave. There was something Langsdon could see, but he was damned if he could put a finger on it.

Langsdon emerged from the bar, followed by Hollis. Both watched as a cab with Sal Pitt stuffed into the back seat pulled away. Langsdon fought a chill that seeped down to his bones. He watched his icy breath swirl around him as he zipped up his coat while rewinding his conversation with Frank through his brain.

"Well?" Hollis asked, honestly wondering what was next.

"Well, what?" Langsdon answered with absolutely no interest in discussing any of this with someone who had questionable knowledge of how any legal system operates.

"We're not going to arrest him?" Hollis asked with an obvious hint of impatience.

"For what? All we have are the standing hairs on the back of your neck and a deputy not hauling him in for drunk driving. You willing to go in front of a jury with just that?" Langsdon explained while the cell phone in his pocket began to ring. "Unless the constitution has changed, he's a compelling curiosity. Find me some probable cause and an arrow that points to him, and I'll park an elephant on his neck."

Hollis was speechless. With his blood boiling, all he could do was watch Langsdon walk off and answer his cell phone in a voice that was impossible to hear.

Frank slammed the bathroom door behind him. Gasping for air, he fumbled with the door lock and backed into a corner, only to then pivot to the sink and turn the squeaky faucets on full into the forty-year-old cracked ceramic bowl.

He'd drown himself if he could.

At a loud banging on the bathroom door, Frank's adrenaline spun him around and nearly ended his life right then and there. He pressed back into the sink as the banging continued.

"Hey, Frank! You okay in there?" Harry barked from the other side of the paint-chipped wooden door. "They're gone . . ."

Frank stared at the door handle as Harry tried to get inside. He wanted to tear his skin off, escape everything around him. Sweat poured down his back, and his conscience screamed.

"Frank?!" Harry yelled even louder now. "Open the door, Frank!"

Only if the door opened to Hell, Frank thought to himself with no immediate intention to unlock anything.

16

"Beau has high-functioning autism," Dana Harper explained with exhaustion. She hadn't slept in days, often having to be coerced away from Beau's hospital bedside by Atlantic's contemptable CEO, who swore he would implicate her in Atlantic's implosion if she refused to haul her ass into the office to shut it down while he hid under a rock in the Caymans. So, through the charity of nurses and an occasional volunteer, including Mrs. Gale, Dana sort of found a way to be in two places at the same time.

And for now, Dana was stuck in a cramped meeting room across from two federal agents at the sheriff's office, which wasn't helping her rapidly diminishing sanity.

"And that means what?" Langsdon asked, clearly ignorant of anything having to do with autism. "He's like Rain Man?"

Andy winced.

"No," Dana answered with flaring annoyance. "It means he's just like you and me, but he struggles with some of the basics."

"Like?"

"Like talking to people, having conversations. He stutters, and he has obsessions."

"Obsessions?" Langsdon pushed, catching on Dana's wording. "Like trains?"

Dana knew she was being led into a corner. "Yes, he has a thing for trains."

"So, what was he doing underneath an overturned 200-ton locomotive?"

"I'd like to ask him the same thing."

Langsdon studied her momentarily before his questioning turned darker. "So, tell me about his other obsessions. Anything violent?"

"Violent?"

"Yes, any obsessions with fire, destroying things? Crashing cars . . ."

Andy had heard enough. "Really?" she said, glaring at him.

Langsdon ignored her and looked on at Dana, waiting for an answer.

"People with autism do not destroy the things they love," Dana answered.

"So, why was he there?" Langsdon pressed.

"He was probably videotaping."

"Videotaping?" Langsdon asked. "Videotaping what?"

"Trains. He lives for it and has a huge collection of them. And lately he's been sneaking out at night to film them."

"And you let him?"

Dana was now thoroughly exasperated. "I'm his mother, not his jailer. And at his age now, the best I can do is try to teach him common sense before I'm not around to do it anymore."

"Yeah, and how's that going?"

Dana tilted her head in his direction, no longer having any interest in answering a single thing.

Andy and Langsdon emerged from the room a few minutes later, leaving Dana wondering if she could go. She had clammed up, no longer wanting to give Langsdon more ammo to use on her and her son.

"Nice Soviet bedside manner," Andy said once they were clear of the room and down the hallway. "What's next, waterboarding?"

"Don't even start with me," Langsdon volleyed in return. "Someone tell me how a mother lets her kid out in the middle of the night to video trains?"

"Probably an exhausted one who has no help," Andy offered with a far more empathetic perspective. "Empathy, noun. The ability to understand—" Andy began to pantomime and Langsdon immediately herded her into a small, empty office and closed the door.

"You really want to do this now?" Langsdon hissed into her grill.

"Robert, you just told a traumatized mother her autistic son killed nine people."

"I didn't say that."

"No. You implied it with a fucking Howitzer. Why do you always have to bludgeon your way through every investigation you're in?"

"Because it saves time, my dear," Langsdon shot back. "And what are you even doing here anyway? You should be up here where I am, not out there playing with … *all of that*," he continued, motioning outside. He then stopped himself, his face softening slightly. Langsdon truly believed she was better than this. Andy possessed an investigative skill that she was more than happy to leave untapped, which aggravated the hell out of him. She had an opportunity to become one of the best agents the bureau had seen in years but chose to stay untangling train wrecks, albeit for a reason he could understand but not accept.

"And yet here you are with me," Andy countered with some satisfaction.

"You know what I mean."

She did. She had known of his frustration with her for a long time. She was actually flattered by it, even though she wouldn't give him the gratification of trying to rub it in. But three months sharing a bed with Robert Langsdon—and his ego—when her life was inverted by the *Sunset Limited* investigation, and everything that happened after it, was simply too much.

"Look," Langsdon said in a warm tone that instantly defused her, "I know why you're here and why you're doing all of this. But you're not going to find Marcus here, just like you didn't find him at the other wrecks you've investigated for the last four years. I can promise you, his trail isn't going through West Virginia."

Andy flinched but said nothing. Mostly because she knew Langsdon was right. She hadn't heard her former husband's name for years, and she dismissed his role in her life to just "him." Or more precisely, "he." She knew *he* wasn't here, and she knew she had been following the wrong trail for years, but Marcus had disappeared like a grain of sand on a beach, leaving nothing behind except nightmares in Andy's often sleepless nights. Emotionally, she believed there was no other trail to follow.

Langsdon left the room and resumed walking down the hall. It was another stalemate with Andy, so there was no point dragging it out. "I'm taking that crowbar you found with me, and I'll let the nerds take a shot at it. Aside from the point-zero-one percent chance Marcus' prints are on it, you might get lucky and someone else's will be."

Andy followed him out of the room and then instantly stopped dead in her tracks. "What do you mean 'with you'? Where are *you* going?"

"Washington," he answered as he turned back toward her, finding her frozen with bewilderment.

"D.C.? Wha—"

"I've been asked to help start up a domestic terrorism unit. So, if you want to find Marcus the Idiot, that's as good a place to start as any."

Andy now moved from bewildered to abandoned.

"Relax, I'll be back." Langsdon walked back to her. "Not that you really need me here."

"Says who?" Andy threw back.

"Says me. This is meat and potatoes for you."

Bullshit, Andy thought. Robert Langsdon was a good investigator who had a bad habit of living Occam's Razor to the letter, so having him here was a blessing and a curse.

"Everything you need to finish this is out there in that mess," Langsdon continued. "If there's anything on the crowbar, that's the cherry on top. Your jackpot is the kid's camcorder. If it's out there and it's in one piece, you've got a great chance of being home by the weekend if you can find it."

"I can't do this on my own, Robert," Andy said with a hint of pleading.

"Why not?" he challenged her. "It's time you stepped up instead of stepping aside. Sheriff Dirty Harry can handle the rest of the motive piece. At least, I think he can."

He then resumed moving down the hall.

"And what if it's not the kid," Andy called after him, "or this Frank Campbell guy?"

"Neither one is yours to arrest, but I'm giving it to you to figure out," he answered with a departing glance.

"But I'm not the FBI!"

"And whose fault is that?!" he shot back.

And with that, he was gone, his broad shoulders disappearing beyond a closing door to the parking lot, leaving Andy up on a high wire without a net.

17

Sunlight poured into Frank's bedroom, landing squarely on his face and disintegrating the deep sleep he was in. When he turned over and away from the audacity of daylight, his mind was immediately active, dooming any hope of returning to the escape of slumber. The guilt had returned, along with the face of Beau Harper seared into his eyesight.

You're a fucking coward, his psyche accused at an inward volume he could not ignore.

Frank tossed again, but now he had to pee. The night was done.

You killed nine people, you piece of shit, his psyche roared on. *And you're hiding from it? You're going to let some kid who can't help himself take the fall? Why? You're already finished. You're just too stupid to realize it.*

And Michael.

The vision of his innocent grandson, shattered and terrified, brought a new layer of anguish he hadn't even reconciled yet.

Who are you? What are you so fucking scared of?

Frank's eyes opened. The punishing illumination of the sun had mercifully moved on, leaving him with a dull morning light in a room that hadn't been cleaned in probably five years.

Why can't I remember that night? I have to have done it, otherwise why was I there?

His eyes closed again, and he was there, at Prowler Flat, in the pouring rain. The excruciating pain in his hand.

And there was the signal lamp.

Wait . . . the signal lamp. Yeah, that's right. I remember that signal lamp . . . it went green. Fucking green . . . okay . . . shit . . . think . . .

He now remembered flinging the crowbar at it and was amazed that he'd actually hit it and blown the damn thing out. Glass exploded everywhere, and the dull green light illuminating him had quickly disappeared.

Frank slid out of bed and stumped his way into the bathroom. He unleashed a burning stream of urine into the toilet that took all of five seconds, which was okay since he would have to go again in ten minutes anyway. With a flush, he turned and saw himself in the mirror. What looked back at him was exactly what he knew himself to be: an old man who should've died when *she* did. His life ended then, but instead, he was stuck in the land of the living, still managing to do things like fight with his son, piss off his daughter-in-law, scare his grandson, and now possibly derail a train.

I have to have done it. Who else would've? Not Beau Harper. He couldn't have. He wouldn't even know where to start.

And the image of Hollis now popped into his head, leading Frank in cuffs into prison with a shit-eating grin on his face.

I'm not going to give that asshole the satisfaction. I'd rather give myself up to the Feds.

And that's exactly what he decided to do. His defenses fell all at once, caving to what felt like inevitability. He was going to put an end to all of this and stand before God and accept whatever doom he saw fit to bestow upon him.

Now committed, Frank gagged down half of a cup of coffee and made for the driveway. He didn't even bother locking the door. It was all going to be gone soon anyway.

Starting the truck, Frank stared at his house. The thought of turning himself in, and to Hollis of all horrors, still made him want to drive off the New River Gorge Bridge, which wasn't a bad idea, really, or even the first time he'd thought of it.

He pulled out of the driveway and drove toward town. Word had it that the pretty little NTSB agent had held camp at Stanley's every morning since she had arrived.

It would be a good enough place as any to impale himself upon the scales of justice.

I'm going to sit across from her. Tell her my name, and that I did it. Or at least I think I did. Maybe. Probably. Shit, why can't I remember?

By the time Frank arrived at the town's edge, capitulation and surrender had given way to annoyance and frustration. The town had now reached a crescendo of congestive ugliness. News crews, the families of the passengers, and the people who actually lived here all piled into the same eight-block area. It was like the town suddenly became Pittsburgh overnight.

Frank pulled up and stopped behind a conga line of cars waiting at a red light on 2nd Avenue. His blood was on simmer. He couldn't even surrender honestly without having some obstacle to overcome. He didn't recognize any car in front of him except for that of Mrs. Hobbs, and her shit-heap Impala two vehicles ahead, stopped short of a railroad crossing.

It's an omen. I should turn around and go home.

The traffic light ahead turned green. The line of colorful metal boxes inched forward, and, of course, there was a dumbass turning left and clogging up everyone behind him.

Traffic had now moved up several car lengths, forcing Frank to stew even longer. It was true; heaven was already punishing him, with the best yet to come. As he looked ahead, Mrs. Hobbs' Impala inched onto the tracks and skulked to a stop. Frank shook his head.

Brilliant, Hobbs. If there was any justice in the world, you'd be the one to get hit by a train.

But out of some shadow of decency deep in his heart, he looked both ways down the tracks, just to be sure the old bat wasn't about to become a statistic by forgetting Driver's Ed 101. The tracks were clear. Not one sign of a freight train, passenger train, or even a handcar in sight.

So much for justice.

And, of course, the traffic light ahead turned back to red, sentencing Frank to another five minutes of brake lights and gridlock, which only sent him sinking into his seat.

Figures.

Frank's eyes drifted down the tracks to the left, which was far more visible thanks to the adjacent paint store parking lot. Standing upright next to the tracks was a signal light much like the one at Prowler Flat, not that he needed a reminder. But it took him a couple of moments to realize it was powered up and glowing green.

Green . . . SHIT!

Frank quickly sat forward. His eyes jumped to Mrs. Hobbs and her idiot Impala, both nicely planted on the crossing with only a few feet of open space in front of her.

The old woman was oblivious to all of it. She was waiting patiently for the traffic light to turn green but jumped when the crossing gates came to life. An instant later, the blare of a locomotive horn snapped her attention to the right as the sight of an oncoming freight train sent her into an immediate panic.

Frank mashed the gas pedal to the floorboard. The truck roared around the car ahead of him and plowed into the Impala's trunk and quarter-panel. The back window exploded and Hobbs screamed, clawing for the door with her foot stomped on the brake pedal. The tires on Frank's truck spun as the Impala remained locked in place.

"GET OFF THE GODDAMN BRAKE!!!" Frank yelled out his window, his eyes on the train that refused to slow.

Mrs. Hobbs lifted her foot and the wheels on Frank's truck spun in a cloud of burnt rubber, pivoting the Impala off the tracks, clear of the crossing and into a line of parked cars.

Frank wasn't that lucky.

The locomotive broadsided him through the passenger door, blasting glass into the cab and lifting the truck onto two wheels. It was pushed for half a block before it became caught on the rail ties and launched upward. It then tumbled through a string of dumpsters and abandoned autos until it was tossed into a building in a bloom of dust and debris.

Frank held on to the steering wheel for as long as he could, and then he just held on to anything. In those fleeting moments, he resigned himself quickly to the notion that this was his end.

And he was fine with it. It was fitting, it was quick, and it simplified everything. Except for one thing: *Kevin, I wanted to . . .*

With a sudden jolt, Frank's world went black.

18

The news took more than an hour to reach Kevin. He was well west of central Ohio in a six-unit mixed freight with green signals as far as the eye could see. It took another hour for him to catch a ride back in the other direction and hours more to make it back to town, grab Trisha and Shiloh, hand Michael off to the neighbors, and make it to the hospital. By the time they arrived, the late autumn afternoon had swiftly given way to a cold, breezy, and dark October evening. And as far as Kevin knew, Frank would find a way to cudgel him with being late to his father's own near-death experience.

Once at the hospital, Kevin and Trisha moved down the corridor with Shiloh close behind. They were soon intercepted by a doctor, who pulled them aside to explain Frank's condition. Shiloh would later recall only that her grandfather was nearly killed, he was incredibly lucky, and he would be out in a couple of days and be in a world of hurt for a while. She tuned out everything else.

With her parents continuing to talk, Shiloh looked around. She wondered where Beau could be, and when she spotted Deputy Preston down the corridor, standing by an open door, she knew exactly where that was. She quietly drifted away to peer into the doorway Preston guarded.

"Hey, Shiloh," Preston whispered.

Shiloh gave him a small wave, then pointed into the room, checking to see if it was okay to go inside. With Preston's nod, she quietly entered. The room was bathed in a soft, clinical light that blended with the deafening silence broken only by the rhythmic beeping of machines that stood vigil around Beau on a bed loosely cocooned by sheets neatly tucked around him.

Beau looked horrible, and Shiloh's heart broke. Deep bruises darkened his face and oxygen tubes laced up his nose. Shiloh's empathy was never in short supply, and to see Beau like this, cruelly beaten by a monster who had fallen just short of completely exterminating him, swelled tears in her eyes.

Shiloh slid past Dana as she lay curled in a makeshift bed, her face worn with the fatigue of a parent whose world had been turned upside down. Despite Shiloh's effort to move by silently, Dana stirred awake as she moved toward Beau's bed. Shiloh's appearance in her son's room moved her deeply, and all Dana wanted to do was hug this young woman and cry in her arms. Beau had managed to find a friend in Shiloh, someone who saw beyond his challenges and connected with the person he was inside. And she was forever thankful for that, far more than she could ever communicate. Even as Beau had developed a less than secret crush on Shiloh, Dana knew Shiloh would always protect the delicate balance of their friendship.

Easing quietly onto the bed, Shiloh slipped her hand under Beau's. He was cool to the touch, and it frightened her. She knew

Beau had a unique way of looking at the world. He possessed an unexpected humor that no one else would ever take the time to see, and his soul was remarkably gentle. Shiloh knew how painfully isolated he was in a world that didn't always understand him. But with her, he had always been just Beau—kind, brilliant in his own way, and endearingly earnest.

Shiloh leaned in and whispered, "Third power equals twenty-seven?" and then waited for an answer that wouldn't come. At least not yet. She knew that somewhere in the depths of his coma, Beau could hear her and was still sandbagging the answer.

Dana looked on from her corner. Shiloh represented a world of normalcy that Beau wasn't even aware of. Her son was a mystery to her. With Beau, she fought an endless battle she could never win. But, at least at this moment, Dana saw the kind of friendship and acceptance she had always hoped her son would find.

Kevin and Trisha entered Frank's room and found him much like Shiloh found Beau: in a bed, bandaged, banged up, and bruised.

Frank looked at both of them and then away. A part of him had hoped they would come, but now that they were there, a larger part of him wanted them to leave.

"Hey, Dad," Kevin said. "How are you feeling?"

Frank looked at him. *Really?*

"Doctor says you're gonna be okay. Just a concussion and—"

"Yeah, I know, Kev," Frank interrupted, not wanting the recap. "No need to repeat it."

Trisha gave Kevin a sour look. She was already done. "I'm going to find our daughter," she said to him and then exited without saying a word to her father-in-law, who wondered if his son knew just how wide and deep his wife's vengeance streak was.

He did.

Kevin nodded and watched her go. He then turned back to Frank and exhaled. A part of him was grateful Frank was still alive and another part was deflated that nothing was different about him after nearly getting killed. And by a train, of all things, while saving the ancient and decrepit Olivia Hobbs.

"Did the doctor also tell you that you look like shit?" Kevin jabbed at him.

Frank cocked his head at Kevin and managed to find enough humor to crack the slightest bit of a grin. This would be one of the rarest moments of comedy they would ever easily share between them. Everything else was just a chore.

"What can I get you, Dad? What do you need?"

"A priest," Frank answered in a defeated tone.

That wasn't an answer Kevin was expecting, and it made him pause for a long beat. He shifted in his stance. "You know," Kevin said with the intent of pulling his father out of the slump he was in, "of all the people you'd risk your life to save, I would've picked Hobbs to be at the very bottom of the list."

"I should've let the Blight of West Virginia get herself splattered all over 2nd Avenue."

"Nice," Kevin tossed back at him. "They're calling you a hero, you know."

Frank scoffed as he raised an arm over his head and hid his face in the crook of an elbow. "More proof that God doesn't exist. Go home, Kev."

Kevin studied him. "You okay, Dad?"

Frank again looked at him. *Seriously?*

"I mean, besides . . . this," Kevin motioned to Frank's physically damaged state.

"Just go home, Kevin. You don't need to be here," Frank said flatly. For some reason, from a dark place inside he couldn't explain or define, something now wanted his son as far away from him as possible. And if he got rid of him with more dismissiveness, all the better. Maybe then his son would learn to just leave him the fuck alone. "You don't have to pretend to be concerned for my sake."

Kevin stared at him. Even after years of showing that he cared for his father, whom he found nearly impossible to love, he was still being rejected. And he still needed to understand why. What was so wrong with him that his own father couldn't tell him?

"Go home," Frank repeated.

While instinct and loyalty told him to stay, Kevin moved toward the door as Frank turned toward the window.

"They're cutting you loose in the next day or so," Kevin said, still with a glimmer of hope that his father would at least acknowledge him caring enough to come and see him. "I'll grab you some clothes, okay?"

Frank didn't respond, and that was unusual. Normally, he would've blown Kevin off and told him he could get his own clothes, mainly because Kevin would grab something he didn't want to wear, which was typical of his son. He'd screw it up, once again missing that bar of expectation. Or at least the expectation that existed in Kevin's mind. But this time, Frank was quiet. Quiet enough to make Kevin realize that something else was very wrong.

19

uck's junkyard was a sprawling expanse of metallic carcasses stacked within a rusted chain-link fence. Rows of abandoned vehicles lay in silent repose, their stories lost forever beneath layers of corrosion and peeling paint. Just outside town, Puck's was the only automobile graveyard for every wreck in a fifty-mile radius. And Puck had just about everything from a replica Scooby Doo Mystery Machine van to a mostly decomposed Model A, slowly being strangled by vines of poison ivy, whose engine Puck had tinkered with over the years, hoping to get it started just for the hell of it.

Today's addition to Puck's collection was particularly unique. His usual assemblage of steel and iron included cars that met their demise by plowing into trees, bears, and boulders. He had a few that had flown off bridges, a novel collection of vehicles that showcased the unforgiving force of eighteen-wheelers, a couple done in by a Sherman tank hijacked by a frat house from Morgantown, and even a convertible Caddie that'd had a Cessna 210 land on top of it, gruesomely removing the heads of everyone within. But he never had one come after getting torpedoed by a freight train and chucked into a building. Once the insurance company was done with it, it would be his to take apart and morbidly explore.

But for now, he had to endure Hollis Peete rummaging through it. Or what was left of it. The cab was a twisted spectacle sprinkled with broken glass. Hollis had to bend and contort to find the blood stains and overall crap simply because Frank was anything but organized. Hollis next went for the glove box, yanking it open and pulling out a piece of crumpled paper.

A train schedule.

He gave it a once over and stuffed it into a pocket.

"He's lucky to be alive, don't ya think?" Puck said, getting impatient for Hollis to get lost. "I mean, most folks don't walk away from shit like this, do they?"

Hollis turned to find a grin break out on Puck's cracked face, which annoyed him immediately. "So how long do ya think it'd take me to find a dead body in one of these fuckin' lawn ornaments ya got here?"

Puck's grin faded.

"Now go make yourself useful and die," Hollis said, dismissing Puck as one would an ugly three-legged stray dog.

Puck scowled and left, muttering an obscenity in a deep, incomprehensible West Virginia accent that even Hollis didn't understand.

Goddamn fuckin' hillbilly, Hollis thought to himself. He then went back to work as rain began to pelt him. He reached the front bumper and felt underneath it, finding the same clay dirt plentiful at Prowler Flat. He pulled a chunk of it out and held it in his hand to watch the rain wash it away.

A faint smile curled across his face . . .

20

Kevin stood amidst the stillness of his father's living room. His eyes were on the disturbing glass fractures of the shattered TV sprayed across the stained shag carpet. This was more than just losing Tom, Kevin thought, or Atlantic cratering into fiscal oblivion. There was something else going on, as coming apart at the seams was not in his father's library of flaws. Kevin was having trouble imagining the emotional chaos that resulted in the violent end of the RCA TV that lay dead on the floor.

He moved on through the house, feeling like a ghost in his childhood home. With his father absent, it was more of a tomb frozen in time. Once his mother had passed on and he'd met Trisha, it never felt like home again. But it didn't stop the random memories that fired at him in all directions, giving his stomach knots whenever he set foot in it. The same knots that had formed as early as he could remember.

The house was also in desperate need of a home invasion of cleaning ladies. Frank was generally not that much of a slob despite his failings, so what Kevin saw around him—stacks of dishes in the sink, cluttered counters, unopened mail—this degree of messiness was atypical of his father.

Stepping into Frank's bedroom, Kevin found a bed spattered with dried blood on the sheets and the reddish dirt from Frank's truck on the floor next to it. In the bathroom . . . well, Kevin decided to spare himself any sort of trauma that awaited him in there.

But, as promised, he went to his father's closet to pull out an outfit to take him home, only to have his gaze drift to the end of the rack, where his mother's dresses still hung, untouched for decades. For a fraction of a moment, he thought he had caught a faint whiff of his mother's last doses of Hubert de Givenchy still on her clothes.

Kevin quickly shook off the emotional cobwebs. He collected Frank's clothes in a small overnight bag before stepping into his childhood room. It was exactly how he'd left it when he was nineteen. Posters of the rock bands Aerosmith, Boston, and Foreigner, and his favorite doe-eyed poster of Linda Ronstadt with a white lily in her hair adorned its walls. Plastic models of classic muscle cars collected dust on the shelves and the dresser top, and a closet stuffed with toys Kevin had long aged out of pressed against its door. His father hadn't changed a thing, and Kevin always wondered why. He also never asked. It was just a subject never touched upon, and Kevin was content to leave it that way.

Turning to leave, he caught a glimpse of a picture on a shelf. Pulling it down, he held a family photo in black and white, probably from 1968 if he remembered correctly. A year before the accident. A family picnic with a younger Frank, Mom in one of her floppy hats, and a skinny Kevin at seven, dripping wet from swimming in the cold Bluestone River.

Kevin lowered the bag to the floor and curled up with the picture on his bed. A bed that felt exactly as it had long ago. And for just a beat, accompanied by the memories of muffled angry voices outside his door that often invaded his childhood slumbering dreams and frightened him to the core of his youthful soul, he was eight years old again.

"Kevin," Fay's voice whispered in her sleeping child's ear, followed by a nudge of her hand upon his eight-year-old shoulder that drew Kevin from his sleep. "Wake up, honey."

Kevin's eyes slowly opened, confused by the darkness of his room and the light streaming in from the hall.

"It's time to get up," Fay whispered further, the smell on her breath curdling her son's young nose.

Kevin pulled himself from his pillow and then looked at the dull green glow of his bedside clock.

It was 2:33 in the morning.

"Let's go," Fay urged cheerfully with a slur and a slight stumble toward Kevin's bedroom door.

The interrupted sleep hung heavily on Kevin as he emerged from his covers, adding to the confusion he still felt when he stepped into the hall. The light stung his eyes, and his confusion was now accompanied by a fear that churned within his stomach. Looking down the hall, he watched the shadows of his mother moving about the kitchen, dishes and glasses clanging against each other.

"What are we doing?" Kevin asked, his voice barely audible.

"We're going swimming, honey," Fay mumbled with the sound of car keys landing in her purse. She then appeared in the hallway, ready to go.

Kevin's eyes narrowed and his brow knotted. "Where's Dad?"

"Let's go!" Fay said, urging him down the hall and not answering the question. But Dad was where he always was: gone.

"But . . . don't I need my swimsuit?" Kevin asked, his voice cracking. His body shook slightly.

"No, no," Fay waved. "You're fine just like that. Come on."

Kevin stood scared in the hallway, looking down at his blue pajama bottoms. "Where are we swimming?" he asked next.

"A friend's house," Fay answered with a more pronounced slur. "Kevin, let's go."

Kevin moved forward as commanded and followed his mother into their blue 1966 four-door Rambler Classic. He took his favorite spot in the back, standing behind the sedan's front bench seat.

In the years ahead, Kevin would remember only snippets of this night. He would recall driving through the empty streets of town and eventually pulling in front of a small white two-story clapboard home with a Ford Galaxy patrol car in the driveway and its big red gumball on the roof.

The home scared him. It always had. The big man that lived there was loud and mean and the few times his mother brought him here he'd always chased Kevin into the backyard that contained a rusted blue and green tubular swing set from the children of owners long departed, sitting loosely in the tall weedy grass. At the time, he never understood the noises that would come from inside the home when he was stuck in that backyard, and he understood even less when she sent him to the front door that warm night in his pajamas.

"Here?" Kevin whispered.

"Yeah, go get your friends," his mother answered.

Kevin caught his mother's sleepy look in the rearview mirror, then turned to stare at the darkened house with a knot in his stomach that felt more like a bowling ball. There were no friends in *this* house, only a monster. And there was definitely no pool.

"Go on."

Head down, Kevin climbed out from the back seat and walked past the banged-up mailbox, dimly illuminated by the streetlamp on the corner. He looked at the letters that spelled H. P-E-E-T-E on the side of the box, then continued up the cracked and uneven walkway that led to a dreary home dressed in shadows on what was a very still night. Only the Rambler's idling motor could be heard. Crickets, frogs, and everything else that usually prattled on during a typical summer's night were absent, and the fireflies Kevin loved so much were nowhere to be found in the ratty lawn and gnarled trees of this home.

His stomach ached. He wanted to go back. To *his* home.

Kevin silently climbed the single porch step, looking upward toward the darkened bedroom windows that housed the monster inside. He then stood before the paint-faded front door and looked at the button for the doorbell.

It glowed with a faint and tired yellow light.

Kevin stared at it. He knew it was late and feared waking the man inside and finding himself the brunt of his anger. The man scared him like no other—far more than his own father did. Kevin quietly stepped away from the door, silently descended the porch step, and returned to the Rambler.

"No one answered," Kevin lied as he opened the door and climbed inside.

At first what Kevin had told her didn't register, not that she was in a state of mind where much would. "What?" Fay said, looking at her son with suspicious disbelief.

"No one's there," Kevin quickly answered, hoping his mother would believe the fib and not yell at him to try again.

Fay's mind drifted. She was so far gone that she had actually forgotten why she chose to drive to this particular house in the first place. She nonetheless pushed on. To where, even she didn't know.

Kevin closed the car door and looked upon the darkened home as his mother drove off into the night. He wouldn't remember how long they drove for, or even where they were going. His mother drove aimlessly onward, often down the middle of a road at any speed she wanted . . . until slumber claimed her over the centerline of old Sumpter Road.

Kevin glanced out the passenger window, watching as the edge of the road came close to them and then fell away as the sedan arced and leaned in a wide left turn. He looked forward just as the headlights lit up the 100-year-old oak that awaited them.

His mind never registered the impact. In just the split of a moment, he now looked upon a shattered windshield and a dashboard bent toward him. Kevin looked toward his mother, finding her pinned against the seat, the steering wheel and column pressed against her chest. He tried to move and climb out of the car, but there was nothing to support him. His left leg was broken, likely from the rear bench seat that had torn itself from its anchors and whipped Kevin's leg as it flipped over.

Kevin cried for help but knew there was no one to hear him. It would be a repeated nightmare that would haunt him often.

He would scream as loud as he could with nothing more than a whisper escaping.

"Kevin," Fay said to her son, straining to turn her bloodied face toward him. "I want to tell you something . . ."

Kevin recoiled. "I can't talk to you right now," he said, "you're covered in blood."

Fay's eyes closed and she turned her head forward. She knew her son couldn't face his mother like that, let alone hear what she had to say.

By the grace of God, a pair of headlights streamed into Kevin's car window. The door swung open and a moment later Sherman Gale, a quiet man with pained eyes whom Kevin had only seen from a distance, opened his door and carried him away from the car. Sherman then fell to his knees next to Kevin as the Rambler's torn fuel line popped into flames. Within seconds the sedan was incinerated.

And with a single scream, Fay Campbell's life came to an end.

21

The following morning, Kevin watched as a slow freight train rolled by the rail crossing on 2nd Avenue. The same crossing that nearly sent his father into the afterlife, a trip that many thought he should've made given how bad his truck looked.

Kevin's eyes drifted to a nearby store where a "FOR LEASE/ SALE" sign hung in the window. He knew this wouldn't be the first of those signs he'd see. Atlantic's end was just the beginning, and he was honestly worried about the gutting this little town would bear in the coming months. From the union perspective, they would be utterly useless beyond finding work for more than forty people. He had pressed for the big carriers to look at the local talent, but much of that was far from where they would be needed, making everything far more dire.

As for the present, the freight train cleared the crossing at a snail's pace with an empty rusted boxcar plastered with graffiti. The gates lifted and Kevin drove on and pulled into the post office parking lot. He emerged with a stack of mail from the union's post office box and then took a step back when he found Puck sitting in his driver's seat, his tow truck blocking him along with a bunch of other parked cars.

"I never get to see 'em this nice, you know," Puck said, his hands caressing the leather steering wheel, wishing it was his. "Be damn kind of ya if you'd let me drive it once."

"Maybe some other time, Puck," Kevin said.

Puck reluctantly surrendered the driver's seat and opened the truck's door. He slipped past Kevin, who had backed up to allow him by. Kevin figured that it had to be at least three days, maybe four, since Puck had an encounter with a bar of soap.

"You know," Puck mentioned as he ran a finger down the truck's fender, "Hollis was pokin' around your dad's truck."

Kevin paused. "What do you mean, 'poking'?"

"He was snoopin' 'round. Lookin' for somethin'. Even pulled somethin' out, too."

"Like?" Kevin asked, motioning him to continue.

Puck shrugged. "Piece a' paper it looked like, I think?"

"You mean the registration?"

"Nah, I pull those out when they come in. This was like one of those things you train guys carry 'round with you."

Yeah, that's not helpful.

A car horn honked at Puck, who turned to see a news van from Cincinnati trying to get around his tow truck.

"You mean a schedule?" Kevin asked.

"Yeah, that's it," Puck answered, a light bulb popping on inside his head. "If ya ask me, sounds like he's prowling."

Yeah, well, that's nothing new.

The Cincy news van honked again, accompanied by a series of impatient hand gestures from its driver.

"Yeah, I heard ya the first time, butt-wipe!" Puck shot back with his own interpretation of hand gestures and arm waving.

Kevin watched as Puck walked off and then spotted Andy sitting at Stanley's across the street. She was visibly frustrated and had a stack of papers in front of her. Kevin tossed the mail in the truck and walked over.

Inside, it was crowded. It was the busiest Kevin had ever seen it, clogged with people he knew and many he didn't. Which meant poor Stanley was likely losing his mind. He usually ran the place by himself since most of the time it was completely manageable. But today it was a zoo.

Kevin made his way toward Andy's table. "You got room for some company?"

Andy looked up from her folders, her clunky government-issued laptop, and a mostly eaten breakfast in front of her. She was surprised to see him, especially after their chilly interaction only a few days ago. "Sure," she answered and cleared a spot for him.

Kevin sat just as Stanley came up to give Andy her check. "Jesus, Stanley," Kevin commented as he took another look around the diner. "Business is boomin', huh?"

"Christ," Stanley answered, exasperated. "I'm about to fuckin' shoot myself." He then pointed around the shop and the counter. "CNN, CBS, NBC, MTV. *Mad Magazine*'s next, for all I know."

"You might actually have to put Karen to work," Kevin quipped, knowing the suggestion would only serve to joyfully needle Stanley.

"Then I *would* shoot myself. Any chance your daughter wants a job?"

Kevin smiled. *Nope.*

"How's your dad?"

"I'm supposed to go take him home this morning."

"May the Lord have mercy upon your soul," Stanley solemnly commented. "Want something to power you through it?"

"Sure. What the hell."

Stanley headed off as Kevin looked over at a nearby table, his eyes meeting the gaggle of old ladies looking back at him and Andy, sizing up new fodder for the gossip mill.

"Small town, huh?" Andy said, picking up on being stared at.

"Yeah, that's Mae Kay Weintraub in the middle. The one with the stringy giraffe neck and beady blue eyes, flanked by her squad of reputation assassins."

"Reputation assassins?"

"Also known as the Ladies Auxiliary Morals Enforcement Squad from our local friendly Episcopal Church of Holy Hypocrisy. They're a nest of vipers who have their noses into everything around here, and there's nothing like a nice cold scandal to warm their little duplicitous hearts," Kevin added as he wiggled his fingers "hello," causing them to look away—all except for Mae, whose nefarious eyes narrowed at him with venom.

She was an imposing woman, well into her seventies, who ruled the Auxiliary of eight with an iron fist. She made Olivia Hobbs look like a children's activity director dressed up as Winnie-the-Pooh in comparison. She was tall and lean with an impeccable wardrobe and a true believer that anyone who didn't have their butt in the pew on Sunday morning had an automatic reservation in Hell. Simply because she said so. Mae made every attempt to control this little town and all the sinful mortals within its area code. She once ran for mayor only to lose when the citizens of Granite Point decided they didn't want to live in an irrational theocracy and be required to stone themselves to death at her every whim. She was also the town's biggest hypocrite. Married and widowed four times, including once to a drunk poet named Shelf, and lastly to Melvin Weintraub, a non-practicing Jew ever since his bar mitzvah, Mae wasn't one folks would throw themselves on the cross for. She was someone they'd throw the cross *at* to save their own souls. Even Melvin, who didn't believe in Heaven and Hell, crossed himself every time she screamed "Oh God!"

Other than that, Mae was very pleasant to be around.

"Rumor has it they have their own private library of Anaïs Nin books they're sneaking back and forth," Kevin went on to add, turning from Mae while scratching the back of his neck with a middle finger.

Andy stared at him. The fact that Kevin even knew of Anaïs Nin took her by surprise, especially since Nin had authored Andy's sexual awakening at the age of twelve, when two minutes after getting into her mother's hidden book stash, she began thumbing through the worn pages of *Little Birds*. Andy never opened a *Nancy Drew* book again.

"What?" Kevin asked as Andy continued to stare at him incredulously.

"The Church of Holy Hypocrisy and Anaïs Nin?" Andy asked, leaning in, quickly clearing her head of the carousel of carnal memories that started to fire off haphazardly in her brain. "What? Did you go to school at Oxford or something?"

Kevin chortled. "C minus in English from Allegheny Community College of West Virginia, thank you very much."

"Maybe you *should've* gone to Oxford. They probably would've loved you there."

"Yeah, they would've loved for me to leave. I'm about as academic as a box of cat litter."

Andy laughed and then glanced back at the Auxiliary, and at Mae Kay Weintraub in particular, who was back to glaring at her with menacing accuracy. "She's still staring," Andy said above a whisper.

"Just ignore her. She's about thirty seconds from folding over and expiring. She's one of the reasons you can't fart around here without everyone smelling it," Kevin answered. "And honestly, I'm surprised Mae's even acknowledging my existence right now."

"The layoffs?"

"Yeah. This town is about to get an apocalyptic zip code, and there's not a single thing I can do about it except arrange job fairs with every big box store between here and Lexington."

"There's nothing the union can do at all for these people?'

"I might be able to get a few hired with some of the Class Ones like CSX, but that's about it."

Andy sat quietly. She knew a company filing Chapter 11 with a relatively viable business and cash flow gives you something to work with. But a company filing Chapter 7 with nothing but hundreds of millions in debt is like a neutron bomb going off with a fiscal blast radius that consumes everyone in sight and beyond.

"I heard about your dad," she said, changing the subject. "That was rather impressive."

"I was more impressed that he didn't get himself killed," Kevin said as he looked over the scatter of paperwork in front of her. "What's all this?"

"This . . . is a headache."

"Have you come up with anything yet?"

"Yeah, you guys have a lot of mud around here."

Kevin smiled with amusement. "That we do."

"I need to get all of this into a basic state of common sense before the FBI steals it."

That gave Kevin a moment of pause and a reaction Andy quickly saw. "FBI's here?"

"They were," she answered with a hint of frustration. "Now I'm it, at least for the time being."

Before Kevin could answer, Stanley returned with his coffee. He could smell it immediately and was instantly suspicious of it. "This isn't one of those Ethiopian Kama Sutra things, is it?" he asked.

"I had this yesterday, and I was MC Hammer for a day," Stanley answered. "If you like it, you owe me $2.95."

"And if I don't?"

"You still owe me $2.95," Stanley answered, moving on with little patience for pickiness.

With a curl of his nose, Kevin took a sip and grimaced. *Oh God . . .*

"And?" Andy asked, waiting for the verdict.

Kevin answered with a sneer and pushed the cup away. "So where do they have you holed up?"

"The Mountaineer over on . . ." she answered, forgetting the address.

"Third," Kevin said, filling in the blank. "You could do worse."

"Yeah, especially since they put me in the Presidential Suite."

"You government types go in style."

"No," Andy shook her head, "I think the guy who checked me in liked my hat. You seem to have a lot of lonely men in this town."

"You have no idea," Kevin nodded. "You're also new, which makes you especially hot and novel."

Andy grinned. "So, what do people do around here besides drink horrid coffee?"

"I dunno," Kevin replied. "Ever been to this part of the country before?"

"No, but I'm still looking for those tobacco-chewing, one-toothed country folk who drive those rusting pickups I keep hearing about."

"Those are actually the women. We hide them up in the hills because they scare the hell out of us men."

Andy was amused by that one.

"We have the same things everyone else has. Except the movie theater has one screen, and there's a shit-kicking country-Western bar down the street that serves the worst watered-down beer this side of the Appalachians. We've got a graffiti problem, football, baseball, and an old lady who steals driveway gravel. We make dinners and babies like everyone else."

"Sounds rather nice, actually."

"Boring as hell when you're sixteen, but when you're an old fart like me, it's not so bad," he said, finding himself gazing at her a little longer than he probably should have. It was time to quickly, and very quickly, change the subject. "So, outside of mud, what else did you find?"

Andy had also realized she was looking at him longer than she should have. Something stirred in her that hadn't been stirred for a while, and it reminded her that it was something she missed. But for now, she leaned back in her seat, a little thankful he had changed the subject, and tried to find something she could share.

"Or you can't say anything?" Kevin asked, picking up on the hesitation.

Andy could only clam up. Regardless of how much she wanted to share anything with him, his presence generated a fog bank in her brain.

"Is my father in any of this paperwork?"

And that cleared up the fog.

"Is he a name I should be looking for?" Andy asked with a hint of probing.

Now it was Kevin who clammed up.

"It was suggested," Andy added. "Did you know he was pulled over not far from where the derailment happened?"

Kevin did not. And since it was the first he had heard of it, he was somewhat annoyed that he hadn't heard of it earlier. "No," he answered, his brain suddenly navigating through some treacherous patches of legal real estate. And he knew precisely where Andy's questions would lead. "My father's a lot of things. But he's not someone who would derail a train."

"What about Beau Harper?" Andy asked, somewhat impressed with how quickly Kevin knew where this could go.

He leaned back with disappointment. "And here I was thinking you're the smart one."

Andy realized this was all going in the wrong direction. Insinuating that he might know something was a tactical mistake, and he was significantly shrewder than she thought he was. The last thing she needed was for him to shut the door on her. With a chortle, she immediately downshifted the conversation to a level of something that didn't build walls. "Smart one? I can't even get out of bed without walking into the bathroom door."

Kevin sensed the change in tactics. And with those dark eyes of hers looking back at him, it worked. She had instantaneously softened up the first round of defense he threw at her. "Well, I don't know about walking into doors, but wearing croissant crumbs on your shirt for later consumption is pretty ingenious."

Andy looked down at her shirt to find a light collection of croissant flakes upon it. She swiped them away with an eye roll. "Shit . . . you see?"

Kevin smiled with satisfaction, which only goaded her into playfully firing back at him. "You're not so hard to read yourself, you know," she commented, leaning in slightly. "You're just like everyone else in this room."

"Oh, really?"

"Yeah," Andy said, winding up to put Kevin in his place. "Like the table at your nine o'clock."

Kevin looked to his left and eyed a young husband at a table with a young wife and her alluring younger sister sitting adjacent to a fussy, food-splattered baby in a highchair.

"He's having an affair with what I can only assume is his wife's sister," Andy deduced with easy confidence.

Kevin looked back at Andy.

"See the way he's sitting? Open stance to the young babe who's not exactly across from him. The sad thing is his wife knows it."

Kevin's eyes revisited the table, finding the clues Andy detailed: the sullen young woman, the young husband obviously angled preferably to her sister, and the baby who was wriggling in his seat.

"Or at your six o'clock," Andy continued as she called out the scene of an older wife sitting amongst a chatty group of ignored ham radio wives, clearly bored with all of it. She was essentially alone as her older husband talked about antennas with his buddies:

"A ham radio widow ready to leave the moment life knocks on her door, only to find she'll be long dead before it ever would."

Kevin looked over at their table, his eyes briefly meeting those of the bored wife dying on the vine, who really did look like someone who yearned for life to come back to her, even if she had to steal it.

"Or the MILF at your three o'clock," Andy nodded in her direction, "who thinks you're hotter than a Denver omelet."

Kevin pivoted to the attractive fifty-something who wore a Pittsburgh news station ball cap and stared right through him, hoping to manifest him into a bed that would likely kill him. She quickly looked off, obviously caught.

"Everyone has a story," Andy said. "Yours is being pinned under some kind of self-imposed boulder, and you're trying to push it up some kind of hill, believing that all it wants to do is roll back over you because you've convinced yourself you're powerless to stop it."

Kevin stared at her, fascinated and taken aback at the same time.

"But that's just a guess."

And it was a good one. Kevin attempted to reconcile being that transparent while his cell phone began to ring.

"And your phone is ringing."

Kevin snapped out of it and looked at the number display. He slumped slightly.

"Your adoring public?"

"Worse, it's my dad. Probably wondering why I'm not there to pick him up yet. Shit . . ."

"You're not going to answer it?"

"Life is better when we keep our conversations to a minimum," Kevin answered as he prepared to depart the table. "He can fight with my voicemail until I get there." He then pulled his wallet out and grabbed the check.

"What are you doing?"

"Paying for my alarmingly accurate psychology session," Kevin responded.

Andy instantly regretted that she'd even opened her mouth. "I shouldn't have done that."

"It's okay. Sometimes, we all need to get hit in the face with a mirror," Kevin said, trying to ease the regret in her. But then again, he saw an easy shot he could get in that he couldn't resist. "Oh, and the ménage à trois and baby over there? The guy is actually married to the babe sister."

Andy immediately looked at the table.

"Hey, Cody!" Kevin called over.

"Well, hey, Kev!" The young husband waved as his wife hauled her baby from his seat to wipe his food-encrusted face.

Kevin looked back at Andy with a satisfied grin as he walked off to the register. Kevin 1, Andy 0.

Andy sat, amused. She watched Kevin pay the bill and leave the diner while attraction brewed inside her.

Dammit. This is the last thing I need.

She then noticed the fifty-something's eyes lasering cold death at her, and then looked over to the Auxiliaries, who were giving her a thorough browbeating. And she couldn't resist the temptation. "Nothing beats dabbling with a married man, huh, girls?" she snarked, having fun with a gaggle of ancient bags with too much time on their hands.

With the exception of Mae Kay Weintraub, the blob of octogenarians gasped loudly at the audacity. Mae sat cold and still, already formulating the end of the pretty little brunette from D.C. Andy then gathered her stuff and left the table with her own shit-eating grin.

22

The ride home from the hospital was intolerably quiet. Kevin held a mostly one-way conversation with Frank, who sat rigidly, staring out the passenger window while waves of nausea and pain ebbed and flowed through his body. His mind was still trying to resolve being hit by a train, thrown through the air, launched into a building, and now, since he was still breathing, going to a family dinner he didn't want to go to. Why the Lord and Master of All Creation had decided to keep him amongst the living with what he had done, and with what he was running from, was a complete mystery. And now he was about to get a noxiously home-cooked meal from his daughter-in-law. It was quite possible God possessed a mammoth-sized cruel streak, and this was his penance. Or it could also simply mean Frank's room in Hell wasn't ready for him yet.

Unbeknownst to Frank, Trisha's sentiment was remarkably similar. She had no qualms telling Kevin she was less than enthusiastic about hosting Frank for dinner. Yet she'd agreed to do it, albeit grudgingly, while still failing to fathom the complex familial tie that bound Kevin to this task.

As they neared the house, Kevin was, unrealistically, hoping the gesture would be a small step toward bridging the vast chasm that existed between them. It was a very small hope—he fully expected the whole episode to blow up in his face within the first thirty minutes at the dinner table.

Kevin pulled into the driveway and somehow banged up Frank was out of the truck before Kevin could shut off the motor. At least he'd thanked Kevin for bringing him a new set of clothes.

Once at the table, the mood was dark and morose. Everyone ate slowly. Michael sat slumped in his chair, the negative energy around him zapping his appetite. Kevin looked blankly through his plate, wishing he had dropped Frank off at a Burger King, while Frank stared through his uneaten dinner, wishing for the same thing. Shiloh didn't know what to make of any of it, and Trisha looked upon her son, hoping he would take at least one bite.

"Come on, sweetie," Trisha nudged at Michael, "sit up and eat."

Michael squirmed with a whine.

"Just a few more bites, and then you can go," she added. "Come on."

Frank watched the exchange. "No point in making him eat if he ain't hungry."

Trisha ignored him and tapped on Michael's plate.

"I'm telling you, if you make him eat, it'll all come back up," Frank added. "He'll eat when he's hungry . . . even if it's this."

Trisha took a good long beat to stare at him.

"What is this? Tuna," Frank sniffed, "or chicken?"

Kevin watched the veins in his wife's head swell. "It's chicken, Dad." He then motioned for her to remain cool. What he received in return was the Icy Stare of Death.

"If you say so," Frank commented with a shrug. "I was kinda worried. Didn't see the donkey outside." Frank knew he was starting to push it. But he also couldn't help himself. This was an old habit that refused to die.

"The horse is at the arena, Dad," Kevin said, trying to deflect what was already boiling.

"If you don't like it, you don't have to eat it," Trisha hissed.

Frank leaned over and nudged his grandson. "Ain't that a relief, huh?" He then pushed his plate back and got up for the kitchen. "Especially for the donkey."

Kevin watched his wife's face tighten. "Dad, come on, Trish went to a lot of trouble to make this for you tonight."

"You mean a dinner I didn't ask for?" Frank answered, dismissing the obligatory requirement for gratitude. "I guess some thanks are in order then, huh?" He then poked his head out of the kitchen. "Thank you," he said to Trisha.

Kevin next spotted Shiloh getting ready to fire her standard shot at her grandfather, only to clam up and sink in her chair as Kevin stared her down.

"By the way, you're not gonna ride that thing, are you?" Frank asked, his voice echoing outside the room.

Trisha stared ahead, her jaw rolling from one side to the next. "*Thing?* What 'thing' are you referring to?"

"The donkey. Sorry, I mean 'horse.' Aren't you a bit old to be riding one of 'em?"

Kevin watched his wife's eyes turn black. It wasn't something he had seen before, and he hoped to never see it again.

"'Let's invite him to dinner,'" Trisha hissed and snarled at Kevin, "'make him a nice home-cooked meal.' Next time keep your great ideas to yourself."

Kevin wisely allowed that one to slide, mostly because he wanted to see the sun come up tomorrow and not wake up with a pillow over his face.

Frank opened the fridge and poked around, looking for something no longer there. "Anybody seen that six-pack I brought over last week?"

"I watered the compost pile with it," Trisha calmly answered with no mercy. She then mentally counted down Frank's reentry into the room with an acidic glare . . . *two . . . one . . .*

And on cue, he was there.

"Cans are in the bin if you're desperate," she added as Frank stood in the doorway.

"Nice," Frank grumped. "I haven't been here fifteen minutes and she's already bustin' my balls."

Michael giggled.

"Hey, Dad," Kevin said as he eyed his child, "watch the mouth, huh?"

"Oh, come on, you really think he's going to remember that?"

"Bustin' my balls!" Michael parroted, proving Kevin's point.

"See?" Kevin said.

Frank rolled his eyes. "Trust me, he won't remember it tomorrow," he said. "You never did."

"Trust *me*. I remember everything you've ever said."

"Bullsh—" Frank was about to blurt out, only to then catch himself.

"Asshole . . ." Shiloh muttered under her breath, but loud enough to be heard by Frank's semi-ancient ears, which earned her a special glare all her own.

"Your reel-to-reel tape recorder?" Kevin said, keeping the subject going.

Frank broke his scowl on his granddaughter and looked at Kevin with no clue as to what he was babbling about.

"Remember when you told me not to take it out, and I did?"

A moment passed before Frank remembered. Kevin couldn't keep his hands off it, no matter how often he was told. "Yeah. And you dropped it on its head like I said you would."

"Yeah, and what'd you say to Mom?"

How the fuck am I supposed to remember that?

"You called me an ass—" Kevin said, cutting himself off. He then looked at Shiloh, who was doing a lousy job of holding back her shit-grin. Kevin then looked at Michael, who was enjoying the new vocabulary lesson.

"The hell I did," Frank shot back. "Besides, you were what, three? You couldn't find your butt if it had a bell on it."

Michael giggled again.

"Honey, why don't you go play now?" Trisha said, nudging him away from the table and the growing adult-sized fray before him. Of course, there was no way that was going to happen. Michael was having too much fun learning new words.

"Why do you have to turn everything into a nightmare, huh?" Kevin asked of his father, trying to get argumentative leverage on him. "Can't we even do one nice thing for you without you turning it into some kind of a horror show?"

"Hey, this wasn't my idea," Frank answered, trying to absolve himself of blame. "But I'll tell you what, Kev. Why don't we splatter the brains out of your best friend, have you get hit by a train with your body feeling like it was stomped on by an elephant, watch everyone around you lose their jobs, and let's see what kinda mood you'd be in?"

Trisha looked to Shiloh, who glowered at her grandfather.

"Shiloh," Trisha called to her daughter. And when she didn't answer, "Shiloh!"

Shiloh snapped out of it and then looked at her mother as she nodded for her to take Michael out of the room. Shiloh scooped him up and left.

Once they were gone, Trisha made sure they were both out of earshot. Then she let the father-son knuckleheaded duo have it. "Alright, that's it. I've had it up to here with both of you. If you two are going to be at each other's throats, that's fine. But you're not going to curse and parade your problems in front of a three-year-old who doesn't know any better and a daughter who does."

Both Kevin and Frank stared at her. Kevin knew she was right, but Frank, on the other hand . . .

"You know," Frank said indignantly, "I'm so glad you invited me to dinner here, Kev. Next time, why don't you just kill me? It'll be far more merciful."

Kevin was about to jump in, but Trisha did it for him. "And you're the worst of all. Kevin's right; no one can do anything nice for you because the price you've gotta pay for it isn't worth it. Pain's one thing, but you're just downright mean."

The words hit home on Frank. She was right. Far more correct than he gave her credit for. But he was far too emotionally constipated to let it show. His face darkened as he fought back the only way he knew how. "Ya got yourself a helluva sympathetic wife there, Kev. Maybe you should start sleeping with an eye open when you go to bed. You might wake up with something missin'." And he regretted saying that the moment the words coagulated in his poorly wired blob of plasma called a brain.

But that did it. Trisha roared at Frank, ready to rip his throat out as the dishes in front of her flew from the table.

Frank backpedaled with genuine fear as Kevin clotheslined her just outside of clawing range.

"LET GO!!!" Trisha howled, dying to crush Frank's skull with her bare hands.

Kevin struggled to pull Trisha away. "DAD, GET OUTTA HERE!" he yelled at a volume that startled Frank even further. He was having difficulty holding Trisha back as Frank remained there, stunned.

"GO!!!" Kevin barked even louder, his voice echoing off the walls.

Frank moved out the back door as quickly as he could.

Once Frank was gone, Kevin released the hold on his wife, who then immediately spun around and slapped him hard enough that it nearly tore his face off. And then she was gone, leaving his cheek sharply stinging and his mind reeling. After the initial wave of pain subsided, he was able to open his eye and look through the kitchen toward the back door, finding his father sitting alone on the lawn, his face buried in his arms.

"You want to tell me what happened to your TV?" Kevin asked as he pulled into Frank's driveway, his headlights illuminating the rotted garage door.

"There was a fly on the screen," Frank flatly answered as he unbuckled his seatbelt. "I missed."

"Well, I cleaned it up," Kevin replied, happy to let the subject of the blasted TV go.

"I didn't ask you to do that," Frank replied as he climbed out.

"I also cleaned up the kitchen," Kevin added. He didn't know why he shared this but felt he had to since it wasn't his house. Or maybe it was just to score a minor emotional point with his dad instead of inflicting more damage.

"Great. Now I won't be able to find anything," Frank complained and closed the door. And before he could turn around, Kevin was backing out of the driveway and accelerating down the street with a tire chirp. That might have been the final *coup de grace* he had been waiting for. Frank had spent decades trying to push his son away, only to have him dig in harder to stay in his life.

The kid was tougher than Frank gave him credit for and far denser than he expected. Most sons would've told their fathers to fuck off decades ago, but not his son. He had to be stuck with a monomaniacal numbskull who couldn't read the signs of "just go away and leave me alone." He had nothing in common with his son, and relating to him was nothing of immediate importance. The kid's wife hated him, which was fine, as he wasn't a fan of her anyway. Why it took this long for his son to finally give up on him and grant him his fatherly independence would go down as one of the greatest unsolved mysteries of his life.

The roar of Kevin's truck faded into the cold night, which gave way to a dark stillness broken only by a single porchlight that awaited Frank at his front door. Frank took another look down the street, now void of life and any sign of his son. And in the deafening silence of the impending winter, he was completely alone.

23

Kevin merged onto Route 3 and kept accelerating, blowing past sixty in a forty-five zone on a two-lane highway out of town. He wasn't heading home. He wasn't heading anywhere. He just stayed on a road that led him far from where he was. And wherever it took him, he couldn't get there fast enough with the twisted lump of lead in his stomach. Over and over, he replayed the evening in his mind, trying to reconcile something that never had a chance of being reconciled.

He whipped past seventy.

His mind was a disarray of contradictions and loyalties that ended in pure gridlock. He was trapped, and what pressed on him more was the incessant self-impalement for a miserable old man whose indecipherable image of a son he could neither discern nor attain. Was there some expectation upon him that Kevin had completely missed, and his father deemed him too stupid to even share what that expectation was?

Eighty.

Kevin's mind raced. *Am I really that bad? Am I really that much of a failure? What is wrong with me that I can't figure out—*

In an instant something large leaped out in front of the truck in the dark.

Kevin quickly cranked the steering wheel over. With a sickening *thump*, a headlight shattered into darkness, and the Chevy skidded, sliding over the double line. He turned the wheel into the skid and straightened out, his heart pounding in his chest. He took his foot off the pedal and caught the helicoptering silhouette of an animal in the rearview mirror.

The truck came to a stop on the lonely strip of asphalt, the yellow centerline dimly lit by the one remaining headlamp.

Kevin turned the truck around and idled toward the lump on the asphalt ahead, stopping just short of it. Taking another few moments to collect himself, he climbed out of the truck and soon stood over a large buck, its breathing labored and crushed flank bleeding profusely. The animal thrashed, its broken antlers clacking against the pavement. Kevin took a step back as a car pulled up ahead of him. A second later, everything was awash in brilliantly lit blues and reds. Kevin turned to see Hollis emerge from the glare of the lights.

"Hey, Kev," Hollis said as he walked toward Kevin.

Kevin's heartbeat picked up again. Of course it had to be Hollis, the mandatory shit-cherry on top of any evening to make it completely horrid.

"Got 'bout 300 pounds on this guy," Hollis noted as he illuminated the suffering buck before turning his attention to Kevin. "What are you doing out here?"

"Driving," Kevin answered.

"Yeah? I can see that. Where to?"

"Anywhere but here."

Hollis cracked a grin. He could appreciate that. Hollis held Kevin in higher regard than most of the clowns in town and was surprised when Kevin failed to escape their little enclave in the valley. If any of them could've done it, it would've been Kevin. Instead, the dumbass had to follow in his father's footsteps.

Hollis moved past Kevin to check out the busted headlight on the truck. "You and your old man aren't having the best luck on the roads lately. Maybe you should both stick to walkin'."

Yeah, that's hysterical, Kevin thought. "What are *you* doing out here?" he asked as he watched Hollis walk by in the opposite direction.

"Headin' to Prowler for a federal confab. Except for the babe in the blue jacket, they'd all fuck up a two-car funeral over there. Ain't much to talk about anyway 'cause we all know who did it, don't we?" Hollis gazed intently at Kevin. For a few moments, he could see the echoes of Fay in the young man . . . and maybe . . . maybe an echo of himself. *If* it was true. At least for Hollis, there was always some lingering doubt concerning Kevin's origins—like a small piece of shrapnel he could never find and pull out.

"What, you think it was an actual accident?" Hollis continued. "Your dad would be a real low-life piece of shit pussy if he'd let that 'tard vegging in the hospital take the fall for it."

Kevin wasn't going to bite. He knew where Hollis was trying to take this and was not interested in going there. Especially as he was now worried that Hollis could possibly be right.

Hollis let it drop. Just sowing the seed of doubt was good enough for him for now. He then took one more look at the busted headlight. "Yeah, you clocked this guy pretty good," Hollis commented and then turned his flashlight on Kevin. "What happened to your face?"

Kevin withdrew from the blinding beam and reactively touched his cheek, suddenly remembering the sting still reverberating like a rung bell.

Hollis moved on, as he really didn't give a shit. He squatted next to the dying deer that writhed in agony and placed a calming hand on the creature's neck. Miraculously, it settled down, finding a peace that took Kevin by wonder. Hollis appeared to have a deer whisperer's touch. *Whoever would have guessed?* "You need help putting him in your truck?" he asked as he stood back up, unclipping his holster.

The question stumped Kevin. "Why?"

Hollis pulled his service issue 9mm and fired two rounds into the buck's skull, ending its suffering in an instant. "Because ya got a couple meat freezers' worth of dinner here, that's why."

Kevin was speechless. His ears rang, and he could only stare at the buck that now bled across the asphalt.

"No?" Hollis continued with a shrug. "I'll give the Bumbling Bimmell Brothers a call, then. They've got a hook that'll fit this guy, and they're not above eating roadkill." He holstered his gun and walked back to his car. "Better get that headlight fixed."

And with that, he drove off, vanishing around a bend. Soon, all that remained of him were the fading lights of his gumballs that he didn't bother to turn off.

Hollis insinuating Frank's culpability remained stuck in Kevin's already cluttered mind. It made a level of sense, which managed to move him from conflict to problem-solving. It wasn't tricky math to equate his father's out-of-the-ordinary behavior to that night. Yes, Tom's suicide and Atlantic cratering had their weight, but the derailment coincided with Frank's amplified intolerability and . . . well, despair. And now he needed to know.

His first stop was Puck's junkyard. With Puck's tow truck nowhere to be seen, Kevin pulled around the back and scaled the fence with a flashlight, landing quietly next to a dilapidated Oldsmobile. It didn't take him long to find Frank's contorted F-150. This was the first time he had seen it, and the sight terrified and nauseated him. By all rights, his father should've been killed instantly. Maybe a kinder god would've made sure of that.

With a dry swallow, Kevin pushed himself to look around at what was left. He picked around inside and found what Hollis had already rummaged through. He eventually reached the front bumper, finding the pushed-up dent and a pile of red dirt that had now fallen below it. Kevin knew that it hadn't come from being thrown into a building; it was the same nasty-ass dirt so prevalent at Prowler Flat. The same problematic chunk of earth that had disappeared under the trackbed just a few years ago from what was left of Hurricane Andrew.

Kevin crouched downward for a closer look but then sprung up at the sound of Puck's tow truck pulling toward the gate. He quickly clicked off the flashlight and retreated into the shadows, watching Puck climb out of his rig.

Puck slammed the truck door shut and walked to his trailer but quickly stopped when he heard what sounded like someone stepping on broken glass. He stood frozen and then peered in the direction of the sound. Kevin, too, remained frozen, not daring to lift his boot. Finally Puck moved inside the gate and toward Frank's obliterated truck, finding nothing but crumpled metal and a cold Canadian breeze that sent a chill over him.

'od-damned racoons, Puck thought to himself before he turned for his trailer to call it a night with a frozen turkey pot pie.

At Prowler Flat, Kevin turned off his one remaining headlight and idled quietly along the trackbed, hoping the blinding work lights would keep everyone's attention on what they illuminated, and blind to anything beyond them. He spotted Andy quickly as she walked through the wreckage, and then stood to watch a crane surgically pull a rail car back onto its trucks. Unfortunately, Hollis was also as easy to find. He followed Andy like a puppy, which oddly turned Kevin's stomach some.

Kevin pulled to the end of the service road and shut off the truck, remembering this was the same road he had chased Beau down the night of the derailment. Climbing out with his flashlight, he waded through the weeds toward the trackbed. He had no idea what to look for except he needed to see what evidence there was to solidify his father as the architect of this horror. He went along the trackbed, witnessing nothing but litter, stones, and mud . . . red mud. Walking became more laborious as he slogged through it. He looked at the mud-caked soles of his boots. In the end, all he found was that the rain had washed away everything.

"You lost?" asked a gruff voice from up on the trackbed.

Kevin spun around with his flashlight, finding and blinding Hollis, who looked down from above.

"Thought you were going home," Hollis asked with annoyed suspicion. "What are you doing here?"

Kevin was caught, even though in truth he was probably doing nothing wrong by being there. "Same thing you are," he answered.

"Yeah?" Hollis said, stepping toward the edge of the melted trackbed. "Then maybe you should leave that to us grownups and get the fuck out." He then pointed. "Door's that way."

Kevin quickly relented. He knew this wasn't a winnable scenario, and even just talking to Hollis was often like arguing with Frank: pointless. He reluctantly moved off, disappearing through the weeds and brush.

Hollis watched him vanish into the dark, satisfied that those seeds he planted were already taking root. He then headed toward Andy as she huddled with her team.

Ryan held up a rusty spike, bent from overuse. "We're finding these all over the place," he said before noticing a brown stain on his hand. "There's like a bunch over there in the weeds. Another scattered all over there in that tie stack. A few buried in the mud."

Hollis snorted. "Jesus effin' Christ, you're as dumb as a bucket of fish bait. Loose spikes are like squirrels. They're everywhere," he jibed before walking off and shaking his head. "Learn your trade, dumbass."

Ryan immediately felt like an idiot, embarrassed to even be there. He tossed the spike into the mud and walked off in the opposite direction.

Andy watched him disappear into the dark before her gaze led her back to the abstract horror and disquieting beauty of the twisted rails, skewed ties, and muddy puddles that vanished into the black of night.

Kevin returned to his pickup and slammed the door shut in frustration. He took a moment to himself, then started the truck up just as a thin piece of reflective metal lodged deep in the weeds caught his eye. Turning off the motor, he climbed out, ensuring he didn't lose sight of it. He waded through the thickets until he stood over the wreckage of a camcorder and the bent tripod it was attached to. It lay entangled in a thatch of thorny vines. He lifted it up, freeing it from what was likely poison ivy, rolled it over, and found it labeled: BEAU HARPER.

In the garage, Kevin lowered the camcorder onto the crowded workbench and stared at it. Once again, the garage was cold—a chill ran down from his scalp to his feet. His mind bounced from powering the camcorder up and possibly watching his father's complicity in what amounted to murder, to the practicality of turning it in as evidence for a federal investigation and ensuring his father's, or someone's, inevitable prosecution.

Kevin chose the former. With a long pause and a wave of trepidation, he moved the camcorder's power switch to "on."

The machine immediately whirred and clicked.

Kevin was surprised he wasn't electrocuted as it came back to life. His mouth went dry. A knot developed in his stomach. *This was a mistake.* He attempted to swallow, suddenly hoping the camcorder would show him nothing but static. But there was no turning back.

With a loud crack, Kevin pulled open the screen. It came loose in his hands, held on only by the thin wires that connected it. He steadied the screen with small chunks of wood, screwdrivers, and the odds-and-ends of workbench junk he could find within arm's reach.

And with a slight wince, he tapped "play."

The screen jittered as the tape spooled, twisted, and snapped loudly just as the camcorder's exhausted battery breathed its last. The machine would keep its secret.

Kevin sagged onto a stool with an exhale of defeat and relief. He knew that proof of his father's culpability in the wreck of the *Limited* could be sitting right in front of him, but it might as well have been light years away. Kevin closed his eyes as this weighed on him, only to then jump as Freedom stealthily approached him from the barn and snorted in his ear.

24

Trisha's fury burned through the night and began to abate by the time the sun rose the following morning. Lying in bed, she replayed the dinner disaster until she drifted off, only to awaken moments later to replay it all over again before finally falling asleep as the day began in earnest. And now, with the early morning sunlight filtering in through the thin curtains, she awoke to a dull headache and a cold, empty bed. Kevin had chosen to spend the night on the floor in Michael's room, well away from his wife's stewing wrath and any possibility of awakening to her pressing a large kitchen knife into his chest. He knew she wouldn't let go of what happened the evening before. She was exceptionally good at going to bed angry and even better at holding a grudge the following morning.

Trisha rolled out of bed and walked toward the window, where the far-away building tops and church steeple of Granite Point poked out above the autumn-colored tree line. Her first year in this horrid little town had been an exercise in painful solitude accented by being crushed-on by computer club nerds—some who later became multi-millionaires, dammit—and a short-lived relationship with Max Durst, a boy who amused Trisha's mother and appalled her third stepfather. Max was an edgy, long-haired bad boy who wore a fat-linked chain from a belt loop of his black jeans, which folded over his nerd-stomping black boots. He was also the one Trisha surrendered her virginity to on a snowy Saturday afternoon, a secret she'd never shared, not even with Kevin.

Max was Trisha's retribution for being dragged to the sticks of West Virginia. For Max, it was like hitting the jackpot, as his only claim to fame at the time was running a Led Zeppelin cover band from his garage when his parents weren't home (because if they were, Max knew they'd likely beat him to death with his cracked-veneer Fender replica). With Trisha at his side, Max's confidence hit such a crescendo that he dropped out of high school and disappeared into the LA rock scene. Over the years he would occasionally reach out to Trisha, something else she would never tell Kevin. He would test the waters of her marriage, hoping for an opening while toying with the concept of scrubbing off his tattoos and returning home to some degree of normalcy and sanity. Even to this day, and this morning particularly, the memory of Max Durst still wandered through Trisha's mind, and what her life could have been if she had followed him into those vague, nefarious dark recesses he sometimes spoke of. What he found in California was not what he had left home for.

Trisha shook her head and made her way downstairs to the kitchen, finding Kevin and Shiloh quietly at breakfast. Even with the hot coffee that awaited her—a minor peace offering from her husband—they kept to themselves and had already loaded Trisha's riding gear into the pickup to avoid being asked, or growled at, to do it. And before she could even sit down and say "Good morning," both had already vacated the premises.

A pang of guilt moved her anger down further.

Without a word, Kevin and Shiloh waited for Trisha in the truck, engine running and Michael already tucked in his car seat. A moment later the front door swung open, and Trisha was down the steps of the porch and walking to the truck in her black racing hat, riding jeans that left nothing to the imagination, and white racing button-down.

Even enraged, Kevin still found her stunning.

Trisha climbed inside and pulled her door shut with authority.

"You look—" Kevin started to say before Trisha responded by pressing a frozen bag of peas against his stung cheek, and then pointed straight ahead in silence.

The date of Bolt Murphy's Western Invitational snuck up on everyone. With the derailment, a pretty brunette from the Feds sniffing for clues, and the drama of Frank Campbell saving the life of the wretched Olivia Hobbs, no one was looking at the calendar except Bolt Murphy himself and Mae Kay Weintraub. She'd tried in vain to shut it all down, as she found such an event distasteful just days after "such a citywide trauma," while clutching the good book to her bosom. And on a Sunday, no less.

Of course, all that did was give everyone further incentive to press on, and to float the prospect of handing Mae Weintraub a shovel for the event so she could prove that "cleanliness is indeed next to godliness."

She found no humor in that whatsoever—or in anything else.

Granite Point Arena was well outside of town and built sometime shortly after Harry Truman left office. It was a dusty attraction that also saw life as a sprint car race track, a bi-yearly tractor pull and truck show, numerous 4-H events, the venue for a one-time concert by none other than Max Durst and his Led Zeppelin cover band that maybe 100 people showed up for, including the soul-saving Ladies Auxiliary, who felt obligated to protest the ear-disintegrating sounds of Satan himself, and the flood of 1965—a disaster of biblical proportions created by a ruptured water pipe directly under the arena. The whole place was turned into a sinkhole the size of Henry Clay's Dodge dealership over on 2nd Avenue.

But today, it was home to Bolt's menagerie of Western sports, made complete with the inclusion of the insane sport of bull riding, where often brain-damaged young men mounted murderous horned bovines who jetted ropes of nasal mucus in all directions. The unlucky few were stomped upon when the bull would whip a rider off its back with the velocity of a swinging hammer.

Bronc riding was another fan favorite. Angry horses sent their riders into traction, as the violent heaving and kicking of the horse was the equivalent of about sixteen head-on collisions within eight seconds. And, for additional fun, parents could allow their children to clutch onto the back of a rampaging sheep in something called mutton-busting. A modest entry fee of an extra five dollars was all that was needed to give Junior an opportunity to be dragged across the dirt and other livestock wonders on the arena floor for the entertainment of others.

And there was the barrel racing exhibition put on by the town's own Trisha Campbell, to be introduced by none other than Bolt Murphy himself.

Bolt had managed to pull in riders and livestock from the four surrounding counties. Once word got out, his phone never stopped ringing. And despite Mae Kay Weintraub's efforts to send him into the bowels of fiscal oblivion, his Western Invitational was going to be a success. He didn't make it as a rider, but just maybe he had a knack for becoming Granite Point's iteration of P. T. Barnum.

The morning was abnormally warm, with a sky such a deep blue it energized Bolt. The backside of the arena was already clogged with horse and bull trailers. Riders streamed into the lot in their pickups, food vendors were setting up, and people were hounding him on the mundanities of where to place trash cans. He loved all of it. The only thing missing was Trisha, who would be the cherry on top.

By the time the Campbells pulled into the parking lot, Trisha's infuriation had eased. Glancing at her husband, she saw the red bruising on his cheek, and it pained her in a moment of guilt. She'd allowed her anger to get away from her, something a woman who preached and prided herself on self-control found difficult to digest, let alone admit. It had felt so satisfying to hit him, but he didn't deserve it.

Silence commanded the cabin of the truck. Shiloh couldn't wait to get out, and she did just that the instant Kevin put the truck into park and shut off the motor.

"I'm spending the night at Ashley's," she flatly announced as she closed her door with teenage authority. She was weary of the increasing number of fights between her parents and her grandfather, and the sound of her mother's slap had carried upstairs, frightening both her and her brother. And as much as

Shiloh would hate to admit it, there was now an allure to Kyle's plan of marital escape.

Before Kevin and Trisha could turn to answer, Shiloh had disappeared into the crowded parking lot.

A few moments passed before Trisha, staring at the glove box, whispered a barely audible "I'm sorry."

Kevin looked at her. Something had changed in their marriage. Something he wasn't sure was reparable. Each sensed a line had been crossed, and it gnawed at them both. But Kevin heard her, nonetheless. "Good luck," he said.

Trisha looked at him briefly and then exited the truck with a soft closing of the passenger door. She pulled her gear out from the back of the truck and walked on toward the arena, her saddle to her hip and rope slung over her shoulder.

Kevin watched her and her slender figure, neatly fitted beneath a cowgirl hat, move off. An abrupt and unexpected emptiness found him. He was, for the moment, falling through a sense of loneliness he had not experienced since he was a child, and it unnerved him. He foresaw an ex-wife walking toward a different life—a life that did not include him.

He panicked slightly and then pushed the feeling away. He collected his son from the car seat, closed up the truck, and walked through the turnstiles, passing Bolt, who was more interested in seeking out Trisha to, no doubt, hit on her mercilessly. At least being related to an event participant spared him the ten-dollar entry fee. In the distance Kevin had spotted Shiloh in the sheltering protection of her friends, who would ensure she stayed far away from her warring parents.

As he walked to the arena's metal bench seats warming in the sun, nothing felt right. Even on a beautiful day like this, he felt like a man trying to claw out of his skin. The world around him had changed, pivoting off into a direction he couldn't gauge.

Michael hung on the railing bars as an announcer babbled incoherently over the P.A. He welcomed everyone in a mush of volume and echoes and then endlessly promised the event would start in "just a short while," which was still a good twenty minutes away. Southern country music filled the balance. There was not a moment of silence to be had.

The stands around Kevin swarmed with people he easily recognized and many he had never seen before. Big-bellied cowboy fanatics in large hats, women adorned in Western-themed shirt tassels and tinsel, flocks of children running loose, and teenagers who were there just to hang out.

He felt completely out of place.

Kevin pulled Michael from the railing and lifted him onto his lap. He looked toward the back of the arena, trying to find Trisha, who was lost in a sea of hats and people. Kevin then thought of Bolt, who was also nowhere to be found, and that created a whole new knot in his stomach. Trisha had more than once told Kevin the man repulsed her. But then there was last night and the stinging on his cheek that had not yet disappeared (nor been soothed by her apology), and his imagination then went on a carnal run he tried to chase from his mind.

After what felt like an eternity, the "short while" finally elapsed. Sixteen-year-old Becky Gale warbled off a wincing rendition of the National Anthem that brought a tear to her grandparents' eyes and drove Kevin to look at his watch. In three hours, he could go home.

Shiloh stuck close to Ashley in a conscious attempt to minimize her exposure to Caitlin, who was in an especially foul mood due to the bovine stink that wafted around her. Caitlin's state was further soured as Shiloh also appeared annoyingly cute in one of her father's oversized plain blue ball caps. Shiloh was not in the mood for any of it and thus found it best to keep her distance.

After a short debate about what to do next, a unanimous decision was made to eat before being witnesses to a few cute cowboys being smushed into the dirt. Given there was only one place to eat, they made their way to the line where hardened corn dogs, greasy fries, over-buttered popcorn, and deep-fried churros awaited them. As Shiloh stood behind her friends, an arm suddenly appeared from the crowd and quickly pulled her aside.

Shiloh spun to find Kyle in front of her, lit up with a smile that stretched ear-to-ear and enough excitement to jump a car with a dead battery.

"Hey!" Kyle said as Shiloh focused on him.

"What are you doing here?" she asked with measured surprise. "I thought you were working?"

"Not anymore," he answered with an enthusiasm that was almost contagious. "I got a new job!"

Shiloh took a moment to register that. "What do you mean, a new job? I thought you were layoff-safe?"

"I was only safe until I wasn't, which could've been next week for all I know," Kyle answered, pulling her further from her friends. "I got a job at U.P.!"

"Union Pacific?" she questioned with suspicion.

"Yeah, fuckin' Union Pacific! Can you believe that shit?! And they're gonna pay me almost twice what I'm making here! Twice!"

"Twice?" she repeated.

"Yeah!"

"That's awesome, Kyle."

"That's awesome for *us!*" he quickly added.

Here we go again. He would pitch her the dream of a little house, a pickup truck, a summer-themed wedding thirty seconds after her graduation, an island honeymoon sometime whenever, and two boys and a blonde-haired little girl in a sundress with dirty feet and two pigtails that stuck out like a pair of ant antennae. For Kyle, it was the picture-perfect Americana he'd always dreamed of.

For Shiloh, it was an escape from the growing minefield of her parents' marriage to picture-perfect mediocrity—about as appealing as a bucket of cold water dumped on her head. "So, what do you have to do?" she asked before Kyle could dwell on the subject of "them."

"Go to Nebraska."

"Nebraska?" Shiloh immediately smelled a rat. A giant, father-sized, Kevin Campbell kind of rat. "Really? My dad got you a job in Nebraska?"

A hint of an insult slid across Kyle's reddening face. "Your dad didn't get me this job," he answered, swiping back at the perceived dig.

"Well, he works for Union Pacific, you know, and now you do, too."

"Maybe I got it on my own," Kyle pushed back. "Seriously, a little faith in me every now and then would be nice, you know."

Shiloh immediately kicked herself for jumping to a conclusion at his expense. "You're right, I'm sorry," she conceded. "So, what's next?"

"I'm leaving for training tonight."

And the big rat feeling was back. "You leave tonight? To Nebraska?"

"Well, Omaha. But yeah . . ." Kyle stalled before taking a life-sized leap of hope. "And . . . and I want you to come with me."

Shiloh stared at him as her life suddenly flashed—and fizzled—before her eyes.

"Just you and me," Kyle added. "We can start our lives right now!"

Shiloh's appetite disappeared and was replaced by a sudden ulcer that grew in her stomach like a swelling black hole. "Kyle, are you serious? I'm not even out of high school yet," she whispered amidst the din of the crowd. "And my father would put a bullet in your forehead if he found out you were planning to take me a thousand miles away from here."

"Who's gonna tell him? You? And besides, you can finish school there."

"In *Omaha*?"

"Yeah, or you can GED out."

And that was the last thing Shiloh wanted.

Kyle read the hesitation on her face and his mood plummeted. It took a few seconds to feel the sickening punch to his chest—the dream he had shared with her was his and his alone. The romance of running away, wrapped in the fantasy realm of young love, was now replaced with the stark reality of Shiloh's cold feet. He took a step back, which pained Shiloh. She knew she had hurt him, and that was also the last thing she wanted.

"I was kinda hoping for a different reaction, you know." Kyle stared at her.

Shiloh held his gaze but said nothing, mostly because there was nothing that could be said. However, her mind raced frantically. In that terrifying moment she saw an escape from this stifling town she lived in and the painful fear of her parents' constant fighting. Kyle's dream had quickly become an albeit illogical solution to the nightmare of her homelife—a problem she was admittedly too young and too inexperienced to deal with. And maybe, hopefully, she was close enough to adulthood to make her own decisions.

"I'm outta here after dinner," Kyle continued, in a notably perturbed state. "That should give you enough time to grow up and figure out what you want to do with your life. And if you want me—or not." He then abruptly turned and threaded himself away through the crowd, leaving her behind.

25

Andy followed the line of people queueing up at the arena's ticket booth. This was unfamiliar territory, and the immediate sensation that assaulted her, beyond a missing Western wardrobe, was the smell of it all. It reminded her of when her parents dragged her to a circus when she was seven and she spent the entire outing with her shirt over her nose.

"Tell me again why we're doing this?" Ryan asked as he stood behind her in the ticket line looking at the mass of people around them. "Shouldn't we be . . . you know, like at the tracks or something?"

"We're here to prove a theory," Andy answered, inching forward in the line.

"What theory? That wearing too small of a cowboy hat gives you a permanent mullet?" Ryan answered above a whisper, his distaste for those around him evident. He didn't go to Yale just to spend an afternoon at a rodeo, let alone wade through the West Virginian accents he struggled to understand. However, the three girls who passed him wearing low slung jeans, bare midriffs, and their straw cowgirl hats might be worth the effort.

"That's not funny," Andy kicked back. Ryan was bright, but his Ivy League snobbery at times was as intolerable as bad gas. "Why don't you say it louder so everyone around can hear you?"

"I think you're reaching," Ryan replied, forcing his attention back to Andy. He was now wondering if he was going to have to pay to get into something that would make him check the bottom of his shoes later. "There's no way we're going to find anyone in here who would want to derail a train." He said that with enough volume to turn the people nearest them around. Ryan backpedaled. "I mean, you know . . . just saying."

Andy looked upward for even more divine help. All she got was two passing pigeons and a lost seagull as an answer. "The goal is not to find a suspect, Ryan," she said. "The goal is to see what life around here is like, which can help you find one. Just like you can't dissect a crash unless you know how whatever crashed works."

"That's what the FBI does?" Ryan asked, not buying the analogy.

"That's what I do," Andy answered.

"Guess that's why you're not in the FBI, huh?"

A moment passed as Andy's patience twinged. "Ryan?"

"Yeah?"

"Shut up."

Ryan shifted his stance and looked off while they reached the ticket booth. Much to his relief, Andy paid for them both, and they were soon walking through the crowded metal stands. He looked toward the arena to find a rodeo clown running for his life from a 1,600-pound, fudge-colored and dirt-covered bull, to the delight of the crowd, who hoped he would be launched into the stands. Ryan's head then craned as he passed a lovely little brunette in an oversized ball cap, staring straight ahead in the middle of a throng of people that brushed past her.

Almost immediately, Andy spotted Kevin. He sat toward the front and near the pens that held animals large enough to bend the earth below them. She made her way through the masses toward him.

At first Kevin didn't recognize her. The NTSB was farthest from his thoughts, although Andy was not. She had managed to play her part in muddling his mind since first meeting her, and he couldn't help but smile and welcome her presence now that she was directly in front of him. "What are you doing here?" he asked.

"Getting a taste of West Virginia," Andy answered with a smile, which crept out without her even thinking about it.

"Well, here it is," Kevin said, motioning to the arena and everywhere around it.

Andy then spotted the purple bruise on his cheek. "Oh my God, what happened to your face?"

Kevin touched it absentmindedly. "Oh . . . nothing. I just used it to keep my wife from tearing out my father's throat."

"With what, a shovel?"

Kevin smiled slightly with amusement.

"I think your wife has anger issues," Andy added. "Maybe duck next time."

"No, that would only piss her off more," Kevin sighed. "She's riding soon if you want to watch her."

"She's riding one of *those*?" Andy said, referring to a bull that was now thrashing a hapless rider against its back.

Kevin chortled. "No, she's a barrel racer."

"And I have no idea what that is."

"Well, stick around long enough and you will. It'll be over in less than thirty seconds, if that."

"Who are you?" Michael piped up from Kevin's lap.

"I'm Andy," she answered, crouching level with his eyes. "Who are *you*?"

"I'm Michael."

"Well," Andy said, reaching out to shake his little hand, "it's very nice to meet you, Michael." She then sat next to Kevin as Ryan looked on.

"Um," Ryan said, getting bounced around by the people passing by, "is this what dissecting a crash is like?"

Andy looked up at him. "Ryan, why don't you go get us a couple of hot dogs."

"Um, you know what's in those, right?"

"Ryan," Andy said and glared at him, telepathically communicating "get lost."

Looking at Kevin and Andy, he now understood even less about the theory Andy was trying to prove. But he did as he was told. He turned and weaved past the tall, scary Mae Kay Weintraub with eyes of steel marching past him, who glared hot holy death at Kevin, convinced the man should be bludgeoned into repentance by Moses himself. She was unnoticed by Kevin and Andy as she moved on toward the back of the arena in her self-proclaimed role as the corrective and punitive fist of God.

Trisha had just tightened the saddle straps on Freedom when Bolt arrived. "You scared the shit out of me," he sighed with a degree of relief. "I didn't think you were going to make it."

"Well, here I am," Trisha said, not sure if her head and heart were into this.

"You don't sound very convincing," Bolt commented, picking up on her mood. "You okay? You're going out in just a couple of minutes after these last two bull rides."

"I'm fine," Trisha lied, now wishing she was home and talking to her husband.

However, Bolt saw an opening. It was a now or never type of moment that he was perfectly aligned for. He moved in close. "You don't seem fine. But tell you what, how about after all of this is done, let's you and I grab some dinner, and you can tell me what's going on. After today, I think we could both use a party night out."

Trisha simply closed her eyes in an inward scream. She needed Bolt Murphy in her life about as much as a bowling ball needed a flat spot.

"She's going to be fine," said an elderly voice that sent Bolt, like a kid with his hand caught in the cookie jar, immediately "bolting" away. "That's right, dear. There's a full trash can that's been knocked over. Please do see about it."

Trisha turned to find Mae Kay Weintraub behind her, shooing Bolt away as one would a stray dog.

"That man is such a pest, wouldn't you agree, Mrs. Campbell?" she said.

Trisha didn't answer. She was suspicious of what this holier-than-thou woman was up to while she stood in her Sunday best, no doubt coming straight from church, where no more than twenty of the town's population were likely held against their will for their weekly sacrifice of a weekend morning to be laid upon the altar of eternal damnation if they didn't show up.

And Trisha was right. Sort of. Mae's Sunday morning was indeed spent at the little church on 5th, where she consistently inserted herself into the morning's service. With a raised fist and the fire of a rabid TV evangelist, she thundered to the handful of captive churchgoers while the Ladies of the Auxiliary guarded the exits. Mae ranted and railed against the endless sins that washed over their enclave with pestilent force.

"It is God's vengeance that brings this derailment to us!" Mae thundered, hammering her fist onto the polished mahogany lectern with enough force to cause the exceptionally nice and welcoming Pastor Rey, in his neatly trimmed beard, to wince, and snap little April Bannister awake with a snort. "With His hands, *He* spread the rails wide and called nine precious souls home. And it is *He* who brings these Jackals of Deceit to our streets!"

From the third row, just inside the center aisle, rose the hand of Natalia Fisker, a slight young woman of Russian descent who somehow found her way into citizenship and West Virginia by marrying Edwin Fisker, a snoozing, heavyset electrical contractor who flew her home after a six-month stint rewiring the U.S. embassy in Moscow and eradicating the bugs within it.

"Uh, yes, dear?" Mae stopped, her personality flipping from the fury of God to that of a sweet old lady in about three-tenths of a second.

"Explain, please," Natalia asked in a thick accent, "what is 'jackal of deceit'?"

"Oh, that would be the press, my dear. The media, people from TV stations."

"Oh," Natalia answered, not entirely sure she understood. But it was enough for now. "Spasibo. I mean, thank you."

"Of course, dear," Mae said with sweet appreciation before snapping back into furious Bible mode with even greater volume, startling everyone. "And now we have this . . . this 'rodeo'! We are affixed to the bosom of Satan with his orgy of sin taking place directly in the face of God on His Holy Day and in our homes! Come with me," she bellowed, throwing a fist upward, "as I climb our own mountain that reaches to the face of the Lord and collect the tablets of His teachings! You will be the divine representation of the mighty Ten Commandments. We shall take them to the arena and stone those who celebrate these cowboys as false idols and deliver the rods of correction upon those who wallow in the filth of animals! They will know the wrath of God, and the mercy of His love!"

If God had any mercy, he'd call you "home" right now with a heel coming through the roof, thought Pastor Rey as he ran a hand down his exasperated face. The woman was a psychotic loon who scared people from his pews with her desire to build a Christian caliphate. And for a moment he could've sworn her face contorted to that of the Grinch Who Stole Christmas.

He then wondered if a career as a beekeeper would be less painful.

Mae surrendered the lectern and marched toward the doors, leading the way to recreate Moses' descent from Mount Sinai. When she realized no one was behind her, she went home, had a cheese sandwich with mayonnaise on white bread, took a quick nap, and forged on to the arena to deliver God's will, where she now stood in front of Trisha Campbell.

"I just wanted to pass along and say how proud we are of you," Mae went on. "How proud we are of your courage to ride this fine mare in the face of such pain."

And here it comes. Trisha stared at Mae, who was about as honest as a drunk Catholic Bible editor. Proud? The only person Mae Kay Weintraub was proud of was Mae Kay Weintraub. And pain? What pain? The pain of talking to *her*?

"I'm sorry," Trisha finally said, shaking her head as she was moments away from climbing up onto Freedom and firing out into the arena. "What are you proud of? And who's 'we'?"

"Why, your marriage, dear."

"My marriage?"

"Well, yes. Your husband and that dreadful girl from the government. The one investigating that horrible accident that God bestowed upon us for all our sins. You know, the pretty one with the dark hair," Mae said. "They've been seen talking and laughing and consorting with each other. And you know what's next . . . if it hasn't already happened. Why, she's even here now, sitting next to him and your son."

Trisha stared blankly at her.

Mae faked a surprised gasp a moment later. "We thought you knew! Oh my word, I am so sorry!"

Trisha looked off, glassy-eyed. She could drive an oil tanker through the bullshit Mae was trying to pull on her. And as far as Trisha was concerned, Mae needed to be flushed down the drain to Hell, where they were certainly waiting for her with a whole barbeque of nefarious horrors and probably a seat right next to Satan himself.

Mae smiled broadly. "Don't worry about a thing, my dear. I'm here to support you through this terrible, terrible time."

"Right. Thanks, Mae," Trisha responded with a tired air. "By the way, your horns are showing."

A long pause passed as Mae tried to digest the insult. Her brow knotted as Trisha climbed up on Freedom and trotted her toward the arena. In Mae's smile she saw not only horns but also a hideous and contorted grin with worms oozing from her twenty-year-old dentures, and a forked tongue that corralled all that back in.

"I'm right here, dear!" Mae called after her with a wave, abandoning Trisha's slight against her. "Be brave!"

Trisha tuned her out and waited outside the arena. She could hear Bolt announcing her ride with breathless excitement, and the short trot on a suddenly amped-up horse already made her lower back ache. For many barrel racing mares, the moments before a run are a wired combination of energy-charged prancing and spinning in circles.

Bolt yapped on, her name echoing across the arena with the long list of her awards and how Trisha Campbell was the best in the state if not the fastest woman in the country.

Trisha lost track of the accolades Bolt rattled off, including those that he had to be fabricating out of thin air. She was good, but not *that* good.

Her back now hurt even more.

Freedom reared on her hind legs, aching to launch.

Trisha looked out over the arena and upon the faces that awaited her. She allowed herself a moment to search for her husband and son, quickly spotting them right near the gate . . . sitting with a young woman she had never seen before. Young, beautiful . . . and brunette.

And her son climbing upon that woman's lap.

Freedom spun about, forcing Trisha to continually twist her neck around to watch Kevin and this woman—this outsider—sit next to him and hold *her* child like he was hers.

"So let's hear it for TRISHA MARIE!" Bolt's baritone reverberated across the arena.

Like a light switch, Trisha snapped into competition mode. It was a conditioned reflex that focused her like nothing else. She became a machine, shutting out everything around her. With a slight kick, Freedom took off, flying straight into the arena at a speed Trisha wasn't expecting. Barrel racing was native to her. With three barrels set apart as points in a diamond, the first barrel would always set the tone for the out.

Freedom rocketed and sharply arced toward the first barrel. Trisha instinctively leaned forward as deep as she could, the mare's mane whipping her chin.

Too fast! Trisha panicked briefly, her brain ripping through the mathematics of the turn around the barrel.

Freedom abruptly slowed, her shoulders heaved upward in a full brake, and she leaned sharply, her muscled legs climbing through the dirt with sheer power as she made the turn, a lean Trisha angled against.

Trisha's boot grazed the barrel, tipping it slightly. If she tipped it over, that would be five seconds added to her time.

It's just exhibition, she reminded herself. *Let it go.*

Freedom jetted toward the second barrel, where Kevin and Michael, and this woman—this stranger—sat close, "consorting," just on the other side of the railing.

Trisha glanced at them for a tenth of a second as Freedom rounded the second barrel, this time faster than the first. This horse could run, and Trisha was focused like never before. But she was still able to lock her eyes on Andy for a fraction of a moment, delivering a glare that could carve a diamond.

Accelerating toward the third and final barrel, Trisha held on and clamped her thighs around the mare's torso. She rounded the third barrel, Freedom's legs spraying dirt outward in the turn.

And then Trisha let Freedom go, accelerating freely back toward the gate with deliberate taps on the mare's neck and instinctive yells that Trisha could never replicate outside of a race. The horse's nostrils flared widely, Trisha's legs extended forward, and her hands clutched the reins in a death grip. Air rushed past her ears in a roar and For the next four and a half seconds Trisha felt seventeen.

Then it was over.

Once past the gate and to the tepid applause of those in the arena behind her, Trisha pulled up on the reins, bringing Freedom into a braking trot as Bolt bellowed, "We've got an arena record! Give it up for TRISHA MARIE CAMPBELL!"

Trisha heard the smattering of applause throughout the crowd, and it did nothing for her. The feeling of being seventeen again faded back into being forty. Her aching back returned, just as everything else did. But for 13.58 seconds, she was young again.

26

ndy had forgotten what it was like to hold a child in her lap, even if it was for less than two minutes. Michael's weight on her legs was a surprisingly welcome salve she wasn't aware she needed, and it was very much a moment to remind her just how much she missed her own son.

As Trisha thundered toward the second barrel in front of them, Michael squirmed free from Andy's grasp and pressed against the railing to watch his mom pass by a second later. He reached out to his mother as she rounded the barrel, and then his arm dropped as she raced away to the third and final one that awaited her. Michael then bounced up and down with excitement as his mother stirred dust and dirt to the end with the cheering of Bolt Murphy and murmurs of encouragement from the crowd.

Andy saw something entirely different. Kevin's wife was imposing and emitted an intimidating level of strength. She possessed an immense amount of power and an air of command as she approached that second barrel. Trisha was tall and regal. Even though they were the same height, Andy felt small in comparison. The brief flash of the woman's eyes completely unnerved her. Andy no longer felt the sensation of being a stranger in a strange land. Instead, she now possessed the strong discomfort of being a trespasser upon holy ground—a space not meant for the likes of her. And as much as Andy wanted to pull Michael back, she absolutely deserved no claim to the nanosecond of peace Trisha's son gave her.

It was time to leave. Not just her spot next to Kevin, not just Granite Point, but the entire state of West Virginia—as soon as possible.

As Trisha's blistering ride ended amidst the applause and Bolt's breathless shrill, Kevin gathered his boy to head toward the back of the arena. He had seen more than fifty of her rides before she hung up her low-brimmed cowgirl hat in retirement for motherhood, and today she appeared just as young as she'd been two decades ago. Trisha rode with fury and hammered home to her husband—and probably the world—that she hadn't lost a thing. And she was right. It was now time to congratulate her on a performance well done, even though she probably wouldn't want to hear it from him.

Before pivoting Michael onto his shoulders, Kevin made the obligatory offer to have Andy meet his wife, although he knew full well that innocently introducing an attractive woman to one's bride was about as idiotic a choice as any husband of any IQ could make. Hence, he didn't push when Andy immediately, and politely, declined. She seemed suddenly eager to depart and vanish into the shifting crowd just as quickly as she had arrived.

Still, a part of him wanted her to stay, no matter how dangerous to his health it might be. "You sure?"

"Uh, yeah. About 100 percent sure," Andy quickly answered, sensing she had about ten seconds before Kevin's goddess of a wife would arrive and drag her around the dirt lassoed to her monster of a horse. And probably to the cheering of the crowd in Old Rome Colosseum fashion. "I'll see you later," Andy added before exiting with definitive haste.

Kevin watched her move off and grab the kid she'd walked in with. Andy snagged him by the scruff of his shirt as he made his return with a pair of hot dogs and condiment packets in his hand. And now he was dragged away faster than he could regain his footing, with a comically confused look on his face.

Kevin felt as if he'd been bewitched. Any shred of propriety and common sense he'd been hanging onto fled in the moments before Andy left. All he knew was that he wanted her to stay. Once Andy disappeared into the crowd, the spell was broken, and his ability to think clearly began making its return. He was also instantaneously self-conscious, now very cognizant of the incredulous stares from just about everyone around him in the stands. It wouldn't be long before this would hit the Gossip Feed, where Trisha would catch wind of it in an over-the-top exaggeration of infidelity based on proximity well before this ear-splitting rodeo came to a merciful close. He then wondered if he could make the Mexican border, following in the footsteps of the long-gone Kitty Belle Braun, before someone would notice a locomotive missing.

By the time Kevin and Michael found Trisha, she was watching Freedom get loaded into a trailer while being hovered over by a pathetically enthusiastic Bolt Murphy, who kept finding ways to land a grimy hand on one of her shoulders. To Trisha's credit, she kept finding ways to escape his possessive grip and slip away from him. But once Bolt saw Kevin approaching, his bravado dug in. He once again placed a hand on her stiff shoulder.

Trisha turned to find Kevin's eyes on Bolt and his patience fading. It was true that Kevin never saw Bolt as a real threat, but he wasn't in the mood for it today. However, Trisha now did very little to alleviate the discomfort of her husband seeing another man's hand on her. At least for the moment.

"She was amazing, wasn't she?" Bolt said, projecting a level of pride that didn't belong to him.

"She's always amazing, *Sebastian*," Kevin answered with a terse emphasis on Bolt's real name. He kept his eyes locked on Bolt. "She doesn't need a horse to prove it."

Bolt was caught with that one. He'd made it easy for Kevin to win that round, and quickly realized he would have to be far quicker to match wits with Trisha's husband of what felt like forever.

Trisha had had enough and gently removed Bolt's hand, then thanked him quietly for letting her ride during the event.

"There's plenty more to come!" Bolt said instantly, suddenly panicked and certainly not willing to give up when he was this close to winning Trisha's heart.

"No . . ." Trisha answered as she turned to Kevin. "I'm retired, and I think I'll stay that way."

It took a moment for this to register with Bolt. He really didn't understand it at first, but then it slowly dawned on him. He knew he had become a tick slower than most, but he truly believed he had not read Trisha wrong after all this time. She didn't ignore him, always talked with him, and she was so beautiful to look at. Suddenly, his perfect day had become a day perfectly wrecked. Everything had seemed to be looking up for him, with Trisha the centerpiece of it all. He'd envisioned their future together and then, just like that, it was gone. Poof. Nothing else mattered now, and the disappointment was etched clearly on his drooping face. That's the thing about delusions. They're real . . . until they're not.

Trisha felt his bubble burst. However, there was no way on God's green earth she would, or could, let alone should, find herself in the arms of *Sebastian* Murphy. He would treat her like a queen, but that was the last thing she wanted. Even when she was infuriated with Kevin, he was still the one she wanted and no one else.

Bolt's mood swung quickly to humiliation. How could he have been so blind? He stood embarrassed next to Trisha—in her skin-tight jeans, her white blouse that inflamed his imagination, her windblown hair, those soul-consuming eyes—and in front of this guy she called her husband. He wanted to run, hide, bury himself, and never be seen again.

Trisha saw Bolt recoil and felt a measured state of awful. She had tried over the years to hold this man at arm's length, and then realized all she did was indirectly lead him on through little effort of her own. And now, taking Bolt up on the offer of riding had telegraphed something far more to him than it ever had to her. Bolt was in love with Trisha Marie Campbell, and as much as she knew it, she'd downplayed it at his expense. She'd just broken the man's heart and now watched as he shuffled away toward the arena.

This was becoming one of the weirdest days of her life.

And Kevin's.

Empathy for a man who was in love with another man's wife was not something that Kevin, or many other men, would have a lot of. But he knew deep down Bolt's love for Trisha did not come from a nefarious place. The man was simple in many ways and so was the affection he directed at Kevin's wife. Knowing Bolt, he would try again next week . . . just like nothing had ever happened.

Trisha pulled Michael from Kevin's arms, drawing her husband's attention back to the present.

"Is that true?" Kevin asked her. "You're retired?"

"Yep," she answered as she swept up her saddle and gear with a free arm. "I've got you and two kids, and the last thing I need is a horse to eat us out of house and home."

"But . . . I've never seen you ride like that," Kevin added.

"I had incentive."

Kevin was afraid to ask what that incentive was, especially considering the level of force with which she shoved her saddle into his midsection to carry.

"So, who was she?" Trisha asked, steaming toward the truck.

"Who?"

Trisha stopped and looked back at him amidst the ebb and flow of people around them.

"Oh," Kevin recovered as fast as he could. "She's with the NTSB."

"She's pretty."

Kevin considered his next move carefully as he walked toward her and took the remainder of her gear from her arm. "Yeah, she is," he said, strategically trying to take things down a notch.

"Did you invite her?"

"No."

"Then what was she doing there?"

"Honey, I don't know," Kevin replied with a hint of exasperation. "She was just there."

"Then why was she holding my son?"

"Ask him," he nodded toward Michael. "He's the one who crawled up onto her lap."

Trisha looked hard into her husband's eyes. She always knew when he was lying, which wasn't all that often, and this time he wasn't. But he was still in a very dangerous place. "You remember what Mr. Gale said to you?"

Kevin did. *How do you say goodbye to those you no longer dream about?*

Trisha leaned closer to whisper in his ear. "Maybe you should be asking yourself how you'd say goodbye to the people you *do* dream about."

Kevin heard the caution loud and clear, and his eyes stayed locked on Trisha's until she turned and walked on, leaving him alone with her riding gear in the middle of strangers and a cloud of arena dust.

Trisha reached the truck and loaded Michael into his car seat. After buckling him in, she closed her eyes and exhaled loudly. The buzz of the ride was now gone, and she had returned to the present, still surrounded by everything that came along with it. Life with her husband was suddenly going in the wrong direction, and she had no immediate idea how to stop it. She knew her son was seeing far more than he should, and she had never felt this distant from her daughter, who was no longer asking to stay over at someone's house but declaring it. Her family was starting to come apart, and that simply terrified her.

Kyle watched the highway sign for Kentucky roll by as he changed lanes. He would soon be across the state line, his life starting anew. He thanked the Lord Almighty for the blessing of not being left behind, for having a bright future, and for the beautiful girl named Shiloh who was sitting in the seat beside him, staring blankly out her window, watching the hills and valleys of Granite Point disappear.

27

A few miles from the center of town lay a pristine natural jewel known as Shale Waterfall State Park. Set on a small parcel of forty-four acres of untouched land, it was an honest run of about forty minutes for Andy, who found the underused park a welcome oasis amidst the growing insanity of the little town she had recently been calling home. The park was the only place, with its thirty-foot waterfall that sailed over a shale cliff onto a smattering of rounded boulders below, that generated enough thunderous racket to drown out any sound and thought from her brain.

In the hours after leaving the arena, Andy had unloaded Ryan back at the hotel and then disappeared in her running gear to jog along the river. She desperately needed to be one with the pines, fresh air, filtered sun, and moss. Once at the bottom of the falls, amongst the boulders, mist, and deafening decibels of brown noise, she screamed in absolute frustration.

The investigation into the *Allegheny Limited* was going sideways, and her hesitation to take the easy road by pinning it all on a single man was making it exponentially worse. There was something wrong with all of it, and she honestly wondered if this guy, this Kevin Campbell with his maddeningly impressive vocabulary and his confounding way of scrambling her intelligence, was screwing up everything by just existing. He fogged her consciousness and was impossibly hard to ignore. It was all further complicated by the nagging guilt of watching from the safety of a parking lot this same man and his wife, this amazing specimen of imposing matrimonial femininity, lock horns for all to see, and then his wife lovingly nuzzle her son as she carried him to their truck and snuggled him into his car seat.

Andy felt herself sinking. She was in a place way over her head and losing herself faster than she could reconcile. And when she complained bitterly up the chain, only to be told to "deal with it" because sending anyone else would only start everything all over again, she felt the subtle reprimand of *stop whining*. It was hers to work and resolve, at least until Robert Langsdon (who'd abandoned her like a box of toys on the side of the road) returned from something presumably far more important.

Her scream lasted until her throat burned, and she found two hikers staring at her from a trail up the steep hill that overlooked all of it. They quickly moved on and away from the psychotic woman below, standing ankle-deep in the cold river water. Andy closed her eyes, exhaled through whatever chakras she could find, and attempted to clear her mind.

That evening she did the equivalent of hiding under a rock. She navigated around the "Jackals of Deceit" who cruised outside her hotel for anything to report, closed the blinds, had room service deliver a salad with strawberry cheesecake for dessert, took the hottest bath possible while listening to Alanis Morissette's *Jagged Little Pill* in her headphones until her ears rang, and was sound asleep by 7:00 PM.

Tomorrow would be focused on closing this whole thing up and getting the hell out of town, starting at the Atlantic Yard office.

28

I t was still the morning of Bolt Murphy's rodeo when Frank opened his one-car garage door. The worn-out rollers complained in their rails as the ancient Sears garage opener strained under the weight of the faded and peeling wooden frame door. As the door lifted, sunlight inched in across dusty boxes and tools that had long gone unused. Frank then stared at a monstrosity that sat in his driveway.

"Mornin', Frank!" Puck said as he climbed out of a tan, banged up two-door 1975 Dodge Dart in sore need of a hydraulic compactor, also known as a car crusher. "Surprise!" he added with enough force and cheerfulness to make Frank cringe.

"Mornin'," Frank answered at a softer and far more appropriate volume. "What's this?"

"'75 Dart. Six-cylinders, automatic. Heat works, air when it wants to. But she's got good bones and solid suspension," Puck listed off while pressing down on a fender. The Dart responded with a squeaky squishiness that would make many seasick if they were to ride in it, starting with Frank.

Frank walked up to the overworked bucket of bolts and looked over its hood. The few paint peels and blemishes of rust reminded him of The Brick.

"Steering and windows are manual, so ya gotta do a lot of crankin'," Puck further added. "But she don't leak oil or anythin' outta the radiator, and she's gotta sunroof, but that takes some muscle to crank open too."

"You got yourself a nice ride here, Puck," Frank fibbed. "Congratulations."

"Nah, she ain't mine, Frank. She's yours."

This took a couple of moments to register in Frank's still drowsy brain. He narrowed his eyes at Puck, then took another look at the Dart with a mind that went blank.

Puck walked up to Frank and tried to hand him the registration, pink slip, and a bill of sale for $0.

"Wait," Frank said, stepping back from the paperwork. "How is this mine?"

"'Cause I'm giving it you," Puck said as he shoved the paperwork into Frank's chest. "You ain't gotta truck no more, and you need something to get around. I gots plenty of cars, so when I was fixin' her up for a quick sale, I was thinkin' you're in need, so she's yours!"

Frank stood speechless. Puck was as poor as they came in the county. The man had little beyond the mountains of rusting iron that polluted the ground beneath his ramshackle home with a leaky roof. Frank was well aware that Puck was often laughed at by many who considered him to be someone who'd launched into adulthood sideways—and they tolerated him like a stray dog running around town. Now, this poor man, who considered everyone in his little hometown a friend regardless of what they thought of him, was giving Frank a car. A disastrous, wretched, tetanus-inducing collection of bent iron on four semi-bald tires that Puck pieced back together with his bare hands and wanted nothing in return for it.

"Christ, Puck," Frank said in a volume that cracked under an emotion that unbalanced him. "I can't take this."

"Sure ya can!" Puck shoved the keys at him. "I already signed the pink slip."

It took Frank nearly a minute to take the keys and receive a gift he felt completely unworthy of.

"'Cept you could, you know," Puck added, "drive me home."

Frank looked past Puck expecting to find his tow truck. He only saw the street and the realization that Puck had even driven Frank's new car to him.

Puck quickly cleared away a pile of old and new car magazines, scattered receipts from who knows when, and a power steering pump for a Buick Skylark from the one and only couch in his small home so that Frank could have a place to sit. Puck was ecstatic having a guest. He then remembered his manners and hopped to the fridge to pull a beer out for Frank.

He even opened it for him.

"Thanks, Puck," Frank said, taking the can and watching the foam run over his fingers and onto the grease-stained carpet.

"She drives great, don't she?" Puck asked.

"Sure does," Frank answered, lying through his teeth. In reality, the Dart was a death trap with a cracked steering wheel and an emergency brake light that stayed constantly illuminated. But it also drove and accelerated past 40 mph, so the piece of junk had that going for it.

Puck opened his own can and sat in his torn leather recliner facing Frank. The chair was covered with a Corvette-themed blanket with tassels on the ends that Puck's mother made for him when he was ten. Frank also noticed the small table next to him, built from a V8 crankshaft and three pistons that held a small glass opera window from a late '50s Thunderbird. And on top of that stood a camshaft lamp with a Speed Racer lampshade.

Apparently, Puck was creative.

Frank looked around the small house. The kitchen was tiny and cluttered with cereal boxes and dirty bowls. The living room was just as cramped, with an old Zenith 19" color TV in the corner connected to a Radio Shack-branded VHS player that could play the stacks of Disney and old Star Trek tapes piled in a corner. The bathroom Frank didn't even want to look at, although he could see enough into Puck's bedroom, which was surprisingly neat with a smartly made bed.

Puck was, indeed, an oddity.

"You don't have many guests here, do you?" Frank asked.

"Nah. People don't come here much. Except for mean ol' Hollis when he's got something to nose 'round about."

Frank's stomach knotted.

"He was 'ere the other day," Puck continued. "Pop hated him as much as sauerkraut."

Frank stopped drinking for a moment and forced the beer down his throat. "For what?" he croaked.

"Huh?"

"What was Hollis here for?"

"Oh, he was fishin' through your truck, but I ain't countin' that as a visit. Never comes by to just say 'hi.' Actually, nobody does."

A twinge of guilt panged Frank's conscience. Not only for what Hollis could have found in the remains of his truck but for being just as guilty as the rest of the town of mostly ignoring Puck. Puck may have been a bit short on the IQ scale, but he made up for it with heart that everyone dismissed just so they wouldn't have Puck hanging on to them as a friend. Puck's parents were simple people, coming up from the core of West Virginia's Civil War days, but they also found their son needy and lonely and preferred him a county's length away. Nonetheless, Puck ran a junkyard. An ugly, ratty, nasty junkyard that was a business. And by the looks of the yard, business was good. For all that Puck was, he may have been Granite Point's most successful businessman.

"Tell me a story!" Puck asked with an excitement that immediately set the bar high for entertainment value.

Frank eyed the door instead. Even though he felt guilty for wanting to leave and escape Puck's clingy clutches, he also just wanted to go home. "Meh, I don't have any stories," Frank said with a wave of his hand, praying that Puck would buy that.

"Yeah, you do. I've heard 'em! Tom Ryder, he told me some."

Frank reacted with surprise. "Tom told you our stories?"

"Yeah!" Puck said, and then admitted, "Well, some. He told me about the submarine in Chicago, and when you got half a cashmere sweater, and even when a bus tore off the door to Hollis' patrol car a long time 'go."

Frank shook his head like he was clearing cobwebs. He had completely forgotten the Greyhound story, when Hollis left his car door wide open after pulling Tom over for going two miles an hour over the speed limit. Thirty seconds later, a double-decker, eight-foot-wide Super Scenicruiser wrenched the door off its hinges and flung it into Old Man McGovern's corn field. Tom told him that Hollis hung his head in shame, and then let Tom go only if he promised not to tell anyone, especially his boss. Tom agreed and the story disappeared into humor legend.

"So, tell me one I ain't heard yet!"

"It kinda sounds like he told you all of them."

"There's more, I knows it!" Puck eagerly smiled and nestled into his chair, ready for story time.

Frank exhaled in resignation and then flipped through his mental catalog of fractured tales of debauchery, idiocy, and pure bullshit. And then he came up with a good one. A true story, if Tom was to be believed.

"Did he tell you the doorman story?" Frank asked.

Puck thought for a moment. "Nope."

"This was back in Chicago," Frank started.

"I love Chicago!"

Frank stopped. "You've been there?"

"Nope. But I love it there!"

Frank closed his eyes with patience and then continued. "Tom and I were in a bar—"

"They always start there, don't they?"

Frank chortled, realizing that Puck was right. "Tom met this woman—they drank all night until they got thrown out."

Puck's grin turned into a huge smile. He reveled in imagining himself as Tom for just a moment, living in another world as someone else and not himself for a change. He knew what he was and often strived to escape from himself. Even if it was in little stories like the one Frank was weaving.

"Since we were out of town," Frank went on, "she took him to her place. Some apartment building somewhere. Tom threw the doorman his car keys and told him to 'park my car,' then they went upstairs and . . . you know."

Puck nodded quickly. He *did* know.

"Anyway, Tom goes down the next morning and he's looking for the doorman but can't find him anywhere."

"Oh no!"

"Right, so he asks some guy in pajamas and robe who's picking up his newspaper, 'Hey, where's the doorman?' The guy looks at him like Tom's got three heads."

Puck snickered.

"'We don't have one of those,' the guy says. So, Tom's thinking, 'Who did I throw my damn keys to?' He heads to the police station and the sergeant who's doing the report stops while Tom is describing his stolen car—"

"Why'd he stop?"

"Because he recognizes the car Tom's telling him about!"

"Wha—?"

"Yeah, the sergeant says, 'Blue Ford with a rusted dent in the trunk?' Tom says, 'Yeah! You know where it is?' The sergeant says, 'Yeah, you threw your keys to a cop last night, so we parked it forty-six blocks that way for ya. Have a nice walk.'"

Puck's body folded and he rolled in his chair in loud laughter.

Frank laughed slightly himself. Not from the story, but from Puck's reaction to it. And for the next few hours, and over a pair of stale French bread pizzas from Puck's freezer, Frank uncoiled many a yarn to an audience willing to enjoy his fables, may they be real or not. It didn't matter. Puck enjoyed having a friend over to his house, living a different life than his own. And Frank felt satisfied in repaying Puck for one of the kindest gifts he had ever received. Even though the Dart might kill him, it was given by a simple man with simple wants who had nothing but kindness in his heart and a yearning for a friend.

Frank later drove home, his head swimming from the endless string of beers Puck seemed to pull out of thin air. He was slightly seasick from the Dart's worn-out springs but weaved his way home to his own well-worn lounge chair before falling fast asleep.

And he dreamed . . .

29

Frank's dreams had become nightmares of late, often drawing him into visions of a dim future down the darkened ruins of Center Street. The sky loomed with a heavy gloom of gray and black clouds that lay above him like an unbearable blanket. Along the sidewalks he could see the remains of long deceased trees and the debris of homes with lives long gone.

Amongst all of this stood the decaying buildings of Granite Point. Those made of brick leaned against those made of rotting wood, their clapboard sidings dropping toxic flakes of lead paint that flittered to the ground. The sidewalks were vacant, and the broken asphalt beneath Frank's feet was littered with rubble.

Frank looked upward to the crushing veils of dark gray that muted all the colors below, but he knew the remains of Granite Point were still full of souls existing in this enigmatic harbor of his dream.

He climbed the steep hill to the old Maude McMillan Victorian, where it stood in a dismal state with its lead-filled windows that had often frightened his son. And yet somehow Frank sensed the lost presence of Fay Campbell within the home. It was a presence he had not felt in decades, but nonetheless the draw of his wife was inside. He swung open the faded picket gate and stepped onto the porch that cracked and groaned under his weight.

Frank stood before the Victorian's double-doors, relics of heavy oak and stained glass. With his fingertips, he pushed them open.

The bottoms of the wooden slabs dragged across an ancient and warped plank floor. Stepping inside, Frank waded into the shadows and past the dark voids that deepened the hollow feeling within him.

And somewhere in this nightmare, a telephone began to ring.

"Can someone get that?" a woman's cheerful voice asked, reaching his ears from some far corner of the home. He knew the sound of that voice instantly. His instincts were correct. Fay was here, somewhere close. He knew it.

Frank moved on, only to stop beside the doorway of a small reading room. What he saw panicked him as his eyes took in the vision of Tom sitting in a window seat, his skull opened up against one of those thick, leaden windows, his eyes staring through Frank.

And still a phone rang somewhere inside this home.

Frank backed away while the wooden floor cracked and splintered beneath his feet. Looking down, he found himself perched upon the edge of a yawning abyss . . . and then it swallowed him whole.

He grabbed onto a fracturing plank of flooring and stopped his fall long enough to see a fifteen-year-old Kevin standing above him, just on the edge of the enlarging breach. His son was just an arm's length away.

And still the telephone rang. Now louder than before.

"Mom wants to know if you're going to answer the phone," Kevin asked, his voice a younger pitch that Frank could barely remember.

The pain in Frank's hand, now dripping blood, had become excruciating—the same hand that had been gouged by the ten-dollar Sears crowbar suddenly erupting through his chest.

A large arm quickly wrapped around Frank's neck and held him in a strangling headlock.

"Hi, Frank," Hollis hissed in his ear and twisted the crowbar.

Frank felt pain and terror. His head pounded from the lack of air, and he struggled against the weight of Hollis' rotund body pulling him into the depths below. Frank's hand began to shred from the splinters, and he fought the pain as long as he could.

He then uncoiled a deafening scream.

And still the phone rang.

"Let go, Frank," Hollis growled, tightening his arm and driving the crowbar deeper.

Splinters carved into the bones of Frank's hand like knives. He looked up at Kevin, who immediately dove for him as the planking broke.

Even through all of this, the gesture of his son trying to save him brought only a moment of confusion. But now that he was falling, Frank screamed again. Except nothing came out. There was no air around him, and suddenly no light. He was surrounded by nothingness; the only sensation was the feeling of his stomach in his throat.

And by now, the phone had stopped its incessant ringing.

Still within his nightmare, Frank emerged from the darkness. He found himself behind the wheel of a ratty old convertible he'd owned long ago. He had exited one of the many tunnels from the old Pennsylvania Turnpike with the wind whipping through his hair. It was a beautiful day. The sky was a collection of large, puffy clouds with the colors of the hills more vivid than one would find in an impressionist painting.

Frank looked over at the beautiful woman sitting next to him. He recognized her immediately. The shape of her face, the build of her figure, the color of her mane that stretched to her shoulders, her signature floppy hat, and the Audrey Hepburn inspired Hubert de Givenchy perfume filled his senses.

He felt serenity. He felt at home.

"I wanted to tell you I was okay," Fay said, looking at him, her hair dancing before her face, providing fleeting visions of her eyes, which Frank desperately wanted to see.

He took some comfort in that, but the old anger of her passing stirred within him. Heaven now possessed her and jealously kept this woman away from him.

Fay turned to enjoy the scenery that rolled by while Frank looked into the rearview mirror and noticed a young boy, no more than five years old, in the back seat.

Kevin glanced at his father and then smiled while the wind flipped his hair about. He was enjoying the ride, having fun with the airstream blasting past his ears.

Frank felt a moment of unease at the sight of his young son. A sense of disconnect. He didn't know what to do with this child—what was right and what was wrong. He hated himself for the realization that he really didn't want this boy in his life. He could not explain it beyond the fact that this feeling came from a void within him. A blank space within his soul. The same place his father lived.

He found his son to be an inconvenience. A chore. A weight that hung around him like an anchor.

And then the sound of a telephone began again—loud and intruding. He glanced again in his rearview mirror and Kevin was gone, replaced by Beau Harper, who excitedly, and innocently, pointed to an ancient freight train, nightmarishly fossilized into the landscape that passed by.

Confusion set in for Frank, who next looked over toward Fay and found *her* gone. She was replaced by Shiloh, who stared outward, her head turned toward the passing landscape. As much as he loved his granddaughter, it pained him to see that Fay was once again lost to his memories.

The ringing of the telephone was now deafening.

"Grandpa," Shiloh yelled over the ringing and turned to look at Frank, "answer the phone!"

Frank snapped awake, his body jolting in the La-Z-Boy as adrenaline blasted through him at a rate that nearly gave him a heart attack. He looked at the phone on the side table and stared at it while it rang at a horrific, nerve-jarring volume. He didn't want to touch it. He only felt like throwing it through a window after beating it into unrecognizable pieces with a twelve-pound hammer.

With a degree of divine mercy, the phone finally stopped ringing when the answering machine picked up.

"Grandpa," Shiloh's voice, rattled and nervous, came across the speaker, "are you there? Please pick up . . ."

30

Frank pulled into the small Flying J Truck Stop just off Interstate 64 about ten minutes after crossing the Kentucky state line. It was shortly after midnight when he shut off the motor and spotted his granddaughter sitting at a table across from Kyle. Frank didn't know it then, but Shiloh had nothing with her except the clothes on her back covered by Kyle's work coat and her beaded blue denim Levi's shoulder purse.

Surprisingly, Frank's blood was not boiling. Although the sight of his granddaughter so far from home soured his stomach, he was calmed by her maturity to fire up a flare to be rescued and embraced the fact that it was he whom she'd called. He opened the door and climbed out, waiting by the car until Kyle made eye contact with him. Frank saw him swallow hard, then straighten up and mature about five years in all of two seconds.

Shiloh was looking down at the table when Kyle tapped her to look outside. Her eyes met her grandfather's, and she was immediately even more guilt-ridden and embarrassed than before. She rose from the table and allowed Kyle to walk her through the doors and toward the grungy Dodge Dart and its ticking six-cylinder motor.

Kyle stopped short of the car, honestly fearful of what Frank would do to him, be it a five-knuckle blow to the jaw or a protective and vengeful pile driver to a kidney. He stood tall regardless, making sure Shiloh was safely to the car, and ready to take whatever Frank was going to unleash on him. His gaze never left her, all the while monitoring Frank out of the corner of his eye.

Shiloh opened the car door, pulling it wide with a rusty groan that telegraphed its long and abused 100,000-mile lifespan. She tossed her denim purse onto the seat and then looked at Kyle, who stood there scared and heartbroken. Shiloh peeled off his work coat and walked it back to him.

Kyle didn't want the coat. He just wanted her.

"I'm sorry," Shiloh said softly as she pushed the coat into his hands. She then walked back to the car and climbed in, pulling the noisy door shut just as quietly as she could. She then watched him through the dirty windshield as he sagged onto a nearby bench, hunched over with his elbows on his knees, his eyes still never leaving her.

Frank said nothing to Kyle. He could easily read the fear in the young man and far more of the pain Kyle was in. Frank knew Kyle loved his granddaughter dearly. He was man enough to stay behind to make sure she was safe, and Kyle stood bravely before him in a true display of honor. That was likely what saved him from the beating Frank would have uncoiled upon him before depositing his carcass at the local sheriff's office for transporting a minor over state lines. Instead, Frank climbed back into the Dart, grateful that Kyle had the maturity to stay with Shiloh until he got there. He put the car in reverse and pulled away from the parking space.

Shiloh continued to look at Kyle as Frank moved the shifter into drive. She felt horrible for Kyle while also incredibly relieved at the same time. The panic that had swept over her as they crossed into Kentucky was more than she could restrain. She felt like a caged animal, but neither side of the bars was where she wanted to be. Shiloh wasn't ready to play the role of an adult. She was still a child inside, wisely cognizant of a future ahead that held very little for her. Something deep within told her there was far more in her tomorrows than following the path of least resistance—or a boy to the plains of Nebraska.

Kyle watched the Dart sputter its way back toward I-64 and felt vacant once it disappeared into a sea of headlights and taillights. A lump of lead took up residence in his stomach, and he sat there for hours before summoning the will to continue onward to the interstate and whatever awaited him in the lands menacingly monikered "Tornado Alley."

The young man felt the isolation of loneliness for the first time with his terrifying adult step into whatever awaited him. He missed Shiloh. The void she left behind in his passenger seat was hauntingly uncomfortable.

Kyle drove on, determined to call her as soon as he arrived at the address sent to him from Union Pacific. But he never did. It would be years before he saw Shiloh again, and that was only when he came back into town for his father's funeral, accompanied by his wide-eyed young city wife from Omaha and their blue-eyed colicky baby that screamed louder than a train horn.

After that, they would never see each other again.

Shiloh's eyes followed the brightly lit "Welcome to West Virginia" sign, then glanced over at her grandfather. They had said nothing to each other since leaving the Flying J, and yet it felt like there was plenty communicated in the fifteen minutes they'd been in the car together. He didn't yell at her, or curse, or expound on the legal peril both she and Kyle were in. He just drove on, his face, still bruised from the accident, illuminated occasionally by the passing highway lights that gave Shiloh a ghostly feeling. She innately knew, somehow, her time with Frank had become incredibly short. How Shiloh knew this she couldn't comprehend, but that ghostly feeling stayed with her even until her last days whenever she thought of her grandfather.

"Are you going to tell my parents?" Shiloh finally asked, breaking the minimal background silence in a car with a thinning muffler Puck had swiped from a totaled 1968 Dodge Valiant.

Frank looked at her briefly. "Why?" he asked. "So they can beat into you what you already figured out? No, I'm not going to say anything to them."

Shiloh took another breath of blessed and thankful relief.

"I'd suggest you not bring it up with them either," Frank added. "Unless you're really lookin' to get pummeled."

"I won't," Shiloh quietly answered, possessing no insane intention of uttering a word about this.

Frank welcomed the few more minutes of ambient muffler noise. He relished having Shiloh in the car with him, even if they weren't having any sort of deep, meaningful conversation. Such things were not the Campbell way, at least as far as Frank Campbell was concerned. He wasn't the grandfatherly type who took his granddaughter on nostalgia trips to a lake for fishing, or played catch, or camped, or even knocked a few balls around at a nine-hole golf course. His interests were in Chopin, Mozart, and Bach, playing the soundtrack to his artistic dreams of becoming the next Gustave Courbet or Andrew Wyeth. All of which would hold minimal interest to a teenage granddaughter who preferred to listen to ear-bleeding noise from bands like Nirvana and Pearl Jam.

None of this mattered to Shiloh. Fishing wasn't her thing, nor was playing catch (although she was good at it) or camping, as that invited creatures large and small into her sleeping bag she'd rather not deal with, or playing golf, which she sucked at. Shiloh was more interested in her grandfather parking himself in the seats for the dumb school plays she was in or helping her at least once learn how to drive, something that wasn't his forte. She loved how he tried to teach her how to count cards in Blackjack, how to read the Daily Racing Form, and how to spot a phony a mile away.

Her grandfather was unconventional, often vulgar, hot-tempered, smarter than most people gave him credit for, impossible to read or predict, and Shiloh was just fine with that. She could be open with him, and, even at her worst, her behavior was met with a grain of salt and a shrug if not an outright snort of amusement. No matter his faults and failings, Shiloh loved her grandfather.

"You know this car smells, right?" Shiloh commented.

"It also has bad seat springs," Frank added. "Ask me how I know this."

Shiloh cracked a smile, which then quickly faded. "Do you think they're going to get divorced?" she asked, firing the question well out of left field. Her anxiety had suddenly surged, and she didn't even think of the question beforehand. It just popped out to an adult who would have an honest opinion, even if it was her grandfather—the root cause of just about every battle her parents had had that Shiloh could remember.

The question surprised Frank. It took him back to a Saturday morning on a date he had no hope of remembering. Exhausted, Frank sat at the breakfast table after a long night of intoxicated quarreling with Fay that lasted well after midnight. He was lost in a bluish haze of cigarette smoke that drifted through a sunbeam when the sight of his frightened young son caught his eye. Kevin, rattled by the parental fighting that had kept him up, had a look of terror in his eyes. Frank remembered being unmoved by it. He didn't know why, but he held no desire to soothe Kevin's fears or calm his son's shaken soul.

And it wasn't until now, decades later, that he realized the fear within his granddaughter was the same his son felt that one morning. Something within Frank cracked. Somewhere deep inside of him, from a corner that was so buried, so lost, so unknown. Frank looked at Shiloh, and for the first time ever, he saw his son's eyes.

"No," Frank said in a voice that was barely audible. "They'll stick it out." The answer was primarily to relieve Shiloh of worry, while he kept to himself the belief that Kevin didn't have it in him to leave a viper like Trisha behind. Someone that Kevin should've avoided like a rancid can of Spam from the beginning. To Frank, Trisha was just evil. Simply because she saw through his horseshit like a plate glass window. "I wouldn't worry. Between your mom and dad there's some degree of common sense."

"You don't like her very much, do you?"

"We just don't get along, that's all," Frank said as he looked at his granddaughter out of the corner of his eye.

Shiloh was waiting for more from him. Far more.

"She's a good mom," it pained Frank to admit. "When you were two, everyone thought you had gotten meningitis."

"I know."

"Yeah, but what you don't know is that your mom stayed awake for four solid days and never left your side. Not once. Couldn't believe it."

Shiloh stared ahead, speechless. She had never heard that side of the story before.

"For moms, you could've done far worse," Frank added as he marveled at the fact he just said that.

His certainty gave Shiloh a moment of relief. She then watched another highway light pass by, this time casting an orangey glow on the skin of Frank's face.

"And don't worry about Kyle," Frank continued. "He's gonna be fine. Consider yourself lucky."

She did, although the image of Kyle with another girl didn't immediately sit well with her. "What about the town?" she asked next. "What do you think is going to happen to everyone?"

Frank shot her a quick glance, not at all expecting the string of twenty questions coming from a girl who usually asked a grand total of zero. "Why are you worried about that? You have other things to give yourself an ulcer about."

"Like what?"

"Like spending another year as a teenager before you don't have any of those years left. Relax. Everyone's gonna be fine," Frank reassured her with a convincing lie. "People always find their way. One way or another, they always do."

Shiloh wasn't sure she believed that. She could sense an impending doom that had befallen a lot of the other towns in the state, many sentenced to death as the reign of coal diminished over the years, each one ultimately meeting the same fate as Prowler Flat.

Shiloh would later see Kyle as one of the fortunate few to escape the impending fiscal apocalypse that would gut Granite Point, an event that would define her path for the immediate decade to come. She would also have to leave much sooner rather than much later.

Her mind then drifted to Beau Harper and what fate awaited him and his mother. She had heard rumblings at school of him being blamed for the derailment and worried what might happen to him if he were to ever awake. Shiloh envisioned the horror of him starving to death on welfare in a world that wanted to avoid and ignore him just as it did Puck. Beau wouldn't understand being prosecuted and he wouldn't last ten seconds in the horrid cruelty of a federal penitentiary. Shiloh's eyes welled at the thought.

"What?" Frank asked, spotting a tear in her eye.

"I was thinking of Beau."

A pang of guilt shot across Frank's psyche.

"Kids at school are saying he probably did it," Shiloh added.

"Yeah, well, most kids are idiots." He paused. "Except you."

"Do you think he did it? I mean . . . there's no *way* he could have done anything like this. I don't think he could even comprehend it."

Frank knew this. He also knew Hollis would possibly hang this on Beau just to smoke out whoever actually did do it, with Frank specifically in mind. And that claustrophobic feeling was soon gripping him.

"Grandpa?!" Shiloh implored.

"No," Frank immediately answered, snapping himself out of the guilt that clouded his common sense. "There's no way he could've done it."

"It's *bullshit* that people think he could have." Shiloh turned toward the passenger window, scrubbing a smudge from the glass with her fist.

Frank looked at his granddaughter and decided to let the vulgarity slide. She was right. It was bullshit. And so was letting Beau go down for something Frank himself might've done.

"Did *you* do it?" Shiloh shot at him, this time coming in from right field. She was half serious with the question and the other half just jabbing at him.

Frank looked at her, his face once again illuminated by the highway lights. But now he suddenly looked tired to her, betraying a faint suspicion of his complicity. His eyes were darker than she had ever seen before, all hiding a storm of turmoil inside. At the time she didn't understand what she had seen nor would she be able to articulate it with any clarity until a time much later. But what she saw frightened her, and Shiloh abandoned the question, not wanting to hear any sort of answer except "no."

"I think *you* did it," Frank deflected, bouncing the question away with a levity that avoided anything having to do with the truth.

And that came with another breath of relief for Shiloh. "Grandpa," she smiled, "you're an asshole."

"That I am, honey," Frank admitted as he drove on. "That I am."

31

Hollis' day normally started a little before 5:00 in the morning. He used to be able to sleep well after sunrise, but once he hit his sixties that all but disappeared. His nights now provided maybe five hours of sleep with a plod to the bathroom—usually after midnight if he was unlucky. Before midnight it was the news at 11:00, followed by Leno and reading in bed until he began hallucinating with his eyes open. He was usually out after a couple of pages, which explained why it took a very long time to get through any book he was reading at night.

It would've come as a surprise to many that Hollis was an avid bookworm. He consumed books the way many consumed popcorn. He possessed a distaste for most of the writers of the late twentieth century and preferred to carve through the likes of Vonnegut, Heller, and Orwell, whose *Animal Farm* he could recite from memory. He plowed through *The Rise and Fall of the Third Reich* with unnerved horror and relished a 1977 biography of Abraham Lincoln. Buried deep in his library, which included a classic set of Kipling, was *Pride and Prejudice*, a secret favorite he would admit to no one.

The mornings were usually the same. Coffee and a three-egg Denver omelet, a short stack of buttermilk pancakes with heavy batter that added layer upon layer of fat to his waistline, all served at a small roadside diner on Bakers Mill Road well outside of town, going south on Route 9. The diner was run by a long-time widow who knew nothing of Hollis from all the years he had come in—nothing beyond the fact that he always tipped well.

But in Granite Point, there was no argument that Hollis was, without a doubt, an utterly miserable sonofabitch. He may indeed have been well read, but he was also mean, disagreeable, and outright foul. He knew it, and it wasn't something he ever tried to conceal. It was in his DNA, likely inherited from generations of mean, disagreeable, and outright foul ancestors.

Not much was known about Hollis, nor did he manage to maintain anything closely resembling a friendship with anyone except the Widow Otis. He arrived in the valley in the late '40s with his father from northern Wisconsin, who departed this Earth at the age of fifty-one. He'd succumbed to Black Lung after working years in the mines that gave birth to the railroad Hollis would ultimately work at for less than three months. His father was known as a vicious drunk, prone to violent bar fights that often landed him in jail. There was no sign of his mother nor any mention of her. Hollis' father was more than content to erase that woman from anything resembling a memory.

But as coarse and cruel as Hollis was, he was highly adept at conflict, both physically and mentally. He was a bruising wrestler in school, a brawling boxer in boot camp, and an exceedingly good debater. He loved them all, with manipulation and squeezing being his personal favorites. Getting elected sheriff was surprisingly easy for him; he just played upon the extreme fears of the everyday county residents like a magician. He expounded on fierce and merciless law enforcement—soothing music to the conservative minds that would pay his salary. He was a man before his time, well ahead of others who in later decades would weaponize fear on a grander scale.

Hollis was not married. Or, at least, no one thought he was or had been. His only love was Fay, the same woman he lost to Frank. An event that galled him to no end. He didn't want to just strangle Frank Campbell; he wanted to humiliate him, then strangle him. And if he could do it by digging his fat fingers into Frank's neck and pulling out his throat, well, so much the better.

Many considered Hollis to be nothing more than a caricature of the worst emotions of those who voted for him. The same who wanted law and order forced down the throats of those malcontents who chose to break it. That is, just as long as it wasn't forced upon themselves.

Law enforcement suited Hollis. A lot more than he expected, although he had to be mindful that such a career had its limits regardless of what he would prefer to do otherwise.

Despite Hollis' aptitude for vicious cruelty, he did have a shred or two of humanity that he kept well locked inside. He had a soft spot for animals, in a way that many never saw. And if they did, it would likely only confuse them. In reality, Hollis experienced fear just like everyone else, but he dared not show it. And as strategic and tactical as he was, he was also vulnerable to errors when he didn't have time to plan an encounter. Now older, he was no longer as good on his feet, and he could only cover that up whenever he threw the weight of the law at someone. But that didn't work all the time either.

On Monday morning, the day after Bolt's Invitational, Hollis skipped breakfast and arrived at the station well before sunrise. It was the only way to sidestep the press camped out across his little town. The only positive from any of this was the mini windfall that would be rolling into the coffers of the Sheriff's Office in the form of parking and speeding tickets and, of course, his nifty new No Left Turn pop-up sign on 1ˢᵗ Street, his personal favorite.

With the station quiet—aside from an occasional deputy pulling an overnighter—Hollis walked the halls with a stale sesame seed bagel loaded with warm cream cheese. He then hobbled his way downstairs to the holding cells, his knees aching from the thick torso they were forced to support, finding all but the one at the end of the row empty. In the unforgiving fluorescent lighting, Hollis leaned against the bars of the cell and looked upon an odorific Bolt Murphy, who lay sprawled across the metal cot bolted to the cell's white cinderblock wall. He had been picked up outside of Rick's Tavern, where he had been thrown out shortly before midnight. A deputy had come across him on 3ʳᵈ, trying to break into his former second story apartment over the old abandoned Western Auto Parts store.

"Mornin', Sebastian!" Hollis barked, loud enough to send his voice echoing through the basement. "How ya' doin'?"

Adrenaline shot through Bolt's body. He rolled over with a groan and dropped onto the cell floor.

"What the hell happened to you?" Hollis asked, keeping his volume cruelly elevated.

Bolt rotated onto his back and squinted upward at Hollis, who had finished off his bagel and wiped his hands on his pants, leaving two greasy streaks.

"She's gone," Bolt mumbled, his forehead resting painfully on a free hand.

"Who's gone?" Hollis asked, now a bit louder.

"Trisha," Bolt answered, his voice quivering and ebbing. "Trisha Marie Pettit Whatever."

Hollis cocked his head at him. It wasn't a secret that Bolt lusted over Trisha. In fact, it was about as public knowledge as the broken clock that hung suspended over the bank down the street. But being on the losing side over a Campbell woman was something Hollis could easily relate to. "You know she's married, right?" he snarked.

"She doesn't love him," Bolt whined as he pulled himself back onto the metal cot.

"Does *she* know that?"

Bolt looked at him, then slumped horizontal. Out like a light and snoring softly.

Hollis shook his head with perhaps a bit more empathy than he would give any other drunk. Bolt was harmless. Stupid, but harmless.

As more deputies arrived later in the morning, Hollis had them rouse Bolt with two cups of coffee. After Hollis gifted him a generic pair of jeans and a gray Bailey's Savings and Loan shirt—courtesy of the Lost and Found Department—Bolt Murphy appeared generally presentable. He smelled significantly better and felt far more human after throwing up the gallons of alcohol from the night before. By the time 10:00 AM arrived, he was apologetically coherent and sufficiently sober to be taken home. Hollis threw a coat on the guy, ordered his old clothes to be incinerated, and led Bolt out the side door to avoid the media.

The moment both men were outside, they took a defensive step backward.

32

Frank settled in at a lonely table in the corner of Rick's Tavern, the same little semi-seedy establishment from which Bolt Murphy had been ejected the night before. It would be a morning that would go down as legendary by Hollis' detractors—a minority who relished anything the good sheriff could be called out on, investigated for, or accused of. With a refreshed glass from the tap, Frank's eyes were glued to the tavern's TV. The local news feed started with Hollis emerging from a side door of the sheriff's station with Bolt, who immediately tried to scramble back into the station with the door slamming shut behind him as both were ambushed by a throng of bored reporters. They had been lying in wait, tired of having nothing to report, and fired questions from all directions the moment they saw the whites of Hollis' eyes.

"Sheriff Peete!" a random reporter called out from the throng that flanked him on all sides. "We've heard that the FBI has left. Does that mean the investigation is over?"

"Uh . . ." Hollis answered in a variable grunt, "no." He was caught completely flat-footed. His brain withdrew, completely unprepared for what was coming at him.

"Why'd they leave?"

"Uh . . . You'd have to ask them," Hollis replied as he tried to turn tail and head back into the station, only to meet a closed door with no handle. He was trapped and cornered.

"Is the FBI considering this no longer a crime scene?" another reporter barked.

"Huh? Who said that?"

"So, it *is* a crime scene?"

Hollis scrambled to pull himself together.

"Do you have any suspects?"

"We're following leads . . ." he blurted out sans thought.

"So you have leads?! So, it is a crime scene!"

Hollis found himself sinking faster than a bowling ball in a river, and the tavern's few patrons howled at his growing misery.

"What a fuckin' dumbshit," a voice cackled from the bar, temporarily pulling Frank's attention.

"I don't believe I've revealed anything more than just the facts," Hollis fumbled, trying to dig himself out of the crater he'd created.

"And that this is now a crime investigation?" another reporter asked.

"Why do you keep saying that?" Hollis snapped.

"If it's not a crime scene, then why do you have leads?" the reporter shot back, completely fearless of the now humiliated sheriff. "Are you going to arrest Beau Harper? Is he your prime suspect?"

Hollis stared at the reporter and quickly found some footing, followed by a horrifying idea that dawned on him that very moment.

"Yes. Based on some evidence we're reviewing, Beau Harper is indeed a person of interest."

It was only a moment, the briefest amount of elapsed time . . . and then all hell broke loose.

If things were a rockslide before, this now made it an avalanche. Hollis found himself buried under more questions than he could hear and process.

Andy's day had started on a far better note. She'd slept twelve hours, had a fruit bowl for breakfast, revisited her action plan, and felt ready for the first day of getting out of this podunk town that was trying to eat her alive. Her first stop would be the Atlantic Yard office to rifle through the place for the soil report that made the yard manager scratch her head. Her instincts told her to start there.

Forget this bullshit of trying to be an FBI agent, do what you do best.

"Follow your gut," her father once told her. "The rest is noise." And he was never wrong, especially after moving to Mexico with his new boyfriend after divorcing Mom.

With a renewed sense of purpose that even Ryan picked up on, she dropped him off at the wreck site and then drove to the yard office. The building was as empty as a school during summer vacation. It felt hollow—a vibe that made Andy want to get out of there as quickly as possible.

And there, sitting in the middle of it all, was Dana Harper— her attention fixed to an old, dusty TV with faded colors—forced to work for the hours she was coerced into while her son lay in a hospital bed surrounded by the kindness of strangers. She was haggard and consumed.

Andy approached her. "Excuse me?"

Dana looked up, remaining completely distracted.

"The geology report?" Andy asked, trying to softly jog Dana's memory. "The one with the soil samplings?"

"Oh . . ." Dana answered, partially coming to. She got up and weaved her way past the empty desks to a rusting beige cabinet. Each drawer opened with a metallic screech.

Andy's eyes moved from Dana digging through the drawers to the TV, where Hollis was being crucified in what would be epically referred to in future legend as "The Hollis Morning Shit Show." She walked to the TV to turn up the volume, and her stomach fell to her sensible sneakers.

"Here it is," Dana announced, pulling a report binder from the bottom drawer and bringing it over.

"That's it?" Andy asked, half of her attention still on the TV.

"It's the only one I know of," Dana answered quietly before sagging into an empty desk chair, this time closer to the TV, more engaged with that than anything Andy wanted. "I swear to God, whenever they figure out who did this, I'm going to put a bullet into their fucking head."

Andy stared at her, digesting the threat. "How's your son, Mrs. Harper?"

Dana ignored her. She was lost in the TV with a radiating degree of rage and angst that dispatched Andy to the furthest desk she could find. She sat down and looked at the cover:

U.S. GEOLOGICAL SURVEY SOIL ANALYSIS
ATLANTIC RIGHT-OF-WAY
PROWLER FLAT, WEST VIRGINIA 1994

But Hollis' TV carnage soon drew more of Andy's attention, underscored by Dana's visible fury—hot enough to burn a hole in the screen. And then she heard Hollis' statement on Beau Harper.

Dana shrieked and pushed away from the TV in horror. Her hands shook while she ran them through her hair.

Andy immediately reached her limit, moved to a discreet corner of the office with her cell phone, and tapped out a number.

"Hey, yeah, it's me," Andy said. She talked as quietly as she could into the phone. "Yeah, I'm watching it too. I need you to get me everything you have on Hollis Peete . . . Yeah, everything you can get in the shortest amount of time. And while you're at it, find a hook and yank this guy off-stage before we're all working at K-Mart during Christmas."

Andy closed the phone and swung her attention back to Dana, who now rocked slightly as she watched Hollis get lambasted.

In his seat at Rick's, Frank hung on every word that bumbled out of Hollis' overtaxed brain. Though pursuing Beau as a suspect technically absolved Frank, the idea of hanging all of this on harmless, pathetic Beau Harper was more than his already cracked psyche could handle. He felt like he was going to disintegrate on the spot.

I have to have done it.

On TV, Hollis retreated into survival mode. "Uh, given due consideration, I feel it's in our best interest to—"

And that's when Preston finally appeared and whispered into Hollis' ear, quickly delivering the word to shut the hell up. Preston then pushed Hollis away from the reporters and back to the front door of the station. "That's all," he said, slamming the door behind him.

Many within the Tavern booed loudly, the fun being over much too quickly, while Frank quietly cursed, drowning in self-loathing.

"Hey, Frankie, you okay?" Rick called from behind the bar. "You look a little pale."

Frank didn't hear him. He just stared off into space.

"Yo!"

Frank snapped out of it and turned his bloodshot eyes on Rick.

"You alright?" Rick asked again. "You want another?"

Frank glared at him, then was quickly out the door with nary an answer. His heart jack-hammered within his chest. He moved to the back of the building as his brain roared. A pair of railroad tracks lay before him, covered with trash from an overturned dumpster long overdue for emptying. Frank's breathing shallowed as voices and sounds of that night thundered through him. It was a noise level that made him want to claw his brain out.

The memories crescendoed through his consciousness, a sickening montage of images: his truck jamming to a stop as it plowed into the rise of the trackbed in a blinding downpour, the fogged-out signal light just a few yards away, but barely visible; swaying and sloshing onto the trackbed, crowbar in his hand; boots sinking into the puddled earth as he struggled through the reddish mud plowed up under his now-bent bumper.

He remembered the rain trouncing him. He could barely see, but he saw enough to jam the crowbar onto a spike and pry it up with a grimace, only to have it slip from his hands. He recalled dropping it and looking at the blood that pulsed from a deep cut in his palm. The signal—he remembered it coming to life, glowing green in all that darkness.

Frank snapped back to the present. The low, plodding growl of a pair of powerful diesel locomotives pulled him from that lost night into the rudeness of now. He looked over, greeted by the sight of Kevin's massive Dash-9s idling by. Their presence pushed him up against a wall, and the sight of Kevin in the cab staring at him was the final nail that pinned Frank to the cross.

As the wind and noise of the train receded, Frank peeled himself from the wall and drove quickly home. He wanted to hide, bury himself under a rock and never be seen again. Once inside, he pulled the blinds down on all the windows, locked every door, and parked himself in his well-worn La-Z-Boy. He swiveled away from the shattered TV and faced the old couch where Fay had often napped, then curled up in his chair and sobbed quietly.

33

Hollis skipped lunch and instead rapped his fingers on the wood of his desk, waiting for the world to come to an end. He'd screwed up. No, he'd fucked up. Far exceeding what even he would consider rational. And what was coming his way was a much-deserved beating beyond what he was already giving himself. Essentially, there wasn't a rock big enough for him to hide under.

The drumming of his digits ended when Andy stormed into his office with about as much authority as she could corral. She didn't even knock. The door swung open and there she was. But even pissed off, she was gorgeous. Hollis could be burned to death by those dark eyes and be perfectly fine with it. But, still, he knew he was in for a shitstorm.

"Guess you're not here for a bike license, huh?" Hollis asked, trying to measure and deflect the heavy shelling coming his way.

Andy looked at him for a moment before she moved through his office, inspecting what he had on the walls, eventually finding a framed National Defense Service Medal. "What's this for?"

"Korea."

Andy nodded. *Impressive.* But there was no way she was going to show that to him. Overall, she knew very little of Hollis. Ryan's hurried search had struck out, so Andy could only work with what was right there in front of her and whatever she'd pulled from Dana. "I heard you used to be a driver for Atlantic," she finally said as she took a chair across from his desk. "What happened?"

"I . . . resigned," Hollis hesitated.

"I heard you got fired," she punted back while tossing a thin folder onto the desk.

Hollis stared at it, his jaw tightening. He didn't even want to touch it.

"I heard it was because you pinned some poor guy into a boxcar," Andy continued, nodding to the folder. "Over a woman, wasn't it?"

Hollis stared at the folder. "Says all that in there, huh?"

"You wouldn't believe what it says," Andy said as she leaned in. "You seem to suffer from a chronic running of the mouth. And while you may have the art of bullshit down, you obviously lack the brains to know when to use it."

Hollis backpedaled. "I was . . . ambushed."

"I don't care if you had hemorrhoids. You talk to the press again without me knowing about it, I'll turn your badge into a doorknob. Got it?"

Hollis stared at her. He was suddenly five again with his father standing over him, the back of his hand ready to fire when Hollis had once again mouthed off one too many times. He remembered the stars that followed as he hit the floor while watching his old man stomp away.

God, he hated that motherfucker.

Andy grabbed the folder and left, steaming down the corridor, where people gave her a wide berth.

Hollis sagged in relief.

Andy turned a corner and took in a loud breath. She was fired up enough to go bench 400 pounds. With one arm. Twice. While dragging an entire NFL defensive line into the end zone with her. This was the first time she'd had to blast anyone on that scale. Oh, he had it coming, and Hollis—despite being a creep—was a force to be reckoned with. Still, she'd done it. She hadn't flinched or stumbled on a sentence, let alone a word.

Langsdon missed all of it. She would've loved to shove this all down his pompous throat, but, for now, she was suddenly starving. Walking to her car, she tossed the folder into a nearby trash bin, a blank piece of paper floating out to be taken by the wind.

34

Andy accelerated out of the valley much like Kevin had done a few nights earlier, except this time in the opposite direction. She was leaving Granite Point in her rearview mirror, even if just for a little while. The goal was to find a place to eat in peace and not be stared at by gossiping locals or endlessly pestered by an information-starved media pool. The news crews were only just beginning to trickle out of town due to the lack of blood to film in breathtaking drama or breathless interviews.

She drove past a few out-of-business hot dog drive-ups and an isolated Dairy Queen before finally settling on a quiet, empty diner the next town over. She pulled into the parking lot near a set of lonely railroad tracks, parked her car, and stepped inside with the soil binder Dana had given her.

At the counter, Andy stared at the menu above her while not registering any of it. Instead of reading the impressive display of six ways to serve hot dogs, four variations of artery-clogging double-cheeseburgers, and something called the "Cardiac Terminator Special" for the bargain price of $8.95—cheese extra—she replayed the scene in Hollis' office, mentally auditing where she'd appeared weak or might have overplayed her hand.

"Ma'am?" a girl's voice from behind the counter called, trying to get her attention. It wasn't working. "Ma'am?!"

Andy finally snapped out of it, her gaze turning toward a young woman with a blonde ponytail and a perky diner-themed polo shirt, along with "Caitlin" on her name tag.

"What can I get you?" Caitlin asked.

Andy's brain remained fuzzy. She may have literally fallen asleep while standing up, likely with a light snore. "Oh . . . um . . ." She scanned the menu with a slight sneer, finding nothing she wanted except to locate the closest defibrillator machine. "Um, do you have any salads?"

Caitlin stared at her. *A salad in a burger place, seriously?* "We have lettuce and tomatoes and onions. Throw 'em together, and you could call it a salad."

Cute, Andy thought.

A moment later, Caitlin recognized Andy. "Hey, wait a second! Aren't you that lady from the government?"

Crap. So much for anonymous dining.

"You're like a celebrity around here!" Caitlin answered with an awe-inspired air.

Andy realized if she really wanted an anonymous meal, she should have had it in Bulgaria.

"No," Andy said with a sigh, "I'm just me. How about a plain cheeseburger?"

"Sure. You want the meal?"

Andy didn't care. She'd eat just an onion ring by now and call it a day, bringing the laborious act of ordering lunch to an immediate close. "Sure. But with water, please."

"No problem. We'll take it out to you."

"Thanks." Andy nodded and turned toward a plentiful collection of tables, choosing one by the window. She dropped the geologic binder onto the thick, scratched orange Formica tabletop and sat, immediately noting the carved graffiti that spelled out: "FOR A GOOD TIME CALL HOLLIS AT 911."

Andy chortled and slid the binder over it. The morning had quickly caught up with her, and though the day wasn't even half over, she wanted nothing more than to crawl back into bed. Verbally throttling Hollis had completely drained her, and the adrenaline buzz was sadly gone, leaving behind a dull ache in the back of her head. The reset she had run herself through last night was now entirely obliterated. Andy was right back where she'd started—her mind a blob of mud. Opening the binder did little to help clear it.

"You must have a death wish if you're eating here," came a voice that sent a bolt up her spine. She quickly looked up to find Kevin standing at her table with a couple of to-go bags. "What are *you* doing way out here?" he asked, somewhat bewildered to find her so far off the beaten path.

"Trying to find a quiet place to eat," Andy answered with a slight sigh. "Anonymity is a little hard to come by around here."

"It is," Kevin admitted as Trisha's not-so-subtle warning took center stage in his mind. "That's why you need to drive two states over if you want any of that." He then glanced toward the doors and spotted Gibson outside, waving his arms.

"You have a cheerleader," Andy commented after she followed Kevin's look toward the window.

Gibson pointed at his watch. *Let's go!*

Kevin gave him five fingers, which sent Gibson off with a flop of the arms. Kevin then noticed the binder. "A soil report?"

"Gotta look at everything."

"Yeah, I guess," he said with a tick of a shrug.

Andy looked at him. And *looked* at him. The draw he had on her completely dragged her in, and the more she fought against it, the harder it fought back—to the point where she just wanted to give in.

I really should have driven to Bulgaria. Or maybe even Kyrgyzstan. She needed to quickly change the subject before she found herself sailing past the Cape of No Hope, and she had the perfect topic to do just that. "I think it's time I talk to your father," she said.

That did it. Kevin sagged into the seat across from her. Being in Trisha's doghouse was nothing compared to the fear of Frank ending up in the Big House.

"You had to know this was coming," Andy said with a slight cock of her head. *What's that look he's trying to hide? Restrained panic? I can read this guy like a dinner menu.*

Kevin eventually nodded.

"Then why are you looking like that?" Andy pressed

"Because I'm curious to know what you're expecting him to say," Kevin said. "'Yep, you got me. I did it'?"

"That would certainly make things easier," Andy answered and then left it there for a beat. If there was anything to reveal, it would happen now.

But Kevin didn't bite. Instead, he looked back out the window and watched Gibson down his shake cup in the midday sunlight. "I don't think you're going to get what you're looking for," he finally answered. "Not from Frank Campbell." *Not that I ever did,* he almost added, but stopped himself.

"Show me someone who usually does," Andy countered before another odd moment of simmering silence between them. As much as she wanted Kevin to give up his gut feelings, his suspicions and intuitions, she knew he would reveal none of it. And for the briefest of moments, she wondered if *he* had done it.

She quickly booted that thought from her mind.

"How often does that happen?" Kevin asked, breaking the heavy pause that sat like a lead blanket around them.

"Does *what* happen?"

"Somebody confesses. You know, they step right up and say, 'Yep, that was me.'"

"Not enough to make our lives any easier. At least mine."

Kevin's brow wrinkled at that. There was a brief sadness about Andy he hadn't seen before. For a moment he saw an exhausted soul, a world's weight of something she had been carrying around inside for what appeared to be a lifetime. "How many of these have you done?"

Andy leaned back in her seat and mulled the answer, weighing the safety of sharing something that had endlessly carved her up from the inside out. "A few," she answered in a tone that sounded more like a confession.

The power in the conversation had turned. Kevin leaned forward in a way that could pry it out of her. "You're looking for someone," he said as the epiphany dawned on him. "Or you are missing someone."

Andy stared at him, taken aback by how quickly he figured that out.

"Who?" Kevin asked and waited for an answer Andy wasn't sure she wanted to give.

35

It was the loud scream of her three-year-old son that hauled Andy back to consciousness. Her eyes opened to the stinging of blood within them and the foul taste of blood in her mouth. The only sensation that ached more than the pain in the back of her head was the growing contusion on her left temple, delivered by the deliberate jabbing of the handle of a 20-gauge shotgun that knocked her cold just a few minutes before.

Andy forced herself awake, fighting through to roll onto her knees. Once up, she was met with the immediate spinning of everything around her. She grasped at anything to give her some semblance of balance. She'd had a concussion before, but nothing like this—ever.

Her son's scream had now moved outside, emanating through the open front door of the modest white stucco Santa Monica home and the April night beyond. Andy's brain focused further, fueled by an anger-driven panic and supercharged by the boy's hysterical cry that had now evolved into complete terror as the motor of an awaiting hot-rodded pickup truck roared to life.

Andy struggled forward, unable to catch her footing, while summoning up the clarity to go after her child. But there, to her left, was Langsdon, lying bludgeoned in a pool of blood fed by a bullet wound in his side. She stumbled toward him, her throbbing head making it nearly impossible to even perform the basic task of walking. A sudden yelling came from outside, mixed with the hysteria of her son, and Andy grunted her way to lucidity. She rolled Langsdon's body over and removed his .40-caliber Smith & Wesson from its shoulder holster.

Andy powered her way through the front door and onto the concrete walkway facing her bucolic picket-fence neighborhood. With a strengthening gait, she steamed toward the men in the street. There were five of them. Big men clustered in the shadows around an obnoxiously loud Dodge Ram pickup jacked up on wheels three times the size of anything normal—at least that was how she would always remember it. Under the light of the streetlamp they all violently argued with the man who held her son tightly to his chest, pinning the toddler's flailing arms and legs into submission.

"MARCUS!?!" The man Andy screamed at, the man who was her husband, had evolved into a horror she was no longer able to recognize.

Andy's shout snapped their arguing and swung their attention toward her. And upon seeing his mother, the child fought the hold of his father even more while stretching his little arms out hopelessly for Andy.

"Give him back!" Andy demanded with Langsdon's gun dangling at her side.

Marcus held their son tighter with no intention whatsoever of letting him go.

"I'm serious, Marcus," Andy again demanded, this time her voice strength quickly fading as consciousness tried to escape her once again. "*Just* give him back."

Marcus Mayland looked on at his wife, eyes on the gun. He considered what she was capable of with an undoubtedly loaded weapon. Marcus was a tall man, on the high side of his twenties. Not long ago he was clean cut, handsome, and neatly suited, blessed with a promising executive career. But then came the insanity: Waco, Texas, 1993. In the aftermath, his left-leaning Stanford business logic took a hard turn to the right. Now the man who clutched their three-year-old son sported an unmarked ball cap, a filthy white Nirvana T-shirt, and an unkempt goatee, and possessed a mindset commanded by an irrational rage driven by the fury of non-sensical hate. He and his posse plundered Andy's knowledge of railroading to derail the *Sunset Limited* in the middle of the worst desert Arizona had to offer. It was their fiery revenge against the government under a ridiculous and ignorant moniker that made sense to no one. They had scored virtuous reciprocity for Waco, only to then disappear like scuttling cockroaches into the dark.

"I told you to come with us," Marcus said calmly as Andy's knees weakened. She stumbled back a step while sounds echoed in her head and a gray cloud enveloped her mind. Marcus took a couple of steps toward her, enough to momentarily settle their son from his hysteria. "But *you* chose this, and I'm *not* going to let our son grow up in your world of hypocrisy and bullshit. I'm going to raise him to be free. He'll never be the pawn you are."

"Please—" she pleaded barely above a desperate whisper. Tears and blood washed down her cheeks. She then jumped as the front door of the pickup slammed loudly, swung by the large arm of a grotesquely obese man with a long beard and a blob of hair boxed in with a John Deere ball cap. The man's name was Alistair Thurmond, a moniker best suited to an episode of *Gilligan's Island*, Langsdon would later joke.

"Man, we ain't got time for this fuckin' Pampers horseshit!" Thurmond howled in a deep Southern accent brewed in the bowels of Alabama. He stormed directly toward Andy, accelerating as he raised his shotgun, still coated with her blood on the handle. "Told ya we shoulda just put a bullet in her gawd damn head."

Before Thurmond could get a free hand under his shotgun, Andy aimed and fired a single bullet from Langsdon's Smith & Wesson.

Thurmond's life ended instantly. The man never knew what hit him as the bullet entered the center of his forehead and exploded out the back of his skull, spraying out nearly half of his skull cap and most of what he'd considered a brain. Already dead, he dropped to his knees, the shotgun falling from his hands. His body sagged backwards and fell, much like a 300-pound bag of dog food.

Marcus jumped and a bolt of electricity went through their son, who clawed painfully at his father, again desperate to escape.

The remaining men around the pickup scrambled, pulling whatever firearms they could find as Andy moved her aim, trying to find somewhere, anywhere to put a bullet into her husband that would be far enough away from her child.

"Think about this, Andy," Marcus continued with a frightened waver in his voice. "He will be the leader our country needs. You'll see. I'm going to teach him everything and what the truth really is. You're going to be so proud of him. He's going to be the second coming."

"Give him back." Her voice barely audible, Andy hoped to appeal to any remaining thread of love between them, anything that still existed from the five years of their marriage that started at California's Monterey Bay and then caustically dissolved in the smoldering remains of an extremist compound.

And oddly enough, for the briefest of moments and a sliver of hope, she saw the shadow of the man she'd once loved as he took one more step toward her.

"He'll be safe with me, Andy," Marcus said, "I swear to God."

"You used me," Andy countered weakly, her ability to simply stand rapidly fleeing.

"No," Marcus answered, "that's where you're wrong. You gave us what we needed. What I needed. Because of you, we were able to strike back. That train in the desert? That's just the beginning. We're going to change our country. Change our world. I'm going to teach our son to fight for us, for our race, for our way of life. But you, Andy, you helped start the revolution. You just wait and see. They're never going to see us coming."

Andy quickly raised the gun and pointed it at Marcus' head. She wanted to kill this man, this thing that inhabited her husband's body, and annihilate this revolution he claimed *she* started.

Marcus backed up toward the pickup, the momentary vision of sanity disappearing just as quickly as it had appeared.

Andy struggled to find a clear shot as Marcus backed away. He was soon in the truck with their son while his cohorts heaved Thurmond's whale of a body onto the truck bed. With a slam of the passenger door, the truck roared down the street and into the night, passing underneath streetlights until it was nothing more than a memory.

Andy screamed and fell to the earth.

36

Kevin sat speechless. What Andy shared was a scenario he could never have imagined. It was truly the fabric of nightmares. He would, in the years that followed, make the emotional connection: his son sitting momentarily on Andy's lap during that one Sunday rodeo, and the resulting expression of peace upon her face.

Andy further explained the story of Marcus, how he'd swept her off her feet at Stanford, chained himself to a fence to protect redwood trees, made love to her on a beach, and then mysteriously overdosed on right-wing news and propaganda until the man she loved disappeared into a dark extremist's hole.

"Not exactly something someone wears around on a T-shirt," Andy said with a sad smile.

Kevin struggled to come up with something, anything, to say. "Where do you think he is now?" he asked, taking a risk by even bringing it up.

Andy took a long time to answer. She honestly didn't know, nor could she see a path to even pursue. The road to Marcus and her son was not on any map. She had gotten close only once, when she had lifted the backside of Thurmond's skullcap from her lawn and DNA'd herself and Langsdon to a shit-hole country roadhouse in Alabama. It was there they found two of the men in that deafening Ram pickup, plotting to drive an eighteen-wheeler filled with C4 into Mobile's Museum of History. But Marcus was nowhere to be found; he was dumped off with Thurmond's carcass at a New Mexico rest stop and hadn't been seen since. Marcus and her son had become ghosts—phantoms that dared Andy to prove they'd actually existed in the first place.

"You think you'll ever find him?" Kevin pressed, asking again to keep Andy moving forward.

"I don't know," she answered honestly. "I know I'm looking in all the wrong places. A small part of me was thinking maybe he was behind this, but he wasn't. No matter how much it looks the same, it's not."

"Maybe you're here to prove you weren't any more responsible for derailing a passenger train in Arizona than you were in Butt Scratch, West Virginia," Kevin offered, taking his turn in the psychiatrist's chair.

"Yeah, maybe." Andy again sadly smiled. "But here. This one. There's just . . . something I'm missing. It's right in front of me, and I haven't been able to find it yet. I mean, if your father did this, it would make no sense he would then risk his life to save someone else's."

"Especially when he hates that someone more than life itself."

Andy shrugged slightly.

Kevin continued, "Not a conversation I wish upon you."

"Your father doesn't scare me," Andy said, trying to regain her appetite by pulling the bun on her cheeseburger to ensure it was edible. She then went for a fry instead. "At least not as much as he does you."

"Is this where I pull up a couch again?"

Andy cracked a smile. "He's human. Built with the same emotions, fears, and frail body like everyone else."

Kevin scoffed. "You obviously don't know my father."

"It doesn't matter if I do or don't. I can already tell you've 'pedestaled' him in a way that's got you mired in the quicksand of inferiority."

"Pedestaled? That's one I haven't heard before."

She smiled. "I haven't even known you for a week, and I can already see how desperate you are for your father's approval. That's the problem. When you latch your self-worth to someone else's opinion, you turn into a knot."

"Great, thank you," Kevin answered, stealing one of her fries.

"No, I'm serious. I heard about what happened to your dad's cab partner. And with your mom gone, maybe that's why he's the way he is?"

Kevin grimaced in defensive amusement.

"What?" Andy raised an eyebrow.

"Why do people think it's always 'one thing' that makes people the way they are? It's not always just one thing. I mean, why is a drug addict a drug addict? Or why is my dad an ass-aholic? There isn't just one reason. There could be fifty. Or two. And sometimes they're a product of their generation—who the fuck knows."

"Okay, so by your logic, we're all echoes of our parents, predestined to repeat the lives they lived before us?"

"I'm not sure I said that, but isn't every child like that?"

"I'm not." Andy shrugged. "But the bigger fact is the two of you are so deep into whatever you're in, you can't even see the time you're both wasting. You're so enmeshed, you're not even aware that every moment is a moment gone forever. It's like a ticking clock, marking every beat."

She then looked off, her emotions surfacing, making her more vulnerable than she was ready—or wanted—to be. Kevin had hit a nerve, punching through her defenses in a way that built emotional trust, and that was the last thing she wanted. Maybe . . .

"We waste so much time," Andy said. After a reflective pause, she continued, "Have you had moments that you're so conscious of that it feels like a heartbeat? I look at the people around me, spending their lives working for something that someone else says has value, and they just don't get it. It's all those moments that have made up your life. That's what you take with you in the end." So much for self-control; she wiped away a tear and drew in a deep breath. "You and your father have no idea how much time you've both wasted. And you're still wasting it."

Kevin sat stunned. Andy had, somehow, smashed straight through the walls of his obvious emotional bullshit. It was something that Trisha could do as well, but her approach was far more accusatory, far more a paralyzing punch as opposed to Andy's gentle takedown, which always ended in a frozen, combative state for him. Trisha was fueled by years of exasperation that never helped to move anything forward, while Andy was gifted with the luxury of not having to live with him for the last two decades. Kevin found Andy's emotional intuition seductively frightening.

He knew he was in serious danger. Kevin felt her pull on him strengthening. He was beginning to fall, and as the ache of Trisha's slap continued to nag at him, it was an attraction he wasn't all that inspired to fight. Andy was light and beautiful and possessed an energy he didn't even know he was lacking. In that moment, Andy connected with him in a way that Trisha never had. It made him genuinely realize the door to his self-imposed prison had always been open. All he needed to do was walk through it.

Sometimes it takes a stranger to validate something one has always known.

Andy left a generous tip on the table, along with her half-eaten lunch. Kevin followed her out, carrying his two bags of takeout. In Andy's presence, everything felt new and just a bit lighter for him. He was able to breathe a bit easier, and that was a sensation he hadn't really ever known—and didn't know what to do with.

Caitlin watched them leave as she leaned over the counter. She'd managed to hear nearly every word they'd said. And as the glass door closed, she slipped back into the kitchen and was immediately on the phone. First call was to her mother, now divorced from Chad Colt's uncle and seeing Sal Pitt's niece in a decision that no one much cared for. The juicy details of this latest encounter, from Marcus' courtship of Andy to the devastating loss of her son, were passed over to her mother's lover, who then told Sal himself, who tossed the news to his wife, who had just become close friends with Bea Amboy's daughter and dropped the gossipy bomb on her. She of course had to quickly call Mae Kay Weintraub herself, who couldn't spell "discreet" if she had a gun to her head.

"Where'd you park?" Andy squinted in the sunlight.

"Back here." Kevin led her around the corner to where his massive twin diesel locomotives sat idling on a siding, spitting air pressure and dwarfing the diner.

Andy stopped and took a moment to marvel at the sight. "I love a man who travels light."

Kevin smiled, fighting the temptation to invite her onboard and see where life would take them. It was through Andy's efforts that he, and many others, had been able to return to work.

With the derailment, the mainline through Prowler Flat had lobbed off a secondary conduit, creating insidious congestion that stretched across two time zones and antagonizing just about every Class One carrier in the country and the shipping lines that fed the Port of Baltimore. The accident had shredded Track One, which wouldn't find a useful life again for at least six months. But with Track Two left relatively unscathed, and with just about every shipper in the Northern Hemisphere leaning on the NTSB, Andy gave the gift of life by having the cranes clear the wreckage just enough to allow traffic to flow once again. If nothing else, she'd at least accomplished one thing through this whole mess.

And as a woman, Andy wasn't asleep through what was happening right in front of her. She easily picked up on what she was stirring in Kevin and took a little satisfaction from knowing she still had "it." The problem was she also found him a calming and grounding presence. His eyes were incredibly deep, and she sensed an even deeper soul that harbored a solid passion for her. And that was trouble. It was big trouble because he continued to cloud her thinking just by standing there.

Snap out of it!

"Again, please," Andy said, breaking the silence between them, "if you find anything or think of something, please let me know."

"You bet," Kevin answered and then watched her walk off. A sudden pang of guilt punched through the moment in the form of Beau's camcorder. It hadn't taken him long to sow the first seed of deceit with her. He climbed the crew ladder as Gibson passed Andy walking in the opposite direction, his face puckered on his second strawberry shake. He swiveled around to watch what moved within her jeans.

"You know," Gibson said to Kevin, "I'd love to get lost in her underwear drawer."

Kevin looked at him. "You're sick, you know that? The only way she'd touch you is with a restraining order."

"And I'd be happy with even that," he fantasized while he climbed the ladder behind Kevin, who whacked him lightly on the back of the head before he stepped through the cab door.

37

When it came to religion, Andy was the poster child for agnosticism. As far as she was concerned, God was, at best, an absentee landlord who should be more scorned than celebrated. And she had yet to find anyone who could explain why God would bestow the miraculous gift of, say, finding one's car keys after saying a prayer, while at the same time allowing a child to starve to death in the cruelty of a dark and forgotten closet. Or why her husband would vacate the rational world with their child who clawed to get to her. The same child who now lived only in her memory or in nightmares that often sent her to the floor with a shriek. She was furious at God and voiced it habitually—usually more than once an hour and endlessly on religious holidays that only held pain for her.

And yet, Andy was grateful for whatever deity delivered the welcoming salve of a few days of benign weather. The mud had dried, and the chill of the impending winter, which had slowed everything to a filthy crawl, had mercifully vacated eastward. It all helped accelerate the clean-up of the wreck of the *Allegheny Limited*.

Andy also knew she was on borrowed time. A new burst of Arctic air was already muscling the abnormally warm weather off to Florida, bringing in the season's first frost and a wave of snow guaranteed to make everyone's life miserable.

By late afternoon the frigid air had made Andy's run to Shale Waterfall State Park exceptionally cold. The blue skies had given way to undulating tufts of gray clouds, and the frozen dew on the fallen leaves cracked beneath her Nikes as she ran to the top of the Falls. Even during the run, Andy struggled to stay warm, and it wasn't long before a light freezing rain pelted her from above.

The wintry air stung her lungs as she worked on catching her breath, making it even harder to clear her head and enjoy the simple beauty of watching water tumble over the rocks into the narrow gorge below. It had been days since she'd heard from Langsdon, and with minimal help from anyone above, Andy now felt like an imposter trying to pull off a charade that no one around her was buying. Somehow, she had let the world in. Her mind was elsewhere, and it was all because of one guy who was screwing up her ability to think straight. At least Kevin Campbell was gone for the day—a nice ancillary benefit of clearing the track at Prowler Flat and getting him back to work. Now she wouldn't have to worry about running into him. At least for the immediate future.

Andy turned and worked her way down the path from the falls, feeling a gust of glacial air pushing her from behind. She had finally gathered enough clarity to at least work out some of the day's agenda.

First up was Frank Campbell. As Andy had warned Kevin, it was time to talk to his father, something she knew she had been putting off for far too long. She was lucky Frank hadn't skipped town, which also drove home the possibility that he had nothing to do with the derailment. She had seen Frank just once, a shadowy silhouette in the gloomy locomotive people called "The Brick," pushing and pulling on the cranes that lifted wreckage from the newly cleared Track Two.

I hope Kevin comes back soon.

Andy quickly shook her head. Without her even being conscious of it, Kevin had found a way to unlock her brain and prop his feet up on the comforts of her emotional couch. She immediately chased the guy out of her mind while gravity accelerated her trot downhill.

But her mind became congested again. The run had done nothing to dispel this attraction—if not infatuation—as Kevin Campbell annoyingly tugged on her focus. It inconveniently bumped her imagination around, creating fantastical visionary moments of intimacy with a man she barely knew.

And it was the same overactive imagination that created momentary nightmares, such as the fleeting vision of Kevin's tall and regal wife awaiting her at the bottom of the trail. Her darkened figure ground Andy's run to a halt in an inch of sneaker-swallowing mud.

"I think you and I need to talk," Trisha-the-Hallucination said with a firm chill in her voice, a voice that Andy could only create in her mind, as she knew absolutely nothing of Trisha's voice.

"I don't think that's a good idea," Andy countered, playing through an instinctive script of self-defense. Her own conscience was now accusing her of wanting to steal Kevin away, or to at least explore what even one night with him would be like. She was caught by her own sense of right-versus-wrong, like a hungry shoplifter trying to sneak a chocolate croissant out of a bakery. She wanted to close herself in her hotel room and then disappear in the middle of the night, never to be seen again.

Andy had allowed her imagination to race away from her, and she immediately chased the scene from her mind, only to find herself alone in the vacant and puddled parking lot, fed by a dirty stream of rainwater that oozed from the muddy hills behind her like a miniature landslide.

By now, Andy's thoughts were all over the place in what had become a descending wintry fog that froze her further. She wanted to run, but there was nothing left in her legs to propel her forward.

But she ran anyway.

Her legs felt like they were being fueled by acid. She was no longer running for exercise; she was now running away from everything—from Kevin and his imposing, larger-than-life wife, Langsdon and his self-righteous Ray-Bans, Marcus and his psychotic trip into the black abyss of conspiracies, this little insane asylum town, the roadblock in her brain that trapped her here, and the horror of this life that now made no sense, all the while missing her son. She raced to be free.

Within thirty seconds Andy's body had had enough. The sprint for liberation abruptly decelerated to a halt at the end of the parking lot. She bent over, hands on her knees, and desperately tried to catch her breath. Sweat, rain, and probably ice dripped from the tip of her nose as she sagged onto the bench of an old picnic table.

She turned her face into the chilling breeze, watching ripples of rainwater in a large puddle nearby, just begging to be stomped in by a playful child. She recalled her son, when he had finally mastered enough balance to walk, dropping into an asphalt pond that instantaneously soaked him from his sneakers to the top of his joyfully mopped head of hair. He was delighted to do something his mother usually told him not to.

Andy smiled slightly, which then faded when a noisy wind gusted the memory from her mind. She had completely misjudged the weather and was now faced with the daunting task of trudging the two miles to town. The warmth of the hot soaking tub in her room gave her at least one goal she could obtain before the day expired. Her attention was pulled upward, her eyes finding the tops of the trees that bent sideways with the wind. The rustling of the leaves filled her ears and rounded out the calm to this small piece of earth she currently occupied. Andy closed her eyes to absorb the moment, deliberately pushing the congestion and noise in her brain aside.

For once, there was stillness.

Andy then felt the cruel north wind shift around her. The bite of the winter air that flowed through those same trees, sending their brittle leaves earthward, burned her face and was followed by a drenching downpour. Soaked to the bone, Andy was instantly angry, fed up with herself most of all. It was time for her to get her head screwed on straight, solve this unsolvable mess, and get the hell out of Granite Point before it irreparably ended her. With her hands shoved up tightly against her torso, she began the long, frozen walk back to town.

Trisha glanced in the rearview mirror and found Michael had slipped off to sleep in his car seat. He had polished off most of the bag of Pepperidge Farm Goldfish crackers, which lay crumpled and empty in his lap. The crackers he hadn't finished lay strewn upon the carpeted floorboards of the Chevy Suburban, awaiting their fate within the belly of a partially charged Dust Buster at home.

The half-hour trip back from the equestrian center that Freedom now called home gave Trisha some moments of mindless peace. She had gone to collect her bridle, although she wasn't sure why. All it was going to do was hang in the garage as a reminder of the life she was putting behind her. But it was hers, and the Amboys had more than enough wealth and did not need a freebie from Trisha Campbell.

Trisha's eyes returned to the road, her view blurred through the slogged mix of rain and hail. It was miserable outside, and a bullet-ridden sign—"Bridges Freeze Before Road Surfaces"—reminded her to take it easy with her heavily leaded foot as she crossed over the Shale River that fed Shale Waterfall State Park. Once she was safely off the bridge, the wintry mix became a deluge, forcing Trisha to nudge the wipers into a frantic pace, smearing ice across the glass and reminding her that Kevin had failed to replace the wiper blades after being asked for the third time.

And somehow, through the curtain of sleet, she spotted a sad, lonely, hunched figure plodding along the road toward town.

Trisha craned her neck to get a glimpse of the pedestrian caught in conditions unfit for even the hardiest of Earth's creatures. Her eyes then snapped to the rearview mirror and her brain practically short-circuited when she recognized the thin, huddled human as none other than Mae Kay Weintraub's "awful woman from the NTSB." The same woman who had held her son, been caught more than once chatting away with her husband, and threatened to destroy Western civilization as Mae knew it to be.

Trisha drove on for a few more seconds before the better part of her removed her foot from the gas pedal and placed it on the brake. The Suburban slowed and came to a stop on the edge of the road, with Trisha's eyes fixed on the SUV's mirrors. And then, with a loud exhale, Trisha shifted into reverse and idled her way back toward this epitome of feminine evil.

A couple of moments later, she stopped and rolled down the passenger window, revealing a doused soul in desperate need of a large towel.

Andy stood beside the large black SUV rumbling next to her. As the window rolled down, her stomach rose into her throat. At the wheel loomed the real Trisha Campbell, who, even bundled up in an oversized coat, presented as an imposing figure of power. Andy would have swallowed hard had her quivering body allowed it.

"Need a ride?" Trisha asked, her hand sliding the Suburban into drive.

Andy experienced a moment of restrained panic. She glanced off toward town and probable hypothermia. She thought of darting into the densely vegetated hillside behind her, where, God knows, she would likely become dinner for a bear or a pack of wolves. She moved her eyes back to Trisha, who still waited for an answer.

"Or would you rather freeze to death while looking like a drowned cat?" Trisha questioned as drops of rain dotted the passenger seat.

Andy shook her head and quietly opened the door. She climbed in, grateful for the warm blast of air and a small diaper towel that Trisha pulled from the back.

Andy took note of the boy in the car seat, content in the crumbs of his recent Goldfish slaughter. "Thanks," she said above a teeth-chattering whisper. She then pulled the towel over her face and fought off a chill. Every article of clothing stuck to her like a suction cup, and she shifted in the seat, contending with a whole new definition of the word "wedgie."

"You must have a death wish for running outside in this," Trisha commented as she rolled Andy's window up and drove on toward town, accelerating perhaps a bit faster than she normally would.

"It wasn't this way an hour ago," Andy answered, now running the towel around her neck and over her ears.

"Welcome to West Virginia," Trisha replied.

"Thank you again for stopping."

Trisha paid Andy her own momentary glance. "No problem."

By the time the Suburban reached the speed limit, an uncomfortable silence sat between the two women. Andy wondered if she could survive stepping out of this 6,000-pound behemoth moving at nearly sixty miles an hour while Trisha contemplated whether a "*Mae made me do it*" defense would hold up in court.

And with nothing better to ask, let alone say, Trisha suddenly broke the silence. "Word around town has it you've been seen talking to my husband."

Andy looked at Trisha and thought quickly. She instantly decided that freezing to death as a flooded feline was indeed the choice she should have made. Too late now.

"I'm talking to a lot of people," Andy answered, now wondering if this would be the part where no one would ever find her body.

"Okay. But you seem to be talking to him more than others," Trisha pushed, staring at Andy for as long as the road would allow. "Is there something you want to tell me?"

Yeah, your husband is percolating my brain cells and turning my spine into mush. You don't mind if he does that, do you? "No," she heard herself say, "except that he's been incredibly helpful."

Trisha again stared at her, this time taking her eyes off the road far longer than she should have while the Suburban dangerously drifted across the double-yellow line.

"Truck!" Andy frantically pointed ahead.

Trisha snapped her eyes back to the road and was met with the glare of headlights. She quickly pulled the Suburban back to the right and kicked herself inside.

Andy exhaled and watched a plain white panel truck pass by, with a possible middle finger just visible behind the darkened glass. This close encounter emboldened her to pitch forth some level of self-defense while smacking Trisha with a dose of reality. "Mrs. Campbell, I'm not quite sure *what* you've heard, but if there are so many holes in your marriage that someone like me can slip through one of them, I'm not your problem."

Of all the answers Trisha could have expected, this was not one of them. And as much as she would hate to admit it, this pretty outsider—regardless of looking like a soddened rodent—was right. By the time word of Kevin and Andy being seen together again had reached her, the encounter had mutated into a farcical, carnal romp, bearing no resemblance to reality beyond that of a plotless adult film. It had been whispered in her ear by none other than Mae, who embellished the fib-filled fable with a slightly stretched tidbit of truth, a gripping, over-the-top rendition of Andy murdering

Nazi skinheads while trying to rescue her kidnapped child. It was that part of the tale that gave Trisha pause.

But still, she wasn't going to back down. "You know, all I have to do is make a couple of phone calls."

"God, I wish somebody would," Andy muttered loudly enough to be heard. She was completely unmoved by the threat, which ushered in another stretch of dense silence, punctuated by the screeching of worn rubber blades dragging across the windshield.

The unspoken détente lasted into town, severed now by the loud banging of empty rail cars being moved from the nearby yard and the incessant ringing of the crossing gate that kept Andy from her hotel, which stood a short two blocks away.

Andy didn't care. She was more than content with the option of standing outside waiting for the train to pass and letting Trisha continue on her way without her.

Her hand moved toward the door handle—

"You know, I got my prom dress from there," Trisha said, breaking the moment and staying Andy's hand.

Andy looked over. "Where?"

"Right there." Trisha pointed to an empty storefront with a pair of bare mannequins behind glass, dust-frosted with age. A "For Lease" sign hung crooked on the doors, with the name of a recently deceased realtor faded to the point where there was no hope of making it out. "They had some of the most beautiful dresses there. Now you gotta go to a mall an hour away to get something made in Thailand."

Andy looked on at the storefront, then at Trisha, who was lost in a moment of nostalgia.

"I always kinda wanted to buy that store, you know?" Trisha added.

Andy didn't, but she appreciated the dream. And it was then she began to see Trisha in a different light. Suddenly Trisha Campbell was no longer this imposing, long-legged beauty queen who could pound Andy into hamburger. She was a woman with her own failed plans, and a girl whose fantasies were dispatched by the oscillating waves of life. "By the way you rode that horse at the rodeo, I would've thought you'd be a forever cowgirl."

"Life is more than only opening one door," Trisha said, her eyes moving away from the vacant store that perfectly embodied a dream now just as abandoned.

"Well, if it makes you feel any better, my prom was spent in the back of a 1964 Impala," Andy threw out without much thought.

Trisha looked at her with a crooked smile.

"Never could explain to my parents why I didn't have one of those stupid prom pictures," Andy followed up, delivering the anecdote with a shrug.

By now the empty freight had passed. The crossing gates lifted, and Trisha continued down the two blocks and stopped in front of the hotel.

"I really appreciate the ride, thank you," Andy said, her hand now grabbing the door handle.

Trisha looked at her for a good, long moment. A moment that unnerved Andy, prompting a part of her to expect a knuckled fist to embed itself in the bridge of her nose. Trisha glanced at Michael, whose head had flopped over in a different direction, the sudden silence beginning to awaken him. She looked back at Andy, who was trying to avoid the anguish of looking at a child who was not hers. Trisha had little to offer another mother in pain, but after reaching down deep, she did have something to give. "Hold on," she said, reaching over to the glove box and pulling out an old pen and an even older envelope. She quickly scratched out something on the back. "Just so you know, this little town has eyes and ears everywhere. Even in faraway diners."

Andy's eyes closed as she shook her head with a slightly facetious grin. *It was that little blonde behind the counter. She probably radioed in before I even left the fucking parking lot.*

"Are you all like a cult or something around here?" Andy sighed.

Trisha bobbed her head with amusement as she handed Andy the envelope. "Yeah, something like that."

Andy looked at the name written on it, along with a 213 phone number. "Who's Max Durst?"

"Someone I also spent some time with in the back seat of a Chevy," Trisha answered. "He lives in some very dark corners of LA now, or at least he did the last time I talked to him. I know you're looking for your son. Could be as good a place as any to start."

Andy stared at the envelope, her eyes welling enough to burn. She then folded the envelope, opened the door, and climbed out, her mind weighing the paper totem that now gave her fresh direction and purpose. And she'd be on it—just as soon as she could extricate herself from this little town she was trapped in.

The moment Andy closed the door, Trisha pulled away and sped off, journeying toward the rest of her own life.

Trisha drove on, crossing through the intersection toward home just as the traffic light ticked to red. The late October afternoon gave way to what remained of daylight, darkened even further by the storm clouds that continued to dump lashes of rain and sleet from above. Her eyes glanced in the rearview mirror to take a last look at the only threat to her marriage she had ever known. And that threat was now absent from sight and no doubt disappearing into the hotel it had called home for what felt like a lifetime.

With Trisha's eyes back on the road, she leaned her head into the headrest, settling into the only immediate comfort she could find. It was on afternoons like this that her mind usually wandered through the upcoming chill of a Halloween evening, Thanksgiving next month, and just how far behind she was on Christmas shopping and how many times she would have to get after Kevin to get the tree stood up.

Instead, she replayed the last few surreal minutes in her mind.

The woman from the NTSB was not what she expected. She was certainly beautiful, and Trisha better understood the hormones she stimulated within the lonely men of Granite Point, and what could be distilling the emotions inside her husband. But there was something else Trisha saw. A look in the woman's eyes when she glanced at the child in the back seat. It wasn't so much longing as it was subtle pain that did not need to be spoken, but it was there nonetheless. This woman was not the murdering snake, reminiscent of the creature in the Garden of Eden, Mae made her out to be. She could even be a friend if enough time allowed, or at least an unbeknownst ally at a time she would most need it.

But still, the sooner the woman got out of town, the better.

Trisha pulled into the driveway and shut off the motor, introducing a sudden silence into the SUV accented by the pattering of droplets of rain hitting the roof. Michael again stirred, this time with a slight whine, as he was no longer lulled by the brown road noise. A whine that would soon turn into a struggle to get out of his car seat while kicking the seat in front of him.

With a sigh, Trisha unbuckled herself, giving a final thought to what she may have just started by giving out Max's number. She wondered if she would ever hear what would come of it, and if the woman from the NTSB would ever find her child. But for now, Michael had moved on quickly to twisting out of his straps, only to be stilled by his mother, who unleashed him from the tyranny of his car seat and carried him inside to his warm house in her arms.

38

I f getting reamed and steamed by Andy communicated anything
to Hollis, it was that she wasn't on board with the theory that
someone intentionally derailed the *Allegheny Limited*. He was
running out of time to prove any culpability on Frank's part, and
his opportunity to crucify him began to close quickly.

Even though it would gall him to admit it, Andy could simply
be right. The act of rail sabotage was easy to imagine but relatively
hard to pull off. It wasn't as easy as laying a penny on the tracks,
but still, Frank would know how to do it. Anyone in the industry
who understood essential physics could figure it out. That took
care of means and opportunity. For motivation, Frank had tons
of it. Hollis knew this right down to his bones.

The last thing he wanted was for Andy and the NTSB to deter-
mine it was some sort of act of God that dispatched the *Limited* to
its demise and for Frank to walk off a free man. The mere thought

of that made Hollis ache to punch a hole through a concrete wall, so waiting for evidence to fall into place was an option now off the table. The only weapon Hollis had left was to squeeze Frank until he popped. And that seemed easy enough to do.

When Frank was released from the hospital for his insane act of bravery, Hollis began shadowing him. It was a piece of cake until Frank was bequeathed that ratty Dodge shitcan by Puck—it was just sound enough to keep Hollis from pulling Frank over for endangering public safety. Even the license plate registration stickers were current. Now Hollis had to tail Frank by a few car lengths. Thank God it was a small town.

Evening had fallen when Hollis tailed Frank into the parking lot of the M&M. Frank was grateful to have wheels and get out of the house, away from the never-ending conflict raging between his ears. Now, he simply hoped to step inside and not get a bullet from Mitch.

Fortunately, the M&M was crowded enough to keep Mitch from spotting Frank slinking in behind a bunch of rowdies and maneuvering his way to a spot at the bar where he settled humbly onto a stool. He then looked up to find Mitch staring directly at him from across the counter.

"Nice face," Mitch said, giving Frank's the once over. He knew what Frank had done saving Olivia Hobbs, so he couldn't, in good conscience, throw Frank out on his ass.

"I'll pay for the jersey," Frank said sheepishly.

"Yeah, no shit you will."

Mitch studied him for a couple of beats, then shook his head and pulled out a glass, which gave Frank a moment to manage a smile. As Mitch poured water into Frank's tumbler, the moment of levity disappeared as Hollis strode through the door.

An instant gloom fell everywhere while Hollis zeroed in on Frank.

"Aw, shit," Mitch said, not caring if Hollis heard him or not. "There goes the neighborhood."

Frank turned, and his stomach flipped the moment he saw Hollis' pocked face.

Hollis looked at Mitch flatly, then sidled up to the bar next to Frank. "Your permits doing okay there, Mitch? Looks like that one over there's a little expired."

Mitch simply stared at him. He was one of the rare souls who wasn't intimidated by Hollis.

"What, no witty comeback?" Hollis snarked. "Beer."

"Aren't you on duty?" Mitch asked dryly.

Hollis glared at him.

Nonplussed, Mitch pulled out a beer bottle, thumped it in front of Hollis, and walked off without even opening it for him.

Hollis watched him go, then took off his hat, opened the bottle, and turned to Frank. "So how ya doin', Frankie?"

Frank just hovered over his glass.

"Jesus, you look like you've been hit by a train," Hollis commented, the only one in the place who appreciated the humor. He took a belt from the bottle and recoiled. "Aw, Christ," he snapped at Mitch, "what the hell's this?"

"Beer."

"It's dog piss."

"Call a food critic," Mitch sneered and walked off before he hissed, "Asshole."

"You see?" Hollis nudged Frank. "Total lack of respect."

"What do you want?" Frank asked, barely above a whisper.

"Relax, Frank. I just need your help, that's all."

"With what?"

"I've been thinking of changing jobs."

"And a chorus of angels sang 'hallelujah,'" Mitch said out loud, still close enough to catch the conversation.

Hollis ignored that as Frank, forgetting what Mitch had poured him, took a big pull and nearly sprayed it out. He fired a look at Mitch, who only returned a quick glance.

"I've been thinking of going back into railroading," Hollis continued. "You know, maybe start up as a driver again. Maybe get into one of those big yellow fuckers your kid drives." He next pulled out Frank's crumpled train schedule from a pocket. "But it's been a while since I've read one of these stupid things, and I was thinking you could help."

Hollis shoved the schedule in front of Frank, who ignored it.

"Like this one here," Hollis tapped the paper. "That sure was one shitty night, wasn't it? Let's see . . . okay, here's one. Clark one-forty-six. I think that's supposed to be the train number, right?"

Nothing. All Frank could think about was hammering Hollis' cranium in with his unwanted water glass.

Hollis read on. "What's this here? Would you say that's the departure time?" He nudged Frank again. "Jump in here anytime, Frank. I want to make sure I'm gettin' this right. Now this says 23:15 . . . fifteen after eleven. Yeah, that's right. Okay, I'm getting the hang of this now. It's coming back."

Frank's eyes moved to Mitch, who looked back at Frank, mulling where this would all lead in the end.

"Come on, this is fun," Hollis playfully said and bopped Frank on the shoulder. "What's this one? It looks like another freight run. Nineteen-sixty-one at 21:38 out of Frederick?"

Frank fumed.

"Huh, you know, now I'm all confused." He crumpled the schedule into a tight ball, its usefulness as a harassment baton having been spent. "Fuck it. I think I'll just stay a cop." He then leaned in on Frank. "Why did Preston pull you over two miles from Prowler Flat?"

Frank's brain froze, and his heart would've stopped right there if it could. He quickly looked at Mitch and around the room as others reacted to Hollis' words. This was something they didn't know about.

"You think saving Olivia Hobbs is going to save your sorry ass? Nope. See, you might be some kinda hero now, but there's blood on you. I can smell it. It's in your eyes. And when I prove it and Beau Harper opens his mouth to-to st-st-stutter it out, I'm gonna drive a freight train straight up your ass."

He shoved the schedule into Frank's water, patted him on the back, grabbed his hat, and tossed a quarter onto the bar. "Thanks for the piss," he said to Mitch before he turned for the door.

Frank's venom crested.

"Don't do it, Frank," Mitch discreetly warned.

One could almost hear Frank's restraint break in two. *Oh yeah, I'm gonna do it.*

"You want to know why it was so easy to steal her from you?" Frank called out, which sent the bar into dead silence.

Hollis stopped short of the door.

"Because you made it easy, you dumb son-of-a-bitch," Frank barked out in a sudden state of fearlessness. He no longer cared what happened to him. Since he knew he was going down, he might as well dish out the vengeance he'd wanted to unleash for decades. Frank moved off his stool and met Hollis in the middle of the bar. "All you had to be was the idiot you are. That was it."

Anger steamed within Hollis; his hand moved to his holster and unclipped the strap, sending the patrons clear.

"And I really didn't steal her. Getting rid of you was a fucking mercy killing for her. And she thanked me every single living day—and night—for it."

The two men were now toe-to-toe.

"Right up to the day she died," Frank said with a twist of the dagger, "you have no idea how much she fucking hated you."

Hollis glared through Frank and began to slide his gun out of its holster.

Frank saw it and placed a finger on the center of his forehead. "Put it right there. You don't even have to count. Not that you could anyway. Do it."

Hollis' instincts ached. It was like dying to scratch an itch.

"DO IT, YOU STUPID FUCK!" Frank screamed.

Hollis envisioned Frank's head exploding like a melon, his brains splattering onto everything and everyone in sight. Mitch's shithole would be painted blood red, and justice would be immediately served. But his eyes moved around the room. He counted off the witnesses who would all testify to the lack of due process he was aching to unleash. He wasn't the most intelligent man. He knew that. But he wasn't a fool, either. Hollis slid his gun back into its holster and then slapped Frank hard on the shoulder with a smile. "Don't worry, Frank. You're not getting off *that* easy." He then returned his hat to his head and headed out the door.

Frank looked on. The door slammed behind Hollis, leaving Frank a loser once again in another battle he had no chance of winning.

39

Next on Hollis' squeezing campaign was Kevin. Unfortunately, there was no sign of Kevin or his pickup when Hollis pulled up to his house. Hollis thought it through, debating staying in wait (Plan A) or lurking outside in the dark (Plan B).

Of course, there was Plan C: knocking on the door, which he promptly did.

After about a minute of listening to the crickets outside, he knocked again and noticed the button for the doorbell. It glowed just like his own had for as long as he could remember, with the same sickly, dull light. He pressed it and the flat, out-of-tune chime rang inside the Campbell home.

This time he heard footsteps on the other side. Then quiet.

"Open the door, Mrs. Campbell," Hollis said.

Trisha opened it a moment later and leaned against the door jamb, a screen door the only layer of protection between them.

The mere presence of Hollis on her porch made her want to grab Kevin's 30-gauge and blast him into the street.

"Ma'am," Hollis said, having at least the manners to take off his hat. "May I come in?"

"Not unless you've got a warrant," Trisha snapped. Much like Mitch, she wasn't intimidated by this grotesque caricature of law and order.

"I don't need one for this. Your husband home?"

"Not yet."

Hollis placed his hand on the latch. "May I?"

It was in that long moment Trisha reached her fill. Dealing with her father-in-law was bad enough, but now having this menacing idiot on her front porch was the last straw. And while Hollis did not scare her, it didn't mean he wouldn't scare her children to death. He was *not* coming into the house.

"Mrs. Campbell?" Hollis' voice took on a dark, authoritative tone.

Trisha stood defiant, but only for a moment, just long enough to imagine Hollis punching through the screen and pulling the door from its hinges. She knew he was capable of it. She unlatched the lock and opened it, allowing West Virginia's local representative from Hell to step over her threshold.

Hollis looked around the modestly decorated living room and found Michael playing with blocks. He crouched down next to him, enough to give Trisha the creeps, while Shiloh looked on from her homework at the kitchen table. "Cute kid," he said, offering a rare honest opinion.

Trisha watched with the enthusiasm of witnessing a dog peeing on her rug.

"Guess you're gonna have to be careful with him, huh?" Hollis asked as he stood up. "I mean with the family history and everything."

"What are you talking about?" Trisha answered with annoyance.

"Well, drinking. Boozing. You know, the Campbell legacy. Shit, the whole town's aware of it. Goes back a long time. Probably started back when the Campbells gave old Willy Wallace the shaft back in Scotland."

Trisha simply exhaled as she crossed her arms and cocked a hip to the side. "And aren't you the hypocrite?" she shot back.

"Come again?"

"You can see it right there in your bloodshot eyes, the nicotine stains on your fingers from the hours spent whining about another one of life's kicks to the head. 'Vodka straight, please. I gotta go kick the crap out of some poor son-of-a-bitch who reminds me of me.' If the irony was any thicker, you'd choke to death on it."

"Sonofabitch!" Michael parroted with glee.

Trisha rolled her eyes. *Great, now I'm doing it.*

"Your husband must find you endlessly charming," Hollis commented.

"He used to."

Hollis was about to respond when Michael spotted Kevin standing in the doorway.

"Daddy!" Michael chirped and sprang to his feet. He dropped the blocks in his hands and latched on to Kevin's leg.

Kevin patted his son on the head and detached him with distraction. The presence of Hollis in his home near his family, especially his son, made him want to find that same shotgun Trisha was still considering retrieving. Or, at least, grab the softball bat that leaned near the front door.

Meanwhile, Michael pointed. "Blocks!"

"Yeah, I see that, bud," Kevin answered as he looked at Trisha. "What's going on?"

"Oh, nothing much," Trisha answered pensively. "The sheriff's just here being offensive."

Kevin looked at Hollis, trying to quickly measure what conniving crap the man was after. "What do you want?" he finally asked.

"A beer," Hollis innocently replied.

Kevin stood for a moment, fantasizing about giving Hollis his beer by throwing the can at his fat head. But a higher state of intelligence prevailed, and he walked toward the kitchen.

Hollis followed Kevin and glanced at Shiloh, who was now fully unfocused from her homework. "Hi," he said with a smug grin.

Shiloh soured at the sight of him. She quickly corralled her homework and slipped out.

Kevin pulled the oldest and warmest beer he could find from the fridge and handed it over. "Anything else?"

"Yeah. I thought we could, you know, chat," Hollis replied before he popped the beer open.

"About?" Kevin responded with marked annoyance.

"Well, how's about the *Allegheny Limited*? What's your take? You think it was an accident?"

Kevin stared at him and did the math. Hollis wasn't exactly transparent, but remembering what Puck had told him, and Hollis' comment after putting two bullets into the brain of the suffering buck, Kevin knew what Hollis was doing. Kevin also knew he was on strategically dangerous ground. "Why wouldn't I?"

"I don't know. Why wouldn't you?" Hollis countered with a degree of playfulness and then waited for an answer, pressing Kevin without words.

Kevin waited a breath while Trisha leaned against the kitchen doorway. "I'm not really qualified to know."

"Sure you are," Hollis tossed back with encouragement. "Probably more than any of us."

Trisha looked at Kevin, honestly wondering how he would handle being pushed by Hollis. And he didn't disappoint—Kevin wasn't taking the bait.

Hollis didn't wait for an answer. "You know, I had the most wonderful conversation with your old man tonight. Sure seems to be taking Tom's death pretty hard. Sorta reminded me of when he took out those strings of mailboxes when your mom died."

Kevin still wasn't biting.

Hollis upped the pressure and reached into his coat pocket to pull out a folded-up arrest report, along with his keys and wallet by mistake. Both fell, hitting the floor.

Trisha stealthily smirked.

Annoyed, Hollis quickly grabbed both from the floor and dropped them on the table. He didn't need to look this clumsy when he was doing so well and having this much fun. He opened the report and read out loud: "Cited, 1983, for drunk driving—this is your old man, by the way, not you—cited again in 1984 for the same thing. Let's see . . . oh, here's one: arrested in '92 for DUI and reckless driving. That must have been a hoot for the insurance company."

"You don't have any friends, do you?" Trisha asked.

Hollis ignored her and kept reading. "Here's my favorite: suspended for a week for operating under the influence. Didn't you bail him out of that one?"

To Kevin's credit, he remained mum, but Hollis could sense his brewing annoyance. Kevin wanted Hollis out of his house, but Hollis wasn't going anywhere. He could move in, and there wouldn't be a goddamn thing Kevin could do about it.

"You know," Hollis said, turning it up another notch. "I don't think Frank has the ability to make a good decision if his life depended on it."

Trisha again looked at her husband, now growing worried about what he would do. She then spotted Michael slipping into the room and snarfing Hollis' wallet off the table. With that, she remained gleefully silent.

Kevin glared at Hollis with obvious irritation. "And you're here telling me this because?"

"Because nine people are dead, Kev. Forty or so injured. Limbs cut off, kids orphaned. It'd be terrible if someone had caused it, wouldn't you agree?"

Kevin still wasn't biting, not even a growl.

Hollis was now impatient. This wasn't working. Frank's son was far more refined, controlled than he had expected—traits he no doubt got from his mother. He was frustrated with himself for underestimating Kevin. This game had moved on to being pointless, and so was his need to be here. Hollis stuffed the report into his pocket and went for his keys, which he found immediately, and his wallet, which had sprouted toddler legs and disappeared. "Where's my wallet?"

Kevin's eyes went to the table and then the floor while Trisha watched all this unfold with glee.

Hollis' eyes darted around.

The floor.

Kevin's hands.

Did Shiloh, the little snot, swipe it? Wait, there! On the floor to the hallway! His American Express card. "That's mine!" He looked ahead and followed a trail that led off into the bathroom, where he found Michael actively dumping the rest of the contents into the toilet. "AHHH! WHAT ARE YOU DOING!?"

Michael jumped about two feet, the wallet bobbling in his hands.

"GIMME THAT!!!" Hollis howled as he snatched the wallet from the boy's nefarious mitts.

Michael's face crumpled as Trisha shouldered her way in to rescue him, her laughter threatening to erupt for all to see.

Hollis quickly fished through the toilet bowl. "Goddammit!" He then caught Kevin smirking at him with contentment. "Yeah, laugh now, smart ass. I know your old man wrecked the *Limited*."

Kevin's smirk faded.

"And you know it, too. As soon as I can prove it, I'm going to wire him straight to hell. And maybe use you as the envelope."

"Get the fuck out of my house," Kevin ordered.

Hollis shoved his toilet-soaked cards back into the billfold and stormed toward the door, brushing hard against Kevin on the way out. Once on the porch, he spotted the Ford through the open doors of the garage.

"Nice ride. Maybe you can sell it to get you and your pop a good lawyer, huh?"

Kevin slammed the door on him and turned off the porch light.

And with that, a little joy returned to Hollis. He grinned, remembering again why he sometimes just loved his job. He turned and stopped. Right there, in plain view on the workbench, sat Beau's camcorder. With a quick look about, he walked into the garage and pulled the camcorder—or what was left of it—off the bench. He immediately spotted Beau's label. "And here I was thinking you're smarter than your dad." Hollis looked over his shoulder and quietly left with it.

Once Hollis hopped into his cruiser and drove off, Kevin turned the porch light back on and emerged from the front door. Adrenaline still coursed through him as he watched Hollis' taillights disappear down the road. He then closed his eyes and throttled himself down. He walked to the garage and stared at the V8 under the hood. He thought about working on it, but given his state of mind, he would likely beat the valve covers into unrecognizable scrap metal. He turned to go back inside and found Frank standing before him. Kevin jumped back a step. "Jesus Christ!"

"You workin' tomorrow?" Frank asked. No "*Hello*" or a "*How are you doing,*" or even a "*What the hell did Hollis want?*"

Kevin quickly caught his breath, and then wondered how long Frank had been lurking in the shadows, waiting for Hollis to hop into his cruiser and drive off. "Why?"

"Kevin, just answer the question," Frank said with impatience. "Are you working tomorrow or not?"

Kevin studied his father. "I have a four-unit mix to Pitt at sixteen-ten," he answered. And then became suspicious. "Now tell me why."

Frank considered confessing right then and there, just to get it over with. But Trisha's footsteps coming out of the house made him turn and exit past her as she walked to the garage. He didn't even look at her. He beelined into the shadows and was gone just as quickly as he'd appeared.

"What'd he want?" Trisha asked as she watched Frank silently pass her.

"I have absolutely no idea," Kevin answered. But he had a suspicion, and his father probably didn't want to make a confession in front of a daughter-in-law who despised him.

"I think you and I need to talk," Trisha said as she leaned against a fender.

A whole new knot instantly formed in Kevin's stomach. "I can't wait," he said, already knowing where this was heading.

"I'm taking the kids to my sister's tomorrow," Trisha said, wasting no time to rip the bandage off. Again, Hollis' visit to their home was the final straw. It was now about protecting her children from the horrors of what was happening to their father—and his.

Kevin shook his head. "Perfect."

"I need to get the kids out of here. You need to deal with your dad, and I don't want it happening in front of them. And Shiloh's already seen more than enough for a lifetime."

All Kevin could do was laugh.

"What?" Trisha asked, surprised by the response she was getting from a man she'd been with for more than half her life.

"Your timing is perfect, Trish. This is just what I need, with guys hitting unemployment, their pensions disappearing like the fucking rain forest, nine dead in a train wreck, and my dad losing what little sanity he has left. And now you're going to Ohio, leaving me alone with all of it. Awesome."

"This isn't my doing, Kevin," Trisha answered defensively. "And the issues with your father are far more yours than anyone else's."

And that hit Kevin right between the eyes. "How is any of this my fault?" he asked sharply with a tone more suited to a complaint.

"Because you allowed this to happen," Trisha pushed back. "You allowed him to treat you this way for far longer than you should have. And I don't care about the doorbells you didn't push or the misguided obligations you feel you have for him, or the fishing trips or campfires or the baseballs you never caught from him. You've been his fucking doormat for decades, and I warned you what would happen if you didn't stand up and change it."

"Why are you putting me through this? I can't change who he is, and I can't abandon him either!"

Trisha hit a blank. She didn't understand his predicament in any sense whatsoever. "Who's telling you to abandon him? And if I had, so what? What has he done to command this much loyalty from you?"

Kevin snapped with a rage he no longer had the energy to contain. "Because he's my father, alright?! That's why! I have a responsibility to him! Just like I have a responsibility to just about everyone else in this fucking town! As his son, I have a responsibility to be there and take care of him! No matter what!"

"That's fucking insane, Kevin! Do you ever listen to yourself?! Your responsibility is to this family! This one, right here in front of you!"

Kevin pivoted, not wanting to hear anything more.

"He treats you like shit, and you keep going back for more! Why?! Just tell me why?"

No answer. Kevin retreated.

Fury stirred within Trisha. She was now determined to drag this out of him, even if she had to use a jackhammer to do it. She punched him in the shoulder. "Tell me why?!"

Kevin finally snapped. "Because he blames me, alright?! As far as he's concerned, I killed her! And he's right! I could've stopped all this, but I didn't!"

And there it was. All of it out in the open. He leaned against the car, head drooped in the embarrassment of admission.

"You have no idea," Kevin continued in a quieter voice, "what it's like to live in a constant state of being disdained as much as he disdains me. Being in a room with someone who can't even stand you being there! You have no idea what it's like to be dismissed as nothing more than a disappointment."

Trisha waited for the emotion to pass, giving her husband a pause to collect himself. "You were eight," she said calmly. "You were in a place your mother never should have put you in. But you're the one who has to believe that. I can't do it for you."

Kevin glanced at her and then went back to looking at his feet and the dirt on the floor that he should have cleaned up three years ago.

"If you're looking for approval from your father, you're never going to get it," Trisha added. "Not from him. He's incapable of it. And until you realize that, you're never going to be free. And neither will we." She then grabbed a handful of his jaw to look into his eyes. "Let it go. Let it go, Kev, or all of what we have will end."

And with a hand softly on his shoulder, she left him with that. Trisha headed back into the house, leaving her husband alone in the garage in the dropping temperature of the evening.

Kevin closed his eyes and shook his head. In complete frustration, he slammed the hood of the Ford shut, which revealed the empty workbench. It took him a moment to realize the camcorder was missing.

"Shit," he said in a whisper.

40

Kevin loaded up his truck in the season's first morning freeze. A thin ice sheet coated everything under a clear, early sky. Even though he was heading westbound later that day, the union had pulled him in early to scour Atlantic's employee records to find anyone who could be picked up on the cheap. Once the loading was done and his hands ached from the cold, Kevin looked back at the house as Trisha watched from the porch, Michael in her arms. He walked toward her. "How long will you be gone?" he asked, hoping she had spent the night changing her mind.

"For as long as it takes," she answered, giving Kevin no hope of a change of heart.

He climbed the porch, ice crunching beneath his boots, and gently kissed her forehead. He then returned to his truck and drove off, his eyes painfully watering.

Trisha wasn't faring any better. She was now second-guessing herself but plowed ahead anyway with stiff resolve. Staying was just ensuring nothing would change. She was done waiting. It was now up to her to control what she could. Once inside, she collected what she needed and then called toward the ceiling. "Shiloh? Let's go!"

There was no reply. In fact, there wasn't a sound coming from upstairs whatsoever.

"Shiloh?"

Still nothing.

Trisha lowered Michael to his feet and headed upstairs. She then opened the door to Shiloh's room. Her eyes took quick inventory of the teenage mess: the disheveled bed; grunge posters peeling from the wall; a pair of distressed jeans forgotten on the floor, her yellow Walkman sitting on top; and—absent from the bedpost where it always hung—her father's borrowed ball cap . . .

. . . but no Shiloh. Trisha closed the door quickly. She knew exactly where to look.

Andy pulled open the door to the sheriff's station and was nearly run over as a drove of deputies hurried behind Hollis down the hall. When Hollis turned to spot Andy, he held up Beau's camcorder like he'd just won a prize at the county fair.

"We've got it!" he championed.

Andy eyed the battered chassis in his hands.

Hollis pushed through his crew and handed her the demolished camcorder, label side up. Before Andy could even give it a cursory look, he snatched it back and led the way into the AV room. Hollis then placed the camcorder with a flourish in front of Fletcher—a deputy hired decades before Hollis and way overdue for retirement. With his patrol days long behind him, Fletcher possessed a talent for electronics and anything with cables. However, he had very little idea of what to do with something like this.

"Fix it," Hollis ordered.

Fletcher looked at him. "This piece of shit? I'd have better luck turning it into a dancing poodle."

Hollis glared at him.

Fletcher plopped onto a rolling stool and plugged the trashed device into a power strip. "It's in pretty bad shape. LCD's shot, lens is busted. Might be able to get the tape out, though."

"Where'd you find it?" Andy asked with suspicion.

"Kevin Campbell's house," Hollis proudly proclaimed as if this proved something. "The dumbass had it sitting right there in his garage on a workbench."

"And you just took it?"

"Don't even go there," Hollis shot back before Andy could get started.

Andy took a long moment to register all of this. Once she did, her mood immediately soured. *Kevin lied to me.*

Fletcher pulled a screwdriver from a toolbox and pried the tape door until it cracked open. "That worked!" he said with almost childlike excitement before pulling the cartridge out along with a stringy mess of tape.

Hollis rolled his eyes. He'd gotten this far only to be tripped up by a tangle of black plastic film. "Can you fix it?" he huffed with exasperation.

"I can fix anything," Fletcher answered with a bit of fabricated confidence. He then rolled over to a tape splicer.

"This isn't going to tell us anything we don't already know," Andy commented.

"What the fuck is that supposed to mean?" Hollis flashed her an angry look, annoyed by her lack of faith.

"Something's still missing."

"Yeah, my patience," Hollis snapped. He then turned to Fletcher. "Get to work."

41

Frank gimped through the beehive of activity at a buzzing rail yard that stretched as far as the eye could see. Workers scurried by on ATVs and pickup trucks around the long string of freight cars coupled to Kevin's four Dash-9 locomotives in the long shadows of afternoon daylight.

In the cab of the lead locomotive, Kevin waited with dread for his father's arrival as Gibson walked up with the manifest.

"A mixed bag today," Gibson said, handing the document over.

Kevin just tossed it onto the console, not even remotely interested.

"Man, who bleached your orange juice this morning?" Gibson asked.

Kevin just looked at him as Frank entered the cab, which was the answer to Gibson's question.

"Never mind," Gibson quipped.

"Christ, this thing's a goddamn RV," Frank exclaimed, marveling as he looked about the cab. His life had been spent in mid-century locomotives that paid little heed to engineer comfort. It was all about utility and to hell with the hapless employees operating it. They were lucky to get heat and a seat cushion.

"Yeah, and we've got a lap pool in the back," Gibson added for humor's sake. "I'll go see if the water's warm yet." He then was out the door, leaving Kevin alone with his father.

Kevin said nothing as he handed an extra headset to Frank, who quickly picked up on his son's foul mood and the reason behind it. The night before, he'd stood in the shadows, watching Trisha walk back to the house, and then heard the decisive slamming of the Ford's hood. Yes, he'd heard all of it. Every single word. And as much as he hated that harpy—this time she was right. He adjusted his headset and sat in the conductor's seat, and for once wisely kept his big mouth shut. His long-rehearsed confession would have to wait.

With the length of freight cars hooked up and their air hoses twisted together, workers ran up and down along the train, each giving a thumbs up. Gibson climbed up on the second unit and gave Kevin his own thumbs up.

Kevin slipped on his headset and looked ahead. The signals before him ran from red to green. He then throttled up.

In a laborious roar, the prime movers of the four locomotives stretched out the consist behind it. The wheels spun, screaming on the iron. Sand automatically belched out as the wheels grabbed, and the train snaked toward the open track. Once on the mainline, the train gained momentum.

Kevin pushed the throttle more, taking it up the notches. He opened the window and leaned out to let the wind press against his face. This was what he loved most about railroading.

To Frank, this was what it was all about. Ahead of him stretched the open track for miles, winding through the graceful curves of the West Virginia countryside. This was also, unbelievably, the first time he had ever ridden with Kevin. The sight of his son at the console, sheer power at his fingertips, shed a whole new light upon the boy—man—he'd raised. Kevin looked different—no longer the pathetic failure Frank considered him to be. That person vanished, and in his place, Frank saw someone he could admire. The more Frank looked on at Kevin, the greater his sense of awe became. It was undeniable: his son had grown into a fully self-sufficient adult, regardless of how absent, questionable, and utterly disagreeable Frank knew he had been over the decades.

Kevin looked over at his father, feeling the weight of his gaze, then followed up with a setting of the throttle and a quick run-through of the gauges. He thought for a moment, knowing what he was about to do wasn't allowed . . . if he were to be caught. "You want it?" he asked of Frank.

Frank immediately shook his head. He knew the rules, and doing something like this would certainly get his son fired.

But he was also dying for it.

"Yeah, come on," Kevin said, assuring Frank it was okay. It was just them and the wind, and no one around would know the difference. He lifted himself from the seat and waited for Frank to take it.

Frank looked at the empty seat. It was there for the taking. A moment later, he did just that. And damn, if it didn't fit him like a glove.

Kevin pointed out the levers. "Throttle, engine brake."

Frank nodded and scanned the console. He then looked ahead while the rails glided by. He felt the throttle handle in his hand, very much knowing how comfortable it was.

"And it's a sixty-five zone," Kevin motioned ahead.

A huge grin crept across Frank's lined face. He nudged the throttle forward another notch, drawing a roar from the thousands of horsepower behind him. Frank swelled inside. He smiled even more as a bunch of kids on their bikes appeared short of the roadbed on a gentle curve up ahead, pumping their arms in the air. Frank looked at Kevin: *Should I?*

Kevin smirked. "Blast 'em."

Frank gave it to them. With the train thundering into the turn, Frank leaned on the horn, carpeting the auditory cells of those kids with happy decibels of hearing damage. They loved every second of it.

Frank kept smiling. With the train weaving through the brilliant autumn colors of the Alleghenies, Kevin was able to witness a picture-perfect postcard moment of his father having one more time in the sun.

In the cooling night air of one of Pittsburgh's many freight yards, Kevin and Frank walked from a roach coach dietary nightmare to a crust-covered picnic table, hot dogs and Cokes in hand. They settled in as the string of freight cars they'd hauled was pulled apart behind them.

Kevin waited a few bites before speaking. "Hollis came by the house yesterday."

Frank stopped mid-chew, suddenly no longer hungry. Kevin was going right for the gut punch, which was fine. Frank just wasn't ready for a confessional at that very moment.

"He says you killed Elvis."

Frank scoffed. His son could be funny every now and then.

"He also thinks you derailed the *Limited*."

Frank swallowed and stayed quiet. He was suddenly having trouble articulating failure on his part to a son he'd dismissed the moment he was born.

"Last night when you asked me if I was working today," Kevin nudged. "Something you wanted to talk about?"

Frank held his silence, then finally released the only words he could muster. "I might need your help."

"With?"

Frank didn't know how to move this along. He got up and tossed the rest of his dinner into the garbage. Instead of a hot dog, he was suddenly choking on pride and not sure he should admit to something he was not sure he'd even done.

"What's going on, Dad?" Kevin pressed.

"Nothing," Frank answered, changing his mind and walking off. "I'll figure out how to deal with it."

"Deal with what?" Kevin asked, close on his father's heels.

"Nothing."

"Dad?" Kevin said as he grabbed his father's arm.

Frank immediately yanked it back out of sheer annoyance that his son would even have the audacity to touch him. He immediately moved off for breathing room. Frank loitered as his son watched him and then eventually sat, looking at his bandaged hand that even then was still throbbing.

Kevin decided to end this. If his father couldn't say it, Kevin would be the man to do it for him. "You really did do it, didn't you?"

"I don't know," Frank rasped out, his throat suddenly as dry as dirt.

"What do you mean 'you don't know'?"

Frank closed his eyes and ran his fingers through his thin hair. He didn't know and wasn't even close to being able to explain it.

Kevin began to pick up on it and was now thoroughly convinced that Frank Campbell had murdered nine people. He sagged to a seat far from his father while trying to find the man within himself to deal with this. He was suddenly no longer the child he had held on to for so long. He saw things as they were, not how he wished them to be. And now his father was no longer on any sort of parental pedestal—the pedestal Andy had so intuitively understood. Any lofty illusions of Frank he'd held were shattered, and at that very moment his extended adolescent age of innocence disintegrated. From that emerged a new identity. Beyond angry and confused, he wasn't exactly sure who this new person was—but he was here to stay.

"You don't need me, Dad," Kevin said. "You need a priest."

"Thanks, Kev," Frank answered with contempt. "Can you help me or not?"

Kevin sat shell-shocked. Even though the man within him had finally shown up, this was all still bigger than him. For a moment he was the little boy in the dead of night, standing before the dim doorbell button of a monster's home. But that was only for a moment. He pushed the feeling aside and accepted he could do nothing for the man. Frank was going down for this.

"Kevin?" Frank pressed, waiting for an answer. But he wasn't getting one. Kevin just sat there, staring into the dirt. Frank quickly realized he'd made a mistake. A grave one. Going to his son was a complete waste of time. Kevin was as useless as he'd always considered him to be. Here he was, in his greatest moment of need, and his meathead son's power to protect his father was nothing more than a hopeful fantasy. "Thanks, Kev," Frank spat with complete dismissiveness as he walked away. "You can go to hell now."

That snapped Kevin's stare. He glared at his father, who was again small in his eyes—a broken man no longer capable of hurting him. "What'd you just say?"

Frank stopped to glare at his son, who now, somehow, was no longer recognizable. He had become taller, if not outright imposing.

"You want my help, and then you tell me to go to hell? Are you fuckin' serious?"

Frank retreated a step as Kevin moved toward him.

"I was wrong. You don't need a priest; you need a goddamn exorcist."

Frank limped off. He had no interest in listening to this shit, especially coming from his son, who wasn't qualified to judge him.

"And where've you been when I've needed *your* fuckin' help, huh?" Kevin thundered at his father's heels.

Frank spun about. He wasn't going to bear witness to this load of bullshit again. It was time he pushed Kevin back down, beneath him where he belonged, and quelled this father-son mutiny. He was immediately in Kevin's grill. "Is that what you think? This is all about you?"

Kevin backstepped, suddenly feeling like a five-year-old again. And he hated it so much that he shoved him back into history where he belonged.

"I kept you fed, put a roof over your ungrateful little head, and never raised a hand to you," Frank snarled.

Kevin stopped retreating and towered over his old man. He had a good four inches on him, and there was nothing Frank could do about it. "Oh, yeah. You're the perfect father," Kevin shot back, closing the gap between them. "Can't do anything wrong, can you? Guess it never occurred to you that there might be something more to raising a son than throwing food at him?"

"Aw, I don't want to hear any of this psycho-babble horseshit. Grow up, Kevin. I was raised the same way and turned out just fine, thank you."

"Oh yeah, look at you. An old drunk staring down the barrel of poverty and a life sentence for murder. Mom would've been so proud—"

At the mention of Fay, Frank slugged his son. He had no idea where it came from, and it happened before he even realized it. The punch nearly tore Kevin's head off, getting him on the opposite side of where Trisha had taken her shot.

Kevin saw stars and a moment of black. That was it. Enraged, he instinctively returned fire. All the years of pent-up emotion, the feelings of parental inadequacy and being dismissed as an idiot, fueled his arm. He caught Frank with a powerful hook that lifted his father off his feet and twisted him into the dirt. Kevin then backed up, ready for a cage fight if it were to go that way.

Frank slowly rolled over and spat out blood as his head swam.

The rage was suddenly gone. Spent, Kevin lowered his guard and stared at his father, who was now a pathetic sight writhing on the ground. He could feel remorse rising, and he immediately banished it to the same place he'd sent the five-year-old. "You want my help, Dad? Thanks to you, I don't know how to give it."

Frank flopped onto the seat of his pants, his cheek and jaw swelling. His son should've been a boxer, he thought. "If this is your idea of help, I'm better off without it."

"You probably are," Kevin answered with a power he never knew he possessed. He then walked away, happy to leave this guy who happened to be his father behind.

Frank climbed to his feet and looked on as Kevin left him in the abandonment of a single floodlight.

42

Trisha arrived at the county hospital in record time after running three red lights, flinging into an illegal left turn, and ditching Preston, who had spun around to try to pull her over. Nothing was going to stand in the way of finding her daughter. With a relieved breath, she arrived in Beau's hospital room and found Shiloh curled up next to him, sound asleep. Just as she'd hopefully suspected.

Although Trisha was furious, she wasn't about to damn Shiloh for her empathy. She would've also given her a hard "no" if Shiloh had asked, which was likely why she'd snuck out. For now, Trisha softly placed a hand on Shiloh's shoulder to rouse her, doing what she could to keep her daughter from jumping through the ceiling.

Shiloh popped awake with a start, pivoting on the bed.

"Shhh . . . it's alright," Trisha whispered, trying to calm her daughter before she flew out the window.

"I'm sorry!" Shiloh panicked above a whisper. She had never been on the receiving end of her mother's wrath and wasn't looking to start.

"You should've told me you were coming here," Trisha said, gently pulling Shiloh away from Beau's bed.

They were soon standing in the far corner talking in low voices while Michael worked on climbing up on the bed.

"I heard what you said to Dad last night," Shiloh admitted, knowing that eavesdropping was something her mother couldn't stand. "I don't want to go to Ohio."

Trisha instantly felt like crap. Shiloh's words reminded her of just how much of a piss-poor job she'd done keeping her arguments with Kevin inaudible. It also hammered home the nagging reality that hauling her children away to her sister's did nothing to fix the actual problem. Trisha took a patient breath, then spotted Michael planted on Beau's bed . . . with Beau looking glassily on at him. She quickly tapped Shiloh to turn around.

However, Shiloh was too busy looking at Preston, who towered behind her mother, ready to haul her in for reckless driving.

It took little time for Fletcher to splice the tape back together and cobble it into something playable. He spooled it up into another camcorder and pressed PLAY. He looked up at the monitor on the bench as it flashed to life.

Hollis moved in behind him, eyes zeroed in on the monitor while Andy watched off to the side. As she'd expected, there wasn't much to see. Hollis had Fletcher fast-forward and rewind, passing over existing train-spotting footage until they finally arrived at the video recording of that one night.

Grainy, low-lit footage replayed on the monitor. It quickly frustrated Hollis. "Make that lighter!" he ordered, eyes squinting at the screen.

"Make what lighter?"

"All of that. You can't see shit."

"Yeah, well, this is as good as it's gonna get."

Hollis' mood fouled . . . until the dark silhouette of a man crossed onto the tracks. "Right there!" he pointed, instantly pivoting to excitement. "That's him!"

The dark silhouette stood amongst the tracks, a large crowbar in his hand. Andy moved in closer to watch that silhouette jam the bar into the trackage and pry upwards . . . until the bar slipped, slicing the man's hand open. The dark silhouette staggered and struggled with the crowbar, only to fling it away off camera, where it landed with a loud crash. The silhouette then floundered away with a limp.

Andy kept her reaction to herself, while Hollis couldn't hide his. He could recognize that limp anywhere. "Gotcha, you sonofabitch."

Shiloh was the first to react to Beau being awake. His eyes immediately went to hers, and, for a moment, he gazed upon an angel. Next to his mother, Shiloh was the perfect ambassador to consciousness he could ever have.

Beau then glanced around the room, his troubled mind trying to make sense of it all. He reeled as he saw Preston, his uniform an imposing presence that unnerved him. Beau immediately scanned the room for his mother—who was nowhere to be found.

"Hey, Beau," Shiloh said quietly with a soft smile, moving toward the bed.

Beau glanced at her briefly, then kept his focus on Preston. He was near a complete panic and immediately wanted his mother, who would protect him from everything and make sense of what didn't make sense at all.

Trisha quickly picked up on all of this. She saw the smile fall from Shiloh's face and watched as Beau recoiled from Preston.

"I think you're scaring him," Shiloh said.

Preston ignored her. He studied the boy, whose breathing intensified with each passing moment.

"I probably am," Preston said, his fingers resting on the foot of the bed frame. "How are you doin', Beau?"

Beau said nothing. His mind muddled down a track of thoughts and emotions . . . and landed upon that night when the train came off the rails. That horrible night when he couldn't run fast enough. The night he thought he would die. His eyes welled.

"I think you should go," Shiloh said, instinctively filling the protective void left by Dana. She moved in closer to stand between Preston and Beau and placed a hand on the bed.

Preston could tell by looking at the boy's eyes the memories of that night were in there. The trick was pulling them out of a kid who struggled mightily just to lace words together to complete even the simplest of sentences. "Beau, do you remember why you're here?"

Beau's eyes darted between Shiloh and Preston. He was a degree short of terror, his brain flooded with emotions and contradictions he had never experienced before. He wanted to run. He wanted to hide. He wanted someone to save him.

"I said, I think you should go!" Shiloh barked with a fierceness that surprised her mother.

Beau began to shiver, his eyes quickly moving back to Shiloh. He knew the answer but fought hard not to say it. But he also couldn't lie. His mother had worked so hard to teach him that, and Beau loved being truthful. But this was different. So very, very different. Suddenly, the emotion of love was at war with the virtue of truth, and he didn't understand any of it.

"Beau, what did you see?" Preston pushed with a firm voice that startled the boy.

Again, Beau's eyes moved toward Shiloh, who was now backing away from him and the bed.

Shiloh easily read the emotions roiling inside of him . . . and suddenly feared the answer.

Beau lifted his hand and pointed to her. "G-g-grandfather . . ."

Trisha watched her daughter's face crumple as she darted from the room sobbing, passing a haggard Dana, who had finally arrived for her long-awaited shift of praying for her son's return to consciousness.

43

Kevin returned to his home rail yard with his twin diesels just as the deepest blue of dawn appeared on the horizon. It had been a crisp night with the clearest air of impending winter when he'd left his father behind in Pittsburgh—and to his own devices—not really caring how Frank got home.

For Frank's part, after the familial exchange of fists, he skunked off to a trackside bar not far from the yard where his now ass of a son had ditched him. It was a setting where Frank flourished. He was more than adept at making friends whose primary purpose was to hold their stools to the rotted wood called a floor while cementing their livers into common stone. If Frank could find a way home, this would be an excellent place to start.

He wooed a heavily perfumed and inebriated Mags Whittaker from the bar for the long drive back to West Virginia. Mags was an industrial drinker with a long history in the railroading industry, handling scheduling and anything the men didn't want to do. She was a throwback to the pre-merger days of the Baltimore & Ohio. Once attractive, Mags was now a survivor and a decades-old widow easily open to the charms of the broken-down Frank Campbells of the world. She was tall and a woman of low discretion, armed with stretched nylons from the '80s, skinny legs with varicose knots, and, most importantly, a car with four fully functional wheels. Frank was back home, in bed, and tangled up in a naked, drunken stupor with Mags before Kevin even idled into the sidings.

With the twin diesels secured, Kevin drove through downtown in the dull pre-dawn light. He was due back in the yard by afternoon again, which would gratefully keep him out of his cold and empty house. The bigger problem was his state of feeling—lost. With last night weighing on him and both sides of his face aching, he drove aimlessly until the Mountaineer Hotel stood before him on 3rd. After a toot of a horn from a news truck behind him, Kevin followed the only draw that took him anywhere: the hotel's parking lot.

The Mountaineer was one of the town's oldest buildings, built during the heyday of rail travel and for the rail executives who'd passed through on their way to places far more important. It was also one of the best-maintained structures in the state and up for recognition as a historical site. Rumor had it that luminaries such as Jack Straus, Henry Ford II, and Harvey Firestone had stayed in the Presidential Suite, and that Mae West had once thrown up in the sink in that very same room.

But now, in the fall of 1999, Kevin stood at the doors of the suite, his hand poised to knock on the ancient, varnished wood. He instead thought better of it and turned to leave, only to find Andy sweating behind him, fresh from a run in the frigid morning.

Andy gingerly applied a bag of ice to Kevin's newly reddened cheek. He grimaced as she pressed lightly and then held it himself before she could kill him with the pain.

"What did your wife hit you with this time," she asked, "a fender from a '57 Buick?"

"No," Kevin answered flatly, "this one's from my dad."

"Might be time to start looking at some of the decisions in your life," Andy said, sitting next to him on the bed. "Your existence might depend on it."

Kevin smiled as much as the pain would let him.

"Why did he . . ." Andy asked, struggling to find the right words.

"He wanted to confess and have me help him do it."

"Confess?" Andy asked, taken aback, as she still didn't believe it was as easy as all that. The tape didn't exactly exonerate Frank, but it didn't condemn him either. In fact, it didn't even identify him definitively. "What'd you say to him?"

"Something along the lines of 'go to hell.'"

Andy looked at him for a good moment. "Why are you telling me this?"

Kevin stared at her, his mind suddenly gone blank. He wasn't sure why he was there himself. No, that was a lie; the emotional nightmare his life had become clearly drew him to the only light he could find in all of Granite Point. Much like Beau's mother, his own mother always had a knack for keeping him focused and explaining things in a way that made him feel safe—at least when she was sober. In his best memories, she was always there, always open, always loving until the day she died—and his life went up in flames. Her death had left an unfillable hole within him ever since. Despite her failings, Fay had been his moral compass, a role Trisha only partially filled. But with the magnetic pull of marriage now reversed, his arrow was spinning, fueled by anger and frustration with everyone he should have been able to trust. He didn't know north from south, east from west, up from down. And now, with his fucked-up father apparently the architect of something so horrific, Kevin found himself at a bitter crossroads with little direction other than wondering what a clearheaded Fay might have told him to do. If there was ever a time he needed his mother, this was it, but she was nowhere to be found, leaving Andy the only soul he now felt safe enough to confide in.

"Kevin, why are you telling me this?" Andy repeated, snapping him out of his trance.

He thought quickly, suddenly worried he had already given up too much. "Because I trust your intuition. Because I trust . . . you."

Andy cocked her head at him. "You don't even know me," she answered in a whisper.

"I know enough." He edged slightly closer to her on the bed.

"No, you really don't," she said, pulling the ice pack from him and taking it to the sink in the bathroom.

Kevin watched her move off, and a hard fog returned to his brain. He found himself standing up to follow her.

Andy dumped the ice into the sink and then caught Kevin's reflection in the mirror. He looked tired but also vulnerable—and beautiful.

Kevin lingered in the doorway, watching Andy untie her tight ponytail, her dark hair falling loosely and imperfectly around her shoulders, her running leggings leaving little to the imagination. His insides immediately knotted. He had nothing left to fight the attraction, and part of him, most of him, didn't want to.

Andy turned and looked up at him. Even at her height, he towered over her, and that same stirring combined with exhaustion and the desire to give in swept over her. Sensing the storm inside him and the passion he was ready to unleash upon her, she retreated against the bathroom counter as he approached. It both frightened and excited her. It had been so long, too long, since she'd had anything like this with someone wanting her as honestly and overpoweringly as Kevin did. Someone she actually wanted in return. Truth was—maybe, for the first time, she'd actually found her equal match.

For Kevin, everything about Andy overwhelmed his senses. He wanted to consume this woman in every way possible, repeatedly, until they were both completely depleted of energy. He, too, missed this desperately. This . . . synergy. His face closed in on hers, and their breathing mixed. His heart hammered in his chest, and he hovered over Andy's lips, his arms ready to lift and carry her to the bed that awaited them.

They stared at each other for a long beat. Andy blinked, feeling her own inner compass spinning. Round and round it went, until the inconvenient memory of holding a child that wasn't hers popped into her mind, the vision of his regal-appearing mother nuzzling him as she tucked him into his car seat, and the destructive familial carnage loving a man that wasn't hers would lay upon all of them. The memory was followed by Trisha's act of kindness, rescuing Andy from ensured pneumonia on the side of the road while providing a possible beaten path to her son.

Andy's conscience anchored her in cement. No matter the degree of loneliness that drove her passion, she was simply caught on the uncomfortable truth. "Is this really who you want to be?" she quietly challenged him, while asking herself the same exact question.

In that instant, everything shattered for Kevin. The rage-fueled passion melted away to a vision of Trisha—Trisha Marie Pettit Campbell—that seared his conscience; he physically felt like a speeding car suddenly thrown into reverse. He pulled away from Andy, the ache of wanting her making it all the more excruciating. Her question hung on him like a scarlet letter, and a moment later, he was gone. He fled the room, and all Andy could do was watch that beautiful man exit through the door.

She sagged to the bed, then curled up on the mattress and sobbed.

44

Kevin pulled up to the stoplight at 6th Street and screamed—until his throat burned and his lungs were empty of air. His fingers were killing him, and he now realized he'd been trying to crush the steering wheel with his bare hands. He still wanted Andy desperately, and he visualized turning his truck around, barging back into her room, throwing her on the bed, and loving her in every way imaginable, her eyes never leaving him, her long limbs wrapped around him as they shared a shuddering climax. But he knew that fantasy would have to remain in his rearview mirror. At the thought, he punched the steering wheel and screamed again.

Suddenly, he felt eyes on him. To his right.

Kevin turned and his eyes met those of the churchgoing, God-fearing, forever polite Millersons as they idled in their 1970s champagne-colored 2-ton Chrysler Newport. They gaped at him in horror.

Kevin waved, smiling sheepishly.

Mr. Millerson replied by rocketing off through the red light, disappearing in a choking blue haze from his exhaust pipe.

As the light turned green, Andy's question haunted Kevin: *Is this really who you want to be?*

The answer was a simple no.

Kevin stormed into Frank's house, shouldering through the door so hard he sent splinters into the living room. He walked heavily toward Frank's bedroom, the pictures on the wall vibrating from his weight.

Would this fury be the way his mother would've handled it? Probably not. But she wasn't here to say otherwise. It was the same thing his father would've done to him. So be it.

Once in Frank's bedroom, he found the reprobate out cold on the bed along with the opportunistic Mags splayed on top of him. Her kohl-streaked eyes opened immediately, and her aged frame scrambled across the bed with an ear-piercing shrill the instant she saw Kevin looming over them.

"Who the fuck are you?" Kevin snapped, taken aback by the sudden odd one-night stand in his father's bed.

"No one, I swear!" Mags mumbled, her hangover slowing her brain but not her body. A moment later, she was gone down the hallway and out the pummeled front door.

Kevin shook his head. That would be a reconciliation for another day. He kicked the mattress. "Get up!"

Frank didn't hear him as Kevin went to the closet, fishing for clothes to throw at his felonious parent.

"I said get up, you sorry, sick sonofabitch!"

Frank mumbled as Kevin pulled him by an arm.

"I said, GET UP!"

Frank began to wake up and retaliate. "L-let go," he said, pushing back on his son.

Kevin hauled Frank onto the floor with a thud and then returned to the closet. "Let's see, what to wear to a confession. Ah! Here's something black." He yanked a worn black shirt and pants and threw them at Frank as he tried to right himself. "Perfect. Matches your soul." Kevin then grabbed Frank and pulled him to his feet.

Frank had had enough of this. He shoved Kevin away—hard, into the dresser, sending everything on it flying. "Get the fuck off of me! What the hell do you think you're doing?!"

Kevin sprang from the old bureau, its one broken leg replaced by a beer can. "You want my help?! Well, here it is!" He then went after Frank again, and both father and son tussled into the hall and finally into the living room. Kevin wrestled Frank, pinning him so hard he cracked the drywall behind him.

"You're not squirming your way out of this," he hissed in Frank's grill. "You're going to tell everybody everything, even if I have to beat it out of you." He dragged Frank along the wall, muscling him toward the door.

Frank managed to get a free hand and slugged Kevin away, sending him to the floor. He then bolted for the bedroom as Kevin shuffled back to his feet. Once back in the bedroom, Kevin stopped cold in his tracks.

Frank stood near the closet, Tom's gun in his hand. He aimed it at the side of his head, hammer pulled back. "I swear to God, Kevin. I'll do it."

Kevin stood there for a long, heavy moment. Sweat ran down his back and across his forehead. Blood oozed from the corner of his mouth. The hatred for his father was never more pure, even though it pained him deep inside. All those years of wanting nothing more than his father's approval continued to disintegrate in front of him. He even hated himself for what he had now become and for what he said next.

"Then what are you waiting for?" The moment these words left Kevin's lips, he turned and left the room.

Frank listened to his son's footsteps fade through the house and disappear outside. He, too, was breathing hard. Nearly hyperventilating. He could smell the booze sweat on himself, accentuating how sick he really was. And now his son hated him with a venom so rightfully toxic it justified his end. He stuck the gun under his chin . . . and pulled the trigger.

Click . . . click, click, click.

Frank dropped to his knees, placing the empty gun against his forehead in anguish. *Loser.* He wasn't even capable of committing suicide correctly.

45

It was around noon at the sheriff's office when Andy closed the binder on the soil report and rubbed her eyes. What she'd read told her everything and nothing at the same time. A few years ago, the tail end of Hurricane Andrew had turned the entire Prowler Flat right-of-way, and other regions like it, into a muddy swamp. What she really needed to do was send the report over to the U.S. Geological Survey, which she was loath to do because getting an answer from them could drag this out into the next decade. But instinct was telling her something different. There was something else about all of this she was missing. It gnawed at her, like a sliver in a finger. She was growing increasingly frustrated with herself; she felt the answer was right in front of her, and she was either too blind or too stupid to see it.

Andy decided a change of scenery would clear her cluttered mind. She collected the soil binder, packed up her laptop, and headed for the door.

The moment she stepped into the hall, she was forced to retreat a step as Hollis corralled his deputies into their version of a muster room. A lot of them were ready to go, all the while not completely understanding why they were treating it like combat.

Andy followed all of them in and stood next to Preston, who watched from the back of the room. "What's going on?" she asked.

Preston shook his head and leaned in quietly. "The kid ID'd him."

"He's awake?" Andy asked with surprise and wondered why she was hearing about it only now.

Preston nodded. "Yeah, this morning. And then word came down about that crowbar."

"What word?" Andy shot back loud enough for Hollis to hear.

"Do you mind?" Hollis snapped and then went back to barking orders at the mob of cops before him. ". . . I want two units at both ends to bottle him up, others are to flank both sides."

"Isn't this a little much?" Preston asked. Hollis was in the process of losing his mind and it was showing.

Hollis glanced at him, not giving a shit. He then pointed to the deputies in front of him. "You three are up the middle. Word is he's at Sycamore Siding, so we'll regroup at the Dollar on route eighty-three. Twenty minutes."

"When did Frank Campbell turn into Dillinger?" Preston added once the room broke up and Hollis walked toward him and Andy.

Hollis was immediately in his face. "Are you going to file out like everyone else or are you gonna file for unemployment instead?" he snarled before storming out the door with the other deputies in tow.

"Holy Christ," Preston muttered to himself, "what the hell is happening?" Before he could follow the rest of the deputies out, Andy stopped him.

She felt like she had just woken up from a deep sleep. Without her having to bang her head against a wall for once, pieces were starting to come together. Her question about the crowbar was suddenly irrelevant. "Deputy, the night you pulled Frank Campbell over, what time was that?"

"Um . . . shit," he said and pulled his notepad from a pocket. He flipped a page to find it. "Uh . . . 23:55. And I gotta go." He was then out the door, disappearing into the sea of deputies forging forward to take down Public Enemy No. 1.

Andy threw her stuff onto the closest table in frustration, her brain in a complete knot. Not only was Hollis running off on his own, but the pieces coming together were still too far away to make any sense.

Why can't I figure this out?! she screamed inwardly.

Planting herself in a chair, Andy stared out the window just as her cell phone rang. While she would've preferred to throw it across the room rather than answer, she looked at the calling number.

It was Robert Langsdon, persona non grata.

"Where the hell are you?" Andy snapped into the phone the moment she answered it.

"Still in D.C.," he replied in a nice, calm voice.

"Yeah, well, shit's hitting the fan over here in West Virginia."

"No sweat. I'm about to make your life easier. Prints on the bar came back as a match for Frank Campbell. Sheriff's going to bring him in."

"And you're telling me this now?! After I already found out?!"

"Hey, it's not like I have a shitload of time over here either, you know. Anyway, you can probably start packing for home. We can debrief when I'm outta here. Until then, I gotta go."

"Wait, what am I—"

Click.

He was gone and so was Andy's patience. Her brain nearly exploded. She slammed the phone on the table, muffled a scream, and fumed, and then stared at the splatter of folders that spilled from her backpack.

And she stared some more, framed by the loud ticking of the old Simplex wall clock from across the room.

With a blink, the image of the Shale Waterfall State Park came to her mind. Water from a seemingly endless river sprayed onto the granite and mud below. Just as it had over a time of thousands of years.

Thousands of years.

And *mud.*

She recalled the dirty stream of water flowing into the puddle in the parking lot, fed by the oozing . . . and eroding . . . mud nearby.

The epiphany hit her hard, the last of the pieces falling neatly into place with a single key thought.

Time.

Andy corralled the folders that were scattered everywhere and opened them all. She quickly scanned through everything.

Time.

She dug until she found the time of the yard derailment: 23:30.

The time of the wreck: 23:50.

Frank Campbell getting pulled over: Preston said 23:55.

One plus one equaling two no longer added up. And that was the best thing she could have ever realized.

Andy quickly gathered her stuff and ran to the dispatcher's desk. Leaning over it, she frantically waved to get the man's attention; his hands were full working the radios.

"I need you to call them back," Andy said, loud enough to drown out the dispatcher's own voice.

He ignored her with a wince and remained on the radio.

"Excuse me! I need you to call them back!"

"Hey!" the dispatcher snapped at her. "I'm busy! Go wait over there!" He pointed to the waiting room and went back to his microphone.

"Shit . . ." Andy said and immediately bolted to the parking lot just in time to see the last of the patrol cars race down the road. She was out of options for anyone who would listen to her.

Except maybe one.

46

Kevin ignored the clipboard on his lap and worked on rounding out his shoulder and moving his sore face in all directions. He felt pain everywhere, and the last thing he was in the mood for was work.

Andy suddenly blustered aboard and into the cab. "Five a second!" she blurted before he could even prepare a defense to her presence and the sure ass-kicking coming his way.

"What?" Kevin asked. She had to have known about the camcorder by now.

"He would've had to pull five a second," Andy continued, not nearly as fast as her brain wanted. "He couldn't have done it."

Kevin looked at her blankly, no clue as to what she was babbling about.

Sycamore Siding was an unattractive stretch of rarely used track near the long-abandoned Hickson Grain Mill. The site was choked with "No Trespassing" signs, illegible graffiti, weeds, and wild, unruly trees, with the only grain silo leaning precariously to one side. It was a favorite for teens to get high and lost in, far from the watchful eyes of parents and law enforcement.

Standing well beyond the long gravel entrance, far from the useless chain-link gate intended to keep vandals and assorted potheads away, Hollis watched Frank sit alone in The Brick. The locomotive idled under the rusted ruins of a conveyor belt, spitting compressed air onto the decrepit tracks beneath. Hollis could see Frank's head resting in his hands, the pain of the morning still running through him.

Hollis took a last drag off a cigarette and tossed the butt. He then unclipped his service issue and motioned his squad forward like he was approaching a beachhead.

Preston found the whole thing almost comical. But the comedy faded when Hollis climbed aboard The Brick and threw the cab door open. Frank looked up and froze as Hollis closed the door behind him. He looked around, feigning a trip down memory lane.

"She's just like I remembered," Hollis said, high and mighty in his moment of leverage and delicious vengeance. This was a moment he had long waited for. "And so are you."

Frank looked out the cab window to the bright lights of patrol cars pulling up in the distance, and watched as a swarm of khaki-clad deputies flanked the scene, weapons drawn.

"I know of this great AA program, Frank," Hollis said while running a finger down a greasy panel. "It's called prison. Perfect for guys like you who operate heavy machinery under the influence. Or crowbars." He then violently hauled Frank from the engineer's seat and drove a fist into his kidneys, bending him in agony. "You've been such a pain in my ass. This is going to be better than fuckin' Ex-Lax." He slammed Frank into the throttle console, cutting his forehead and drawing blood. Hollis then yanked him up by the throat, hatred fueling a strength normally not his own. With Frank dazed and choked with pain, flailing at Hollis' hands, Hollis jammed him hard into the wall. "I heard a kid died in that wreck. You know what they do to kid-killers in the hole, don't you? Compared to what's waitin' for you there, this is a slow dance." He drove a hand into Frank's crotch and squeezed, drawing a grimace and a groan from him. "But for now, you're mine."

Frank's face turned dark, the veins bulging in his head. "Then . . . I . . . might as well . . . earn it," he scratched out and found enough strength to spit blood into Hollis' face.

Hollis smiled and then hammered a fist into Frank's kidneys again and easily tossed him against the cab wall, only to then unleash his baton on Frank's curled body.

Frank was completely defenseless. Anywhere he tried to protect himself, Hollis landed a blow elsewhere. Frank managed to get a leg free and jam his boot into Hollis' knee, drawing a sickening crack from it.

Hollis screamed and buckled. He fell away from Frank as Frank plowed a fist into Hollis' face, breaking his nose. Frank then ripped the baton away as Hollis fumbled for his gun, only to have Frank club it away, nearly shattering every bone in Hollis' hand. Frank, with his own hatred-fueled strength, blasted Hollis out the cab door with his boot.

Hollis crashed onto the crew walk and landed on his back. Blood began to sting his eyes, blinding him to the blows Frank continued to deliver mercilessly upon him.

The sight of all this froze Preston for a moment. He then pulled his gun and aimed at Frank. "FREEZE, FRANK!" he yelled with an authority that echoed against every surface around.

The sound of Preston's voice was strong enough to break Frank's rage. He stopped instantly and then withdrew from Hollis, who immediately rolled under the locomotive's crew railing and tumbled down onto the trackbed.

"Put the baton down and place your hands on your head!" Preston ordered, holding that same authoritative volume.

With the pain that shot through his body, Frank was in a fog. Hollis had disappeared overboard, and all Frank could see now were deputies aiming to annihilate him.

"Do it now!" Preston again ordered.

Frank opened his hand and the baton clattered to the crew walk. He then saw a slight figure emerge through the line of deputies, passing Preston and walking directly toward him.

It was Dana Harper.

Preston turned as Dana dropped a chattering police scanner at his feet and raised a small pistol at Frank. An odd stocking stuffer from none other than Randy on their first Christmas together.

"GUN!" Preston shouted as he moved to bring Dana to the ground.

He wasn't nearly fast enough. Dana unloaded the gun at Frank, the loud popping ringing in her ears.

Bullets clanked off the metal around Frank except for the one that plowed through his arm, spraying blood onto the faded paint behind him. He dove into the cab and scrambled for the throttle. Bullets sprayed through the cab window, shattering the glass and torpedoing the engineer's console. Frank battle-crawled for the throttle and jammed it forward.

The wheels spun on the iron. Sand belched out and The Brick grabbed traction as Preston drove Dana into the mud, wrenching the now empty gun from her hand. She screamed in protest while the deputies wrestled handcuffs onto her flailing wrists.

Hollis rolled clear of the locomotive and immediately went for his gun.

Which was still in the cab.

Shit!

With a deputy trying to help him to his feet, Hollis wrenched the man's gun away and slipped aboard The Brick just as the back crew ladder slid by.

Kevin continued to stare at Andy, trying to make sense of what she kept rattling on about. It was enough to shatter the anger inside him and enough to make him question the reality of his father. He was also oblivious to Gibson outside the window below, whose walkie-talkie remained plastered to his ear, his eyes growing wide; he couldn't believe what he was hearing.

"Kev!" Gibson shouted to the cab window, drawing Kevin's attention. "You'd better flip to the Atlantic frequency, man."

"Why?" Kevin asked, distracted by Andy.

"You'd better just do it."

Kevin stared at him and then flipped the radio channel and turned up the speaker. The chatter he heard was going on faster than he could process. He tried to unscramble the rapid series of arguments over switching settings and setting derailers, but what he heard more of was the squealing of people that keyed over each other, compounding the confusion. "What's going on?"

"I don't know," Gibson shrugged with urgency, "something about your dad beating the living shit out of Hollis and taking off. Last I heard he was out of Sycamore."

Kevin's mind raced. He tried to imagine what went down to create a scenario where his father and Hollis would come to blows, and the answer was obvious. He then looked at Andy, and some of what she was saying began to gel.

"I also heard he got shot," Gibson added.

Kevin immediately tossed the manifest aside. "Cut 'em," he ordered out the window.

"Huh?"

Kevin pointed back to the fifty-three loaded coal cars behind him. "CUT 'EM!"

Gibson took a step back. Kevin's order didn't register at first, but the look on his face drove his intent home. Gibson ran to the lead car and severed the brake line. With a deafening hiss the line popped free. He then opened the coupler and gave Kevin the thumbs up.

Kevin ran the throttles up, stirring the prime movers behind him into a roar. "You'd better get out," he said to Andy.

"Think about what you're doing," she cautioned, making sure he knew what going after his father could result in.

He did. The infuriation that was there five minutes ago had disappeared. The boy in him was still gone, banished to a place of memories. He wasn't sure, when asked years later, if it was love, but it *was* family. For another first in his life, he wouldn't be doing something to elicit demonstrable gratitude from a man incapable of it—he was doing it because he wanted to, simply because it was the right thing to do. He was going to save his father.

Andy saw that in Kevin's eyes and through the bruises on his face. This was a man different from the one she'd met only a few days ago. There was now power behind him. Resolve. It drew her in, and she was going to be a part of it. Andy descended to the front cab door and closed it. She was all in.

Kevin nodded. *So be it.* He released the brakes, sending his pair of locomotives onto the mainline.

And about thirty seconds later, Dispatch hollered for him on the radio. "U.P. ninety-three eleven, dispatch. Kevin, what are you doing?"

Kevin pulled on his headset. "Clear everything between here and one-fifty-five," he radioed in return.

"It's not our right-of-way, Kev," the dispatcher fired back.

That was all that Kevin heard. He pulled off the headset, unplugged it, and tossed it aside.

47

Frank pulled the first aid kit off the cab wall with his one working arm as The Brick moved onto the mainline a couple of miles from the siding at Sycamore. He cleared off the glass from his seat and landed hard on it. The pain was excruciating, both from the bullet and the beating Hollis had laid upon him. He fought through what felt like impending shock, or at least that's what he thought it was.

He pulled his shirt aside and revealed not one, but two bullet wounds. One a graze across his left bicep, the other clear through his right shoulder. It still worked, but the hole within it gave him a pain that was nearly blinding.

As for Hollis, he held on to the crew railing. The cold wind went right through him as The Brick accelerated past thirty. The girl was old, but the GP-9 could still move. Hollis ripped a piece of his shirt off, exposing the skin beneath it to a wind chill well below freezing. He created a makeshift bandage around a cut on his arm, then eyed the cab door banging freely in the wind.

He also saw Frank, who was focused on bandaging himself, oblivious to the threat that now crept up behind him.

With the diesel horns blaring through what was left of the wreck site, the crews that were working on clearing the disaster watched Kevin throttle the pair of Dash-9s past them with a deafening roar, sending some of them scurrying for safety.

Kevin stole a quick look at a route map and then folded it away while Andy settled into the conductor's seat and held on. She honestly did not know where this would go, let alone the repercussions of being a part of it. She just knew this was where she needed to be. *This is what Langsdon gets for leaving me in charge.*

Hollis eased up along the crew walk, Frank still oblivious to his presence, just as Hollis was oblivious to the oscillating headlamps of the Dash-9 locomotives approaching from behind.

The blood in his eyes had now given way to tears from the cold wind in his face. The Brick was now easily past forty and closing in on fifty. The pain from the damage Frank had done to him started to claim more of Hollis' attention. But stopping now wasn't an option. Frank was going down, even if he had to kill the man to do it.

"I need you to go up front and open the nose coupler," Kevin said as he watched the distance between his Dash-9 and The Brick up ahead. "You know how to do that?"

Andy nodded. "I think so." She moved down the steps and out the forward crew door. She needed to push against it, and once it was open, the wind before her pushed her back into the cab. Ahead, she could see the black and ominous shape of Frank's locomotive rapidly approaching. It was a moment she could only allow herself to take in for a second. She then reached below the crew railing for the coupler release and pulled on it.

The knuckle opened with a groan. Andy disappeared back into the cab and away from the cold wind that cut right through her.

Frank swiped the first aid kit off his lap and grimaced. There was no hope of getting comfortable, and there was no hope of turning himself in while Hollis was intent on beating him to death as painfully as possible. He'd rather just take another bullet and be done with it.

He almost got his wish. Hollis had slid his way along the steel hull of The Brick and now aimed at Frank, steadying himself against a steel door panel and the incessant rocking motion of the locomotive. Taking his best shot, he fired, clearly missing Frank by a country mile.

"Fuck!" Hollis shouted as he rushed toward the cab. The moment he was inside, Frank slugged him from behind, catching Hollis behind the ear and causing him to tumble into the cab. In an instant, they were both back to beating each other to death.

Kevin peered as far ahead as he could and backed off on the throttle as the Dash-9s slid up on The Brick. He felt the couplers latch and lock.

"What now?" Andy asked, not quite sure what strategy Kevin was working on.

"I become the drag my father always thinks I am," Kevin replied. He pulled his hands off the console and stepped back from it. Six seconds later an obnoxious bleating of the locomotive's alert system ricocheted about the cab. A moment later the locomotives lurched forward, the throttles shutting down, creating an 8,000-horsepower decelerating ball and chain.

"Let's go," Kevin said, motioning forward and leading Andy back through the forward crew door. The sound of The Brick's prime mover laboring against the dead weight it was dragging was nearly deafening, accentuated by a planet-killing black cloud of diesel exhaust that funneled out from the locomotive's exhaust stack. Kevin knew this wasn't going to last long, regardless of how much heart Frank's little locomotive had. He quickly became concerned about the V-16 behind the steel panels blowing apart and shredding them before they could even reach the cab. With the locomotives rocking against each other, Kevin hesitated to cross over just long enough to witness a siding sign whip by:

COLEMAN

The locomotives lurched to the side, nearly sending both him and Andy onto the graveled roadbed that streaked by below. Kevin quickly turned to watch the mainlines stream away.

"Shit," he said, knowing where they were just shunted off to.

"What?" Andy shouted, her voice rising over the rush of air and the screaming of the wheezing GP-9 in front of them.

"They've shunted us off to Coleman!"

Andy shrugged. "So?"

"It's an old missile base with about twenty dead-ends!" Kevin answered and pulled her over the couplers and onto The Brick. He then led the way down the crew walk. The thought of Andy following behind him crossed his mind. He should've made her stay back in the cab, but now the fear of getting annihilated by an exploding steel panel door quickly dismissed that.

Kevin looked ahead at the flapping crew door in time to witness Hollis deliver vicious blows to Frank's head, sending him to the floor in a concussed daze.

"You have the right to remain silent—" Hollis hissed as he hauled Frank to his feet and drove him into the wall, his arm behind his back. "Anything you say can be used against you—"

Frank snapped his head back and caught Hollis on the bridge of the nose, stunning him enough for Frank to drive him into the throttle console, almost knocking it off its mounts. With his good arm, Frank plowed a fist into Hollis' stomach and then threw him into the back wall. Hollis' head cracked loudly against the steel and his legs went limp. Frank then saw the gun on the cab floor. He instantly jammed it onto Hollis' forehead.

"YOU LOSE!" Frank screamed, glaring death at his mortal enemy. His eyes were dark with wrath.

Hollis sat frozen and beaten.

Frank pulled back the hammer. There was no rational thought in his mind. Just blind rage. Pure blinding fury.

"Dad . . ." Kevin said, moving in slowly. "Dad, it's me . . ."

The sound of his son's voice broke Frank's fixation on Hollis. His eyes moved to Kevin, who cautiously reached for the gun in his hand but couldn't take it. Frank looked back at Hollis' bloody frame and slowly backed off from him, never letting up his aim. His face crumpled for a moment as everything suddenly caught up with him. He then quickly regained his composure.

"They've sent us down to Coleman, Dad," Kevin added. "There isn't much time."

Frank's mind cleared. He finally lowered the gun and looked out the cab window and noted the screaming of The Brick's engine.

Without a fight, Kevin now took the gun from Frank and released the hammer; he then handed it to Andy as she came in behind him.

"Mr. Campbell," Andy said, raising her voice over the noise, "I know you were there at the derailment site before the accident. I'm here to tell you that you did nothing to cause it."

Frank's eyes narrowed at her in confusion.

"He still had intent!" Hollis thundered through the pain that wracked everything from the top of his skull to the balls of his feet.

"Just like *you* did when you tried to kill him all those years ago?" Andy shot back.

Hollis didn't answer; she got him on that one. He just eased his head back and closed his eyes in defeat.

Kevin moved to the throttle console and quickly pulled the throttle back. He looked at the shattered gauges, alarmed that nothing had changed. The Brick screamed on. The cab began to stink of burnt oil as fumes poured in. Kevin then pulled on the engine brake and the reverser levers. Still nothing. He placed a hand on the bullet-ridden control stack, and it easily fell from its mount.

They were screwed.

"We need to go," Kevin said. He moved his father out of the cab and rapidly down the crew walk, followed by Andy, who had helped Hollis to his feet. They were over the couplers, leaving the shuddering GP-9 behind them.

But as Frank moved over, he looked down at the over-stretched coupler arms. He knew the moment he saw them they would never easily release. "You've jammed them," he yelled at Kevin.

"What!?" Kevin answered, not following what his father was pointing to.

"You ran them out of their housings!" Frank again yelled, hobbling over to the release lever that wouldn't budge. He then moved back over to The Brick and took a few steps down the crew ladder, immediately next to the release lever and a foot over the roadbed. Kevin moved in on the opposing crew ladder as Frank moved the release lever. It was stiff, but it moved. It was going to take everything to lift it.

Kevin turned to Andy. "You know where the throttle lever is!? I need you to push it all the way forward!"

Andy nodded and was about to disappear into the cab.

"STOP!" Frank yelled.

He saw in that very instant a vision ever so clear. Frank looked upon Kevin, whose hair whipped in the wind, determined to save his father, to save all of them from the destruction that loomed ahead. Frank no longer saw an inconvenient child to be dismissed out of annoyance, nor a frightened ten-year-old lost without his mother. Frank saw his son as a man. A man who somehow, despite Frank's fatherly failures, raised a family with a daughter who had the courage to call her grandfather exactly what he was. A man who was a leader for those who worked around and with him.

Frank finally saw who Kevin really was, and for the first time in Frank's entire life as a father, he felt something he had never experienced before.

Pride.

Andy froze while Kevin turned toward his father, still determined to rescue him.

Frank suddenly grabbed his son by the front of his coat.

The move startled Kevin. He irrationally envisioned his father discarding him, or them both, onto the tracks below.

"If you remember anything," Frank yelled over the roar of his locomotive, "remember this! You'll always be the best thing I've ever done!"

Kevin's mind went blank. Words escaped him, and in that moment everything around him disappeared.

Frank pushed Kevin back against the crew ladder and pulled up on the release lever. With a metallic scream, the couplers parted.

The Brick accelerated away as the Dash-9s braked hard toward a harmless idle.

Kevin fell forward, only to be grabbed by Andy to keep him from falling onto the rails. "DAD!" he cried. He had finally heard the words he had spent his entire life hoping would come his way. Now that he'd heard them, all he could do was watch his father race to his end, a broad-shouldered figure growing smaller and smaller as he was carried into oblivion by an ancient locomotive where he had spent most of his life.

Epilogue

My father eased himself into the engineer's seat of that GP-9. I knew, without a doubt, that for him it was peaceful and quiet. I knew the screaming of The Brick's prime mover had disappeared, replaced by the tranquil droning of a smoothly running diesel motor that ran like new. It was probably all brown noise while the old rails into Coleman streaked by as they mowed down the tall weeds that grew unchecked from the trackbed. I knew he slid open that pock-marked cab window and felt the cold wind of winter, which probably felt more like spring air pressing against his face. Maybe, for the first time ever, he found peace.

Andy said it was memories that we get to take with us. I never realized what those words meant until now. And as much as I could guess, I still wonder what memories went through my father's mind in those final moments of his life. I'd like to think he was a young man again, cruising through life in the engineer's seat of a new locomotive with clean glass that reflected the spring morning. I remember once, a long time ago, he mentioned to Tom, I think, that he loved to look out the cab window while the sun peeked through the thick trees as they streaked by. He was living his dream. He loved railroading. Far more than I ever did or could.

Stories from my father were few and far between as we both got older. At least the good ones were. I remember at my wedding, which now feels like a lifetime ago, he shared the story of his first date with Mom, and how they spent an afternoon cruising down a country road in a convertible that could barely run. She held on to her Sunday hat while the wind tried to steal it from her. She was the most beautiful thing he had ever seen, and even more beautiful as she enjoyed her moment in the sun. I can still clearly imagine that even now.

I only saw Andy once more after that day. She asked me to come by the airport, which I agreed to do with equal parts excitement and reluctance. It was important for me to be there, she'd said over the phone the day before she left. It wasn't something I shared with Trisha until much later, when the time was right. Even to this day, Andy's draw on me is just as powerful as it was back then. I had visions of her asking me to climb into that small plane to go with her to anywhere but here. A part of me would've gone if she had asked. When she hugged me, I felt a warmth that I'd never felt before. She completed a part of me I wasn't even aware existed, and she saw through me in a way no woman ever had, not even my wife. When we held each other, I didn't want to let go. In my mind, I begged her to stay. But with her arms around me, she whispered the same thing she told me in the cab that day.

"Five a second," she said.

"I don't know what that means," I answered.

"That's how many spikes your father would have had to pull," she continued, "in the time he had to compromise the rail anchoring along a hundred feet of track."

I now saw what she had only been able to articulate at the end.

"From the time he left the bar to when he was pulled over was only twenty minutes. So how could an impaired man who's nearly seventy remove enough spikes to derail anything in the middle of the night and in a downpour?"

And she was right. I envisioned my father in the middle of the tracks in the dead of night, landing on his ass, defeated in the dark and pouring rain, failing to get even one spike, let alone hundreds, out of the roadbed while nearly slicing his hand in two trying.

It was in the time that followed that I saw the findings report Andy had filed. She had implicated Mother Nature and the now long gone Atlantic Eastern Railroad, whose CEO had vanished south of the border into Mexico with what money he could abscond with. With a Tonka-like bulldozer rented from Puck, and dirt swiped from a nearby housing development, Atlantic Eastern repaired the trackbed at Prowler Flat for the price of a Yugo with four flat tires. It was only a matter of time, and the right amount of soaking rain, before it would all fail again.

My father's horrific timing was always impeccable.

Andy placed a hand on my cheek and kissed me softly. And then she was gone. And with her, a part of me.

Later that day, once I returned home, I found Trisha waiting for me on our front porch. The day had turned much colder, and yet she'd waited for me there regardless, bundled up in one of my heavy work coats. As much as Andy was something new, Trisha was where I belonged. I climbed up the creaky steps of our porch, and she held me as I buried my face into her and fell to the emotions inside me.

As for Hollis, he died a few months later. Those few days, now so long ago, somehow changed him. People found him far more tolerable, even polite and eerily kind at times. He refused to press charges against Dana and allowed her to bring Beau home, much to the shock of everyone within a ten-county radius.

Mom once told me Hollis was a handsome young man a long time ago. But that streak of cruelty had contorted him, which was surely what had driven her to my dad. In a way, part of her still loved Hollis. I caught a glimpse of why she may have loved him one afternoon while driving through town when he waved at me. I nearly rear-ended Mrs. Hobbs and her rusted shit-box Impala. What brought the kindness back I couldn't say. Maybe it was the beating my father laid upon his thick skull or the fact that Hollis' mortal enemy was finally gone.

It was a bright winter's morning, with a fresh layer of snow that rested on everything outside, when he sat across from me at Stanley's. The reflected sunlight poured in through the windows and onto the same table I'd sat at with Andy. Hollis had lost weight and oddly looked younger. I honestly didn't know what to say to the man who had spent his life menacing my father and had frightened me as a child. He chatted with me, kindly asking about the kids before finally bringing up his regret at my having to witness the endless war between him and my father.

And what ultimately happened to my mother.

It was a surreal moment that I haven't quite reconciled yet.

It was then I told Hollis of that night. The night of the accident, when a scared and confused eight-year-old boy stood upon his darkened porch, staring at the doorbell that he never pressed. I told him of the anchor's weight of guilt I'd been carrying in the years since that night and how my inaction was responsible for ending my mother's life. A crime my wife insisted I was innocent of.

Hollis looked at me. "You were eight," he said, sharply echoing Trisha's words in my mind. "Your mother asked you to do something she never should have."

I drew in a deep breath. The man was right; I was eight and in an impossible situation.

"Besides," Hollis continued, "that damn doorbell never worked anyway."

I stared at him as my mind instantly went blank.

Hollis downed the rest of his coffee, suggested I find more useful things than guilt to carry around with me, tossed a tip onto the table, and walked out the door. I watched him climb into his cruiser and drive off into the morning light and toward the kindness that ended his life. He was hit by a drunk driver while changing a tire for a stranger stranded on the side of the road in the twilight of that same winter's day. He died a gentler man.

Dad would've loved the irony.

After Atlantic's collapse, Granite Point was forever changed. By the grace of God, a larger regional carrier swooped in and bought everything for pennies on the dollar. They hired some who were laid off, and a few retired onto welfare with dreams of fleeing to Florida that would never come to pass. Others moved away to chase factory jobs with the big three car makers, still hoping to make enough between the endless strikes.

Karen's Coffee Shop is still around, where Stanley continues to poison people with bad brews as he competes in vain with the Starbucks and Caribou Coffees of the world. Still, the town manages to scrape enough together to hang Christmas decorations on the lamp posts and spread a little holiday cheer every year.

As for me, I never worked for Union Pacific again. I'd violated just about every regulation and policy imaginable, and I was fired immediately. Not that I blame them. I would've fired myself for what I did. But I also wouldn't have done anything differently. I was there when my father needed me, and I think he saw that. That alone is worth ten careers.

It was also the end of me being the local union president. That part of my career came to an end just as fast, and in all honesty, it was a complete blessing. I hadn't realized how much I was done living and breathing the laws of the union and embodying the pains and woes of its members. Every time the railroad had the slightest wrinkle, it ended up as my problem to solve and left no one happy. So, by the grace of God, I find myself now running operations with Dana at that same larger regional that came in to consume the scraps of our little railroad.

But every now and then, when they're desperate, I find myself behind the throttle. And every time I'm there, my father's presence weighs on me.

He and I were the end of a familial cycle that started long before either one of us was born. I couldn't say when it all began. I never knew my grandfather, and Dad refused to speak of him. But as I watched my son sit alone on a swing outside, bored and lonely even with his big sister there, I knew this wasn't something I could perpetuate any further.

As the days and months passed, it finally came to me: my life was not my father's to judge or condemn. I've lived in a constant state of war in my mind. There are days I win the battles, finding solace in the pressing of the wind in my face with open rails ahead, and others when the bitter cold of winter lays heavily upon me. Often I find myself wary of what I pass on to my children, making sure what I give them is not rooted and formed in my past, a past that is just now fading into notions of a lifetime long ago.

I know if it weren't for Trisha, I would fail miserably.

With my father gone, I'm now able to breathe. But only because I realized I chose to suffocate myself in a self-imposed familial prison while he was alive. I do still find myself imagining his final moments running into Coleman, where the rails raced by and The Brick blasted through an endless series of chain-link gates at the old missile base. I can see the collections of tunnels waiting for him, swallowing him into the darkness as he closed his eyes, remembering a different life from long ago.

It's then that I reach for my son's hand and make a feeble attempt to show him the world around us from my own flawed perspective.

Andy was very much right. We do, in some way, take our memories with us, the ones we choose to keep, and the ones that choose us. Her gift to me of that realization is something I can never repay. Life really is a collection of moments. I mean, it just takes one second of stillness and quiet to really hear the moments of life passing by like a heartbeat. Once that happens, they're heard forever. The real gift is knowing which memories to make because they really are the only things we take with us.

I'd like to think that one day I'll see my father again, and maybe, just maybe, together we can ride upon a magic carpet made of steel.

an excerpt from the sequel to *Power & Way*

Shiloh Campbell-Auclair . . .

. . . shifted in her seat at a corner table in the Old Ebbitt Grill on Washington D.C.'s 15th Street. She fidgeted with her utensils while looking restlessly about the restaurant. The Grill had yet to receive the noisiest of the crowds given the time of day, which gave Shiloh more quiet time to sit with her rambling thoughts and amped-up anticipation.

The day had already been a long one. It was stiflingly hot and humid outside, with temperatures forcing the trains out of Manhattan to an agonizing crawl. A trip that should've taken two-and-a-half hours as advertised took just over four. Her journey was also not well supported by her brother, who saw no point in exploring a past he had scant memory of in a little town that now existed as a hub for recreational hikers, bike riders, railroad nostalgia buffs, and a collection of bed and breakfast inns.

The inhabitants of Granite Point had found a way to survive and thrive, just as her grandfather had told her so very long ago.

A prophecy she would have to remember to add into the book she was writing.

Shiloh's trip to D.C. was also not enthusiastically supported by her husband. Andre Auclair preferred she stay at home and finish her book with what she already had. It was close enough as far as he was concerned. He also wasn't a fan of his pretty wife running off to meet someone who was far younger and whom Andre considered to be far better looking than he was. It was a paranoia Shiloh had learned to live with for the nearly fifteen years they had been together. With a soft kiss on his lips, a hug of his slightly plump frame, and a hug for her ten-year-old daughter, Sarah, Shiloh embarked from their Stony Brook home on Long Island just the same.

It was coming up on five in the afternoon when Shiloh looked at her phone. She endured a moment of panic, fearing she would be stood up after all this time, chasing down the son of Andrea Mayland, a woman Shiloh knew little about beyond what her father had told her over the years, and the emails Andrea's son would eventually send her. Shiloh's own knowledge of "Andy" existed at a time when everything was turned upside down and came crashing down all at once.

There was very little left for Shiloh in Granite Point in the years that followed. Her friends had moved off to different corners of the country except for Caitlin, who found herself on divorce number three with four monster children and living on a career collecting child support and skimpy welfare. Ashley had moved to London with a vow to never return to the United States and its sagging hope as a nation. But Mom and Dad still lived there, harboring dreams of retiring to a beach home that may or may not come true.

The large doors of the Grill opened, drawing Shiloh's attention to what had to be four White House interns, recently set free for the day from the confines of the West Wing.

But still no Christian.

Shiloh's fear of being stood up returned. She looked at her phone again, expecting a "sorry, not coming" text, but instead found a reminder text from Andre further declaring his love for her and beseeching her to please come home.

"I will and I love you too," Shiloh quickly typed back, reassuring her nervous husband, whose imagination was likely running wild. She would FaceTime him later from the hotel room, which would hopefully quell his queasy stomach.

A low voice. "Shiloh?"

She looked up to find Christian Mayland standing before her. She jumped slightly, then her brain went off-line for a moment. Christian stood very tall, six feet plus a lot of inches, and looked just as he did in the social media pages she had stalked to hunt him down. He had his mother's eyes, she noted from the pictures she'd seen, along with the shape of her face and the color of her hair. He was also stunning. Andre had good reason to be concerned—not that he had anything to fear.

Maybe.

But still, the energy that existed between Shiloh's father and Christian's mother now reached out to her. The instant draw was undeniable, and for the first time Shiloh fully understood the battle of emotion her father had contended with per the stories he imparted upon her.

"You're Shiloh Campbell, right?" Christian asked.

Shiloh snapped out of it. "Yes, sorry," she said as she stood, offering a hand. "You're Christian."

"As much as I would like to deny it at times, I am," he answered with surprising humility and gave her a perfect handshake with just the right amount of pressure. He pulled his chair out and sat.

Even sitting in a chair, he's tall, Shiloh thought to herself as she retook her seat. *His knees must be up against the bottom of the table.*

"How was the trip down?" Christian asked, breaking the verbal ice. Emailing with Shiloh was one thing; talking to her was entirely something else.

"Long," Shiloh answered. "The heat really raises hell with the trains."

"Yeah, I've done that trip up to Boston and New York enough in July and August, and it can be excruciating."

"Fortunately, I don't have to do it that much," Shiloh replied, doing what she could to keep her brain from tripping over itself. "I really appreciate you coming here to meet me."

"Sure," Christian answered, fighting his own brain that oddly started to fog up. "Mom mentioned your dad a few times, so I thought it was only fair to meet you and compare notes."

And ask you out to dinner if you weren't goddamned married, he thought.

Shiloh smiled. "Did you just come from work?"

"I did," Christian replied. "I'm getting ready for a symposium with the Center for Missing and Exploited Children next week, so there's a lot going on."

"You're speaking at it?"

"Yeah, can you believe that?" Christian said as he leaned back in his chair.

Shiloh was about to speak when the waiter arrived, frustratingly snapping their conversational flow. She wanted to kick the man's knees out from under him.

"Welcome to the Grill," the waiter said, lowering a couple of waters onto the table. He was tall and skinny with a neatly trimmed beard, impeccable hair, and Clark Kent-style rimmed glasses. "My name is Trent, and what can I get you on this gloriously roasting day? Or do you two need a little time?"

"I could go for a Cosmo," Shiloh answered, now thinking a drink would calm her racing brain.

"And a Negroni for me," Christian added.

"A Cosmopolitan and Negroni. Very good. A couple of my favorites," Trent the Waiter replied before moving off toward the bar.

"What's a Negroni?" Shiloh asked.

"It's a mix of vermouth, gin, and Campari," Christian answered, desperately needing a shot of something to clear his own brain.

"It sounds . . . busy."

"That it is," Christian agreed, finding himself following the lines of Shiloh's hair. His mouth quickly went dry, and he reached for his water glass.

Shiloh wasn't doing much better. She had already eyed his long torso and the day-old scruff and felt like she was on a sinking rowboat. She needed to get this conversation re-railed before she began speaking in tongues.

"How's the book coming?" Christian inquired, helping Shiloh keep the conversation moving.

"It's almost done. I'm just missing a couple of things."

"Like my mom?" Christian cut directly to the point.

"Yeah, and a title."

Trent the Waiter returned with the drinks in record time, placing each one where it belonged on the table with flair. He then lingered, a part of him wanting to hear what this conversation was going to be like.

Why don't you just pull up a chair and join us, Shiloh thought with annoyance.

"Enjoy!" Trent the Waiter bubbled. "I'll come back for your order in a little bit."

"Thanks," Shiloh said. *Now get lost, dude.*

Christian took an immediate sip of his drink. Sitting down with Shiloh wasn't something he'd really wanted to do, but he'd felt it would be good for him regardless. He hadn't been quite ready to revisit the subject of his mother or how he was freed thanks to her relentless war to find him. Christian also knew it wasn't something he could always run from either. As much as Shiloh had researched him, he had done the same on her after she had reached out to him. Shiloh made it easy due to her much larger social media footprint. He found her pictures warm and inviting, and in no way did they portray her as being insane, psychologically disturbed, a rabid stalker, or criminally inclined. She appeared normal and safe—and distracting.

Shiloh reached for her glass and took her own sip.

"You have a tat," Christian commented, spotting a small round tattoo on the inside of her wrist.

"Yeah," Shiloh replied as she set her glass down on the table. She rolled her arm over for him to see the small circle with a curved railroad track within it. The same design Frank Campbell had created as his painting logo—but situated within a compass rose and north-pointing inward to herself. Shiloh's own personal touch.

"A keepsake for an old friend?"

"Something like that," Shiloh answered with a hint of sadness. She rolled her arm back over and waited through a couple of moments of silence before asking, "Christian, what happened to your mother?"

Christian looked at Shiloh for a long moment. A moment that felt like a good hour. His first reply was taking another sip, which didn't satisfy. He then pulled down the remainder of the glass. The alcohol burned his throat. Christian set the glass down on the table, a little too hard, and again looked at Shiloh, who waited patiently for an answer. He was surprised when she didn't flip her phone over to record anything or whip out a pen and paper to impersonally scratch down everything he uttered, or even have a camera crew magically appear out of nowhere with glaring lights that blinded his eyes. All of which he'd had to deal with before. No, it seemed Shiloh honestly wanted to know. Maybe it was for his sake, or maybe her father's, or maybe it was simply to round out her book, chronicling those days he had only heard about. He next hoped Trent the Waiter with his ridiculously square jawline would return soon to refill his now starkly empty glass. Until then, he summoned the courage to revisit the years behind him, calculating out an appropriate place to start.

With an exhale, he leaned forward, folding his large hands together, and began to speak.

Acknowledgments

One of the biggest challenges I faced in editing and evolving this story was the desire of some to affix a root-cause origin to its plot. I guess I could have added one, but doing so would've been a disingenuous ode to the emotional cold war my father and I waged against each other. To this day I still do not know why we were the way we were. It sure would have made things easier for both of us if, say, my diaper had leaked upon his favorite Christmas tie and he never forgave me for it, or I sang a foul rendition of a nursery rhyme during Thanksgiving dinner for no other reason than "just because," leaving my fragile grandmother appalled and my sister witnessing an ensured thumb-thump to my skull.

For those who have never experienced disconnect with a parent, consider yourself fortunate to be a member of such an exclusive club.

I was really taken by surprise by how many nerves I touched as this story's audience broadened over the years. I honestly, and naively, thought I was the only one to have experienced this unique disconnect I had with my father. This is something I've since been corrected on. So, in many ways, this book is very much dedicated to us men, women, and the children within all of us who have fought, lost, and have yet to settle these lonely unresolvable wars.

While I have lugged this story around like a weighted suitcase for half my life, I've carried the heart of it for as long as I can remember. The characters inhabiting the fictional river-hugging town of Granite Point are a composite result derived from the people and places and stories I've come across throughout my years. Many of the nuances within the chapters are actually quite true, and the emotions expressed come from the heart.

It's important to note that this story isn't meant to be a full indictment of my father. It is a recount of the emotional battles we waged or sometimes painfully ignored. We were both a part of the same problem, and neither of us reached victory in the end. But as I write this acknowledgment, I've officially placed this weighted suitcase upon the ground and left it behind to fade into the lost memories of yesterday.

And while I possessed the proverbial pen and heart to create *Power & Way*, there were many hearts that helped shape the story into what is now captured within this book's bindings. I would be remiss not to recognize Julia Bobkoff and Thomas Fiffer for their long nights and weekends editing and refining the story's prose, and for Julia's unrelenting passion for the soul of the characters and the very heart of *Power & Way*. I also want to acknowledge Dr. Austin Hayden Smidt for his long memory of this story he read so long ago, Paul Emami, whose love for *Power & Way* helped evolve the screenplay version over the years, and finally to Conner and Sarah and my wonderful wife, Karen, whose never-ending, endlessly energetic support of me is something that still fills me with wonderment. The woman is a true gift from the angels that look over me.

And finally, I need to acknowledge my father, whose presence in my life, for right or wrong, made this story possible. In fact, I'm sure he's turning in his grave at the notion that I, his son, had the actual wherewithal to even write a novel, let alone with him as an antagonistic protagonist.

It's a feat he would undoubtedly laugh and shake his head at.

N

9 781960 865366